HERA

Also by Jennifer Saint

Ariadne

Elektra

Atalanta

HERA

JENNIFER SAINT

FLATIRON
BOOKS
NEW YORK

HERA. Copyright © 2024 by Jennifer Saint. All rights reserved. Printed in the United States of America. For information, address Flatiron Books, 120 Broadway, New York, NY 10271.

ISBN 9781250855602

*For Mum and Dad, much better parents
than are often found in Greek mythology*

I sing of golden-throned Hera whom Rhea bare. Queen of the immortals is she ... the glorious one whom all the blessed throughout high Olympus reverence and honour even as Zeus who delights in thunder.

Homeric Hymn XII to Hera,
translated by Hugh G. Evelyn-White, 1914

A SIMPLIFIED
(BUT STILL COMPLICATED!)
DIVINE FAMILY TREE

Note: the family relationships in Greek mythology vary depending on the version of the myth being told. No attempt has been made here to create a comprehensive family tree – only deities relevant to this novel are included, to avoid it becoming too unwieldy to be of any help. Some gods are born of parthenogenesis (a goddess conceiving a child entirely on her own with no male input at all) and many are the offspring of sibling marriages.

PRIMORDIAL DEITIES AND TITANS

TITANS AND OLYMPIANS

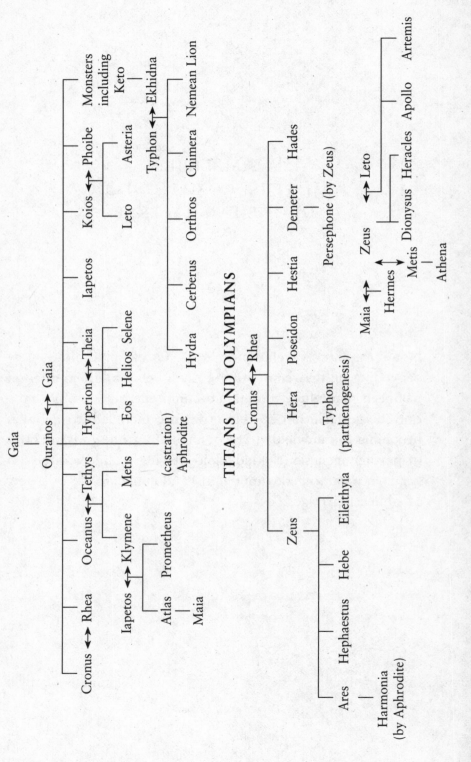

PROLOGUE

The earth streams with molten gold. It flows in every direction, around the scattered rocks, gleaming in the light of the fires that rage all around. *Ichor*, the blood of the immortals, seeping into the soil.

Smoke hangs heavy in the air, obscuring the stars. Thunder rumbles in the distance, and the horizon flashes with lightning. It dances across the sky, leaping between the clouds, a glare that dazzles, white and blinding, and is gone, only to reappear somewhere else a moment later.

Hera glances up at it, narrowing her eyes to chart its progress as she steps across the ravaged battleground.

The falling dusk and swirling ash make it hard to see. The ground is churned up, great gashes in the earth where boulders have been heaved and trees torn up by their roots. Some of the mounds she skirts are these shattered rocks and mangled trunks, but some of them are not. Some are golden-stained, sprawled, staring glassy-eyed up to the heavens. Every now and then, one might stir painfully as she passes, let out a whimper of agony so that she raises her spear. She is swift and merciless, leaving silence in her wake.

Lightning sears the sky directly above her, its livid glow rendering every detail of the carnage in stark clarity for the space of a heartbeat before it dies away into darkness again. She listens, trying to distinguish the shrieking of the winds from another scream, one of anguish and rage. The earth is scarred and brutalised, but it is quiet at last. The fighting is in the heavens now.

The euphoric rush of victory still tingles through her body, but she senses something else too. As she walks on, her gold-spattered tunic damp against her skin, she feels the soft melancholy that hangs on the mist and drizzle. It rises from the vast craters; the wounds carved deep into the ground. It is the sorrow of Gaia that she feels. Gaia, the first of them all. The goddess of the earth, who bears the pain of this violation.

Hera glances around her, making sure that nothing else is still moving. Satisfied, she kneels, and rests her palms on the gold-stained mud. Her touch is gentle and reverent, her eyes closed, as she prays. One goddess to another; a holy moment of gratitude to the mother who had birthed them all: the Titans who lie bleeding and the warriors who fought at Hera's side.

There has been so much suffering.

Hera opens her eyes and looks to the heavens, where the thunder is reaching its crescendo. It growls from the furthest edge of the horizon, the rage building as it echoes across the mountaintops, loud enough to split the rocks apart and send them tumbling down the steep slopes. Lightning shears the skies over and over, hurled by Zeus to bring down the last Titan still standing.

Her brothers and sisters are up there with him, fighting side by side. Hera's battle-mates on the ground were not gods;

they were Gaia's monsters. Creatures of nightmare nurtured in the deepest caverns of Gaia's womb, broken free to aid in this war against the Titans. Before Gaia had sent them, the two sides were evenly matched. Cronus and his five brothers had ruled the heavens since they overthrew their own father, Ouranos. Hera, Zeus and the other four children of Cronus had the advantage of youth – they were full of fiery rebellion, eager to seize the world. But the six Titans were experienced, they were crafty and they were long-enduring. And so, years of war have passed in spasms of frantic, boiling chaos punctuated by desperate councils where the gods proffered the same tactics over and over, and Hera saw her own frustration at the unending stalemate mirrored in Zeus' eyes.

And then the three Hecatoncheires lumbered forth from the earth, sprouting fifty heads from each thick neck and a hundred arms bulging with muscle. The three Cyclopes followed, each with one vast eye in the centre of their craggy forehead. The gods turned their perfect faces away from them in distaste. But to Hera, their strength was beautiful.

Now Hera's monstrous warriors come forth again, clanking bronze chains as they walk, their silhouettes massive against the incandescent sky. They spread out across the battlefield and begin to bind the defeated Titans, who have fallen to Hera's blade or been crushed by the monsters at her side. Not that they can truly die; she knows that. The same golden blood runs in her own veins, and ichor is strong enough to sustain her through any injury, however grievous. It will sustain them too, just enough to keep them alive in this broken, battered state. It is the closest to death that an immortal can ever come. They are beyond resisting, unable to move or make a sound, drained and beaten to almost nothing.

3

The ground shudders. This is the end. Cronus, their father, who battles now against Zeus in the mountains, cannot stand against them alone. His allies are shackled at Hera's feet, his children united against him, and even as his howl of fury rings out across the vast sky, she knows he is already beaten.

The age of the Titans has collapsed.

The rule of the Olympians begins.

PART ONE

Come, blessed Goddess, fam'd almighty queen,
with aspect kind, rejoicing and serene.

The Hymns of Orpheus XV: Juno [Hera],
translated by Thomas Taylor, 1792

1

After the war is over, Gaia's earth heals. In the years that follow, the plains where Hera cut down the Titans become meadows, and flowers grow in wild profusion where their blood soaked into the soil. The raw edges of the craters soften into gentle, grassy slopes. Hera strolls over them, and she remembers, *This is where I led my monsters, this is where I plunged my spear into my enemies' flesh*, and the sunlight warms her skin. When she comes across pools that once glistened with golden blood, she smiles at her unchanged reflection in the clear water. Birds fly across skies that were once fractured with Zeus' lightning, skies that now stretch blue and cloudless to the horizon.

In the war, time was measured in skirmishes and strategy. Now, Hera charts its passing by the trees that grow where the battlefields were; thin saplings becoming forests of broad-crowned oaks and towering pines.

It's from such a forest that she emerges now, slipping out from between the wide trunks into the afternoon sunshine, her cheeks flushed and her eyes sparkling. She shakes out her hair, plucking a leaf from the dark waves tumbling down her back.

Her skin is still warm and tingling as she hurries towards the mountain that rises up from the landscape, higher than any around it. She pictures the river-god she leaves behind her in their secluded glade; in her mind's eye, she sees him bathing under his foaming waterfall, his thick chest gleaming in the spray, droplets glistening on his strong arms. She casts a longing glance back. These hazy days of peace afford a freedom that Hera never knew before. But today, she has somewhere she needs to be, and she moves briskly on.

When Cronus ruled, Hera was hidden away and raised in the darkness of the house of Oceanus beneath the waters. She can remember what it was like, hearing the great river above her, its distant thunder surging over the rocks, trickling down through the mud, tingeing the air she breathed with the scent of damp earth. Now she is free, and every joy is hers to discover. She is a goddess revelling in the infancy of the world. A warrior who fought side by side with giants. A girl delighting in birdsong. Reigning in the heavens alongside her siblings; laughing in the woods with her lovers. A sister, curled up by the fire, exchanging confidences, her face open and warm in the glow of the cosy flames.

She eyes the distant mountain. She can traverse great distances and never tire, but she decides to take the form of her preferred bird, the hawk, to get there now. Her body ripples in transformation, and she takes to the air, the ground dropping away. Since the war, no god has seen Gaia, but she has rewarded them with more and more bounteous life, and all of it is laid out beneath Hera now: silver schools of fish in the waters, bears and lions to prowl the forests, creatures that creep and slither and scamper, furred and feathered and scaled. On the plains, horses run wild, kicking up dust behind them, and Hera sees her brother Poseidon, darting between them, swinging himself on to their backs, seemingly just for the joy of galloping. He's on his way to Mount Olympus too, the seat of the victorious gods, the mountain home that has given them their name. Up the steep slopes, past the ragged pines whose branches are stripped by the wind that whistles through the peaks, beyond the rough boulders, where the fresh tang of scattered snow is sharp in the air and the clouds wreathe around bare rock; from here, they can watch the world beneath them. The palace they have built is a feast for the eyes: shining white marble and gleaming gold columns so cold and smooth they could be carved from ice, every line and corner straight and sharp and flawless. It's nothing like the rugged perfection of Gaia's creation, Hera sometimes thinks. Its glory comes not from the wild and beautiful chaos of the earth below, but from order, and that's more pleasing to her than anything else. After the tumult of war, they lift themselves now beyond the grasp of any possible usurper.

No one can challenge us, Zeus had said when it was all over. Hera thought no one would dare.

The victorious Olympians chained their father and four of his Titan brothers in the deepest bowels of the earth, a pit called Tartarus from which they can never escape. They will live out eternity in its darkness, sunk so deep that all their power and ferocity can't shake even a pebble on the surface. Only one of Cronus' allies, his nephew, Atlas, was spared the pit. He stands at the western edge of the world, the crushing weight of the heavens resting on his shoulders. His bowed, weary stance serves as a reminder to the other Titans – the

Titans who didn't fight, who now live free under Olympian rule – that they were right not to join the battle. A warning to them in case they ever doubt it; in case their allegiance to the Olympians should ever waver.

Hera keeps a close eye on these peaceful Titans. When Zeus consigned the five brothers to the pit, their skills went with them. Hyperion, who had commanded the sun, will never see its light again. It's his children who perform his role now. Hera oversees, makes sure they never deviate. And sure enough, each morning, Eos appears, Hyperion's daughter, Titaness of the dawn. The horses tethered to her chariot whicker softly, and Hera looks for the glitter of their wide, dark eyes reflecting the light of the morning star as they emerge from the banks of Oceanus and begin their climb through the dim air. Far above, Eos' sister, Selene, withdraws slowly, the great silver orb of the moon gliding away with her as Eos makes her ascent to the heavens, strewing radiant sparks of fire through the dying night. Her rosy fingers trail through the sky, the bottom edges of the clouds blooming with pink feathery streaks of light where she touches them. Eos will give way to her brother, Helios, whose horses will charge forth, a crown of rays flashing atop his head, his gaudy procession through the skies relentless and unstoppable. But for a moment, the world is held still on the cusp of a new day and Eos, mother of stars and winds, laughs as her sons wreathe around her, their caresses lifting her hair and fluttering across her face in a scatter of gentle kisses. It unfolds the same way each time: regular, predictable, *ordered*. The days stack up, and no one cares to count how many. What matters to Hera is that each one happens as it should.

* * *

The sky behind the palace is white, merging with the shining stone. Wisps of cloud flutter past the graceful columns as Hera ascends the final stretch of the mountain. She has taken her goddess form again, preferring to climb. She likes to feel the rough surface of the rock beneath her smooth feet, the bracing shock of snow between her perfect, immortal toes. Sometimes a snake will dart from its hiding place, coil around her ankles and be gone again, and she'll laugh out loud, relishing the sensation of its sleek power against her skin.

A bird swoops past, its wingspan wide enough to blot out the sunlight for a moment. An eagle; hardy enough to brave this bleak, rocky elevation. Hera likes its hooked beak, its sharp claws and the vast sweep of its wings, though she loves smaller birds better, the ones that rest on her palm, their heart-beats thrilling against her thumb.

The eagle is Zeus' choice, and of course he is here with it now, on the wide marble steps that lead up to the gates of Olympus. It dives towards him, landing on his outstretched arm. It ruffles its wings, tucking them at its side as it dips its head into his palm. Zeus smiles at the bird as it stretches its throat back and swallows his gift. Something crushed and bloody, still warm.

When he sees Hera, his face brightens. 'Where have you been?' he asks her. The bird's long black claws sink into his forearm, but of course they cannot puncture his skin.

'Nowhere in particular.'

He gestures to her to walk with him, and the eagle, affronted, takes to the skies again.

Zeus' appearance still takes Hera by surprise sometimes. Part of her expects to see the boy-god she knew on Crete, before the war. When it was only the two of them, hungry to claim their birthright. On Olympus, he has assumed a more regal dignity. A thicker beard, an air of authority. His words don't tumble out so quickly anymore. But she still sees his delight in her presence, just the same as the first time they met and each of them realised they weren't alone.

On the other side of the gates, the courtyard shimmers in the soft light of the sun. A haze hangs in the sky beyond, cloaking the other mountaintops in the distance. Hera would lean over the low wall, letting the cold breeze lift her hair – there is almost nothing she likes better than to survey the world from up here – but there are nymphs draped across the benches, giggling together, and she stands up straighter.

'Isn't there something they should be doing?' she asks, and Zeus shrugs.

'There will be.'

It's frustratingly vague as an answer, and a challenge is already forming on her lips as she whips her head around towards him, but the words die in her throat when she sees his eyes are already locked on her, warm with amusement.

'Is this what you do all day, check up on all the Titans and the nymphs, make sure everyone is usefully occupied?' he asks. 'Is there no better use of your time?'

She doesn't think there is anyone in the world who speaks to her as directly as Zeus does. Nobody else would dare.

'Don't you think it's important to know how your subjects spend their time?' she counters. 'And that they're kept busy?'

'In case they use their freedom like we did?' he asks, and it takes her by surprise. To make even a joking reference to an imagined rebellion – it feels shocking, profane even. 'These girls,' he goes on, and he shakes his head, smiling. 'There's no cause for worry.'

There are a dozen retorts she could make, but he's probably right about the nymphs. Hera watches them chatting breathlessly to one another, winding their hair around their fingers, their voices high and thin as they lean inwards, flutters of their conversation drifting across the perfumed air. They don't look as though they're intent on toppling any regime. They're not like Zeus and Hera were.

'Perhaps I shouldn't, then,' she says. 'Worry, that is.'

He takes her arm, easy and confident. 'Of course not.'

He doesn't give any indication that he knows where she's been, or what else she might do on her wanderings. There's no teasing insinuation about her riverside trysts – today's or any other – no raised eyebrow, no jokes like the ones he makes with his brothers about his own dalliances.

She's glad. She likes to have secrets. Maybe she grew used to that in the old days, perhaps it's a habit she can't shake – the desire to hold something close to her heart and keep it just for herself, not for anyone else.

They pass through the columns, into the megaron. Four golden pillars in the centre hold up the ceiling. Hera's eyes are drawn immediately to the seven golden thrones that line the far wall; they are new and startling, the sight of them sending a little thrill through her body. Poseidon is here already, ahead of her. The hearth burns bright as always, crimson flames casting dancing shadows on to stone. Hestia glances up from her low seat beside it and smiles at Hera as she enters. A flurry of voices and a clatter of steps announce the arrival of Demeter and Hades. Now the six siblings are together, and only Aphrodite is still to come.

'Where is she?' Zeus sounds annoyed.

'You know she does as she pleases.' Hera slides on to the bench next to Hestia.

'She'll be here,' Hestia assures him.

There's a tension in his shoulders. Demeter and Hades chatter on blithely, and Poseidon scowls into the fire. It's only Hera who recognises Zeus' mood, and she can't resist provoking him.

'Do you think she'll miss it, though?' she asks, her eyes round with innocence. 'Because that would mean . . .'

His eyes darken, but at that very moment, Aphrodite sweeps in. Hera smiles sweetly. Nothing will puncture her good spirits today.

Zeus clears his throat and the gods fall silent. He gestures to the new thrones. 'Sit,' he says. 'The Titans will be on their way.'

He takes the centre throne. Hera sits at his right. Poseidon sits on the other side, Hades next to him and Aphrodite at the end. Demeter takes the throne beside Hera, and Hestia the last. For a moment, they are silent and still. The gold feels cool where it touches Hera's skin – the hand she rests on its side, the backs of her arms and the shoulder left bare by her draped dress.

Then one of the nymphs from the courtyard, her face serious now, opens the arched doors and ushers in the Titans.

The gods of the old world stand face to face with the new. Helios stands among them, crowned with golden rays; there is silver-horned Selene, and Eos clad in a rosy gown. Oceanus and Tethys, risen from the depths of their vast river, their robes trimmed with coral and pearl. Styx of the underground river that branches from theirs. Klymene, the mother of the beleaguered Atlas, her sweet face shadowed. Her husband languishes in Tartarus with Cronus; her son strains under the weight of the sky. But she is still here, in the Olympian palace.

'Styx,' Zeus says, and the Titaness steps forward. 'You were the first of the Titans to come to me in the war and swear your loyalty to us instead of to Cronus and his brothers.'

Her gaze is steady, her dark eyes fixed on his.

'You preside over the river that flows from the upper world to the lower,' he goes on. 'In gratitude for what you did for us, we will honour your stream now. Its waters will be the waters that all gods will swear oaths on from now on; oaths that will be as unbreakable as your word.'

He takes her hand, and looks out across the watching Titans. 'We are all descendants of Gaia.' His voice rolls across the silent hall like distant thunder. 'A family, coming together in peace now the suffering of war is over. We welcome you here on Mount Olympus.'

No Titan betrays their thoughts. Every immortal face in the room is smooth, devoid of expression.

'But,' Zeus goes on, 'we must make sure that the mistakes of the past are never repeated.' His thunderbolt is tucked into his belt; the slender, pronged weapon that the Cyclopes forged for him, that could crumble the mountain beneath their feet if he wished. 'The rule of the Titans that came before us was cruel. Ouranos, the sky-Titan, subdued Gaia in marriage and imprisoned her children. The world was crushed beneath his weight, stifled by his tyranny. It was only when Gaia gave her youngest son, Cronus, the sickle he would use to slice his father apart and scatter the pieces to the winds that the world would know freedom.'

For Hera, his words conjure the drifting fragments of the vanquished Titan; diffuse and weakened, floating on the breeze, an echo of the powerful king he once was.

'The castration of Ouranos gave us Aphrodite.' Zeus nods

towards the goddess on her throne, and she smiles, lifting the solemnity in the room for a brief but dazzling moment. 'His blood mingled with the seawater, and she was born from the foaming waves. But Aphrodite's loyalty was never to Cronus. She would join with us against him.' He nods emphatically. His thunderbolt is a warning to anyone who would not fall in line, but Aphrodite is an enticement. Her beauty, her allure, calls to everyone in the room far more seductively than Zeus' lecture.

Still, he recites their history, one they all know intimately. 'After Cronus toppled Ouranos, he married Rhea, his sister. But in fear that his own son might do to him what he did to his father, he plucked each infant she bore him from her arms and swallowed them whole. Hestia, Demeter, Poseidon and Hades. Only Hera and I were saved, spirited away by Gaia – Hera to the halls of Oceanus and me to Crete, to be raised by Metis.'

Hera catches the eye of the Titaness of whom he speaks. Metis looks back at her, the same grey eyes that Hera remembers from when she came to Crete to join her brother. Zeus spoke of Styx as though she was their first Titan ally, but before her there were Oceanus and Tethys, who had taken in Hera, and Metis, who hid Zeus away in the foothills of Mount Dicte. It was Metis who trained the two of them together for war. Metis who prepared the emetic herbs that she would use to trick Cronus later, so that he would bring his swallowed children back up. Hera wonders why it is only Styx that Zeus honours here today; perhaps he holds some other reward in store for Metis.

In this airy hall, where the gold shimmers in the firelight, where the gods are strong and young and glorious, the old savagery seems so very long ago – an age of darkness they have banished forever.

'No Titans will rule again.' Zeus echoes her thoughts. 'We will never return to those days. Every one of you will swear today, just as Styx once did, that your allegiance is to us. The oath you swear will bind not just you, but your children as well, even those not yet born.'

There is no dissent. Hera doesn't know what each Titan thinks as they step forward, one by one. It doesn't matter, so long as they pour the water from the jug held by Styx, and swear upon its silvery stream that they will serve the Olympians. The peace they have won will be eternal.

When it's done, the Titans depart and the atmosphere lightens. The Olympians descend from their thrones and sit instead on low benches, cushioned with shaggy furs, and sip sweet nectar from polished horns. Hera breathes in its fragrance. The honeyed spices rising from the thick, amber liquid are rich and intoxicating. Outside the palace, the sun sinks low behind the mountain, the sky alight with the same fiery shades as the nectar that she swirls one way then the other, watching it gleam as it catches the torchlight.

The gods are convivial, congratulatory as they talk and feast. Serving-nymphs bring platters of roasted meat, honey, cheese and figs, followed by the sweet ambrosia that is the privilege only of the gods. Demeter is animated, expressive, gesturing with her hands in the air to sketch out the shape of growing plants, and when she shakes back her hair, it ripples down her back and Hera thinks of leaves swaying in the breeze. Her sister smells of the earth after rain, fresh and vital and invigorating.

'And how was your watch today?' Hestia murmurs to Hera.

'Is the world still in order, like always?' She leans in close, the scent of smoke, a crackle of embers, a comforting sense of home and safety emanating from her.

'Everything is the same,' Hera answers, and she feels a fierce gladness at her own words. A satisfaction as she looks around the table. Aphrodite curves her lips at some private thought. The aroma of rose petals rises from the smooth, bare skin of her arms and neck. She has them crushed in golden oil, rubbed into her flesh when she stands up from her fragrant bath, and it always drifts behind her, a seductive trail in the air.

Hera notices the dust clinging to Poseidon's forearms where his elbows rest on the table, his fingers interlinked beneath his chin. His eyes are dark and surly as ever, but tonight they seem fixed on Hestia, who keeps her face determinedly turned towards Hera.

'And you?' Hera asks, flicking her gaze to their brother and back, a pointed gesture for Hestia and no one else. She wants to know what's going on, why Poseidon stares so.

Hestia shakes her head a fraction, rolls her eyes. 'The same . . . for now.' Perhaps she has no explanation either. She's looking at Zeus and Hades now, the two of them deep in their own conversation. Every now and again, Zeus' booming laughter rolls around the hall, an echo of thunder.

The conversation turns, as it always does, to their victory over the Titans. They never tire of bringing out the same stories, each of them eager to speak of their own bravery and decisive action at each moment of peril. Hera enjoys it just as much as the rest of them. She appreciates it all the better – the magnificent hall, the attentive nymphs, their seat in the clouds – when she remembers a time before these luxuries.

*   *   *

When Hera ascends to her chamber later, it is in a haze of contentment. Their seven thrones work. The continuation of the world proves that it works. Power shared between them, not one tyrant growing ever more solitary and ferocious.

Hera sleeps. The nectar and ambrosia she consumed replenish the ichor in her veins, strengthening her. In repose, any trace of wary watchfulness drops away from her. Her face is unchanged since she grew to womanhood. Aeons of war and an infinitude of peace have left no lines, no mark on her immortal flesh.

2

Demeter prefers to spend her time roaming rather than staying too long on her throne in the airy megaron of their palace. Zeus, Poseidon and Hades sprawl there more often than not, while Hestia prefers the cosy warmth of the hearth. Hera divides her time equally between the outside world and her royal seat. But when Hera wanders, she doesn't forget how they won this freedom, and how closely they must guard it. She is ready for any sign of dissension, for the Titans to stray from their allotted tasks. They never do.

Other immortals swell their ranks; another tier of deities born. Zeus is busy consolidating their alliances. The Titaness Mnemosyne gives him nine daughters, and he calls them Muses. They aren't charged with responsibility to keep the sun in the sky or the rivers flowing; they are blessed with beautiful voices that they lift together in song. What they sing of most often is the victory of the Olympians. The battle of gods and Titans will never be forgotten, Hera realises. The old rule of Cronus is hazy now, his cruelties left far behind in the past. But the Muses will keep the celebration of the gods alive. Hera thrills a little when she hears her own name in their songs.

She notes when more are born; when Zeus invites the Titaness Themis to counsel him – Themis, whose clear sight and foreknowledge of the future must have given her an inkling of what the outcome would be – and with her come her daughters, the graceful Horae who tend to the earth, and the three Fates. The task of the Fates will be to allot the lifespans of the mortals Zeus and Prometheus are bent on creating. Hera hears the two of them discussing it whenever she comes back to the palace, and she wonders at their vanity. It is Gaia who brings forth creation; it is goddesses and Titanesses who give birth. Zeus and Prometheus shaping dolls from clay is not how life is made. Cronus had attempted it before them, and his mortals had been too feeble to survive long in the world. She thinks that Zeus should be satisfied with his divine offspring, and leave Cronus' failed experiments in the past with the rest of his rule.

Even their sister Demeter bears him a daughter, an infant called Kore. Hera wonders at this liaison more than any of the others. The gods do as they please, act on their whims and follow their desires, but somehow she is still surprised when Demeter swells and ripens like the fruit trees she nurtures, and attributes it to Zeus.

Hera is relieved when Demeter whisks the child away to an island and speaks no more about her. It would complicate things, Hera thinks – it could disrupt the order they've established. She doesn't know what a child of Demeter and Zeus might grow up to be, what claim she might want to lay, and she can't help but bridle at the prospect. Hera knew Zeus before any of the rest of them did.

That it was Hera and Zeus who first formed an alliance against Cronus goes unspoken, but acknowledged. The victory belongs to them most of all. Hera doesn't want this superseded by anyone else. So it is only when she realises that Demeter isn't going to speak of what took place between her and Zeus, or mention her daughter, that Hera is content again.

The family of gods grows ever larger, and Hera can see the advantage. They establish more loyalty, closer ties, and make it less likely that their rule will ever be threatened.

Zeus makes his mortals, and Hera finds them as unimpressive as she expected. They huddle together in small hamlets, easy enough to avoid. They're afraid of the vast open spaces of the plains, the depths of the forests and the wild seas. They don't dare to wander off alone, terrified of prowling creatures with sharp claws and fangs, for they lack any such defences. Without fur, they shiver, naked and pathetically ill-equipped for the world into which Zeus has brought them.

Hera ignores them, but Zeus is too pleased with his creation not to seek out her admiration. She finds herself faced with his expectant expression, trying to summon up an opinion.

'It's a feat,' she says at last. 'To create life from nothing. Like Gaia herself.'

He puffs up with pride. 'That's right.'

But what a pale imitation of her creations these are, Hera thinks. 'What are they for?' she asks out loud.

'Cronus' mortals worshipped him,' Zeus says, his tone off-hand. 'It pleased him to have their devotion.'

But Cronus' mortals, unlike their creator, were more peaceful than these. Perhaps Zeus was not so careful; perhaps in his eagerness to press ahead, he didn't take the time to get it right. These mortals seem peevish, fractious, easily inclined to argue with one another. They fight over their trinkets, their poor wooden shelters, the crops that Demeter so patiently encourages to grow near their settlements. They don't spend their days in quiet gratitude like the mortals who had lived before.

'Why *do* you help them?' Hera asks Demeter, her curiosity piqued.

Demeter sighs. 'Pity, I suppose. They can't seem to manage alone.'

Better Demeter's interference than Aphrodite's. The renewed existence of mortals has delighted no one else more; even Zeus is not so tickled as Aphrodite by the opportunity for entertainment they present.

Hera can't imagine what possible allure these grey, weary creatures have for the shining, resplendent goddess. Their skin is stretched thin over purple veins, their eyes watery and their limbs weak; they don't present any sort of attraction that Hera can conceive of. They begin their lives mewling and tiny, even more hopelessly dependent than the full-grown versions, and within the blink of an eye they are withered and wrinkled, their meagre existence snuffed out.

'If you concentrate,' Aphrodite tells her, 'if you pay attention, then their lifespans aren't quite so fleeting as you think.'

The Fates, at last occupied with something, are busy spinning and measuring and cutting the threads that determine just how fleeting these lifespans are. To Hera, it seems that no sooner have they spun a thread than they slice it, and another mortal slumps over into death.

'But what is there to hold your attention, even if you try?'

23

Aphrodite smiles. 'They have passions,' she says. 'Desires I can inflame, a little flicker I can stir into an inferno if I want.'

'Why do you want to, though?' Hera pushes, but Aphrodite doesn't answer. She's infuriatingly languid, always giving the impression that she doesn't care about anything beyond her pleasures: a scented bath, an attendant-nymph's fingers combing through her hair, a cup of sweet, honeyed nectar.

'It gives her a way to flex her power,' Hestia murmurs to Hera later. 'A way to play without consequence.'

Hera isn't the only immortal to be wary of Aphrodite. Her taste for pleasure is one she can spread to others, her influence so beguiling and irresistible that no one realises how strong she is until they're already under her spell. Hera has wondered sometimes if Aphrodite is nearby when she's found herself overcome by longing for a handsome god in the forest; has found herself looking from side to side, alert for the scent of roses just in case the goddess has followed her in mischief. Gods don't like to lose control of themselves; they're all a little suspicious of Aphrodite. From the moment she joined them – neither Titan nor Olympian, but something else – they could all feel it. They could sense the promise within her: *I could tear the world down, burn it to ashes, and make you long for more.*

Gods recognise strength and they respect it. It's why Aphrodite has the seventh throne, although she is no child of Cronus like Hera and her siblings. And it's why Aphrodite veils her power, holds it back from them. It makes sense that she would enjoy the freedom that the creation of mortals lends her, to exercise it at her whim without risking divine revenge.

'And what do you think of them?' Hera asks Hestia.

Like Demeter, she looks sympathetic. 'I'd like to give them fire,' she says. 'They're so cold at night, so afraid of the dark.'

'They'd burn their villages to smoke,' Hera says.

'Zeus forbids it, anyway,' Hestia says, a tinge of regret in her voice.

Poseidon appears to be as little enamoured of the mortals as Hera is, and Hades won't be drawn to comment. She sees him sometimes, watching them, perhaps a shade of her sisters' sympathy in his eyes, but she doesn't really know.

A pointless experiment, she decides, and maybe a sign that Zeus is restless. She thinks he'll tire of this project soon and move on to something else, but instead he finds further diversion in his mortals.

Specifically, in a king, or so he calls himself. When Zeus tells her about him, Hera can hardly believe even a mortal would pride himself on ruling over such scraps, but he does. He's taken a wife, but when the wife's father came to visit them, this king took offence at one thing or another, and murdered the man.

'They're always fighting one another,' she says. 'Why do you care?'

Zeus shrugs. 'I like this one,' he says. 'He has ambition.'

Hera makes a face. 'I don't even know how you tell them apart,' she says, and Zeus laughs.

'You know nothing about them,' he says. 'If you watched them for a while—'

'Well, what of it?' Hera interrupts. She doesn't care to hear him rhapsodise again about his creations.

'They've chased him out of his village,' Zeus says. 'They curse him for his treatment of his father-in-law, for his lack of respect, both for his elder and the fact that the old man was a guest in his house.'

'And?' asks Hera.

'I've decided to offer him sanctuary,' Zeus announces. 'Here, on Mount Olympus.'

A mortal, in the home of the gods. If Hera thought the very creation of them was an act of foolish ego, this is beyond anything she could have foreseen.

She swears to stay away while the mortal is there – it's hardly an inconvenience. Mortal lives are over so quickly, she'll barely notice the time until either Zeus tires of his new plaything or the man dies. But she can't quite believe that Zeus will actually allow it to happen, that he would really bring a mortal to their palace. Besides, she doesn't want to be the only god that doesn't see it for herself, to listen to their stories later without having anything to offer. So, with a grudging fascination, she lingers.

He's hunched, wearing dirty, ragged skins around his body. Hera smooths down the soft fabric of her tunic, the flowing folds that move against her skin like water, golden threads glimmering in the sunlight. Weaving belongs to the gods; a skill as yet undreamt of by humans. She notices the grime rooted deep beneath his bare nails, his matted beard and the salt stink of him. Next to him, Zeus gleams with divine vitality; the comparison could not be more stark. *Surely Zeus can't feel any sense of pride in his creation* Hera thinks. The gods have to dim their radiance for the benefit of the mortal; his eyes are too weak to withstand their glory, and he would burn to ashes if he looked upon them as they truly are.

When an eagle soars over the palace, it is magnificent. Never mind that it is of the earth, to which it will one day return. It's beautiful and harmonious, perfectly in its own element. This man – Ixion, as Zeus introduces him – struggles even to breathe up here. The air is too thin for his lungs; his chest heaves as he tries to speak around his shallow panting. He's forbidden to consume the nectar and ambrosia on which the gods dine, so he eats a lumpen bread, dense and dark. She wonders what immortal hands have grudgingly made it for him. He flings himself upon it in disbelief, never having tasted such a thing. The crumbs fall from his mouth, mingling with the juices of the berries he's been brought. Hera wonders if Zeus gathered the berries himself. She can almost picture it, so hearty is he about this strange joke; she can see him laughing in the woods, preparing for this unprecedented guest.

At first, the mortal king is cowed by their presence, but he begins to relax as he realises he isn't about to be struck by Zeus' thunderbolt or hurled off the peak. He stares around at the golden pillars and the bright stone, all impossibilities in his limited experience. He knows browns and muddy greens, he knows toil and discomfort, he knows cold and hunger. When he sees the fire burning in the central hearth of the megaron, his mouth drops open and he can't tear his eyes away. He's hypnotised by the dancing flames, drawing nearer and jumping back in comical astonishment when he feels the heat on his skin.

'You said you would keep the secret of fire for the gods alone,' Hera mutters to Zeus.

'What can he do with it?' Zeus replies. 'He doesn't know how to conjure it himself; he'll hardly have the words to describe it when he goes back.'

She takes heart from this. At least Zeus intends for Ixion to go back.

And when he does, overwhelmed by the majesty and miracle of the gods, he'll live out the rest of his life never being able to recreate the wonders he saw on Mount Olympus. Is that part of the appeal for Zeus? After all, what good is it to deny these privileges to men if they don't even know they exist?

Part of her had feared that Zeus invited the king here in order to blend their worlds more closely. Instead, it seems that he wants to impress on the man how inferior he is, and how very powerful the gods are in comparison.

But Ixion begins to lose his stuttering awe. She sees him begin to look more closely at the riches of their home. The necklaces that tumble from Aphrodite's neck, polished amber and lapis, shining metals and delicate pink quartz – stones he has never seen before, wrought from divine craftsmanship that humans will not learn for centuries still to come. A rock-crystal bowl, glowing in the firelight. His eyes turn covetous, resting on one treasure and then the next, and then his gaze creeps towards Hera herself.

It feels like a creature scuttling across her skin. She looks at Aphrodite, indignant, and Aphrodite looks back – the realisation dawning on her at the same time as it does on Hera. This isn't her work; she has cast no spell on Ixion. It wouldn't even occur to her – to any of them – that a man could lift his eyes to a goddess.

Aphrodite is caught between horror and delight, her eyes wide and her fingers pressed across her mouth as though to suppress a smile. If Hera wasn't so profoundly insulted, she might laugh too, at the sheer, insane presumption of the man. But his gaze lingers on the outline of her breasts, and it makes her want to plunge into an ice-cold pool to scrub off every trace of his stare.

As she considers smashing Ixion's skull on the marble tiles, Hades' voice breaks into her thoughts. 'Our guest must be tired,' he says. His tone is soft and measured; his face unreadable. 'It must be exhausting; the only mortal to have ever dined with the gods. I'll take him to his chamber to rest.'

Zeus looks as though he might object, but then he waves an arm in dismissal. He hasn't noticed Ixion's impiety. 'You're right,' he says. 'Let him sleep, so he can marvel again tomorrow with a clear head.'

The mortal king has the good sense to do as he is bidden. He follows Hades meekly enough, and he lies down in a bed softer than anything he's known before, in a room beyond all imagining. But this is a man who has lived his life taking what he wants. He clawed his way to power through violence and greed, leaving weeping women in his wake. He sees Zeus, Poseidon and Hades, and understands their strength: the way they stand head and shoulders above him, the breadth of their chests and the power in their strides. But when he looks at Hestia, Demeter, Aphrodite and Hera, he trembles with excitement. Ixion knows what to do with women; he knows how to stifle their screams and force them down beneath him. In the house of the gods, his mind runs wild with visions of Hera. He sees her haughty, lovely face contorted, his forearm pressed against her throat. He thinks of her smooth, divine flesh laid bare, and the flicker of contempt in her eyes giving way to panic.

In the megaron, the gods talk about it too. Zeus is unconvinced at first. Hera was against him from the start, determined to think the worst of any mortal. Her anger is just a product of her displeasure. But the other gods chime in, agreeing that Ixion's desires could not have been plainer. What kind of man would even dare to look a goddess in the face at all they argue. Aphrodite tells Zeus what she felt, the waves of lust that rolled from the king. Not the kind she instils, not the heady intoxication and wash of desire in which she revels, but a darker longing: to break and conquer and ravage. Hestia comments with disgust on the sheen of sweat across his forehead and the way he ran his tongue across his lips. Demeter says nothing, only puckering her lips with distaste. Poseidon smirks and stays silent, and Zeus ponders.

'You liked him for his ambition,' Hera says. 'But you need to remind him of his place.' In the dirt, among the other humans, is what she means.

Something is dawning on Zeus' face. A realisation, a recognition. 'I wonder,' he muses, 'just how far he would go.'

And he smiles.

The cloud-nymph Nephele is summoned. 'You can make illusions,' Zeus says. 'You can shape a vision from clouds, and anyone who sees it would believe it is real.'

Her face is cast down, demure and sweet. 'I hope I am so skilled.'

He claps a hand to her shoulder, his hand lingering on the bare skin at her neck. 'Make Hera.'

Her head darts up at this. 'Hera? But – I could never dream of replicating her beauty—' She stumbles over her words, casting an anxious look in Hera's direction.

'Try.'

Hera gives a slight nod. She doesn't like this plan, doesn't see the need for it. But she thinks that perhaps it will convince Zeus of what she's always said about the mortals. It might end his interest in them altogether, and they can carry on as before.

Nephele is gifted; Hera remembers that from her earliest days. This nymph is a daughter of Oceanus and Tethys, and she lived in Oceanus' halls beneath the river when Hera did. Nephele had the freedom to come and go as she pleased; she was not trapped below the thick mud and rushing waters. She could ascend to the upper world, where the dark smoke of night met the rosy light of dawn, where Eos still harnesses her chariot every sunrise, and there, at the edge of the earth, she practised her creations. Drawing water into the air, gathering it together and setting it afloat in the skies in whatever shape was her whim. That was how she began. But then Iris, charmed by her sculptures, would come to help. The winged goddess offered to lend her the colours from her rainbow, and Nephele would mix and blend the shades, letting them bleed into her cloud-shapes so that they took on a startlingly realistic aspect.

In the time since, Nephele's gift has become an impressive accomplishment. She practises it for her own delight and that of her sisters. Now she has the chance to please the Olympians, and she takes it.

The result is beyond anything Nephele has created before. Hera is fascinated by the cloud image of herself. The same smooth arch of her forehead, delicate eyelids fluttering closed over her eyes – round and full and dark, fringed with sweeping lashes like those of the famed cattle of Helios – her lips plump and perfect. Nephele's work does not displease her.

Nor does it displease Zeus. He eyes the false Hera with appreciation. 'Superb,' he says.

'It's very convincing.' Hera folds her arms across her chest. Impressed as she is by Nephele's sculpture, she can't feign any enthusiasm for its intended use.

Zeus glances at her. 'It's a shadow compared to you.' He hesitates. 'But it will fool the mortal well enough.'

She swallows. 'It will.'

Abruptly, he takes her hand in both of his. His gaze is sincere. 'I would never let him touch you,' he says.

She snorts. 'He couldn't come close.'

'And I'll make him suffer for even thinking that he might.'

She pulls her hands free of his. She can't abide any more delay. 'The sooner it's done, the sooner that mortal is gone from our palace. Let's get this over with.'

They leave the sleeping phantom in Hera's chamber and they wait.

It doesn't take long for Ixion to rise from his own bed, stupefied with fantasies, intent on his purpose. Sweat dampens his hairline, froth gathers at the corners of his mouth, and he creeps across the marble tiles to where Hera sleeps. He thinks of nothing but his own desire; his mind is incoherent, dazzled by the impossibility of everything around him. He has convinced himself that he is here because he deserves to have what the gods enjoy.

He slips into Hera's chamber, her holy sanctuary. Silver moonlight spills through the window; the breeze is cool against his damp skin. The air is fragrant with the scent of lotus blossoms. The peace feels sacred. A thrill shudders through him; this is a violation greater than any other.

And then he strikes. The phantom twists in his grip. She isn't the warm flesh he was expecting, but he thinks perhaps this is what a goddess feels like. He feels a surge of power, an incredible rush that he can subdue her, that she gives way so easily, that she almost seems to dissolve as he tears at her dress and forces his way into her, light exploding behind his eyes as he gasps and judders to a stop.

And then she is gone, vanished into vapour, and he is lying foolish and alone on an empty bed.

From the corridor, the gods draw closer. When he rolls over and looks up at them, he knows there is no escape.

The fire that so intrigued Ixion becomes his torment. Zeus binds him to a great wheel, sets it aflame and sends it spinning into the heavens.

Still, Hera won't let it lie. 'What if any of the other mortals are as greedy as him?' she asks. 'What if they, too, lack fear? What if they try to ascend to our palace again?'

Zeus looks discomfited. 'These men are bolder than the ones who came before, it's true.' He thinks for a moment. 'We must have misjudged, in the making of them. In case any are as rotten as Ixion was, we'll get rid of them. A flood, maybe.'

For the other gods, there was a certain amount of entertainment in Ixion's downfall, but Hera found no enjoyment in watching him in her chamber. The cloud-phantom wore her face, and it made her uneasy to see those filthy mortal fingers splayed across it to silence her cries. She could almost feel his hot breath in her ear; his greasy skin on her own. She found she couldn't laugh it off so easily as the others.

But Zeus keeps his word. He summons a great wave from the ocean and it washes the mortals away in a tide of divine vengeance. When the waters retreat, the earth comes back green and vibrant and renewed. Everything goes back to how it was before. She hopes Zeus has lost his enthusiasm, that he won't try again.

She could live forever like this, in a world that never has to change.

3

It's an impossible hope, although she doesn't know it yet. The earth is changing all the time; Gaia breathes and the world shifts, imperceptible but unstoppable. Far faster, her fellow gods look for the next diversion, moving in whichever direction desire sways them.

Swooping down from the twilit skies, hawk-clad, Hera sees Metis hurrying from a forest. Shortly after, Zeus saunters from the same gap in the trees. Hera narrows her eyes.

The next morning, a divine council of gods gather in the megaron, and Hera watches Metis closely. The Titaness says less than usual, and Zeus doesn't look to her for advice as he talks. Afterwards, Hera detains her in a bright-frescoed corridor, the two of them alone while, in the throne room, the gods laugh and drink together.

'I saw you and Zeus earlier,' Hera says.

Alarm flashes into Metis' eyes, but she's quick to gather her composure again. 'What of it?' she asks.

'Was there something . . .?' Hera hesitates. She doesn't know how to give voice to what she's thinking.

34

'What?' says Metis.

'Zeus can do as he wishes,' Hera says. 'You as well. It's just – you were his nurse.'

She can't discern any reaction. Metis keeps her gaze cool and steady. 'Zeus is no longer a boy. He's a king.'

Everything is different now, Hera concedes, from those days spent in the shade of Mount Dicte. When Zeus would perch on a rock in the sun-dappled light beneath the trees, the goat whose milk had nourished him in the absence of their mother always at his side. Nothing else is the same, so why not this change too?

'So you are lovers, then?'

Metis is silent, gathering her thoughts. She always used to do this, the young Hera watching her, spellbound, waiting. 'When Gaia asked me to take him in, I saw that he could be great – greater than his father,' she says. 'I sensed the power in him. And I trusted Gaia. She wanted an end to the savagery of Cronus. I saw the prospect of a better world in Zeus.'

It isn't even close to being an answer, not as far as Hera can divine. But then, Metis has the most powerful intellect of any immortal in the realm, and Hera knows she's keeping whatever has passed between her and Zeus hidden for a reason. She's talking about kings and dynasties, about power and ruling. Not about love, or even just desire.

And there is something hunted in her expression, something more disconcerting to Hera than the idea that, of all of Zeus' possible conquests, he would turn to their childhood mentor as his next.

Hestia appears at the end of the corridor. 'Hera?'

If there was a moment when she could have pressed Metis further, it is shattered. The Titaness nods to Hestia. 'You have things to discuss,' she says. 'I'll leave you both to it.' And she strides away.

'Did I interrupt?' Hestia asks.

Hera shakes her head. 'Never mind. What is it?'

Hestia glances up and down the empty corridor, making sure they aren't overheard. Her face is serious. 'Poseidon.'

Hera wrinkles her nose. 'He wants you in his bed?' she guesses.

'Worse,' says Hestia. 'He seeks a wife.'

'A wife? You?'

Hestia shudders. 'Imagine it.'

'But why does he want a wife at all?' Hera can't understand it.

'He looks to Cronus.' The name seems to stick in Hestia's throat, a flash of panic in her eyes, as though saying it could conjure his presence. It startles Hera, to see her sister's fear. She knows that Hestia isn't weak, even if her calm and quiet nature might give the impression she wouldn't fight back. 'Think about it, Hera. Our mother was Cronus' sister. Cronus married her to consolidate his power – so that he wouldn't just be the son of the king, but married to the king's daughter too. Poseidon thinks it would be the same if he marries me.'

'But we all rule together.'

Hestia holds her gaze. 'For how much longer?'

Hera shakes her head. 'You think Poseidon would take a lesson from Cronus? Cronus, who we put under the earth?'

'I watch them. From the fireside, I listen to what they're saying. I hear the words behind what they say out loud. And you should be careful, Hera.'

'Of Poseidon? When you refuse him, you think he'll come to me?'

'I'm thinking of Zeus.'

The idea is absurd. She won't think of it.

If Zeus were to look to any of them, surely it would be Demeter, who has already borne him a daughter. Or he could choose Metis, with whom he could form a bridge with the old world. It would create a more formal alliance of Olympians and Titans, one that would bind Titan loyalties ever closer to the new gods.

Not Hera: his sister, his first co-conspirator, his equal.

'I know him better than you,' Hera says. 'The old ways are dead. We buried them with Cronus.'

'I'll tell Poseidon no,' Hestia says, and there is a ring of authority in her voice.

Hera knows Poseidon is no match for her sister. Like the flame she tends, she is comforting and warm, but she is powerful too.

'You should heed what I've said,' says Hestia. 'Think about what your answer will be.'

After such unsettling conversations, Hera is eager to get away from Mount Olympus. She finds a distant pool, and bathes in crystal waters. The water is cold, bracing, a welcome contrast to the sun that beats down on its glittering surface. She surrenders herself to its buoyant embrace, letting herself drift. A bird lands on the bank, darting its sleek little head into the damp earth, searching for food. It pauses for a moment, casting a beady yellow eye towards the goddess, then resumes its hunt. Its wings are folded back along its body, its sleek feathers blue-grey, darkening at the tip of its tail. A cuckoo. It finds what it's looking for, puffing up its chest and tipping back its head to gulp down its prey. Then it turns back towards her, its curious gaze intent upon her for a few moments more before it ruffles its wings and flies away. In a pleasant state of dreaminess, Hera waits for more.

But it isn't a bird that descends next from the clear blue sky; it is a miracle. A rainbow, faint at first, then brightening into something more dazzling and vivid as it arcs towards the grass.

Hera lifts her head, and Iris is there, gold-winged and as beautiful as the rainbow that conjured her – the messenger goddess, sent from Olympus. She dips her head respectfully to Hera.

'Is there news?' Hera calls.

'Zeus summons all the gods to gather at the waterfall of the river Styx,' Iris answers.

'All of them? He said nothing about it at the council today.'

'He announced it just now, and sent me here. He said this is where you'd be.'

Hera's curiosity is piqued. Her strokes are swift and efficient, bringing her to shore, her feet bare on the mud. Iris holds out the tunic she discarded on the grass, and the goddess shrugs it over her wet skin. The heat of the sun is already drying her; by the time she reaches the Styx, she will be immaculate again.

She realises that Iris is waiting for her dismissal. 'Go, tell the others,' she says, and Iris smiles gratefully before disappearing again into the ether. Hera curses Zeus for not giving her any prior warning. It would serve him right if Iris hadn't been able to find her – and besides, how did he know where to look?

She's too eager to know what's going on to dwell on it. And so, like Iris, she takes to the skies, her tunic transformed to feathers, her bones hollowing and her body shrinking as she takes on the shape of a hawk.

The earth falls away beneath her, the delight of flying over-shadowed by her impatience to arrive. She follows the broad, winding curves of Oceanus to the horn of the Styx, where the waters tumble over a high crag, falling through a wide fissure into the depths of the earth itself. Some instinct tells her not to reveal herself at once, but to hold back and get the measure of whatever is about to take place first.

She perches on a rocky outcrop at the peak of the crag, watching as other deities file down the steep slope towards the underground cavern. Her wings are tucked down at her side, her eyes focused on the immortals, but she feels a stirring of feathers on the back of her neck and turns her head.

The impossibility of Gaia, here and present on the peak, in her goddess form. For a moment, Hera is overwhelmed by the memory of her standing in the twilight halls of Oceanus. The first time that Hera could remember seeing colours that weren't veiled in grey shadow and dim light. Like then, Gaia is cloaked in green, a swathe of verdant cloth, and there are ivy leaves woven between the points of her golden crown. Hera knows that if Gaia lifts the hem of her robe, she will see the roots entwined around her ankles, coiling and uncoiling with every movement, keeping her anchored to the earth. In the bright, clear air of the upper world, Gaia brings the scent of the earth with her.

Hera hadn't understood at first what Gaia was, that the woman she saw before her was only a form that she borrowed every now and again. A shape she shrugged on and off, like the hawk form that Hera wears now. But Gaia cannot lift herself from the roots that tether her, because Gaia *is* those roots, and the ground from which they grow as well. Gaia, the earth itself, the mother of everything. Even though Hera

39

comprehends it better now, still she struggles to hold the idea of Gaia in her head. That Gaia stands before her, but is spread beneath her at the same time, holding the weight of this very cliff. That she is the cliff too, and every rock and fern that grows upon it, every mountain on the horizon and every valley that dips between them. It's even more difficult in this form, her hawk-brain aching as it tries to contain her thoughts. With a shudder, she steps free and is Hera again.

'You were summoned too?' Hera asks. 'But how?'

Gaia smiles. 'I'm here for you,' she tells her, and Hera furrows her brow. This is Gaia's way. She's always mysterious. Maybe it's a consequence of being the first to be born of Chaos. Gaia spent an eternity alone before there was anything else, before she shaped the world and brought forth the primordial forces that would give way to the Titans and the gods. Gaia isn't used to explaining herself, or remembering that no one else shares her perspective. No one else can see all the way back to the start of everything. For Gaia, every ancient mountain was only recently a pebble. She only takes an interest when a monumental shift is taking place.

Hera, like every other god, has not seen her since the fall of Cronus.

So why is she here now?

Gaia nods towards the waterfall. 'It's time,' she says, and Hera sees that no one else remains out here. They are all assembled below; it only remains for Hera to join them.

Iris must have spread the word to every corner of the world. Beneath the earth, where the water from above crashes into the subterranean stream, Titans jostle with nymphs for space. At the front, by the bank of the dark river, stand Hera's brothers: Zeus, Hades and Poseidon.

Hera scans the crowd for her sisters. They're standing to the side at the front, and she peers at their faces, trying to discern if they know more than she does. Aphrodite stands apart from them, her beautiful face smooth and serene.

It is like the assembly of allegiance oaths, except the seven of them were together then, in front of everyone else, seated upon their thrones. This cavern is more crowded than the megaron had been, populated by all the newer gods born since, but Hera can see the old ones among them. No sign of Oceanus or Tethys, though. She pictures them in the dim depths of his river, submerged in their echoing caves. They came to swear loyalty, she can imagine them saying, and that's enough. They have largely stayed out of the affairs of the gods, remaining neutral in the battle against Cronus. They sheltered Hera from him when she was a child, but they did not fight alongside her when she was grown. Perhaps yet another summons from Zeus is too much. For their service to the young Hera, they might think their absence today will be tolerated.

Everywhere Hera looks, she can see Zeus' stamp. So many of his children are gathered here: those with the power to stir weather from the skies and to coax forth the stars each night to twinkle against the inky dome of the heavens; those with gifts of wisdom and poetry, bright-haired nymphs who bow their heads before him now.

Metis joins him, and Hera sees that they have plans about which she knows nothing.

On Crete, Zeus and Hera had always made their plans together.

He lifts a hand and the throng falls silent. His thunderbolt is clenched in his raised fist, its sharp prongs glittering in the single shaft of sunlight that falls on him through the cleft in the ground above their heads, like nothing else that exists on earth.

Hera glances at Helios. His face is impassive, but she finds herself wondering what he might be thinking. What kind of conversations take place in the Titan halls, where the roar of the river muffles all sound? What will they say about this summit when it's done?

'It's pleasing to see how our divine family flourishes,' Zeus says. 'Our numbers have grown since we came together last. Back then, I brought you to Olympus to swear your oaths to me.'

To me, Hera thinks. *Not us?*

'But things have changed since then, and our rule must change with it. It is time,' Zeus says, 'to divide the world into realms for which my brothers and I can take responsibility. While Oceanus has control of his great river, we must take charge of the seas. Another land lies beneath the earth itself, here where we stand now: the shadowy caverns of the Under-world. It will be the realm of the dead, for the new mortals we create will not simply rot into the earth, but will go there after they die: a shadow kingdom that will worship us in death as they do in life. That kingdom will need a ruler too. And finally, the heavens: one of us will rule the skies and all the land we see from above.'

Fury surges in Hera's breast as his words sink in. Three realms, three rulers. She looks to Hestia and Demeter, and does not see the same shock wrought on their faces as she feels within her. Nor on Aphrodite's. Did everyone else expect this? For her, it comes from a clear blue sky. She won't stand for it.

As strong as rock, Gaia's hand clamps around her forearm. Hera looks at her, bewildered, thrown off course as she was about to charge forward, but Gaia does not let her move. She is tethered to the ground, as surely as if she were held by tree roots, unable to take a single step. She feels the weight pulsing from Gaia's touch, dragging her down, anchoring her where she stands, the ichor in her veins thickening to sap, and her eyes widen in horror as she realises she cannot move to stop this from taking place. Frantic, she searches Gaia's face to understand why the goddess would betray her like this, but there is no clue in Gaia's wise, kind eyes.

Metis brings forth a bowl containing three polished stones. One glimmers blue, one is sleek and black, and the third is a bright crystal. She shakes them into a square of cloth and draws the corners together, holding the edges of the fabric so the stones within it swing concealed beneath her fist.

Hera hears the rippling of Iris' feathered wings before she sees her. Swift and graceful, she stands before Zeus with a golden pitcher in her hand. Styx steps forth to dip it into her waters, and hands it to Metis. Metis takes it, tilts it, and a silvery stream of water falls to the ground as the brothers swear their unbreakable oath to abide by the outcome. Hera opens her mouth, knowing she cannot speak, and of course no sound comes out. Her throat is as dry as bark.

Poseidon is the first to draw his stone from the pouch. He scowls at the blue gleam but says nothing. Hades pulls out the black pebble. And Zeus' eyes meet Metis' in triumph as he reaches in and brandishes the crystal.

There is no doubt in Hera's mind that the two of them engineered it this way. Zeus, with his thunderbolt, was never going to be consigned to the waves or beneath the earth.

But Hera, daughter of Cronus, has nothing. The world is divided between her brothers, leaving her hands empty.

Gaia's voice is in her head, so low she doesn't know if the goddess speaks the words out loud.

Don't let them see your anger.

It isn't in Hera's nature to hide it.

But already, Hestia is moving. Her voice cuts across the crowd, and for a wild second, Hera thinks that her sister is about to do exactly what Gaia has prevented her from doing.

'Zeus, as king of the heavens, I ask you to grant me a favour,' Hestia says, and Poseidon lifts his head to stare at her as she goes on. 'You brothers have taken your share; I want mine.'

A ripple of excitement runs through the spectators at this.

'You have the land, the sea and the Underworld between you. I only ask for the hearth to be my domain. Entrust it to me, let me be the goddess of its flames in every immortal home.'

Zeus shrugs. 'Of course.'

She hasn't finished. 'And let me devote myself to that entirely. Swear to me now that I can stay as I am, untouched by anyone else. Swear that I will never be compelled to take a husband to distract me from my purpose.'

Zeus cannot fail to see Poseidon's outrage. He smiles. Then he takes Hestia's hand and speaks. 'I'll swear it, sister,' he says. 'The hearth is yours, its sacred flame your responsibility. And no one will claim you as a wife, if that's what you want.'

Poseidon's face contorts, but there is nothing he can do. Hera feels no sympathy for his position, but she shares his helpless rage.

'Hestia is goddess of the hearth,' Zeus says to the crowd. He turns back to Hestia. 'Gods will honour you every day, sister, when they come together at the fireside. And Demeter.' He brandishes his arm towards their sister. 'Demeter, who has taught the mortals to cultivate grain and who smiles on their crops, you will be goddess of the harvest, and they will owe their gratitude to you for what you provide them.'

If she could only break Gaia's hold, if she could only interrupt him . . .

'Aphrodite,' he goes on. 'Your domain is desire. Be the goddess of love, for gods and mortals alike.' He makes it sound like he's bestowing her power upon her, the power she already wields. As though it is in his gift to decide.

Hera can only wait, powerless and seething, to see what he has in store for her. What domain, what aspect, what role does he think she will accept when he has taken it all for himself?

It's worse than she could imagine.

He says nothing about her at all.

Without so much as a glance at her, Zeus talks about the glorious future that lies ahead, of the plans he and his brothers have for the three realms they command. There are cheers, some enthusiastic, some dutiful. At last, Zeus brings it to a close. As the crowd of immortals starts to disperse, Gaia's hold on Hera finally begins to loosen.

Hera is too experienced a warrior to make any headlong rush now that the initial burst of anger is dissipating, hardening into something else within her. She lets Gaia lead her away, the two of them concealed behind the waterfall, their words drowned in the crash and hiss of its torrent. She will hear an explanation before she decides what to do next.

From where they stand, she can see the departing Titans. Some of them move faster than others – *Eager to get away*, Hera thinks. Zeus made a show of consolidating the alliance between Olympians and Titans, but the purpose of it was to demonstrate his strength and make more explicit the hierarchy that separates them.

'Why did you stop me?' she demands of Gaia. 'I'm the daughter of Cronus too. Why should my brothers take the power that is rightfully mine?'

'You should learn from your sisters,' Gaia tells her. 'Hestia, Demeter, even Aphrodite – they didn't object. They didn't need me to prevent them, either.'

'I rescued my sisters from Cronus,' Hera says, and her voice is colder than it has ever been. 'We stood against him before Aphrodite did. My claim is greater than theirs; greater than Poseidon's and Hades' too.'

Gaia's face is contemplative. 'Aphrodite can wield more power than anyone, without ever bearing the responsibility that Zeus has assumed. And she'll never face the threat he does now.' This gets Hera's attention, as she knew it would. 'Hestia and Demeter see that too,' she goes on. 'Hestia has been clever to defend herself like this, and to make it so public. Demeter has acted more quietly, but she makes herself invaluable without drawing attention to what she's doing. She nurtures plants and flowers, tends to my lands to make them beautiful and fertile. Hestia has the fire; she makes Mount Olympus a home, and could render it cold and lightless if she chose, just as Demeter could blight my earth if she had cause. Zeus has no wish for the thankless chores of keeping the hearth or growing things. He gives them these tasks without realising their importance. Instead, he has put himself above the rest, and his subjects' eyes will turn to him in times of trouble, not towards your sisters.'

'So?'

'Cronus was cruel to his children,' Gaia says. 'But there were Titans who lived happy lives when he ruled. Some that remember Ouranos, and how much worse their existence was then. Once, it was Cronus who saved the world from tyranny. Zeus overthrew him. Now he's king of the heavens, so if anyone comes for Olympus, it will be Zeus they topple.'

'Is that why you didn't want me to put myself forward?' Still, she is haughty.

'There are other ways to rule. Sometimes the true power is in the shadows. Someone who stays out of the light, and watches others shrivel and burn in its glare.'

'What power do I have when my brothers have taken it all for themselves?'

Gaia's gold-flecked eyes are searing. Hera feels a giddiness when she looks into them. She remembers that Gaia is ageless, that she was the first to exist and that she will endure when everything else is gone. She has watched two regimes rise and fall already, and still she walks free.

'I saved you for a reason,' Gaia says. 'And I know you would be foolish to put yourself where Zeus is now.'

And although Hera recognises the truth of what Gaia says, still she grinds her teeth together at the thought of it.

4

He waits for her in her chamber on Mount Olympus. She doesn't give away her surprise when she opens the door to see him there. He looks young, strong, unapologetic. In his hand, he turns the thunderbolt over and over.

Did she expect something different? A spiky defensiveness, maybe, that would prove he knew he was in the wrong? But there is none of that. She's sure that, for him, everything has gone exactly as he planned.

'Why didn't you tell me?' she asks. It's the first question that comes to her lips, out of many more. He's standing right in the centre of the room, like it's his to command. She walks past him as though he isn't there at all, so that he'll have to turn to face her, crossing to the window cut out of the stone wall, letting the breeze cool the heat rising in her cheeks. She won't hover in her doorway like a guest, when it's he who is the intruder.

'What would you have done?'

'I should have drawn one of those lots,' she says. 'It was my right.'

He looks amused. 'How could I let that happen? If you

had drawn the sea or the Underworld, you would have been consigned to salty depths or dark caverns, where I could not see you from here.'

'Or I might be in the heavens,' she points out. 'And you in one of those.'

He shakes his head, his eyes sparkling.

It confirms what she already knew: Metis made sure that Zeus drew the heavens.

She keeps Gaia's words at the forefront of her mind. Aphrodite chose her realm before Zeus granted it to her. Now Hestia and Demeter have staked their territory too, just as clearly as her brothers did. For someone so watchful, Hera didn't see this coming.

'I haven't taken anything from you,' Zeus says. 'There's no need for you to rule the sea or the Underworld. You can rule the skies with me. As a queen. As my wife.'

She stares at him.

'You're Cronus' daughter,' he says. He's moving closer to her, and she feels like she did when Gaia temporarily incapacitated her, only this time it's because she's too stunned to respond. 'You fought the Titans. The two of us together will be more powerful than one of us alone.'

Hestia and Gaia, both of them knew. They knew what was in his mind. Her thoughts are racing, but one comes through clearly. *He doesn't want me to challenge him. I have as much claim as he does to the heavens, and he means to add mine to his to strengthen his position.*

'We were together in Crete,' he says. 'Just we two.' His gaze is full of intent, of meaning that makes her stomach churn.

'The two of us and Metis,' she reminds him. 'Plotting to attack our father.'

'And now you can have everything you wanted, everything you dreamed of back then.' His words are relentless, his tone loaded with insinuations she has never considered. He's standing so close that her skin prickles. 'You want to rule; it's why we fought Cronus. You don't want a portion of the world. You want all of it. That's what we'll have together.'

'We wanted to be rid of Cronus, not to be like him.'

'We won't be.' He reaches out, his hand on the back of her neck, and she jerks away. 'Cronus is gone and the world is ours. You want to be queen, don't you?'

She pauses. 'I did. With all of us together, as we were.'

He isn't deflected. 'Now everyone else has made their choice. What will you do?'

'You have a host of daughters,' she tells him. 'All your Titaness and goddess consorts, all your nymphs. Even Metis. Why would you need a wife?'

For the first time in this conversation, she thinks she sees something sincere in his face. Some ripple of true emotion. 'I always longed for you,' he says.

She is blindsided, for the second time today, and it makes her furious. 'Nothing needed to change,' she says. 'We were ruling better than the Titans ever did.'

He raises his hand, batting her words away. 'The world is already different to the one we took from the Titans. If we want to keep it, we have to be ready to defend it. There is no one I could choose who is stronger than you, Hera, no one who would be better than the two of us together.'

It is a warping of what she knows to be true. They *were* better together than anyone else could be. When she came to Crete, freed from the dim halls of Oceanus, when the world around her was bathed in light for the very first time, and she saw the possibility of a future she hadn't even known to dream of, it was Zeus who shared her ambition. Zeus who saw the same possibilities. But it was never like this, never what he's saying now.

She takes a step away from him and watches his face change. 'I won't marry you, Zeus.' Her voice is clear, her words decisive. 'You need to leave my chamber now, and never speak of this again.'

He's between her and the doorway. The light fades from his eyes, his face closed and unreadable, and she has no idea what he's going to do.

The moment passes, and he shrugs. 'As you wish,' he says.

And he leaves. But she can still feel his presence lingering in the room: the stillness before a storm.

She tries not to think of him. She stays away from the palace, plunging deep into her beloved forests and valleys. Sometimes she runs through them in the skin of a lion or the shape of a bear, taking respite in the feeling of uncomplicated freedom – only thinking of the stretch of muscles in unfamiliar limbs, the sun warm on her fur, the storm of emotions muffled by animal instinct. Even so, Zeus' face will rise up in her mind, unbidden. The flash of honesty she saw when he told her he wanted her.

Hera thinks back and tries to recall a time when Zeus has had his desires thwarted. She can't. Zeus always gets what he wants, in the end.

And so she stays away, unwilling to hear another entreaty, another proposal, another demand.

But she can't leave the palace forever. She's consumed by fury over the coup, her unease about Zeus burning away like mist in the heat of her rage when she thinks of it. The longer she stays away from Olympus, the more she can see whatever power she still has diminishing. She won't let it go.

She sighs, a loud huff of breath disturbing her whiskers and ruffling the grass where she lays her shaggy head. She sits up, the lion shape falling away, a goddess again, and hugs her knees close to her chest. She stares at the horizon, at the distant mountain peaks, and she wonders what to do.

She has to go back. She has to retake her throne. But the world has been divided up, and she isn't sure which realm she can have for herself. The only one offered to her is wifehood, and she doesn't want it.

There is, of course, no sign of Gaia. No chance of questioning her again, asking advice on what to do next. What had Gaia meant by wielding power from the shadows? Did it mean becoming Zeus' wife and ruling behind him? She frowns. It isn't only that she can't think of Zeus as a lover; Zeus, who was her friend on Crete, her friend and ally when there were only the two of them. She doesn't know how long he's been nurturing his fantasies of her. For all his rapacious appetites, she never dreamed he would see her like that. He might be handsome, might have charm or power enough to conquer a hundred other goddesses, but he is her brother. She doesn't want him as anything else. She doesn't want to be his wife, or anyone else's either. Her freedom is the greatest gift she won from the war.

From what little Hera knows of her mother, being wife of the king of the heavens means servitude. For Rhea, it meant bearing Cronus' children and having them torn away from her arms so they couldn't grow up and threaten him.

Hera didn't escape her father only to find herself in her mother's role.

It can't be what Gaia intended for her, not when she spirited her away from Cronus as a baby, and not when she held her back from challenging Zeus at the assembly. Gaia hasn't saved her to be subservient to Zeus. Gaia chose Hera, and there must be a reason.

If she could ask her ... if she could even ask Rhea. But Rhea disappeared after the trickery with her last-born child, the infant Zeus. There are countless hiding places for a beloved daughter of the earth if she doesn't want to be found.

Hera thinks of the maternal line: Gaia, Rhea and now Hera. The goddess who created the world, the goddess who nurtured it and the goddess who will protect it. But stronger than that line is its dark twin: Ouranos, Cronus and Zeus, who only care for what they can take.

What does Gaia hope for? She can only think it must be for Hera to break the pattern. To prevent another tyrannical king from crushing everyone else under his heel in his pursuit of power. To bring about the kind of world Gaia would have ruled if Ouranos hadn't overpowered her, the kind that she would have handed down to her daughter if Rhea's spirit hadn't been broken by Cronus. A world under the rule of benevolent goddesses, instead of power-hungry gods.

She gets to her feet, energised by the realisation.

Her mother and her grandmother couldn't do it, but perhaps Hera can.

She lies in wait for Demeter. Hestia rarely leaves the mountain summit, but Demeter will never stay confined. Hera hovers in the foothills, a watchful hawk, and hides among the trees, coiled serpentine around a branch, until at last she sees her, and takes her own shape once more.

Her sister wears a band of plaited flowers around her head and a robe of flowing green. She glances towards the forest, where Hera stands shaded by the wide sweep of an oak tree, and her eyes widen.

'Hera?'

She casts a look around her, then hurries towards Hera. In the sun-dappled greenish-gold light of the woods, she is beautiful, and Hera feels a surge of affection. Since Zeus left her chamber, she has been alone.

'Why haven't you returned?' Demeter asks.

'To marry Zeus?' Hera retorts, and the look of astonishment on her sister's face is almost comical.

'Is that what he wants?'

Hera nods. 'I won't.'

Demeter looks thoughtful. 'Hades is gone,' she says. 'He left for the Underworld after they drew the lots, and he hasn't come back.'

'Was he angry?'

'I don't know. I don't know what he thought.'

Hera imagines the banishment. From the highest peak in the clouds, to the gloom and shadows under the earth. 'Poseidon?' she asks.

'He's taken the palace of Nereus, a golden mansion beneath the waves,' Demeter tells her. Nereus, the bearded fish-tailed god, who until now has ruled the seas. 'He chased the old god from his halls, and now they belong to him. He wanted the sea-nymph Amphitrite for his bride, but she fled. He sent the other sea-gods after her, and Delphin found her and brought her back to him. He still comes to Mount Olympus frequently – he and Zeus have much to discuss.'

But Hades has stayed away. Hera wonders why. 'So there is only Zeus, and some of the time Poseidon,' she muses.

Demeter looks wary. 'What do you mean?'

'Aren't you angry?' Hera asks. 'The world wasn't theirs to divide between them – it was all of ours!'

The leaves above them flutter in the wind. Hera tenses, looking for any sign that Zephyrus, god of the west wind, hovers close, listening for snatches of their conversation that he can carry back to Zeus.

The swaying leaves cast a ripple of green-tinged shadows across Demeter's face, and it's hard to make out her expression. 'I have my share,' she says at last.

'It's not what you were owed,' Hera says. 'Daughter of Cronus.'

'I have my own daughter now.'

Her own daughter, yes, and the bounty of the earth in her hands besides. Is she happy enough with that?

'We could take it from them,' Hera says, a last-ditch attempt to convince her. 'You, me and Hestia.' She wants to explain the revelation she had in the meadow; the vision not yet fully formed in her mind of a world where the daughters hold power and not the sons. 'I think that Gaia wanted me to see what Zeus was capable of – she wanted me to know what was in his heart.'

'Gaia?' Demeter asks, confused.

'She was there,' Hera says. 'At the assembly, with me. Didn't you see her?'

Demeter shakes her head.

'Never mind. She held me back, she stopped me from challenging him.'

Demeter is unconvinced. 'If she *was* there . . . you say she stopped you then,' she says. 'Why do you think she wants you to do it now?'

Hera searches for the words. 'She wanted me to understand. I need to stop him from taking what's ours – like Ouranos did to her, like Cronus did to Rhea. Think of it, Demeter. The world we could make, compared to him.'

'And how would we do it? With another war?' Demeter shakes her head. 'How would that be any better?'

Hera flounders, unable to answer.

Demeter meets her eyes at last and sighs. 'If you want to fight,' she says, 'I won't join you. No one will.'

And she walks away, leaving Hera alone.

Hera is stricken by her sister's rejection, but she doesn't allow herself to dwell on it for long. She takes the hawk form again and, determined, flies to Mount Olympus, where she watches the palace gates, wings tucked and beak nestled into her soft breast-feathers. It's a hive of activity; a constant flow of comings and goings. It isn't long before she sees Zeus striding out past the Horae, down the marble steps, with Metis on one side and the tall, thoughtful Titan Prometheus on the other.

She takes her chance, gliding in overhead on a thermal current and circling the roof. In a quiet square, where only a small fountain tinkles in the centre, she swoops down and steps through the surrounding columns as herself. She's in the back corridors of the palace, with the uncanny sense that she is an intruder here.

While the courtyards outside were busy, here it is cool and silent, sunlight streaming through the openings in the roof, falling in honeyed rectangles on the floor. She doesn't know how long she has, so she makes her way to the hearth as quickly as she can.

Hestia is alone in the throne room. Hera's last hope of an ally here. She takes a deep breath, and enters. Her eyes are drawn to the row of thrones, the majestic seat that has been hers since the fall of the Titans.

Hestia looks up, sees her, and at once enfolds Hera in her embrace. She holds herself stiff at first, unprepared, but Hestia's hair is soft against her cheek, and the warm, smoky scent of it smells so much like home that it fills her eyes with unexpected tears.

'Have you come back?' Hestia draws away, pulling Hera down to sit among the pile of furs propped up on the low benches by the hearth.

Hera shakes her head, resisting for a moment as she glances towards the high arched entrance.

'Zeus is gone,' Hestia says, 'Poseidon is in the seas – no one will be back for a while.'

'I saw him leave, with Metis and Prometheus.'

'It's the mortals,' Hestia says. 'It's all they talk about; they'll be preoccupied with it for who knows how long. You don't need to worry.' Her voice is low and gentle, a voice that invites confidence, that coaxes out secrets. She has a gift, a way of creating calm in this cosy little circle. Hera gives in to it now – the only place that she can bear to be still, where her restlessness feels soothed.

It emboldens her to ask her sister's advice, rather than challenge her like she did Demeter. 'What do you think I should do?'

Hestia's gaze is meditative, trained on the fire. 'You could marry him.'

This is worse than Demeter's refusal to join her. It knocks the breath from her body for a second, before she can recover her equanimity enough to retort, 'You wouldn't marry Poseidon, how can you advise me to marry Zeus?'

'Zeus didn't care about letting me have my freedom,' Hestia says. 'He didn't want me, not like he wants you. I don't think there's anything he wants more.'

Hera shakes her head. 'Is that really what you think? That I should give in?'

'You've heard what Poseidon did to get his bride,' Hestia says. 'He sent his sea-gods to search for her and they brought her back in chains.'

'But she wasn't an Olympian. Zeus wouldn't dare do that to me.'

'Maybe not,' Hestia says. 'But things have changed; Zeus has more power now than Poseidon did when he sought my hand. Poseidon had to accept my refusal. You don't know that Zeus will accept yours. But if you agree to his proposal, he would make you queen. You could carry on, the same as before.'

'As his wife? How can you say that?'

'What else is there? If you fight him and lose . . .'

The spell is broken, the peace between them hanging in tatters. Hera gets to her feet. 'I've told him no, and he can't force me.'

'So what will you do?'

Hera holds her sister's gaze. 'I'll find a way.'

Hestia shakes her head, her eyes dark with sadness. 'If you run again,' she says, 'make sure he can't find you.'

*   *   *

She needs a plan. Angry as she is, she isn't quite ready to storm Mount Olympus alone. Not yet, anyway.

She's returned to her distant meadow, the quiet lake where she can sit on the bank and think as long as she needs to. She's gone over and over Demeter's rejection, Hestia's advice. The anger is bile in her throat, a burning poison that eats away at her from within.

Swallow it down, she tells herself.

A cloud drifts in front of the sun, dimming its light. Hera feels a drop of rain, then another, gathering pace. She glances up. The whole sky is grey and darkening rapidly, the clouds swelling. There is a growl of thunder in the distance, low and ominous, building to a dull roar.

Lightning flashes, its livid scar pulsing bright white across the heavens, and for a moment, Hera thinks she sees a ragged gap tear open in the clouds. The rain drums down in freezing sheets, and she is running towards Mount Olympus, dodging the lightning that stabs down from the sky. Soaking wet ferns slap against her calves, branches tangle in her hair, and she pays no heed.

There have been storms since the war, but not like this. She hasn't run so fast since she was plunging into the fray against the Titans. Her body remembers what that was like: heat and passion and determination propelling her forward. She doesn't know if this is an attack, a rebellion, striking back at Zeus' power grab on Olympus. Gaia's warning, that all eyes would turn to him: could that have happened so quickly? Or is it some other threat that she hasn't seen coming, something that flourished in her absence?

Even as she runs, she is undecided. If someone is raising a challenge against her brothers, will she fight against them or with them? If she defends Olympus again at their sides, will they honour her with what she deserves or will she find herself isolated and with nothing once more?

All she knows is: if there is a fight, she wants to be there.

She expects to see chaos, a din of battle-cries, boulders torn from the earth and hurled up the mountainside. But as she reaches its base, she sees no sign of fighting. Already, the sky is clearing. The rain slows and steadies, the thunder dying away in the east and the wind softening into a breeze.

Cautious of what she will discover, she begins to climb.

Her hair clings to her shoulders in sodden ropes, trickling water down her back and over her collarbones. Overhead, an eagle circles, its silhouette black against the grey.

She reaches the upper slopes, and all is still and quiet. Above her, the steps to their palace begin, but she sees a figure standing further down the mountainside. His head is bowed, rivulets of rainwater streaming from his crown.

She takes a step towards him, and then another. She reaches out to touch his arm, and his head jerks up at the brush of her fingers.

His face is hollow, his eyes bleak. Despite herself, she feels a flash of sympathy for him. A leftover from their days together on Crete, the pull of the bond that holds her to him, one forged in the flames of battle. She wonders, for a moment, if his pain is caused by her absence. If he has realised what he has lost in driving her away; if he regrets, at last, what he has done.

'What is it?' she asks.

'Metis,' he answers.

He isn't the cocky god who brushed off her concerns about mortals, or the untouchable ruler seizing control of the heavens. This is a Zeus she has never seen before, perhaps never will again.

'A prophecy,' he says, 'from the earth – I heard it whisper from the trees, rise up from the valleys.'

Hera feels a cold twist of fear, strange and unfamiliar. 'What did it say?'

'That she would bear a child stronger than its father.' His eyes meet hers. 'I knew it was too late already. That if I let him be born . . .' He breaks off, but Hera knows what he thought.

'The same fear our father had about us,' she says. 'But you wouldn't do as Cronus did.' She's sure of it.

'I was overcome with rage,' he says. 'I stirred up the sky, thinking I would strike her down.'

'And what, chain her in Tartarus next to Cronus?'

He shakes his head. 'Her baby would still be born.'

'You should never have taken her as a lover,' Hera says. 'She has a mind like no one else.' Though for all of Metis' genius, she thinks, she didn't stay away from Zeus. His impetuous nature, as unpredictable as the thunderbolt, should have repelled the cool-headed, grey-eyed Titaness. Hera can't understand why it didn't.

He doesn't seem to hear her. 'I pictured a son as depraved as our father, even more powerful, bent on taking the heavens. And I wasn't just raising a storm; I *was* the storm. I was the sky itself; I filled its dome as though I was Ouranos.' He grasps for the words to explain. 'I could feel the horizon tethering me, as he must have done when he lay upon Gaia, and I saw what happened to him. Cronus tore Ouranos apart with his sickle, scattering the pieces of his father into the ocean. And then I rose up against Cronus and cast him into Tartarus. The same history happening again. Father deposed by son, twice over.'

If he hadn't pushed Hera aside, if he'd kept things as they were, with the power shared between them, then he would never have had to fear this. He's made himself a tyrant like his father, and his father before him, and now he thinks his own son will come for him. This is all Zeus' fault.

'I couldn't let the child be born,' he says. 'I was as vast as Ouranos, and everything was below me. Metis – I took her into the sky. I *was* the sky.' He pauses. 'There is no other way to describe it. And when I was myself again – she was gone.' As he says the words, she can see his eyes beginning to lighten. His horror at himself is passing, alchemising into something else. 'The threat was gone.'

A brief expression settles on his face, gone as quickly as it landed, but Hera shudders. For that moment, Zeus resembled their father. A crafty, cunning gleam in his eye. His satisfaction that he was safe, that he would remain unchallenged.

Zeus looks out across the mountain, at the clouds swirling around the peak above their heads, and Hera recalls Metis at their last meeting, the flash of something concealed in her expression when she spoke to Hera of Zeus' power and the prospect of a better world. Did the Titaness think she could bear his child and bring about a new rule that way – to take power back for herself? Had she tried to conspire against him, and been outmanoeuvred by his brutality, greater than she had anticipated?

She can hear Hestia's words again: that Zeus wants Hera more than anything, and that nothing will stop him. She makes the decision before she can question herself any further. She leaps forward, springing into the shape of a dove, and swoops down into the empty air. She's gone before he can call her back.

They owe no small part of their victory to Metis. She was

the reason Zeus thrived in secrecy in the caves of Mount Dicte, hidden from his father's eyes. Now Hera knows there is no loyalty Zeus won't betray in order to defend his position.

The thoughts she'd had about returning to Mount Olympus, demanding her own share, seem too precarious now. She needs time to work out a better plan.

She's leaving Olympus. She's going back home.

5

Her first home – the first she can remember, at least. There are only flashes from before: a fuzzy light before her newly opened eyes, a rush of air against her face. Then darkness. A descent beneath the earth.

Gods grow quickly, their infancy short-lived. It isn't long before a god becomes what they will be forever: strong, powerful and fully grown. Hera came into her true self in the caverns that yawn beneath Oceanus, a place where daylight could never reach her.

It's a place where she can hide from the sky.

Tethys sighs when she sees her return, though she embraces her, Hera's body tense in her arms. She has a chamber prepared for the goddess; she brings her nectar and ambrosia, and speaks of inconsequential things, her voice calm and soothing. Hera doesn't listen to the words she speaks, only the rhythm of her chatter. In it, she can hear the murmur of water over rock, the ebb and flow of gentle waves splashing on to a pebbled shore.

'I won't let anyone know that you're here,' Tethys says.

'The nymphs would be so excited to know we have such a guest, they wouldn't leave you alone, and perhaps you don't wish for endless company.' There is a delicate silence before she continues. 'Perhaps you would prefer to be left alone.'

It hovers unspoken between them. The question of Hera's presence here, what it means for the careful balance between the Titans and the Olympians. The recent memory of Poseidon, sending his gods up the river to chase Amphitrite here, to the edge of the world. The peace that has seemed so solid for so long, suddenly as fragile as thin ice, bowing and cracking and ready to give way at the slightest pressure.

'Don't tell anyone,' Hera says. Whatever Poseidon did, she still thinks the idea of Zeus following her here is unlikely. She tries to picture him descending through the dripping caves, the sizzle and spit of his thunderbolt in the murky light, and it doesn't fit. Zeus is fire and air; he doesn't belong in the mossy earth. But she won't make Metis' mistake; she won't assume she can predict his actions any better than she can know what shape the lightning will take before it strikes.

Tethys nods and rises to leave, but before she can, Hera can't help but ask a question.

'When I came here before,' she says, 'why did you take me in?'

Tethys hesitates, then sits back down.

'Gaia asked me to,' she says, and Hera remembers Metis saying something similar. 'She's my mother – mother of us all. And it was for my sister Rhea too. Your mother.'

'Did you ever see Rhea again?'

Tethys shakes her head. 'No one has, not since she bore Zeus.'

There is a silence.

'What do you think happened to her?'

Tethys looks at the dark stone wall. 'I think she disappeared back into the mountains and the forests that she loved. She was the only one of Gaia's daughters who could create them – she could summon them up from the earth, just for the joy of it. She would be happiest there.'

'Do you know why she married Cronus?'

Surprise ripples through Tethys at this shift in the conversation. 'I don't know what she thought, not really. Oceanus and I were always here, in the waters that have always been ours.' She pauses. 'The two of them were the strongest of all of Gaia's children. I know Cronus thought marrying would make them stronger still.'

'I know what he felt. But not her. Did she want to marry him? Or did he force her?'

'I can't say.' Tethys' lovely face is calm, her voice sweet and steady. 'I only know that when Hestia was born, Rhea never dreamed what he was thinking. I remember Gaia told me how Rhea handed him his daughter, wrapped in swaddling, so he could see her sweet little face.'

All Cronus had seen, Hera knew, was a child who might one day rise up against her sire.

'Even Gaia didn't know what was in his mind with the first. When Demeter was born second, she tried to appeal to his pity, but he refused. It was when you were born next that she tried reason: "Another girl," she said to him. "A girl won't cause you any harm."' Tethys smiles at Hera. 'Wrong, of course.'

'But he let her take me.'

'Gaia argued that it had taken him, a son, to overthrow his father. Not a daughter. While he thought about it, she brought you here in secret. And for her sake and Rhea's sake, I kept you.'

Cronus had devoured two more sons before Zeus was born, and by then Rhea had come up with her own plan. Wrapping a stone in swaddling, she gave that to her husband instead, and gave the baby to her mother. Gaia spirited the infant Zeus away to Crete, just as Hera had been smuggled here to Oceanus.

'You had to hide from Cronus then,' Tethys says. 'But why have you come here now?'

Hera sighs. 'Zeus wants to marry me,' she says. 'He's stolen the rule of the heavens for himself, and he thinks I'll be content to be his wife instead of queen.'

Tethys frowns. 'Wouldn't you be both?'

'Was Rhea?'

Tethys looks as though she's choosing her words carefully. 'You aren't very like your mother,' she says. 'Rhea was gentle – timid, even. She just wanted to dance in the forests, she didn't care about power. If you were married to Zeus, it would be diff—'

Hera cuts her off. 'I won't be.'

Tethys shrugs, the movement graceful as water. 'Do you know he won't follow you here?'

'I promise,' says Hera.

She veils herself, covering up her shining curls, and wears the simple garments Tethys leaves for her – robes that belong to her nymph daughters, flowing and unfussy, made with fine, soft wool and dyed the same shades of green and blue as the streams above. Necklaces of shells threaded together, pearly white and rosy pink. Hera wanders unnoticed in the day, just another nymph visiting the fountains or gathering wilflowers. When the gods gather each evening to drink together in Oceanus' halls – gods of the rivers and the seas, gods of the wind and stars, the moon and sun, from the most insignificant deities presiding over a barnacle-covered rock to the mighty Helios, who drives the chariot of the sun – she keeps herself hidden. She thinks of more carefree days, long lost to her now, when she could wander in the woods and do as she pleased. Now, she can't risk recognition – as a conqueror, a queen or a passing lover. All the possibilities she used to revel in are shrinking away, and none of the paths before her seem inviting anymore.

But in the corners, in the corridors, she listens. The river-gods talk of Poseidon's rule, of the bronze-hoofed horses with golden manes that he drives into the sea before his chariot, towards the palace he took from Nereus.

'But my cave, of course, is more than ample for me now,' she hears Nereus say, his voice a rippling gurgle. When she peers into the hall she sees him, seaweed straggled through his beard, drinking from a wide fluted shell.

There's a murmur of agreement, but Hera wonders what lies beneath the gods' smiles.

Everywhere she steps in the halls of Oceanus, she is assailed by memories of the past. Here, in this wide hall, where moss creeps across stone and the torches burn low, this is where Gaia visited her the first time. When Hera asked her who she was, Gaia's answer was as perplexing as everything else she would say.

'I came from Chaos,' she told Hera, eyes glittering in the firelight. 'There was nothing – no cave like the one we stand in now, no river above, no earth around. There were only swirling shadows, shapes that formed and dissolved before they could become solid, a great emptiness that lasted forever. And then me, in the centre of it.'

Young Hera had strained to understand. Her life so far had been confined to these caverns. She had seen nothing of the world, and now she tried to imagine its absence.

'I stretched my new-formed limbs,' Gaia went on. 'I wrenched myself free of the elements that were drifting around me, and I spread out and sank down so that I could hold myself steady. I made oceans to fill the spaces where I was not, and I girdled myself with the fresh river that flows above our heads now. I lifted the air to fill the dome above me, to make the sky and the heavens, and so I made the world.'

Hera longed to know what there was outside the sunken palace of the river-Titans. It was only from Gaia's stories that she could imagine it at all – a world created by Gaia, a world that was Gaia. The land above that rested on her broad bosom, and the caves and tunnels inside her vast body. But more than that, Gaia created another world for Hera – a world filled with immortals, a world of legends and history that Gaia had seen and shaped herself.

She was teaching her about the world, just as over on Crete, Zeus was being educated by Metis. The two of them, learning the world's history and composition so that they would be ready to rule it.

Now Hera has held that power and watched it crumble from her fists, and she is back here again – but Gaia does not come.

She goes back over the lessons she learned beneath the river, hoping she can prise out something that will help her now. She's bolder than she was back then; she no longer confines herself to the dark, damp underground, climbing the banks of Oceanus and wandering through the water-meadows, the earth squelching between her toes, lush flowers and long grass brushing her legs. Fat bees tumble from bright petals, springs bubble and surge from the ground, and fish leap from the water, flashing silver.

Black smoke drifts up from the horizon, dissolving into the cloudless blue, from the palace of Nyx, sunk deeper below the ground than the halls of Oceanus. Hera sees other nymphs filing out in procession from there when Helios wheels his chariot around the final descent of his arc. Their long black dresses distinguish them from the Oceanids and the Aurae, the nymphs of water and wind that live here. These nymphs carry torches; their hair is loose and unbound, and their eyes shine silver in the starlight. They are attendants of Hecate, who strides out ahead of them, her black dog barking at her heels. Hera lowers her head when she sees them.

Later, when Tethys comes to her chamber, she asks her about Hecate. 'Why did she pledge her loyalty to us?' It had been a great boon to the Olympians in the war. First Styx had come to them, bringing her children to swear allegiance, and then more of the ancient Titans had followed, but Hecate was the ally who had most delighted Zeus. A wandering goddess, who held sway over the heavens and sea as well as the Underworld, she would have made a formidable enemy if she had chosen to side with Cronus.

'It was a time of panic.' She sounds stern. Tethys is usually so gentle that Hera sometimes forgets her streams have carved their way through solid rock. 'Everyone had to declare one way or another. Families were divided – no one knew who they could trust. I wouldn't know what was in Hecate's mind any more than anyone else's.'

Hera muses. 'Zeus never interfered with her power, afterwards.' Other Titans had been reassigned, kept in line according to what the Olympians needed, but Hecate carried on as she had always done. 'Perhaps he didn't dare.'

Tethys looks at her steadily. 'No one here wants another war.'

Hera opens her mouth, but another voice rings out in the corridor, calling for Tethys.

'It's Klymene,' Tethys says, and Hera snatches up her veil.

She catches a glimpse as Tethys goes to the door to greet her daughter, a round-faced goddess, her hair braided and coiled around the crown of her head and her skin fresh and glowing as though she has only just sprung into the world. Klymene doesn't glance into the room from which her mother emerges, and the pair disappear into the heart of the palace, leaving Hera with her thoughts.

Tethys might insist that no Titans seek war, but the sight of Klymene reminds Hera that there are gods here who have suffered more than others. Klymene's husband is chained in Tartarus; her son is sentenced to hold up the sky. How must she feel about Zeus?

Hera needs allies, more than anything.

She lights a taper and sets it upon the damp wall.

'Won't you come?' she whispers into the empty air. 'Come back, and tell me why you saved me then, only to leave me now.'

She knows there will be no reply.

Hera wanders from the palace, not up the rough steps that lead above the ground, but into the dank tunnels that twist through the earth. The scent of moss and flowing water changes the deeper she goes. The air becomes thicker, heavy and stagnant.

Slime oozes from cracks in the rock, forming fetid pools on the ground. The dark encloses her, embraces her.

She is far from the surface now, far from the cool comforts of the Titan's halls. She is sure that neither Tethys nor Oceanus have ever ventured here. No torches blaze on the walls, and the stone is rough and jagged to the touch.

Far beneath the earth, there is the Underworld, and deeper still is Tartarus, where Cronus and his brothers are imprisoned. Hera's old battle-mates, the Hecatoncheires, live there now, guarding the great bronze doors. They were her allies once before; perhaps they will be again.

She is tired of waiting, of hiding in Tethys' chamber, undecided. She misses the world that belonged to her, and she knows now that she needs to claim it back again. Gaia's old lessons were stories of violence and conquest; the only way that power had changed hands before. Hera came back here hoping to find another way. She isn't sure, now, that there is one.

She reaches out a hand to trace her way through. Her other hand drifts in empty space. She steps forward, blind and curious, the rotting earth sloping downwards beneath her feet.

But before she can follow it deeper into the dark, she feels a shudder in the rock at her fingertips. The rattle of pebbles and clods of soil shaken free and scattering, and a slow grumble building from above.

She hesitates, torn between exploring further and returning to investigate the disturbance. The grumble gives way to a dull roar, echoes in the tunnel, then dies away.

The darkness will wait. She'll find out what's happening at the surface first.

6

Oceanus and Helios sit on carved wooden thrones in the megaron of Oceanus' palace, the grey stone walls illuminated by Helios' crown of rays. Around them, nymphs are crammed on to every bench, spilling over on to the tiled floor, squeezing water from their hair and wringing it from their dresses. A faint cloud of steam rises from the crowds, and their laughter and good-natured shouts echo across the vaulted ceiling. Among them are river-gods, broad-shouldered and handsome, Hera notices with a wistful pang. Others are fantastical, bare chests giving way to fish-scaled tails, barnacles clinging to their beards and tiny crabs scuttling over their fins.

'Take a cup,' someone urges her, thrusting a goblet of golden liquid into her hand.

When Hera looks to thank her, she sees it is Klymene. Her hand flies to her veil instinctively, checking that her own face is still hidden. Klymene betrays no sign of recognition.

Hera takes the goblet, murmuring her thanks, looking to find a way through the crowd and out of here. It's busier than she's ever known it. The presence of Helios tells her that night

73

has fallen outside. Ordinarily, Hera watches the twilight from the quiet coves of the rivers that branch away from Oceanus, only creeping back to her chamber when everyone has dispersed and the palace is slumbering.

She can't see a clear route to the doors. Everywhere she looks, immortal faces are shining with merriment.

'Why do you wear that veil?' Klymene asks her. She leans in closer, conspiratorial. 'If it's to hide your pretty face from those old rogues, there's little use in it.' She jerks her head towards a particularly briny cluster of gods. 'They'll see it as a welcome challenge.'

She could knock them all aside, but she's trying not to draw attention to herself. She can't help but give voice to her frustration. 'Why are there so many of them here?'

'The storm has driven more of them in than usual,' Klymene answers. 'You must have escaped it.'

The storm. Was that the rumbling she'd heard underground? That would explain the nymphs' soaking hair, and the smell of damp wool that mingles with the incense and petal-scented oils in the hall.

She searches for Tethys. If Zeus has brought a storm to the banks of Oceanus, if he means it as an act of aggression, the mood in here would not be so convivial. No one seems concerned that this might be an act of wrath from the heavens.

It might be unconnected – but then again, if he has sought her here, if he knows or suspects that this is where she has come, then the last thing she wants is to draw him any closer.

Hera gives up on discretion, pushing her way through the revellers to the high arched entrance of the throne room. There are some rumbles of irritation, which she ignores, though every instinct in her body wants to snap back at their disrespect.

They don't know that it's an Olympian goddess they're muttering about.

Outside, rain streams down the wide steps that lead to the riverbank, drumming against the stone. The wind sighs, eerie and mournful, and Selene's light is lost behind the clouds. If there was a storm, as Klymene said, it has blown itself out. While the leaves still tremble on the branches and the stars are swallowed by murky gloom, this is not the fury of the heavens. *It is just rain*, she thinks, *no worse than that*.

Still, an uncertainty lingers. Zeus might be here. And for the sake of Tethys, who craves only quiet; for Klymene, who has lost those that she loves; for Gaia, who counselled peace, Hera will lead him away.

She follows the curve of the tributary to a cove, where the fresh waters mingle with salt. The cold sting of the rain feels like a gift, a revival after the stifling humidity of the crowded megaron. A lock of hair plasters itself across her forehead as she turns from side to side, looking for him.

There is a plaintive cry, small and despairing, only just audible above the tides. Hera tilts her head, and just as a cloud slides away from the moon, she sees it. A bird, perched on a rock, its feathers sodden. In the silvery glow, she recognises the grey-blue stripes on its front white feathers, and she reaches out towards it. The cuckoo lets out a little trill, trying to flap its wings, but only one will move smoothly. The other looks bent, painfully folded in, and she moves closer, her hand still outstretched.

It takes a small hop, then another into her cupped palm. She wonders if the winds have blown it off course, tangled it in a branch or dashed it into the hillside, and that's how its wing has been damaged. She feels the rise and fall of its body

75

against her fingers, heaving with its rapid breath, and she pities it for getting caught in this struggle between the gods. If that's what this is.

The bird shivers, and Hera cups it between her hands, stroking its head with her thumb. It closes its eyes in bliss, opening them again to look into hers, and then it tries to stretch out its injured wing again. She nestles it against her breast, warming it, as she concentrates on picturing the wing as it should be, encouraging it to take its proper shape again at her command.

Feathers flutter against her skin in a sweeping caress. Her lips curve in triumph at her success, but the cuckoo's wings stretch out wider than they should, the weight suddenly heavier in her hands, and she stumbles, caught off-balance as it wraps around her – not wings now, but powerful arms that imprison her against his body.

His eyes glitter in the moonlight as he pushes her down on to the pebbles worn smooth by the endless ebb and flow of the water. She gasps, twisting in his embrace, pushing her hands flat against his shoulders and shoving as hard as she can.

Her elbows dig into the scattered stones, and she can't find the leverage to get him off her. 'Zeus,' she splutters, 'what is this?'

His face isn't that of the brother she found on Crete. There is a blankness there, a horrifying strangeness, and although the shock has slowed her down, she finds her anger and drives her fist into his cheek. It knocks him to the side, so she can wriggle from underneath him, pulling herself up on to her hands and knees and scrambling up the beach. Zeus has become accustomed to weaker goddesses than her, she thinks, but she has always been as powerful as him. They trained together, under

Metis' guidance, and as many of their fights ended with him bruised and beaten as the other way around.

His hands clamp around her ankles, dragging her back.

He has had more practice in violence since those days than she has.

Still, she doesn't believe he will do it. Not to her. It's her disbelief that confuses her reflexes, her conviction that this cannot happen, even as it unfolds. The rage that fuelled her in battles before was clean and precise, not muddied by shock and bewilderment.

She's pinned beneath his body, the weight of him crushing her lungs, and still she is sure he will stop. His forearm squeezes down on her throat, his other hand wrenching at her dress, but it's only when her eyes roll up to the sky that panic truly seizes her. It's like plunging into an icy pool, the breath robbed from her body and the terror holding her frozen. The sky is vast above her, the sky whose shape she knows he can take as easily as he did the cuckoo's. She is paralysed by the know- ledge that Gaia must have felt this too, spread under the wide heavens, with nowhere to escape.

She thinks of Metis, once loved and trusted and revered by them both, then consumed by his greed, lost to his terrible desire.

She doesn't want to disappear into that same abyss.

Later, she will torment herself about those awful, terrified seconds in which she froze, when she couldn't fight back. She'll curse and rage against herself, imagining all the things she could have done to stop him. She won't forgive herself for her fear, or for her faith that he would stop.

But as he looms over her, blocking out the sky, it seems that he is everything in the world, that he is bigger than that sky. He is too immense and too strong.

There is nothing that Hera, the warrior who felled the Titans, can do to save herself.

I always longed for you.

Zeus always gets what he wants.

If you want to fight, I won't join you.

The rain stopped long ago. Eos has awoken, casting a soft, rosy glow on the lingering mist, and the calls of seabirds ring out across the waves. The air tastes of salt, and the tide laps at the shale. The rest of the world feels washed clean, brand new and sparkling after the storm.

Hera thinks it could rain forever, and it would never be enough for her.

Her immortal life has split into two. If she moves – if she stands up and walks away from this cove – then she will be in the new part of it. The part that is *after*.

So she stays where she is, as though she can conjure back the *before*. Gods can do so many things. They can manipulate the weather, take on any shape they choose, change the landscape. But they cannot change the flow of time.

She can't go back.

Gods are proud, defiant, always righteous. She has felt divine wrath, she has known frustration and fury. Gods can be afraid, they can exult, they can be repulsed or thrilled. Bored, much of the time. This emotion – the one that crawls across her skin – is new. It is a stinging tide seeping through her body, a slow and painful burn. *Shame.*

This is what he has left her with. A humiliation she feels so deep it curls her toes and makes her clench her fists until her fingernails pierce her palms. When she flexes her fingers, the crescent marks will disappear, as though they were never there.

A gull swoops low above her head and soars over the waves. She doesn't flinch. If anyone is watching her, they will see her sitting as though carved from rock, like the cliffs overlooking the cove. Her face, hard as stone, staring out to sea.

A scrap of fabric dances on the wind, fluttering this way and that across the pebbles. It's her veil. She remembers unhooking it when she was clear of the palace and tucking it into the woven belt looped around her waist. She watches it drift. She wonders now why she ever skulked around the Titan halls with her face covered, hiding underground. A daughter of Cronus with a throne on Mount Olympus, creeping in the shadows.

This is what comes of such cowardice, she tells herself. This has happened to her because she fled.

The mistake can't be undone, but no one ever needs to know. She'd thought that what she wanted mattered, but that seems like a childish dream now. What she wants isn't as important as what she is owed.

She's had it muddled all along, thinking of sharing the power, of ruling together. Of finding another way, different to the old ways.

She was born to be a queen.

The sun is setting over the western edge of the world. Atlas watches the golden orb sink through the skies, its beauty a fleeting distraction from his pain. The deep crevices of his craggy face have been carved by his eternal grimace. The weight of the domed heavens crushes his back, his weary shoulders buckling as he braces against it. His is a suffering without end, unrelenting and unchanging.

This evening, though, there is something different about the sunset. It gleams brighter, more fiercely, than he can recall ever seeing before.

With a monumental effort, he moves his head a fraction. The weight shifts on his neck, finding a new and tender place to press down on, and Atlas squeezes his eyes shut, the agony too much to bear.

Sweat beads on his forehead, tears form in the corners of his eyes, but he bears it as he has always done. He opens his eyes again, and he sees it.

There, in the wild garden spread beneath his feet, a new tree has grown. The garden-nymphs – Hesperides, he has heard them called – clad in rosy gowns with starlight in their eyes, are clustered around it. He can hear their voices lifting together as they marvel over it.

It's an apple tree, but the fruit it bears is shining and golden. The apples catch the glow of the falling sun and reflect it back, casting dazzling rays that render the sky fiery and molten. Atlas has stood here for a long time. This is the most spectacular sunset he has ever seen.

In the gorgeous light of the evening, the gods come forth.

The Hesperides fall silent, watching the fleet of chariots approach. Atlas feels as though the world itself holds its breath.

The immortals gather in the garden. Atlas sees among their number Titans he once knew, who he has not seen since his exile. His mother, Klymene, makes her way to stand beside Tethys, and tears blur his vision once again. He blinks them away, not willing to miss a single moment of this extraordinary event, this break in the unremitting loneliness of his existence.

The crowd shifts, mingling and merging, though some figures stand apart from the rest, even when they are in the centre. Poseidon, come from the depths, brandishes the trident he was given by the Cyclopes. Now jewels are pressed into the handle: white coral and pearls, gems of the sea. Hades, cloaked and indifferent. Demeter, ripe and beautiful. Hestia, radiant in the evening air. Aphrodite, the raw, primal power of her beauty astonishing even to Atlas in his beleaguered state. Another walks with them: a newborn goddess, tall and grey-eyed, her breastplate glinting silver. Together, they move through the other gods like oil freshly pressed from olives gliding on the surface of water: lustrous and rich and always separate.

Last to arrive are Zeus and Hera. She has no trouble keeping up with his long, confident strides. Her smile is regal, sweeping across the crowd with only a hint of disdain. She only falters when she sees the tree.

It's so glorious and impossible – a part of the landscape, but magical – and she knows at once it has come from Gaia. She breaks away from Zeus' side, ignoring his frown, and touches a leaf. It's green and fresh, a lush and growing thing. She reaches towards one of the apples, its metallic surface gently warmed by the sun. For the first time, her smile is real.

Zeus looks pleased. He doesn't know where the tree has come from, what the meaning of such a strange thing might be, but he is glad that Hera looks joyful at last.

His dark eyes sparkle with the light of victory as he takes it in – his bowed and vanquished enemy, Atlas, holding up the horizon, and his subjects gathered in his honour. Hera, meanwhile, counts how many of his former lovers are in attendance, how many of his children.

But she is the one he cannot walk away from. Titanesses

from the dawn of the world, daughters of Gaia, even her own sister Demeter, are long discarded. It is Hera who will be at his side; all of them are present to bear witness to it, and she will never let him forget.

He takes her hands in his, but she can still feel the weight of the apple in her palm.

On the beach where he had left her, Hera had hoped that Gaia would come. In this wild garden where she will marry Zeus, she looked for her again. The tree is the first sign she has had, a message she cannot miss. She felt it thrumming through the leaf, the stem, the fruit – Gaia's power imbued in every part of it – and she knew the moment she touched it that it is a gift for her.

She cannot see Gaia, but now she knows she is here. Here to see Hera take what is rightfully hers.

On that beach, that's where she realised the truth. She can never make Zeus pay from the shadows. In front of all the gods of the world, she unites herself to him. It is a declaration that she is no fleeting conquest like all the others, no victim to be forgotten. And while he gazes at her, captivated, in the falling dusk, she makes her own silent vow. She will be his wife, the Queen of Heaven, and she will use every resource she has at her disposal to bring him down.

PART TWO

Lastly, he [Zeus] made Hera his blooming wife: and she was joined in love with the king of gods and men.

Hesiod, *Theogony*, translated by
Hugh G. Evelyn-White, 1914

Marry him and become the bridge he could never burn, never forget.

Great Goddesses, Nikita Gill

7

On the journey back to Mount Olympus, she notices the fires scattered across the earth below them. Dozens of little smoke spirals winding their way up into the air.

'Prometheus disobeyed me,' Zeus says.

'How so?'

'He helped me to make a new race of mortals.' He glances at Hera, who looks steadfastly ahead, her profile strong and straight as the horses pull their chariot through the sky. 'It was Athena's idea to help him, so that they could take care to instil them with a more temperate nature than last time.'

'Athena,' Hera repeats. 'Your daughter.'

He shifts, momentarily uncomfortable. 'Metis' daughter.'

Now she can't stop herself twisting around to stare at him. 'How?'

'Well,' he says. 'When you were gone, I had a terrible pain in my head, behind my forehead – an agony I couldn't understand. I had no injury, none that any other god could see.'

'What was it?' She's puzzled.

'It was Athena,' he says. 'Prometheus could feel something

bulging under the bone, and the pain was insufferable. I told him to cut it out with an axe.'

'An axe?' She stares at him.

'I wanted it gone. What else could I do?'

Of course he'd never stand for a moment's discomfort. She can imagine him giving the command, all the other gods shrinking away, fearful of being the one to strike a blow into Zeus' immortal skull. 'And it was . . . Athena?'

'I didn't understand either,' he says. 'Prometheus swung the axe, and freed her. I saw straight away that she was Metis' child. Her eyes.'

Hera shudders. Her focus had been on getting through the wedding itself. She'd seen Athena, and Hestia had whispered that this was Zeus' daughter, but she'd assumed some new and unlucky Titaness had fallen prey to him before he'd tracked her down, and here was the result. But now she summons the goddess to mind, and she can see it too. Those cool, grey eyes she used to know so well.

'Athena explained it,' he continues. 'When Metis – when I – she became part of me, you see. And the child she carried grew within me. When Prometheus split my head open, she was fully formed, clad in armour – all her mother's wisdom, all my fighting spirit.' He laughs.

Hera's face is cold.

'Anyway, she helped Prometheus with his scheme to make more mortals. But he took pity on the new ones they made, as he had done with their predecessors. It wasn't enough for him to teach them and help them; he wanted to give them fire. He stole it from Hestia's hearth.'

Hera frowns. 'Why don't you just forbid mortals from using his gift if you don't want them to have it?'

Zeus puts his hand on the nape of her neck, stroking her skin with his thumb. She forces herself not to recoil. 'Can't you smell it?' he asks.

'What?'

'The savour,' he says. 'The fires you see, the ones in the open – they're altars. Altars the mortals have built to honour us. Prometheus showed them how, and when they feast, they burn a portion of their meat for us.'

Hera breathes in. The smoke does carry the scent of roasting flesh. Later, she'll hear that Prometheus told the humans to wrap the thigh bones of the animal in fat and burn that – the part that would give them no sustenance. It's an empty gift to the gods, another insult from the Titan to Zeus. But it still pleases Zeus to have the dedications, to hear the prayers they speak in praise of the Olympians.

'How did you punish him?' she asks.

'I haven't decided yet.'

Hera watches the fires twinkle below them. It's pretty, like an inverted sky, she thinks.

The palace of Olympus is the same as it has ever been. Demeter and Hestia are there to greet her. Hera fixes on a smile, and when the memory of Demeter under the tree rises unbidden to the surface, she doesn't let her body betray her. She lets her sisters comb her hair and pour scented oils into her bath.

When she rises from the water, she lets them anoint her with yet more fragranced oil, jasmine and lotus, so that the sweet scents waft in an intoxicating cloud from her skin, and then she goes to Zeus.

When she draws him to her, she tells herself it will undo

the violation of the time before. By the low, flickering flames of the tapers in his chamber, she guides his hands across her body, erasing the tracks of his bruising grip, snuffing out the memory of his crushing force as though it's as easy as smothering a fire. She will drive it out, she tells herself, extinguish the pain, and if its embers still glow hot and burning somewhere within her, no one will ever know. Least of all Zeus, who is delighted with his receptive wife. It seems he's forgotten more of their history than she has, for he never questions the change in her, only seems grateful for his good fortune. She wonders if he ever knew her at all.

Demeter comes to her chamber in the morning and offers to help her dress. Hera bridles at the hint of sympathy in her eyes. When her sister fastens a jewelled clasp in her hair, she asks about Kore, her daughter.

Demeter looks wary. 'She is happy,' she answers, 'living among flowers on her island. She likes the peace.'

'Is that why she didn't attend my wedding?'

'She has a shy disposition,' Demeter says. 'She has always lived away from the other gods.'

'Now I'm so happy in my marriage,' Hera says, keeping her tone light and free of irony, 'I wonder that you haven't considered a husband for Kore. Zeus might want to share his own joy. He might want to see his daughter married, following in our example.'

Demeter's hands go still in her hair.

Hera has no intention of saying anything to Zeus about the girl. He's probably forgotten her existence altogether, it was so long ago that she was born. But she wants Demeter to think about how she refused Hera once, when Hera had lost her power. Now there is a new hierarchy on Mount Olympus.

She has no veiled threats to hold over Hestia. She finds that she's glad as ever to see her at her hearth, a comforting familiarity in the world that is *after*. She goes to sit with her, and tells her about the sunken halls of Oceanus. Hestia is enthralled by her description of the sea-gods, the mer-gods, the multitudes of nymphs, and the place where the dark smoke of night rises from the palace of Nyx and mingles with the bright air of day. She knows better than to ask Hera why she came back.

The closest she comes is telling Hera that she's happy to have her in Olympus again. 'Happy for me, that is,' she says. 'Not if you would prefer to be in Oceanus.'

'I'd far rather live on the mountains than under the earth,' is all Hera says.

'You make it sound like such an interesting place, though,' Hestia says. 'So different to here.'

Hera laughs at the wistful note in her voice. 'You had your chance to live in the sea,' she reminds her. 'You could have been queen of your own underwater palace and swum to Oceanus any time you liked.'

Hestia laughs too. 'And only the small price to pay of sharing that palace with Poseidon.' On the heels of her laughter, concern flashes in her eyes, and Hera speaks quickly to stop her from having time to apologise.

'Well, only his unlucky bride has to endure his attentions now.'

Hestia looks at her curiously. 'He still takes other lovers, you know.'

'He does?'

'Even mortal ones,' Hestia tells her, and Hera is incredulous. 'It's true! He reared up from the waves once just as a human girl named Coronis walked along the beach, dreaming of her handsome lover. When she saw Poseidon bearing down on her, she ran – she'd have had no hope of escaping, but Athena saw and intervened.'

'Athena stopped him?'

'She transformed the girl into a crow so that she could fly away. Poseidon was furious, but Coronis was so thoroughly disguised he couldn't find her.'

Hera swallows. It's so like what happened to her, but in reverse. 'Did Athena turn her back into a girl?'

Hestia pours another cup of nectar. 'I don't think so. It's another reason that Poseidon stays away from here as much as he can. He can't bear to be near Athena. And he can't do anything about it.'

Of course. Athena's power is equal to his now. The throne that once belonged to Hades has been given to her, for Hades has his own in the Underworld. Hera wonders that Zeus isn't concerned about bestowing such power on his daughter, that he apparently pays no heed to the prophecy that led him to devour her mother in the first place.

Maybe it's because she is a daughter, not a son. Maybe he thinks that because he bore her from his own head, the prophecy has been evaded. But as Hera watches them together, she thinks it is simply that he loves her. This clever, imperious daughter somehow commands his adoration. When she refuses a husband, insisting she will stay unwed like Hestia, he acquiesces without question. Athena, it seems, can do as she pleases.

To spare Demeter from attending to her again, she asks Zeus for a handmaid. Of course, he tells her, there are dozens of serving-nymphs in the palace; she can pick any of them.

It isn't fitting, she replies, for her new position. The nymphs who braided her hair and prepared her baths before, the ones who wait on Demeter and Hestia or on Aphrodite, are not suitable anymore.

He tells her to choose whoever she wants.

She picks Klymene. She remembers her kindness in their fleeting encounter, how motherly she seemed.

It also won't hurt, she thinks, to have someone else with her on Mount Olympus who has suffered because of Zeus. Someone who lost her husband and son to his wrath.

The Titaness is summoned from Oceanus and she obeys, as Hera knew she would.

Selene's moon waxes and wanes in the night sky, and before it grows full again, her own child stirs in her womb. Although Zeus has visited her bed many times since, she knows this child took root inside her that first time on the beach. She could have gathered the yellow-flowered silphium for the draught she always used to drink by the light of the full moon to stop this from happening in the times before Zeus, but she chose not to. Not because she has any wish, especially, to bear him a child. But Zeus has Athena, his motherless daughter whose loyalty is to him alone. Now that Hera is back on Mount Olympus, she feels more isolated than ever before. She can't forget that no one would help her before, that no one would stand with her against Zeus, not even her sisters.

Perhaps a child of her own will be different.

On a starless night, she feels him coming, and she won't lie on her couch, tended to by Klymene, Hestia or Demeter. This infant belongs to her, and she won't let anyone interfere, even with well-intentioned ministrations. She can't stand the thought of anyone else's hands on her body, of anyone touching this baby before she does. She imagines Rhea, her children seized from her arms no sooner than they were born, and she vows that she won't be so vulnerable. Instead, she runs to a desolate Thracian plain and births him alone in the darkness, to a chorus of shrieking owls and hissing serpents. He's angry and squalling, an infant god given to fits of rage from the very start. His black eyes are hollow pools, and Hera feels the scarlet edge of his fury when she looks into them. She recognises it. He was conceived in violence and nurtured by the fermenting bitterness of her blood. When he suckles at her breast and she remembers how he came to be, she thinks he is nourished by venom, the curdling of her resentment against his father.

'He'll be a war-god,' Klymene pronounces, and what else could he be? Not the cool-headed, tactical part of war that is Athena's realm, but the hot-blooded din and roar of combat: the savage battle-lust of clashing armies intent on destruction.

Hera calls him Ares, kisses him on his furrowed brow, and dreams of the day he will bring her triumph. He grows quickly, and his fury does not diminish with maturity. When weaned from her breast, he pushes her away, refusing to tolerate her caresses any longer. His shouts echo through the palace as he tosses vases to the floor and overturns delicate carved stools in his rages.

'Can't you find a way to restrain him?' Athena asks Zeus, exasperated.

Zeus shrugs. 'The boy is full of spirit, like his father.'

Hera suppresses a shudder.

'He has no self-control,' Athena says. 'He's too volatile, too unpredictable.' It's anathema to her; Athena, who was born in armour, who never lets an emotion disturb her iron-plated composure.

'He needs a throne,' Hera announces.

Zeus draws his heavy brows together. 'A throne?'

'He should rule over matters of conflict,' Hera says.

Zeus snorts. 'If there's a fight, he wants to be in it,' he says. 'Not sitting up here and overseeing.'

'He's your son. Yours and mine. He has a right to it, more than any other.'

'I don't think—' Athena begins, and Hera raises a hand to stop her.

'It's not your decision to make.'

Zeus takes a sip from the polished horn in his hand. No doubt he's enjoying the tension between his wife and daughter, and the opportunity it affords him to choose which one to favour today.

'It could be wise to have Ares' strength on my council,' he muses.

'He's strong, yes,' Athena says. 'But he won't listen. And you're strong enough without him. Your thunderbolt is more devastating than he is, and that's under your control.'

In these golden halls, Athena is a glinting column of silver, from her helmet and her breastplate to her shield and sandals: a mirror, cold and sleek, reflecting back to Zeus what he wants to hear. Hera's sure he's about to agree with Athena, but his words surprise them both.

'If Ares answers to me,' he says, 'if I can harness his power and make him exercise it in my name, under my direction, then that's all the better. I'll give him his own throne and make him the god of war. He can direct his anger on to mortal battle-fields, instead of taking it out on our home.'

This isn't how Hera intended it at all, but she can see how pleased Zeus is with the idea that Ares will bring more glory to him. He grants his son the status of an Olympian – the status that is his birthright, Hera insists – and Ares, still a beardless youth but armed with lethal sword and shield, joins their council.

Now the ruling gods number eight, and Hera eyes the thrones lined up in the megaron. Surely Ares, who refuses to wear a crown in favour of a crested helm, won't be swayed to his father's side over his mother's in exchange for a shining seat in the heavens?

She can't be certain. When she sees Ares descend in his black chariot, his horses racing to wherever the mortals are waging war, his hollow cry echoing to the clouds, she feels like he is the embodiment of her anger. Everything she pushes down inside herself, every violent impulse she's felt since Zeus attacked her on the beach which she keeps cloaked behind regal composure, is made manifest in her son. But he's as unreachable to her as he is to any of the other gods, who draw away from him in the bright halls of Olympus. She wonders sometimes if he's born of such hatred that he's incapable of love. He certainly shows no great affection towards his mother, nor gratitude for the throne she won for him.

She braces herself. If her plan to bear a child to be her ally on Mount Olympus hasn't worked this time, she'll have to try again.

8

In her chamber, Hera leans out of the window, her elbows propped on the stone sill, her chin resting in her linked hands, looking down on the world spread out below them. Zeus comes up behind her, places his hands on her waist and his cheek against her hair.

'Do you listen to their prayers?' he asks.

'Why would I?' She wrinkles her nose, remembering Ixion, and he laughs.

'To hear what they say about you.' He sounds light and teasing. He really has no idea what she thinks about. 'Listen,' he says, pushing her hair behind her ear.

She can only hear the sounds of the palace: water tinkling in the courtyard fountain, the crackling of flames at the hearth, a snatch of conversation floating on the breeze.

'Not like that.'

'Then how?'

'Just – you have to close your eyes,' he says. 'Like this.'

She looks at him. The cold air of the mountain summit

ruffles his hair and a smile hovers around his mouth. She sighs. 'Fine. I will.'

She closes her eyes, letting the breeze caress her face. It's nonsense, she's about to tell him; there is no sound but the rushing wind and the distant flap of an eagle's wings.

But then she hears it. A faint, whispered chant. A voice so soft it almost dissolves into the air, but another overlaps it, and then another. She hears tantalising scraps and tries to concentrate harder, forgetting that Zeus is even present. *Hera, the queen*, she hears in pleading, worshipful tones, and *Hera, so perfect in marriage*.

They praise her beauty. They beseech her favour. They call her the bride of the Thunderer and the queen of all goddesses. And as she listens more intently, lifting out individual strands from the mass of overlapping voices, she hears what they ask for.

Please smile on my wedding day and bring me happiness.

Teach me how to be a good wife, so that my husband will be kind.

Oh Hera, let the man I am to marry be even-tempered and gentle.

Bless our marriage with children, so that I can have something to love.

She opens her eyes. Zeus is looking at her, curious and amused.

'They're all women,' she says. 'Asking about their weddings and husbands.'

'They honour you at every marriage ceremony,' Zeus says. 'Wives keep an altar to you in their homes. Every girl raises her eyes to Hera, the queen of all brides, and hopes you will send her a good husband and grant her a marriage as glorious as your own.'

She blinks.

'See how they revere you?' he asks.

'They're mortals.' She shrugs. 'It hardly matters.' She pauses for a long moment, then can't resist asking, 'Do they burn sacrifices at my altars too?'

'Of course. Watch a human wedding; see the cattle they bring to slaughter in gratitude to you. Look for the smoke that rises to the heavens, the gifts they devote to Hera, goddess of marriage.'

She frowns.

'Doesn't that please you?' he asks. He's watching her closely.

'Is that what they call me?'

'It's what you are,' he says. 'It's the title I'm giving you. What else could you be?'

She starts to speak, and falls silent. *Once*, she thinks, *there were so many answers to that question.*

'You'll preside over immortal weddings,' he says. 'Gods will seek your blessing to marry, and you can decide if you'll give it. On earth, the wives will pray to you as they already do; you can listen to them or not. They'll keep on praying, regardless.'

It's an insult wrapped in honour. A realm assigned to her, the last of the Olympians to have one. While Zeus gets to be king of the heavens, she gets this.

A reminder, now and always, that no matter who she was before, in the eyes of the world, she is only his wife.

He slides his finger under her chin, tilting her face up to his so he can kiss her. She can still hear the soft tide of voices from below drifting upwards, and she lets them wash over her as though they could lift her up and carry her away. His hand slides to the back of her neck, his fingers tangling in her hair, his other hand warm on her back.

She makes a space inside her head for this. His touch, practised and assured, is not so bad, not something she has to endure. It will never be like the first time, when he overpowered her. Now she pushes him to the low couch alongside the stone wall, unclasps the brooch that holds her dress at her shoulder, and feels a thrill of triumph at the helpless desire she sees in his eyes. In the throne room, in front of other gods, Zeus is always in control. But Hera knows how to weaken him.

She never lets herself remember the lovers that came before him. She doesn't want to think about a time when this was only about pleasure and nothing else, an easy exchange instead of a complicated game that she cannot afford to lose. She knew when she married him that there would never be others again; that there would only be Zeus. When he pulls her down, his skin hot against hers, flawless and immortal, she empties her mind. She lets her anger burn like passion, desperate and intense, until everything is aflame.

Afterwards, when he is gone, she rises and leans out over her windowsill again. Bathed in silver light, she listens once more for the prayers.

Despite her disdain for Zeus' creatures, there is something gratifying about their devotion. The tide of adoration rolls up towards her and she feels powerful. Zeus thinks he has the upper hand. He's made her the goddess of marriage, thinking she's nothing more than a dutiful wife.

But he never imagines the mistake he's made in making her his enemy and inviting her in so close.

She lifts her arms above her head, luxuriating in a long, deep stretch and then letting her hands drift down. She rests her palms against her stomach, her gaze wandering towards the stars as she dreams of the baby she might have, of the son or daughter who will stand with her against him, of the seed of his own destruction he could unwittingly sow.

Zeus doesn't forget how Prometheus defied him. Thanks to the gift of fire, alongside the instruction Prometheus gave them in agriculture and metal-working, in shipbuilding and animal-rearing, in foraging and navigation, mortals have proliferated further and wider than ever before. But even though their increased numbers bring more honour and glory to the gods, Zeus is intent on punishment. He chains Prometheus to the desolate face of Mount Kaukasos, sending an eagle each day to tear out his liver.

For Klymene, it heaps more cruelty on top of what she has already endured at the hands of Zeus. Another of her sons, condemned to an agony that will never end. It's even worse that it is Prometheus, who joined the Olympians, who gave them his wisdom and his foresight with the same quiet gener-osity that made him tend to mortals, a far kindlier father than their creator has ever wanted to be.

Hera holds Klymene's hand while she weeps.

At night, Hera dreams of the caves beneath the river of Oceanus. She walks down the tunnels, and when the storm above shakes the earth, she ignores it. This time, she doesn't turn back. What-ever waits down here cannot be worse than what is up there.

It's so real, she can taste the corruption in the air. She can feel the slime under her fingers, noxious and putrid. She knows that the heavens are wild; she can sense the winds buffeting the trees, the frenzied lightning and the chaos of thunder, but she is safe from it here, deep in the ground. She breathes in the foulness, inhales it deep into her lungs. It feels like poison, and she imagines it running through her veins, mixing with her golden ichor. *Give me your strength*, she urges wordlessly, and the silence pulses like a wave.

She is alive, she is ready, she is eager for whatever it is that waits down here. She is sure it waits for her, that she can feel it calling from the depths.

Gaia told her of Tartarus, of the Underworld, of her monstrous sons, but Hera knows there are more secrets within the earth, secrets that Gaia holds close to herself. *I'm ready*, she thinks. *Show me.*

She hears the hissing before she sees the beast. The drag of its scaly coils slithering through the dirt. Her eyes widen, strain to see further in the darkness. A light flickers into existence, a greenish glow, and as she gets closer, she sees that the tunnel twists. She hastens towards it, rounding the bend, and then she stops short, awed into stillness.

The tunnel widens into a cavern, vast and echoing. The hisses reverberate from the high walls and domed roof. Along the floor, she sees a tail is coiled in great loops underneath a body. Where scales meet flesh, the rotting black diamonds give way to smooth skin. The serpentine curves become a woman's waist. Long, dark hair spills over her breasts. Hera looks up at the creature's face, and her wide eyes, framed by thick lashes, meet Hera's gaze. She holds it, sure and steady. Her lips part, revealing teeth that are sharp and jagged, and Hera holds her breath, waiting for her to speak.

Light floods her eyes and Hera jerks awake, sitting bolt upright. Klymene, in the middle of parting the drapes, freezes, alarmed by the sudden movement.

Hera's chest is heaving, the fine woollen blanket she sleeps under pooled around her legs.

'What is it?' Klymene is staring. 'A nightmare?' She sounds dubious. Epiales, son of Nyx, is known to haunt sleepers with his terrifying visions, but she doubts he would dare to creep into any of the chambers of Mount Olympus, far less the queen's.

Hera shakes her head. 'Something else.'

'A vision? A prophecy?'

Hera pats the bed, gesturing for Klymene to come and sit beside her. 'I want you to tell me,' she says, 'what it is that lives under the halls of Oceanus.'

Klymene doesn't know what she means at first. But when Hera presses her, she confirms there are tunnels and caves apart from Tartarus and the Underworld – that Gaia has carved innumerable passageways into her own body, and that no one except Gaia herself could ever know how many there are or where they lead.

'There are other gods of the sea,' Klymene tells her, 'gods that always dwelt in the depths, beyond where even Nereus would dive. In the deepest, darkest waters of the ocean, where monsters are born.'

'But this is in the earth,' Hera says. 'I saw her there, in a cave.'

Klymene casts a sideways glance at her. 'I only know the stories I heard from Tethys. I've never seen her. But there is a sea-monster goddess, Keto, who is mother to sharks and whirl-pools, to Gorgons and the grey sisters that drift on the sea-foam and share one eye between the three of them.' Hera nods along;

she knows of these. 'But she had another daughter – woman-headed and serpent-tailed, just as you describe.'

'Then that's what was in my dream. Keto's daughter.'

'Tethys called her Ekhidna. A snake-goddess who has never seen the sunlight. She could have swum up from the ocean depths and crawled into the earth, I suppose. No one knows anything about her.'

'Tethys never saw her? Or Oceanus?'

'The sea is full of mysteries,' Klymene says. 'Even the river-gods can't know every deity or spirit or creature of the waters.'

Only Gaia would know. And she's given sanctuary to such creatures before.

The face of the serpent-goddess is vivid in Hera's mind. The black void of those eyes still bores into her own.

After this, when Hera sleeps in the starry heavens of Mount Olympus, her dreams lead her back into the putrid darkness. A hidden world that no god would care to visit.

Hera keeps her dreams of the snake-woman to herself, a precious secret tucked away. Until she knows what they mean – and how she can use the knowledge they've given her of this subterranean monster – she needs to move forward with the plans she already has. That means finding a way to bring Ares to her side. Now that she carries his sibling in her womb, she has an ally for them both if she can convince Ares to stand with her against Zeus. And so one morning when she awakens one bright morning from her serpentine dreams, she goes in search of her son, finding to her irritation that, yet again, he is nowhere to be seen. She passes Aphrodite, gliding down a corridor, and asks her if she's seen Ares anywhere.

Aphrodite's eyes are wide and limpid. 'I don't think so,' she answers.

It's not an answer that satisfies Hera, but luckily Athena is more helpful. 'He's building his own palace,' she calls over to them. 'On the slopes of Mount Haemus.'

Hera purses her lips. She doesn't want to thank Athena for, as always, knowing the answer, and she certainly won't give her the satisfaction of asking any further questions. She'll have to go to Ares herself to find out his reasoning. She doesn't bid either of the other goddesses goodbye. Athena barely notices; she's always busy, her gaze perpetually distant, as though she's thinking of a hundred other things and Hera is only a brief distraction. Aphrodite does watch, however, as Hera stalks out of the palace, wrapping a cloak around her shoulders that transforms into tawny feathers, and she follows the curve of the nighthawk's flight out towards the far-flung dark forests that ring the mountain where Ares has chosen to make his new home.

9

It's a bleak, forbidding mansion; an iron-dark twin of the bright Olympian palace. As Hera glides above, she can feel the chill of cold metal, the way the structure seems to suck the light out of the air, as though Helios himself turns away.

From the villages below rise the chanting and rhythmic drumming of the mortal clans that live here, the clash of spear against shield in a repeating pattern, the hollow notes of metal ringing upon metal, carrying on the wind up to Ares, bringing him praise.

The wind whips her skirt, its breath icy on her skin, as she takes her own shape again at his gates. She takes a long, lingering look around. *He's made quite a fortress here*, she thinks. A place to retreat, or to make a stand if need be. She's impressed.

'Why are you here?'

She turns around and, for a moment, he takes her breath away. Under the cloudy sky, his face in shadow, he looks so like his father for a second that she's lost for words. But the bird on his arm is a vulture, not an eagle; it hunches its midnight-black shoulders and gives her a baleful glare. Ares' expression isn't any more welcoming.

'Athena said you were building your own palace here,' she says. 'Aren't the comforts of Mount Olympus enough for you?'

He doesn't answer her, just unlocks the gates and jerks his head for her to follow. As he passes through, he strokes the bird's head and it leans into him, closing its eyes in blissful affection before it hops down to the ground. 'Has Zeus sent you?' he asks.

She's confused. 'No.'

'Did you follow someone else here?'

'Who? Who else has been here?'

He doesn't answer, his face settling into its familiar scowl.

Hera doesn't know her way into conversation with her son, so she changes the subject. 'The sound of the spears,' she says, nodding down towards the side of the mountain. 'The noise they're making, it reminds me of Crete.' The memory comes as a surprise to her. 'They weren't mortals, they were mountain-gods – Kouretes – and Gaia charged them to beat their shields and spears together to cover up the sound of Zeus crying when she first hid him there. He was a baby, of course. They used to raise a great din so that he'd never be detected by Cronus. They still did it when I arrived, though Zeus was grown by then. I remember them dancing.'

It feels as though she's talking about someone else's life. But she can still hear it: the snakelike, relentless insistence of the drumbeat and how their bodies moved to echo it, dressed in shaggy furs, their faces alight with sheer joy behind their long beards. She recalls the heat of the sun, its rays blinding after her years spent in the dark, and the brimming excitement she'd felt standing on the precipice of a new world.

Here, in Ares' barren courtyard, the wind shrieks through his desolate towers.

He looks bored by her presence. 'They do it here to honour me,' he says. 'To give me gratitude for their victories in war.'

'You could hear their prayers from Mount Olympus,' Hera says. 'Why come here to live among them?'

He draws his brows together. 'This is where I belong. With the mortals who love battles best. Why would I want to watch war and combat from Zeus' thrones when I can be here, in the heart of it.'

'One of those thrones belongs to you.' Her tone is sharp. 'You're my son, and Zeus' progeny too.'

He casts his eyes down her body, pausing on her rounded middle. 'You'll give him more.' He shrugs.

This is her opening – her chance to offer him her proposal, that they join together as three against Zeus. But this isn't going the way she intended; she can feel her own temper flaring in the face of his antagonism. If he won't even come back to Mount Olympus, if he doesn't care for the power he could wield, how will he help her to take it? 'You'd rather be among mortals than your family?'

'Poseidon has his own palace in the sea. Why can't I have mine here?'

Her anger boils like acid in her throat. 'I'll bear another child so you can have a sibling. An ally.' That's the whole point, she wants to tell him: two children to stand beside her against Zeus. It's a dangerous tactic, but the only one she has. She never forgets Metis – how could she, when Athena is always there with those same grey eyes and measured tone? – and she won't be outwitted the way the Titaness was. If Zeus takes it into his head to fear the child in her womb, she knows what he'll do. But she needs more sons of her own on Olympus; she can't refuse to bear any at all, or who will be on her side?

'I have no need of a sibling,' he mutters scornfully. 'And no ally born from you.'

It's the reason you exist, she wants to scream at Ares, *to stand with me against Zeus.* But he has been intractable since birth, his furious spirit never tempered – and how can she start a battle of wills against a war-god? She'll have to count on his hunger for conflict to be enough when it comes to it.

'Never mind.' She keeps her tone as icy as the wind. 'Perhaps this one will know his responsibilities better.'

The insult glances off him like a spear against his breast-plate. He barely seems to notice as she stalks away, taking flight again and dipping back through the valley where the war-cries ring out, a hollering up to the skies for the glory of her infuriating son.

As eagerly as Ares has embraced his domain of war, so Hera resents her own. But even so, she can't ignore the fact that Zeus has made her the goddess of marriage. It's become her responsibility, though she finds it immensely frustrating. Demeter's role is an active one: she coordinates cloud-nymphs to nourish thirsty soils with rain or else withhold it; she populates bare fields with waving ears of corn, ripens figs on laden branches, tends to apple trees and pear trees, instructs the shy dryads and the pretty flower-nymphs. Her benevolence feeds the mortals, and she punishes them with broken ploughs, dry earth and blighted crops if they displease her. Poseidon is busy with storms and earthquakes, governing sea-gods, wrecking boats and splintering rafts, or else guiding them to safe harbour as he chooses. She imagines Hades in his Underworld, ruling over a kingdom of ghosts – and even *that* she could envy in comparison to her own dispiriting tasks.

Weddings, a steady stream of them, which she must bless. Immortal brides, turning their hopeful eyes to her for a promise she can't make. She oversees the rites, commands nymphs to lift their voices in bridal-song, to light torches and burn incense, but she can't grant them any more contentment than she has found in her own union.

'Shouldn't you be present sometimes?' she asks Aphrodite, who laughs at the very idea.

'My domain is love,' she answers. 'Not marriage.'

Hera draws herself up, summoning all her composure in response to Aphrodite's impudence. 'Zephyrus, the wind-god, marries the nymph Chloris today. He spoke most charmingly of her when he asked me for permission. He praised you for bringing such love into his life.'

Aphrodite scoffs. 'He spied on her in her father's garden for weeks. She thought it was just the breeze stroking her face, ruffling her gown, lifting her skirt.' She gives Hera a meaningful look. 'He pounced on her among her own flowers, crushing all the violets and clover underneath her. Yes, he's offered to marry her now, but his method of courtship owes more to Zeus than it does to me.'

'The lovers you inflame hardly behave with decorum,' Hera says, her voice tart. 'You've overseen plenty of outdoor trysts, plenty of' – she pauses – '*impulsive* moments.'

Aphrodite shakes her head. 'He forced her; it's no fun. If he'd come to me first, prayed for me to intoxicate her with the same desire . . .' She looks dreamy for a second, then snaps back to attention. 'He didn't care about that. Why would I go to their wedding?'

So Hera oversees the wedding alone, with even less enthusiasm than normal. She narrows her eyes at Zephyrus as he enfolds his new wife in his arms. Soot blows from the torches, the nymphs' voices falter on the high notes, the roses garlanded around the trees wilt with her displeasure, but she doesn't halt the ceremony. Afterwards, she can't assume her hawk shape quickly enough. She flies back towards Olympus, letting the clamour of mortal voices from across the world rise up to drown out the memory of the bride's stony face. It's a chaos of fragments; entreaties and flattery and laments, overlapping and intertwining, drowning each other out in a wild cacophony. Narrowing her eyes and tilting her wings to keep her course steady, she lets them all fall away except the ones to her. In the quiet of night, there are so many women sneaking from their beds to their altars, or lying still and silent, staring into the dark while they send their thoughts up to the goddess.

She slows in the air, hovering high above a wide river. The moon shines silver on the rippling water, a fractured path that shifts and shimmers with its gentle movement, and she listens.

From huts nestled in pine-forested peninsulas, from villages standing on fertile plains, from wild olive groves and rocky islands, they beseech her. Their praise for her beauty and benevolence is a soothing balm, but among the chorus, she begins to hear a familiar refrain. Mothers, their voices strained and cracking with faint hope, beg her to watch over their daughters in marriage. *Don't let her husband beat her, don't let him grind her beautiful spirit to dust. Let her have some joy in their union.* New wives kneel in ashes, brides pour out milk and honey to likenesses of Hera carved in wild-pear wood, and their pleas are threaded with the same note of disappointed dreams. She falters, her buoyancy lost for a moment before she recovers herself, and still the tide of voices pours forth. Complaints of cruelty, suspicion and heartbreak, a thousand instances of neglect and unkindness, all of them carried on a surge of yearning for another life; one they hope she'll grant them.

When another moon passed and my blood still didn't come, I thought I would bear a child at last. But there was only pain and loss again.

She was so small and precious; perfect and mine. I loved her from the moment she was born, but before the sun rose again, she was still and cold and gone.

If I could keep just one, if one of my children could live, please just let me keep one.

He didn't know why I cried when we have two living sons, why I grieve for the one that died. But it breaks me into pieces and I don't know how to bear it.

They call out to Hera the bride, Hera the wife, Hera the mother, with every grief and sadness they hold. Each of them is a stream flowing into an ocean of despair, deeper and vaster than she could imagine, and she follows them one after the other, each woman's suffering so familiar she can barely tell one anguish from the next. Until, abruptly, one leads her to the shape of a girl crying under a willow tree, and Hera knows that pain before she can put a name to it. Her body remembers it: the way she clasps her knees into her chest as though she is trying to hold herself in one piece; the way she tries to shrink into herself as if she could disappear; how numb she is to the scrape of tree bark against her back, her ragged breath the only sound on the silent riverbank.

Hera banks sharply in mid-air, taking to the skies again. These girls cry out to her too, their outrage palpable; the raw edge of their agony and their shock horrifying in its insistence, demanding that she hears them, that she helps them survive the violence she once survived herself. It flings her back, against her will, to a memory around which she has built a wall. But as hard as she pushes it away, she can still feel the rough stones under her body and the weight of his arm crushing her throat.

She's seen Athena delight in the prayers that spiral up towards her, noticed how she'll lean attentively towards the distant altars far below and set her mind to planning. Athena views the mortals as vessels for education; she takes a keen pleasure in watching them acquire the skills she deigns to teach them. Demeter too enjoys distributing her bounty, letting her cornucopia overflow with plentiful abundance and basking in the endless nourishment of human gratitude for her generosity. Aphrodite takes delight in hearing the appeals from lovers, in the seductions and the games, in the chases and the conquests that seem so far away from the broken women who pray to Hera. Even Hestia, so quiet and unassuming, takes her portion of glory. The women who turn their misery and anger to Hera give thanks to Hestia first of all for the hearth that sustains their homes, the ever-burning light and warmth that makes their existence bearable: the centre of their lives.

And it's left to Hera to pick up the pieces. To hear of the commonplace tragedies that blight their existence. She never asked to be the goddess of marriage, she thinks; she never wanted to be the patroness of brides. It was forced on her, like the roles of wife and mother she plays herself, and she seethes that her realm is one of empty promises, of stunted hopes and ruined faith. That the women who pray to her do it from the ashes of their optimism, the smoking remains of their ambitions and ideals. Their bruised and aching bodies, their tattered souls reaching to her for comfort and salvation.

She has none to give them.

She blocks out the sound of their prayers, and carries on home to Olympus.

For the birth of her second son, she doesn't flee to a barren plain. This time, she submits to the helpful hands of Klymene and lies upon a cushioned couch in the palace to bring him into the world. She had permitted herself to be hopeful about this one, but she's no more enchanted with the sight of the infant than she was when Ares was born – less so, perhaps, for when she looked into the eyes of the squalling little war-god, she at least felt a kinship to his boundless fury. Hephaestus, as she calls him, is lethargic and ugly, his cries weak and pitiful, as though he can't summon the strength to howl the way his brother did. He turns his head away from her breast, sending a fountain of milk spattering through the air, and when at last he latches on, he barely suckles. His head lolls and his eyelids flutter, and she finds an unexpected storm of tears burning behind her eyes, tears she won't let fall. What kind of existence awaits this unprepossessing, misshapen little creature, who doesn't possess the instinct to sustain himself?

Aphrodite wanders past, a vision of beauty; Athena, strong and clean and precise in every movement. Zeus, full of boundless energy, insatiable appetite and vigour. Ares, despite his sulky disposition, is awe-inspiring; capable of stirring terror in the hardiest of onlookers. There is no place on Mount Olympus for any blemish, for anything tainted or lesser in any way.

This fretful, anxious child stirs her pity, but ignites a flame of anger too. How can this be the product of the union between her and Zeus, she wonders. How can it be that each child has fallen short; the first lacking in temperament and the second one in strength? It taunts her, the thought that Zeus has nothing to fear from her children. That somehow her sons will never be willing or capable of overthrowing the tyrant, like their father did, and his father before him.

She broods over the cradle of Hephaestus, a dark cloud of motherhood. She is supposed to be the perfect example: the image of wife and mother to which everyone should aspire, a divine realisation of the ideal. She cannot understand why she has failed again.

Just as she did with the praying women, she tells herself to harden her heart against this forlorn infant. If he is to grow strong, it must be through his own determination. He will need to find reserves to call upon, the source of power that he must have, that must be in him somewhere.

'Another son!' Zeus remarks when he sees them, and Hera grinds her teeth at his joviality. He's pleased, she thinks, to see how unimpressive this one is. He doesn't linger. There is nothing in the room to interest him: an irascible mother and whining infant are unlikely to offer any amusement. He leaves them alone, and Hera looks out towards the star-strewn skies, disappointment lodged in her throat, as hard and immovable as stone.

10

Like Ares before him, Hephaestus sheds his baby form swiftly. By the next moonrise, he is a cumbersome child, lumbering towards Hestia in the megaron. He loves to watch the fire; he's fascinated by its sparks. Hera is surprised he isn't afraid of its heat or its unpredictability. He shies away from everything else. The sound of Zeus' sandals striking the marble floors makes him jump, as does the ring of Poseidon's trident against a pillar when he arrives, smirking as he glides past them to his throne. The child-god drops his head, his unlovely face hidden by his hair. Poseidon snorts, and walks on.

Hephaestus looks up at Hestia, who keeps her expression mild as always. 'I can tell you a story about it,' she tells him, nodding towards the flames, and he dares to smile and snuggle in closer to her to listen.

'It belongs to us,' she says. 'It was always ours alone. Out on the hillsides, the mortals would shiver and freeze, but the fire only burned in the palaces of the gods. It was our sacred privilege, and we were forbidden to share it.'

'So how did they get it?' Hephaestus asks her, enraptured. 'Did they steal it?'

She laughs. 'No mortal would dare.' She glances up at Hera, who is watching. 'They would be too afraid of our punishments. It was Prometheus, a Titan who loved them, who wanted to give it to them. He came to our palace, hiding a fennel stalk.'

Hera raises an eyebrow. She's surprised that Hestia goes on, even telling Hephaestus of the eagle that feasts on Prometheus' liver with every sunrise. His face crumples when she gets to that part.

'Why did Zeus let them keep it?' he asks.

'They've learned to live better lives with it,' Hestia says. 'They live longer and praise us more for it.'

'There's more they could do with fire,' Athena interjects. 'I could show them how to melt down metals, which ones to combine together to make them stronger.'

'For what?' asks Hera.

'They could make better weapons,' Athena answers. 'Sharper, more robust, less prone to snapping and crumpling in battle.'

Hephaestus looks anxious again, and Hera catches Hestia's eye. 'More secrets that belong to us,' she says. 'How many of the gods' arts will you give away?' She remembers Ixion, and the way his greedy eyes feasted on the glories of their palace, how much he wanted to take for himself. Athena looks as if she's about to argue, but Hera knows better than to get into a battle of words against her. 'Hephaestus, leave us,' she commands and, catching the brusque tone and sharpness of her manner, he rises and hurries away. He's already taller than when he sat down at Hestia's side, however much he rounds his shoulders and hunches into himself.

'What will he do?' Hestia asks as Hera sits on the bench that Hephaestus has just vacated.

Hera sighs. 'What can he do?' She props up her elbow on the carved back of the seat and rests her head against her hand. She rubs her temple, the caress of her fingers soft and soothing. She doesn't have anything as mortal as a headache, of course. Gods don't have to contend with such pains and inconveniences. But somehow she feels as if she might; as though the thick black tangle of thoughts in her head is swelling, about to burst free from her skull. It makes her think of Athena's birth from the forehead of Zeus and that only intensifies the irritation. 'He's so timid.'

Hestia reaches out and wraps her fingers around Hera's. 'He's gentle,' she says. 'But he's eager to learn.'

Hera rolls her eyes. 'What place is there here for gentleness?'

Hestia pauses. 'It's one of the things he'll have to learn,' she says, at last. 'To be careful how much he shows it.'

'Why—' Hera stops herself from finishing the sentence.

'Why is he so different to Ares?' Hestia suggests.

'Not just that.' He's so ungainly. Not just diffident and awkward. His broad forehead, his heavy brows and dull eyes, the thickness of his neck and the way his arms dangle at his sides. Hera wonders how he was born from her, with her graceful limbs and wide, clear eyes. Or from Zeus, for that matter, who crackles with vitality like the thunderbolt he carries.

'A splendid fire can burn from just a feeble spark,' Hestia says. 'Ares was himself from the moment he was born. Hephaestus might just need a little more time.'

Hera hadn't noticed Athena leave the room, but she must have done, because now she's back, her face alight. 'Come and see,' she calls to the sisters, 'in my workshop, now!'

Hera and Hestia exchange glances. Athena so often has a new scheme, a new wonder to show everyone that is of more interest to her than anyone else. But the delighted urgency in her tone piques their curiosity, and they rise to follow her.

Her workshop, as she calls it, is a large, airy hall. Her loom stands tall at one side, surrounded by baskets of fleece and yarn. Hera notices the tapestry she's working on; the first panel complete and the second half-done.

Athena waves her hand impatiently. 'Look, look at Hephaestus,' she says. And there he is, leaning over a stone block, his forehead creased into lines of concentration.

'What's that?' Hera asks, and he looks up at her. She notices the breadth of his shoulders, the swathe of hair climbing from his chest to his wide neck. He is nearly fully himself now. Still, there is a shyness in his smile as he proffers what is in his hand, and she comes closer to see.

One of his meaty fists almost swallows a delicate-looking hammer. His other hand is outstretched, a disc of gold gleaming on his palm.

Hera pushes a curl of hair back from her forehead, hooking it behind her ear. It isn't a disc, she sees, it's a curved triangle – a tiny serpent's head, with diamond scales carved across its surface, two little indented eyes and a forked tongue she could swear flickers from its mouth. He tilts his hand so that the light catches it, and it seems to come to life, appearing molten and wriggling for a brief moment.

She laughs, faintly puzzled but amused nonetheless. He looks so pleased, pride shining across his ruddy cheeks, and it's like a stab to her heart, a physical pain that stops the laughter dead in her throat. The pleasure he takes in her approval, the way his eyes turn to Athena, soft and adoring, horrifies her.

He is so open, he might as well be laid bare in front of them, all his vulnerability on display.

'So,' she says, her voice stiffer than she intends. 'An artist.'

He brings her gifts, starting with the snake. He turns it into a necklace, a double-headed serpent to coil around her throat. The body is a thick golden rope of overlapping scales, each one fitted perfectly to the next. He's placed tiny rubies in the eyes that stare out from her collarbones. Hera can't deny that she loves it. When she walks past Athena's workshop, she sees him so intent about his anvil, solid and focused on his creations. He makes more tools, more equipment, and one day she notices he's constructed bellows to blow cool air on the glittering, molten streams of metal he pours into shapes. He carves different-sized hammers to beat gold into thin sheets and smooth them down; he shapes moulds from wax, and makes bolts and rivets as his creations grow bigger and more ambitious. She notices Aphrodite lingering at the doorway, her gaze covetous as it takes in the shimmering crowns and delicate bangles, while Athena offers suggestions and helps him to puzzle out problems as they melt copper into bronze, shape wide bowls with intricate carved handles, work silver into goblets decorated with elaborate curving patterns. She's delighted when he fashions two great gold and silver dogs that look so lifelike Hera expects them to bark. Yet she can't help but notice how he looks up at Athena's face, as immaculate and polished as a bright coin, so eager for her praise.

It feels like a knife between Hera's ribs, every time. Zeus' daughter, so radiant and sharp, and Hera's son, lumbering after her. Athena is alive with the passion of discovery; her mind racing to the next idea like liquid silver, her joy in his talent so pure that she doesn't notice how he stares at her.

Hera can't hide her disappointment. What kind of a god has she created this time? Lovesick and yearning, with a gift for creating beautiful things that can only ever throw his own ugliness into sharper relief. Instead of thanks, she finds herself snapping at him, and the way he stands and absorbs it only angers her more. Ares would rear up at her, she thinks, his fury would blaze over. Neither of her sons seem to really understand her.

She hears his heavy footsteps outside her chamber, where she's retreated to get away from him and all the rest of them. Without a moment's hesitation, she transforms, hopping up on to the broad marble sill and spreading her hawk wings to the sky. She hears him falter on the threshold, uncertain and confused, as she soars away.

The day is warm and golden, like it always is. Far below her, mortals wipe sweat from their brows as they go about their toil. Whispers of their prayers float up towards her in fragments, but she lets them drift on the breeze unheard. Her mind is preoccupied, dark shadows swallowing up her every thought. When she thinks of her old freedom now, when her power felt light and careless in her hands, she only sees its looming end; the shape of her brother blotting out the sunlight, consuming the sky itself in his greed. The routes she'd charted to her own escape, uncertain now.

Her body tilts in the air, her wings carrying her back towards the Thracian hills. She'd hoped to go back to Ares with his brother, to set out a plan for the three of them together. Perhaps, she thinks now, she should try again with Ares alone. He has the strength, if she can only find a way through his resistance.

But as she sees the silhouette of Ares' palace ahead of her, she notices the graceful swoop of a white dove as she lands on the fearsome metal spikes of his gates. The dove lets out a melodic trill, her song sweet and full-throated, and its notes tumble into a peal of laughter as she jumps down on to the black-tiled steps to his bolted doors. Her dress spills over her body like water, every curve unmistakeable as she shakes back her hair, her face eager and expectant.

The doors swing open to the gloom within, and Hera can't quite believe her eyes when her son steps out and takes Aphrodite in his arms. It's his face, but not as she's ever seen it before. The sullen scowl in which she thought his features were permanently fixed is gone, transformed by a smile he's never worn for anyone else. Somehow, he looks like nothing more than a young warrior clasping his beloved. There is something exquisite and painful in the scene for Hera: his fine, muscled arms around Aphrodite's soft, yielding form. It is as if there is no one else in the world but the two of them: a perfect tableau of romance in front of his stronghold of war. It makes her flinch. And somehow she can't tear her eyes away from them. Even when Ares tugs Aphrodite through the door – Ares happy, Ares *playful* – still Hera stares at the empty space they leave behind, not able to put a name to the loss that aches inside her.

She's on an island beach, white sand sifting between her toes, her head tilted back to watch stars fall through the night sky, each one a vivid streak of light in the darkness, burning into nothingness in between her fixed sisters that twinkle steadily in position. Hera has never thought to find out why it happens. She doesn't know if it's the whims of the Titaness Asteria, who is in charge of these darting stars, or if it serves some other purpose. Even the queen of all the goddesses doesn't have the answer to everything.

She's lost in hazy contemplation, the feel of sand beneath her elbows and the play of light in the dim bowl above, when her body stiffens and she lifts her head, suddenly aware. The atmosphere has thickened and every muscle in her body tenses. A god approaches.

But he's not aware of her. It takes her a moment to make sense of it, for her mind to race ahead of her physical response and unscramble what she sees. If she looked up again, she would notice that the sky has become still. No more falling stars.

But all Hera sees is Zeus, his arms wrapped around a struggling figure. They've tumbled to the ground from above, and even though she can't see his face, she knows him at once. She recognises the way he pushes the woman down on to the beach. Her body remembers what that was like and turns to ice, freezing her in place. She wants to scream for him to stop, to leave her alone, but she can only stare as his fingers dig into the flesh of the woman's upper arm and she flails under his weight. Her head turns from side to side, searching for escape, and her eyes lock on to Hera's.

This is the moment, Hera thinks, that she will be jolted into action, that she will intervene. But the woman looking at her – a goddess, with dark gold eyes and midnight hair – reacts as though she's seen another horror. The terror in her gaze intensifies, then all at once she is gone, and Zeus is clawing at the air.

A tiny bird flutters through his closing fist. A puff of soft brown feathers taking flight. The bird casts one final anguished glance at Hera, and in that moment, Zeus' hand swipes at her, knocking her off course. Hera watches as the little quail zigzags through the air and tumbles into the sea.

The waves close over her head and Zeus is panting, his face alight with frustrated rage. Hera is transfixed by the lapping water; how quiet and calm it is, with no sign of the goddess it swallowed up. The goddess who, moments before, had been painting the sky in streaks of light.

'Asteria!' Zeus bellows, as though she would come back at his summons.

Hera turns her head to him, disbelieving. 'What are you doing?'

He starts, noticing her for the first time. Guilt hovers on his face momentarily, but he lapses back into a sulky frown. 'Why are you here?'

There is a buzzing in her ears; a lightness in her head that makes her feel unsteady on her feet. 'That girl,' she says, and she stops. What will she say? They both know what he was going to do.

'What about her?'

She can feel the confusion creasing her forehead. His anger has cooled like a summer storm, blown out before it gets going. Now he looks impatient, as though she's boring him. 'Do I really have to say it?' she asks.

'Say what?'

'I'm your wife.' She waits for him to respond, but he says nothing. 'I'm the goddess of marriage.' Does he need this clarification? It seems he does. 'Brides pray to me; wives pray to me. Why am I watching my husband chasing a goddess down from the sky?' *That was the point of all this*, she thinks. That was the reason for their sunset wedding in the Garden of the

Hesperides: to make something worthwhile out of what he did to her; to melt down her pain and transform it into power.

'Well, marriage is your domain. Not mine.' There is nothing shifty in his demeanour. He's looking at her, his eyes open and honest. He truly believes what he's saying to her, she thinks, and her stomach curdles. 'Did you expect something different?'

Yes, she thinks, *I did*. She's always expected something different of him; it's always been her mistake, and now she's made it again. 'So, you made me the queen of marriage,' she says slowly, 'and you ignore what that means?'

He pauses. The moonlight silvers the broad outline of his shoulders, and she notices the thunderbolt gleaming at his waist. Everything about him radiates power and control, from his easy stance to the disinterest in his eyes. 'I love you,' he says, 'but marriage is something different for you than it is for me.'

He has her, is what he means. Love for him is about possession, she knows. It's not something that will bind him.

The shame she felt on the beach where he left her all that time ago roars back. It burns through her: another humiliation, heaped on top of the others. Will she be the goddess of faithful wives to faithless husbands? The role she'd never wanted in the first place, degraded even further to this?

'She wasn't the first,' Hera says, and he looks almost pitying. 'What do you tell them about me?'

Keep quiet, she can hear him whisper. *Don't let Hera know what I've done to you, or you'll have her wrath to contend with next.* She can imagine it, can almost feel the warmth of his breath in her ear, and it sickens her to think that this could be why Asteria looked so afraid.

He comes closer to her, his hands on her shoulders as he leans down to kiss her, and when she jerks her head away, he only seems amused. 'Come on,' he says, 'back to Olympus with me now.' His meaning is clear, his body pressed against her, and she's revolted to realise that having been thwarted with Asteria, he wants her instead.

She shoves him away. He laughs, unrepentant. The night's events are nothing but a joke to him, her fury an entertaining diversion. She is trapped, and he is free.

'Never mind, then,' he says, and he becomes an eagle and disappears into the skies.

She is left with her bitterness, and the conviction that he will find another victim instead.

She must have known, really. He hasn't hidden what he is. But to survive, she divides her life into compartments in her head; to keep on going, she has had to pretend, even to herself, that she doesn't know, until she can't any longer. No doubt the other gods have been mocking her. The sea sparkles in the moonlight; the air is fresh and salt-scented, and the peaceful dark feels as though it's mocking her too. Whenever she has thought power is within her grasp, it has slid away from her.

Out towards the horizon, the waves break around new-formed rocks. An island floats up from beneath the surface. While Hera tries again to wrestle down her impotent fury, to hold it within her and somehow not let its poison burn her from the inside out, this island that was a quail that was a girl finds its precarious home atop the water. Unanchored, it drifts from side to side with the movement of the currents. Hera takes a long, shuddering breath. If she let the tides within her loose, they would rise up and drown the world in an ocean of blood-red violence.

She lets her gaze follow the fractured path of silver light across the sea. The little island is far out, but her divine gaze can distinguish it from the enveloping blackness of night and dark water around it. There is nothing to distinguish it as the goddess it once was. But Hera knows, all the same. She feels it tingling in her mind, a hum of understanding.

Asteria was a Titaness, more ancient than Hera or Zeus, with the power to melt the stars. But her fear of the two of them had been so great, it had driven her first panicky transformation into the little bird. From then, Hera can only guess. Disorientation, bewilderment, her feathers waterlogged and the waves sucking her down – it might all have been enough to compel her to transform again, but to find herself this time, instead of a living animal, an insensible rock. With the golden ichor hardened into mineral, perhaps she had been unable to change again. Or something else could have occurred in the depths of the sea. It looks peaceful enough, but Hera knows too well the nature of the gods who lurk there. One of them, maybe Poseidon himself, might have detected the fluttering of the terrified creature, heard the frenzied beat of her immortal heart, and known what she was. His brother's would-be victim, escaped from his clutches, only to plunge straight into the realm of the other. Desperation to flee another attack might have compelled her to shed her warm, vital shape and assume one that is unyielding and impenetrable instead.

Hera has tried to bury her resentments deep inside; every time they rear up, she forces them back, but it has done no good. She's denied them sunlight, but instead of withering away into something manageable, they have embedded their roots far down into her soul and grown strong. Now they tangle together, thick and poisonous. Ares and Hephaestus, subsumed by the shadow Athena casts, are no use to Hera at all. The cage of her marriage and her role, the trap she walked into. Meanwhile, Zeus is unconstrained, the world laid out before him, full of glittering prizes. And he gives her nothing at all. There is so much that she cannot reach out and take for herself, not anymore, and it's this that compels her now. With a force that comes from all her pain, a power greater than one she's ever felt before, she cries out to Gaia. It's a howl of wild desperation to the silent earth that has brought her nothing since the tree of golden apples: no sign, no comfort, no help. Her arm is raised to the sky, and the anger surges through her body. She thinks that if she sliced her skin open, her blood would run in rivulets of black venom. She brings her hand crashing down to strike the ground with her open palm.

Her scream echoes in the silent air, and for a moment nothing happens at all.

Then, beneath her feet, she feels a distant rumbling. A low growl emanating from far below, somewhere in the depths of the earth.

It is an awakening. And even though Hera wanted nothing more than to make this happen, there is a sudden flash of fear in her bones.

11

The moments slide by, and slowly Hera's stance relaxes. Nothing has emerged from beneath; no Gaia, no serpent-tailed goddess. Whatever it is that she felt awaken does not come forth. She exhales a long, trembling breath and waits for the disappointment to flood her.

But instead she feels a curious elation. A thrum of power, transferred from the shifting ground to her body.

Gaia has heard her howl of rage, the wordless prayer she shrieked aloud, and although Hera doesn't yet know how, she has answered it. Hera can feel life flickering inside her womb, the stirring she has felt before with her goddess intuition. But this is something different.

The sons I bore to him felt at first like tiny flames inside me, she thinks. The creation of a new god is a sparkle of light in a dark abyss; heat and radiance where there had been nothing at all. For all that Ares and Hephaestus have failed her, she had sensed the presence of a new power within her as soon as they existed.

And she feels it again now. Power, potential, the possibility of greatness that her body will nurture. Only whatever this is, it comes from her alone. There is nothing of Zeus in this one. Instead of the flutter of a new-kindled fire, she feels a dark slither, twisting inside her.

Gaia heard me, she tells herself. *At last, she listened.* This is a gift of the earth, and she knows in her heart that it is something never seen or dreamed of before.

In his rapacious greed, Zeus inadvertently gave the world Athena: a goddess formed from the galaxies swirling in his body, the galaxies that had sucked her mother into their centre and torn her to shreds, building the wise warrior from the remains. Now Hera's outrage, the pure and steely force of her anger, has harnessed the power of creation from Gaia herself, and she calls forth something new. Something more fearsome than Athena – a monster that will make the gods quake.

She knows him from the first shudder. How could she not? He is made of her, and only her. If she felt affection for her babies before, it was a pale shadow of this. The children that were part-Zeus never commanded such a rush of protective instinct, such a fierce desire to keep them safe.

She can't go back to Olympus. That much is obvious. She thinks of Athena's clear-sighted gaze and shivers. If anyone were to sense what she carries within her – and if anyone were going to, it would be Athena – she doesn't know what they might do. It's not a risk she can take.

Zeus knows she is angry with him; he won't be surprised if she stays away. His suspicions won't be raised for a while, at least. He will imagine that she sulks, that she hopes to punish him with her absence, to make him regret what he's done.

That he will regret it, she is sure.

There is no question this time of going back to Oceanus.

No home of the gods is safe for her now. Hera thinks of the world spread out beneath the peak of Mount Olympus: the thick forests, the deep lakes, the hidden caves and valleys where she could hide. None of them are beyond the eyes of the heavens. The seas can offer her no sanctuary either – they belong to Poseidon – and the subterranean realm is ruled by Hades.

It would never occur to her under any other circumstances, but Hera thinks she knows the last place any god would look for her. Somewhere she has always disdained; a world for which she has never cared and in which she has never found anything of interest.

A place where she is sure she'll never be found.

The village lies by the northern banks of a river that has carved out a valley at the foot of sloping hills. Barely more impressive than the inhabitants' humble dwellings is the temple they have built to honour Hera. Its columns have been sculpted from the oak trees that grow here, and for all the care that has been taken, they are still rough and weathered. The villagers come with their offerings: sweet-smelling flowers, which they heap at the base of the statue in the centre, and rich wine, which they pour out before her. From the cool shade of its interior, Hera can hear the low bleating of the sheep they lead to the altar to sacrifice in her name, and she breathes in the smoky scent of roasting meat while they sing to her in praise.

They never know how close they come to the goddess they worship. The priestesses who perform her rites don't dream that, as they mix their libations, they could reach out and touch her robes. They lower their voices in reverence around the temple statue, but if they knew who was inside it, they would not dare speak at all.

Their belief is a complicated thing, she has learned. They yearn for her to hear their words, they send their prayers so fervently to the wooden figure that gazes sightlessly ahead, its wide eyes and serene expression a clumsy imitation of her beauty, and they long for any sign that she is there. But if she showed herself, they would crumple in terror.

Athena moves among mortals, Hera knows. She loves to veil herself in the form of an elderly woman, to dispense her guidance as a wise old crone with only a twinkle in her cool, grey eyes to betray herself. But it's not for Hera to put on human flesh, to make herself move as slowly and ungracefully as one of them. She doesn't care to dim her divine radiance or speak in their hoarse tones.

So she keeps herself separate. At their centre, but always apart. She can't show herself for what she is, but she can't be anything else. This new isolation might make her feel lonely, if it weren't for him. She feels him, always wriggling, in her womb, the strange, unknown shape of him, and she rests her hand against her swelling skin, sure that he is the one who will change everything.

Still, she finds herself in moments of weakness longing for the comforts of Hestia's hearth, wishing that she could look into her sister's warm, brown eyes and hear her soothing tones. Or that she could see Klymene's sweet face and listen to her stories of Oceanus while she combs Hera's hair into intricate braids and swirls around her head.

She has to make up her own stories to keep her company. In the long passing of the year she spends in her temple – a spell that would seem fleeting on Mount Olympus but that here, in the home of the mortals, slows and stretches – she finds her favourite one. The story of a son born to a goddess; a monster shaped of his mother's righteous fury, who grew strong in secret, strong enough to topple the heavens. She whispers it in the somnolent haze of the endless afternoons, to the glittering motes suspended in the dusty air of the temple, hovering in the shafts of sunlight as they slant towards evening. Days ooze into one another like slow-flowing honey, and Hera counts each one for the first time in her existence.

Perhaps in the heavens they haven't even noticed her absence yet. There is no need to track time in the same way there, but even so, Hera knows that when her body ripened with her sons before, it was a much quicker process. That it is taking so much longer now heartens her. It only confirms that the baby she nurtures is so very different to them. She knows her patience will be rewarded.

She charts the seasons, the mild transition from the summer heat to the gentle warmth of autumn and the wintery cool. Nothing very much changes between them, but Hera is attuned to the subtle rhythms of the year. When spring emerges with an ever greater abundance of flowers, she senses it is time to leave her sanctuary. She was right that no god would look for her in a mortal village, hidden within her own cult statue, but it is no place to birth this child. She needs to find somewhere more secret still: a cave sunk far into the earth where no one will disturb her.

During her time at the temple, she has noticed how mortal women have far more trouble with birthing their babies than the goddesses do. Even Hephaestus, who had seemed so reluctant to be born, too weak and limp to aid his own passage into the world, had been little more than an inconvenience to her. She has a presentiment that this one will be more difficult, and her observations of the women that come to pray cloud her mind further. It is a great trial to them, and sometimes, the pregnant women who come to make their hopeful offerings don't return. Those who do bear the look of someone who has walked through fire. She looks down at the roundness of her own belly, at the impressions her baby makes against her flesh from within. There is nothing so discernible as a foot or an elbow. The writhing tumult he makes when he turns around inside her, that cannot come from arms and legs. She cannot be sure of what he will be and what that means for this birth, only that she must find somewhere secret.

Under the cover of a moonless night, she makes her way to the mountains to find a cave set deep enough, with tunnels that lead her into the earth. In the pitch black, she grits her teeth against the clamping pains that beset her. He is fire and pain and blood: all the elements that made him. He is the darkness of her soul; the horrors she has kept inside. Hera doesn't have to fear, like the mortal women do, that either one of them will not survive this. But the torment is enough to make her worry that it will crack her mind into fragments, that the agony will burn away her sanity and her knowledge of who she is or what existence she knew before this pain.

If time passed slowly at a mortal pace, it seems to stop dead now. *He was never meant to be*, she thinks, and it is the only thought that has clarity, worse than the pain. *Gaia gave my suffering a shape and made me bear it*. And she thinks of her rage made flesh, how vast it must be, and she is sure she cannot do this.

But Hera is an Olympian goddess, the highest of them all. In the silent midnight of this empty cave, she draws upon every reserve of strength in her body and, at last, with all of her effort, the monster is born.

The cavern flickers into light as he exhales his first breath. A tongue of flame flares bright from his mouth and sputters out, plunging them into the dark again. Hera watches with fascination as, with each breath, another fire pulses, illuminating the shape of him in fractured flashes. With each one, she sees what this baby is.

She'd thought Hephaestus ugly, because he is such a poor imitation of the gods. Hephaestus shares their form, but his features are lumpen and displeasing, while the other gods are perfect. This creature would be called hideous by them; in comparison, they would no doubt declare Hephaestus handsome. But Hera remembers how they turned in disgust from the Hecatoncheires and the Cyclopes – the vast, wild giants who brought them victory in battle against the Titans. She has always had a different measure of beauty. What she sees in this child is another victory, and as such he could not be more beautiful.

The sight of him ignites a love she never dreamed of knowing. Perhaps it's because she laboured so hard to bring him forth, and the relief that it is over is so great. Perhaps it's because he is the first thing that has ever been only hers. No other creature in the world knows of his existence – except, she thinks, for Gaia, from whom nothing can be hidden. He belongs to no one else but Hera. And to her, he is flawless.

He could be the kin of the snake-goddess Ekhidna. Like her, his flesh gives way to rolling serpent coils at his waist, though he has two sinuous tails rather than one. Each one curves and glimmers black in the fleeting firelight, the scales shifting as they ripple with his every movement. Where the scales meet skin, his torso is that of an infant god, though when he lifts his arms, she can see the leathery stretch of wings joining them to his back. And his fingers are not plump, pink fingers ending in white-tipped nails. Instead, from each hand grows a cluster of miniature serpent heads that twist together, forked tongues darting from their hissing mouths. His hair curls dark and thick around his skull, over his pointed ears, and his eyes flash crimson and malevolent when he looks up and meets her gaze.

He is warm in her arms, fierce and vulnerable all at once. She is grateful for her own foresight in hiding so well. If Zeus were to see him, he could crush him in a moment. Just like his mother before him, this baby must be raised in the secret dark. And if he grows as rapidly as his half-brothers did, he will attain his strength soon.

When she feeds him, she can feel the sharpness of his teeth at her breast, and the burn of his breath against her skin. She looks down at him, his eyes drifting shut, and she marvels at the difference between him and the babies she has birthed before. There is no trace of Zeus in this one.

The monster sleeps, peaceful and content, and Hera tucks him under her cloak. She steals away, back through the tunnels she had made her way down, tormented by labour pains. Now her body holds only the memory of an ache, and she moves swift and sure as ever. Outside, a mellow dusk is falling. A dim veil is drawn across the sky, and the first lights of the stars are glimmering.

Hera sits at the entrance to the cave, her fingers twining with the shoots of grass that grow in clumps around it. Deep-red petals brush against her calves: the nodding heads of poppies, heavy and drowsy. She closes her eyes, letting her thoughts wander. She sends them roaming across the meadow, floating through the flower stems to the rich soil beneath, a silent call to the earth. *Now that I have him, how will I keep him safe until his time comes?*

She listens to the breeze rustling through the leaves, sighing among the reeds and stirring the velvety petals, and she feels it taking shape.

The cave of the snake-goddess ... under the ash-strewn plains, shrouded in mist ... a dismal place at the farthest banks of Oceanus ...

Her eyes snap open. It's Gaia's voice, she's certain. Of course, she must take the child to Ekhidna. Surely, she will feel some kind of nurturing instinct for the creature that is like her. The only being in the world that Hera could call upon to protect him; the only one who would not turn from him. This time she can't make her way through the halls of Oceanus to the branching caves that lead off from his underground home. Gaia is telling her of another way to reach the serpent-goddess's caverns. Perhaps Gaia won't come out again in full support of another assault on the heavens as she did before. But she is giving Hera a chance, at least. The opportunity to try.

She'll have to return to Mount Olympus. She'll have to allay any suspicions that her absence might have raised, to pretend a reconciliation with Zeus. She'll have to tell him that she can see that her role is to be goddess of women and to know her place beside him, that she accepts it now. He will believe her. He'll have no reason not to.

And all the while, she will nurture her monster beneath the earth.

*　　*　　*

She smuggles the infant creature in her cloak, mindful as she does so of how she and Zeus were spirited away by Gaia from their father Cronus. She wonders for the first time if Rhea had wrapped her in a robe of her own. If the cloth that concealed her had carried the scent of the mother she would never see again.

Gaia had seen something in the infant Hera that made her worth saving. She'd known that with Hera, things could be different. Otherwise, why take her away? Hera knows, with the same certainty, that this will be a new rebellion – that this son will be capable of what Ares and Hephaestus are not. This child was given to her by Gaia; he is chosen, just like she was.

When she was taken, it was to the home of powerful allies, and she had the protection of the earth herself. She takes heart from the knowledge that Gaia watches over her still, that she has given her the gift of this monster and a haven for him, but she feels a pang nonetheless that Gaia has not come to her as she used to. Hera longs to see her take her goddess form, to see her green-robed figure and tumbling hair woven with flowers and ferns. She knows that she has evoked Gaia's sympathy, but not her unreserved support. Not this time. Hera can't run back to Oceanus; she can't call on anyone in Olympus to stand with her. Whatever is coming, she has to face it alone, with only her son.

She knows the plain that Gaia described. It's a bleak and lonely place, charred and inhospitable. Most mortals would shun it, and most gods too. Nothing about it has ever piqued Hera's interest. She likes to seek out far-flung places, but none as featureless as this. It makes sense that it would harbour an entrance to the subterranean world where Gaia keeps her secrets.

Hera

The river of Oceanus runs black and sinuous beneath the clouded night skies here; a wavering beam of moonlight falls ghostlike across the water. Hera holds the sleeping bundle in her arms, close to her chest. The mountains rise tall and forbidding, and here and there a gnarled tree sprouts from the bare ground, its branches skeletal.

Here, in this desolate place at the end of the world, she will make her son's first home, with a monster so ancient she has almost been forgotten.

12

It's just how it was in her dreams. The long, twisting tunnels through dripping rock. The fetid smell of slime, oozing between the cracks. And at last, the vaulting cavern where the serpent-queen lives.

Her eyes are dark and unreadable as Hera speaks. She doesn't know if Ekhidna comprehends a word she's saying. But her expression changes when Hera unwraps the swaddled thing in her arms and she sees what he is.

'Typhon.' It's the first time Hera has spoken his name aloud. She's named him for the most ferocious of winds; the powerful gales with the strength to tear trees from their roots. A force that will upend everything, a chaos unleashed.

The serpent-goddess reaches out for him, and Hera takes a step back.

'You can't take him to the heavens.' Her voice rasps in the shadows. Hera wonders how long it is since Ekhidna has spoken aloud to anyone else. 'Zeus would destroy him.'

She cradles her son closer to her chest. It's true, but she can't bring herself to let him go.

Ekhidna's tail drags along the rocky floor as she moves closer. This time, Hera stays still.

The serpent-queen reaches out a hand towards the baby's face. Her finger strokes his cheek, so softly that he doesn't stir at all.

Hera's heart is in her mouth. But there is so much tenderness in Ekhidna's touch; she takes such gentle care not to disturb him. Hera wouldn't have thought there could be such maternal instinct in this solitary monster.

'He belongs here,' Ekhidna says.

'How can I know you'll keep him safe?' She's used to giving commands. This kind of negotiation doesn't come naturally. But she can't threaten Ekhidna, not when she's here to hand over the thing she holds most dear.

'Why would I harm him?'

'I don't know. Before today, I didn't know for certain that you really existed.'

Ekhidna laughs: a horrible, gurgling sound. 'I have no love for the gods,' she says. 'You among them.' Her hands slide around the baby's body, one beneath his head and the other where his serpent coils split apart. They twitch, and wrap around her wrist as she lifts him from Hera's grasp. 'But Typhon isn't one of you.'

Hera feels his absence in her arms, but she quells the impulse to take him back. 'You'll take care of him,' she says. 'For his sake, not mine.'

Ekhidna nods, but doesn't look at Hera. Her gaze is intent on the child, drinking him in.

'I'll be back,' says Hera. 'As often as I can.'

'He'll grow strong with me,' Ekhidna says. Her voice is a

cold hiss, but Hera believes her. What other choice does she have?

When she crosses the river again and makes her way back towards the familiar meadows and forests that she loves, she tells herself she must forget the whole experience, be as convincing as she can be, as though none of it has happened. On Olympus, it all goes just as she predicted. Zeus is unshaken by her brief disappearance, and is as unrepentant as ever. The gleaming gold of her cloud-wreathed palace and the bite of the cold, thin air restore her.

The only change is a distance that has sprung up between Athena and Hephaestus. There is a coolness now that was not there before, and a new mournfulness in her son's demeanour. Hera doesn't yet know why, but she feels relieved to see it.

When she goes back to the caves, at first she's afraid she'll find nothing there at all. Ekhidna might have vanished into the gloom, taking Hera's son with her. But Typhon is still there, thriving in the dark, growing swift and strong. His chest grows thick with muscle, his coiling tails capable of whipping gouges in the solid rock of the cavern walls. His face becomes bearded, the hair matting and tangling in foul clumps, and the snake-heads at his hands provide a constant hissing chorus. It delights her, every time she returns, to see what he has become.

Even with the thought of Typhon to cheer her, she can't make herself sweet for Zeus, can't control her bitter temper when he comes back to the palace from his own wanderings. Although if she did, it would probably only raise his suspicions.

Their divine acropolis has expanded; Athena has built her own, smaller palace apart. Aphrodite has her own cosy quarters too, and Hera can hardly contain her curiosity about what she keeps hidden there. She hasn't managed to banish from her mind the image of her sullen elder son transformed into a giddy lover, nor of Aphrodite's perfect face gazing up into his. When the gods assemble for a feast in the wide hall of the main building, she looks up and down the table, wondering what each of them hides behind their smiling expressions.

Zeus takes his seat at the head of the table, Hera at his right hand. He reaches lazily for her, twining his fingers through hers, and she pictures Typhon growing ever more powerful underground. The two conflicting images jar against one another in her mind. Zeus, so self-satisfied, never dreaming of her plans for rebellion. He has such an easy command of the room, such a relaxed confidence in himself, and when she watches him, she can almost imagine a world in which she would be glad to be his wife. A world that might have been open to them once, when they were young gods on Crete and had only one another. When they thought they could shape the future as they wanted. When it would never have crossed her mind that he would shut her out of it, take it all for himself and expect her to be glad of what scraps he had to spare for her.

Athena talks with vivid animation, gesturing as she explains some new idea or another, and Hephaestus stares into his goblet, the tips of his ears reddening as he determinedly keeps his eyes from hers. Hera must ask Hestia about that later, she thinks. It's only Hestia, of course, who has enquired after her disappearance from Olympus. Hestia, tethered to her hearth, with the time and interest to pay attention to what the rest of them are doing.

She's given her sister a truncated story. She included the Asteria episode, up to Zeus leaving her on the beach. After that, she didn't feel like coming back too soon, she's told her sister. It seemed prudent to show Zeus her displeasure, not that he seems concerned.

'Oh, he is, though,' Hestia had replied. 'When you aren't here . . .'

They were interrupted by the entrance of Poseidon, flinging open a heavy door and casting a scowl in their direction, and Hera never heard the end of the sentence.

Now, she takes a long draught of wine, sweetened with nectar. Pulls her hand away from Zeus' grip and turns her face to the other side. Unfortunately, it's Aphrodite who sits there, and Hera can't think of a single thing to say to her.

Aphrodite, though, has her sights set on Poseidon. 'You seem angrier than usual,' she remarks to him. 'Any reason?'

'How can you tell?' Demeter murmurs.

Poseidon glares at her.

'Since I taught mortals the art of shipbuilding,' Athena says, 'it's annoyed him that the seas are busy with boats.'

'Hardly busy,' says Hera. She flies across the waters all the time, between Mount Olympus and the entrance to Ekhidna's cave. It's always an empty blue expanse. Little boats – hardly more than rafts – might tentatively navigate the coastlines, but it can't be much disturbance to Poseidon.

'He sinks half of them, anyway,' Aphrodite says.

'If they asked for my favour,' Poseidon mutters, 'they might receive it.'

Aphrodite laughs. She knows that Poseidon won't turn his irritation on her, he never does. 'If only all sailors were pretty girls, they might stand more of a chance.' Her voice is light, a teasing tone that Hera has never been able to get the hang of. From her, it would sound like an accusation.

'And who's to blame for that?' Zeus interjects. 'Poseidon can shake the earth until mountains become rubble, but he can't withstand your meddling, Aphrodite.'

She raises an eyebrow. 'I have nothing to do with half of it,' she says. 'Who was that woman – Iphimedeia? You came to her as seawater, submerged her and swept her away, am I right? It was inventive, certainly. Not something that ever occurred to me.'

Hera frowns. *Iphimedeia*. She thinks she can remember a prayer, an entreaty for her help. There are so many, they all merge together, but this one stood out for the creativity of his cruelty if nothing else. 'Wife of a mortal king,' she says. 'Not yours to take.'

Her words drop into the flow of the conversation like boulders crashing into a bubbling stream. The gods turn to stare at her. She's sure she catches Aphrodite rolling her eyes, and she can't mistake how the beautiful goddess meets her son's gaze; the thus far disengaged Ares brought into the moment by a brief flare of connection between them. Aphrodite and her eldest son, united against her.

'Well,' Hera continues. 'Poseidon defends his waves against sailors, why can't I defend my realm? I'm bound to preserve marriage, after all.' She looks pointedly at Zeus. 'You entrusted me with the role.'

His smile is wide and lazy, his eyes glinting in the torchlight. 'I did,' he says softly. 'And a key tenet of marriage is that the wife obeys her husband.' He pauses, glancing at Poseidon. 'And her gods, of course.'

'But—' Hera begins, and Poseidon sits up straighter, keen with anticipation. There is a hum of tension in the air: all the

Olympians caught between Hera and Zeus, poised to see how he'll respond if she argues further.

'The mortal queen gave birth to fearsome sons.' Athena's voice cuts across hers, smooth and cool. 'This Iphimedeia. They were normal infants, but quickly grew to a vast size. Both are giants now.'

The growing smirk vanishes from Poseidon's face. He stares at Athena with deliberate insolence. 'So?'

Athena leans forward, her elbows on the table and her chin propped on her linked hands. Either she doesn't notice his hostility or, more likely, she doesn't care. She's eager to share her thoughts, and Hera knows well enough that nothing will dissuade her once she starts. 'It's interesting, don't you think, that some children born to mortal women from gods are simply human, but others are more powerful? If there was some way of predicting ... could it be something within the mother? Surely not.' She shakes her head, an airy dismissal of the very idea of any kind of maternal influence on a child. 'It must be the father; it must come from the divine element – but then, why the variation?'

'Why not the mother?' Hera can't prevent herself from asking.

'Why does it matter at all?' Poseidon growls.

The surprise on Athena's face is utterly sincere. 'Giants are unruly,' she points out. 'And they're strong.'

This stirs Zeus' interest. 'Two giants,' he muses. 'That's not so hard to contain.'

'But if there were more,' Athena says. 'How many liaisons of gods and mortals would it take to form an army?'

Poseidon scoffs. 'Of course Athena would look at it like that.' He doesn't address her at all, turning to Zeus as though she isn't even there. 'She's so cold . . . so unnatural. She sees everything as a logic puzzle. She can't understand the forces at play – the chase, the lure, the conquest.'

He's practically licking his lips, and his palpable hunger makes Hera feel queasy.

'You still haven't forgiven her for Coronis,' Demeter says, amused.

'The crow,' Hestia whispers to Hera, and she remembers now. The girl Athena rescued from Poseidon's advances, who became a bird.

'Athena turned down Hephaestus.' The rare sound of Ares' voice joining the conversation strikes all the gods dumb for a moment. It's the most animated that Hera has ever seen him at dinner. It must be the spark of conflict that's enlivening him; the prospect of the simmering resentment boiling up into something more violent.

'That's hardly unnatural.' Zeus' laugh echoes from the marble pillars, loud and hearty.

Hera thinks Hephaestus couldn't hunch further into himself than he already is, but somehow his shoulders droop and she sees the tops of his ears flame even redder. He doesn't look up at his elder brother or his father as the mirth spreads among the rest of them. *Speak up*, she urges him silently, but he says nothing.

Now she understands, at least, why his worship of Athena seems to have come to an end. It was absurd of him to think it could be any different.

'We'll keep an eye on Poseidon's monstrous sons.' Zeus waves his hand, the laughter dying down, though his cheeks are still ruddy with enjoyment and wine. 'We won't allow them to become a threat.'

The rest of them nod in fervent agreement. Athena, unfazed by the mockery of Hephaestus or Poseidon's insults, seems pleased. 'That's right,' she says. 'If we monitor them, if we anticipate any danger before it can emerge . . .'

'That seems like a job for you,' Zeus says, and she nods, satisfied.

Hestia's fingers brush Hera's forearm, warm and gentle. 'Mortals know better than to defy us. I hear the stories they share at the fireside.' Deftly, she steers the conversation to safer ground. Somehow, the legend of Ixion has made its way down the generations, she tells them, and the mortals say he suffers his eternal punishment down in the realm of Hades now, his shade strapped forever to a flaming wheel as his body was when Zeus flung him into the skies. 'They fear what might become of them after death in the Underworld,' she says, 'if they offend us while alive.'

The gods agree this is a good thing. But Hera thinks that they learned something from their experience with Ixion too. Not to let the mortals too close. Not to let them think they can behave as the gods do, with impunity. Ixion had no worse intentions than Zeus, after all. He just didn't have the strength to get away with it.

The hypocrisy maddens her. Aphrodite, inciting infidelity everywhere she goes. Zeus and Poseidon, riding roughshod over the bonds of marriage. Athena, warning them that giants can be monsters – a threat to squash at any moment – when Hera thinks, looking up and down the table, that the true monsters are here, clad in beautiful immortal flesh.

What would the world look like, she thinks, if Hera wielded the thunderbolt instead of Zeus? If the gods followed her commands and her example instead of his? If the dispossessed and hated creatures – the giants, the Cyclopes, the hidden serpent-gods, her son, *the best of them all* – had their say. If her sisters – and maybe the preening Aphrodite, perhaps even the cold and calculating Athena – made up her council. Without the coarsening influence of Zeus and Poseidon, without Ares riling them up to violence, they could be better. Hera could be better too, out of the shackles of her marriage.

She doesn't argue any further, not here. She stays silent, sipping wine and ignoring them, lost in her own thoughts. She tries to speak it aloud when she goes back to Typhon again, giving shape to the tentative ideas in her head formed of every grievance, every injustice she's suffered. 'We can make a different world,' she tells Typhon, and Ekhidna listens in the shadows.

His heavy brows are furrowed as he listens to her, and she's struck by the memories of Gaia coming to her in the caves of Oceanus, filling her head with visions of the life that awaited her above the ground. Now she's the one coming from the world outside, sketching out the triumphs ahead and the pitfalls to dodge.

'But you think you can keep the Olympians?' Ekhidna slithers towards them, her tone laden with suspicion. 'You think things would change enough if you only banish the Thunderer and the Earth-Shaker?'

'That's when things went so wrong,' Hera says. 'When they pushed us down, made us inferior to them when we'd been equal before.'

Ekhidna narrows her eyes with contempt as she winds one long, slender arm around Typhon's broad shoulders. Her hair falls across his bare chest, his serpent-fingers nestling around her wrist as he reaches up to take her hand in his. 'And the war-god?' she says. 'Your other son. You'd turn on him so easily, would you?'

The way she presses herself against Typhon's body, how she wraps her other arm around his waist and stares at Hera with defiance, makes it so clear. She's not protective of him like a nurse to her charge, not anymore. The love between them has become something else.

'Ares can make his choice,' Hera says.

'We can't trust them,' Ekhidna says. *Or you* hangs in the air, unspoken.

'If I wanted,' Hera says, 'I could tell Zeus about your existence. He'd destroy you without a second thought.' She looks at Typhon. 'I bore you alone,' she goes on. 'You were a gift to me from Gaia. But he'd never believe that, even though he should know better than anyone. He makes a mockery of our marriage every day, and the earth is populated by his bastard offspring by dozens of mothers. But I can't break the vows I'm charged to protect. I wouldn't.' He'd never tolerate, not for an instant, the prospect that she might have done. 'I've kept you hidden all this time, never breathed a word. You must know I'm on your side. This isn't some kind of trick.'

Typhon nods. His matted beard brushes the crown of Ekhidna's head and she lifts her chin with a faint smile. The cautious façade she maintains against Hera dissolves as she looks up at him.

'Zeus had a nurse once,' Hera blurts out. 'Her name was Metis. And when I realised they were lovers, I blamed her. I didn't know why she didn't say no to him. Now I know there was nothing she could do to stop him.' A flush of shame rises in her body, and she holds her voice steady as she speaks. 'You two aren't like that. You're the only two creatures in the world of your kind. I knew that, Typhon, when I brought you here, to give to her.'

'Of course we're nothing like Zeus,' Typhon says.

'It's how I know things will be different.' Hera takes in a breath. The air down here is damp and fetid, but lately it's more invigorating to her than the fresh breezes of Mount Olympus. There is an honesty to its foulness; no pretence or concealment. 'I thought once that maybe Gaia wanted me to rule with my sisters alone – a world under goddesses. But we weren't enough. Then she sent me you. And I realised what it was she wanted me to see.'

'Which is?' Ekhidna asks.

'Gaia loves all her children,' Hera says. 'Gods, Titans and creatures like you. She created a world where we could all live peacefully. First Ouranos stifled everyone beneath him, then Cronus brought strife, now Zeus. They only want to dominate and despoil. Monsters must be exiled, women used and crushed. Zeus and Poseidon set the example, and others follow.'

'So an alliance of goddesses and monsters will change it all?' Ekhidna still sounds disdainful. 'You should leave us where we're safe. I've dwelt in the underbelly of the world since time began to exist. It makes no difference to us which gods rule the earth. Nothing changes here. There's no reason for me to risk it now, not for you.'

Hera doesn't recoil at the rejection. She isn't watching Ekhidna at all.

Her eyes are on Typhon. And she doesn't think he looks convinced by his lover's words.

*   *   *

149

Nothing changes here. It would have been true, if Hera had never come with her infant. The serpent-goddess could have lived in darkness for eternity, locked in stillness, untouched by the rise and fall of the gods.

But the moment she'd handed her swaddled creature to Ekhidna, Hera had disturbed the peace of centuries. And change is inevitable now.

The Hydra is born first: her nine snake-heads weaving between one another, her long necks twining, tongues flickering in the dim green light. Hera gasps in astonishment when Typhon folds back the cloak she once wrapped him in to show her his daughter, cradled proudly in his thick arms.

Ekhidna is at his elbow, cold and distrustful, unwilling to take a step away from the baby while Hera is there.

'May I?' Hera asks her, extending her hand towards the bundle and, reluctantly, Ekhidna acquiesces with a tight nod.

She's composed all of coils, a thick rope of sinuous muscle wound into curves in Typhon's hold. Hera strokes a finger along one neck. The Hydra's scales feel rough against her skin, and a chorus of hissing rises from her heads as she twists to see the goddess.

'Ouch!' Hera pulls her hand back, startled. She raises it in front of her face, staring in fascination at the double puncture just above the knuckle of her forefinger, and the two tiny drops of golden blood welling up.

'She's powerful,' Ekhidna says. There is a satisfaction in her voice, and a smile on her face that she can't suppress.

Hera feels herself smile in return, a giddiness springing up inside her as she watches the ichor trace its way down her finger in two narrow streams.

When she leaves, the bite still burns and tingles. She feels

an urge to scratch at it, to scrape away the venom, and out in
the sunlight, she can see there is no way she can go back to
Mount Olympus with such an injury. The blood still trickling
from it is tinged with noxious green that's sure to raise all kinds
of questions. What manner of creature could have pierced her
skin, and how strong must its poison be to fester so?

She finds a remote lake and plunges her hand into the cold
water with relief. Her bright, shining ichor swirls into the
eddying ripples, and she holds her hand there until it ceases
to flow. Then she lies back on the damp grass of the bank and
looks up into the sky.

That Typhon was born was a miracle in itself – a perfect
miracle from Gaia, a reward for her anger and her pain. That
he goes on, that he can make his own family, that there can be a
brood of beautiful monsters made from her wrath is better yet.

But the need for concealment is even greater now.

When Hera leaves Mount Olympus next, she gathers
wriggling eels, frogs and toads to take to her granddaughter.
The Hydra bathes in stagnant cave waters, her heads poised
above the dirty foam and foul bubbles, her eyes intent on these
intriguing gifts that writhe and hop on the damp rocks, until
one of her necks will whip around, her fangs bared as she
strikes. Hera learns to stack shining bracelets on her wrists,
and artfully swathes tunics to drape across her upper arms,
concealing the bites and scratches.

Ekhidna and Typhon's caverns soon ring with barks and
yaps when the two-headed Orthros and three-headed Cerberus
are born – both serpent-tailed like their parents but otherwise
with the bodies of hounds. Hera laughs at their puppyish
enthusiasm, how they lick her face when she kneels down on
the floor and opens her arms to them. Their needle-like teeth

are sharp against her ankles when they cavort around her legs and bite at her skirts, but her scrapes and grazes no longer ooze and sting so much.

She's becoming immune to their poison. And her joy in this clutch of hybrid things that would so appal any of her fellow Olympians overcomes even Ekhidna's reticence. It's hard to stay cold and detached from this goddess who is so rapt and radiant in the presence of her children, whose regal dignity falls away when they rest their heads in the crook of her elbow and look up into her face, who spreads out her fine dresses across the dank floor of the caves, not caring for the stains that seep through the fabric, ushering the little beasts close to nestle against her, to snap and growl and play-fight with one another around her.

It's Ekhidna, not Typhon, who presents their youngest child to Hera, eager to introduce the strangest of her offspring, the Chimera, with her body comprised of lion, goat and serpent all at once. She's gratified by Hera's enchantment.

Hera has her happiest moments in the Tartarean caves with her monsters. She barely thinks of her Olympian family when she comes here. It's this family that matters most; this family that seems more real.

But Typhon, although he is her son, is not hers to command any more than his half-brother Ares has been. His shoulders sweep the roof of their vast cave, his breath rumbling hot and fetid in the swampy air, and he grows restless from waiting.

His children are grown, he says to Hera, they cannot hide here forever, and so the time has come to strike. To put Hera's vision into action; to overthrow these tyrants that he's never seen.

Ekhidna draws to his side. Her voice is still hoarse, still

always seeming close to collapse from the eternity of silence down here that preceded their arrival, but it thrills with ancient power, with hints of stories she could tell about the world before the other gods were born. 'We will be heard,' she says. 'We cannot hide here forever.'

It's true. The shrieks and growls from their brood echo up through solid rock, and they won't go undetected for much longer. If the Olympians discover them first, they won't leave them alone. Why would they? Hera's entire purpose has been to create a threat to the gods, and they will recognise it as such. Now that they are tangible, now that they are alive, now that they are not just the hatred and grief and fury locked inside her heart, she feels protective of them. She fears the risk of unleashing them.

'It isn't your decision to make,' Typhon warns her. 'We have to protect our children, before they're discovered.'

He looms above her, snake-fingers hissing and eyes burning, and she knows how terrifying he will be to the others. It would be cowardice for her to hold back now.

He was born of rage. Of course he wants to fulfil the destiny she set for him.

She imagines the gods slumbering on Mount Olympus, replete and complacent. She remembers Zeus shoving her down into the pebbles, the powerlessness she felt. She thinks of the way he divided the world between himself and his brothers, and snatched away what was rightfully hers.

'We'll burn it down,' she tells her son. 'Together.'

His smile is horrifying and magnificent.

'Just give me time,' she says. 'Let me work out a plan.'

'Why wait?' he says.

'Zeus is strong. Don't underestimate him.'

'Not stronger than me.'

'You don't know that. You've never left these caves,' she says.

His teeth snap together, fire streaming out from between them.

'He's powerful,' Hera insists. 'But he has his weaknesses. And other enemies besides us.'

Ekhidna looks wary. 'Don't bring anyone else into this,' she warns. 'We can't risk betrayal.'

'We won't,' Hera says. 'All you have to do is trust me.'

'Fine,' says Typhon. 'Come back with your plan. I'll hear it. But don't take too long.'

'I promise,' says Hera.

And it's only when she's left that it occurs to her, too late, that she should have made him promise too.

Hestia is the only one she will warn. Not Ares, not Hephaestus. She knows where Ares' loyalty lies now, and it isn't with her. If he were to tell Aphrodite, it could all fall apart. And she can't trust Hephaestus to keep her secrets either. If he thinks there is a way back to Athena, or a way to wheedle into Zeus' favour, he might take it. He's at the bottom of the Olympian hierarchy right now, and Hera won't give him the chance to tip the scales.

After it's done – after Zeus is toppled, and she is ruling – then she can rebuild with them. If they choose to follow her.

Hestia looks grave when Hera finds the words, stumbling over the absurdity of them as she speaks. She wonders if her sister will disbelieve her, but Hestia listens with her usual air of quiet calm, and then she gives her answer.

'I could sense something,' she says. 'Not only with you – not just that you weren't telling me everything about your disappearance. But I knew that something had shifted.' She pauses. 'I felt it when Hephaestus was born – that he has a kindred connection to the fire. It's in his blood, like it is mine. But your Typhon, he is different. What I could sense – it was fire, but not like ours.' Her brows draw together, concern writ across her lovely face.

'He isn't like us,' Hera interjects quickly, but Hestia won't be rushed.

'I can feel his anger,' she says quietly. 'I can feel it burning deep in the earth.'

'It's what we need,' Hera says. 'His size, his strength – alongside me, and you if you will fight with us – the others won't be able to withstand it. I took down four Titans with the Hecatoncheires and Cyclopes on the ground while you all battled Cronus in the skies. And Typhon is more powerful than all of them combined.'

She can read the doubt in Hestia's face, and she is desperate to convince her.

'Truly, he is. He can bring down Mount Olympus, with our help. And when we're rid of Zeus and Poseidon – think of the rest of us together. What we could be.'

Hestia says nothing. Hera notices how she wrings her fingers together, betraying her anxiety, but she has no idea what her sister is thinking.

'Please,' Hera says, when she can't bear the silence any longer. 'Tell me if you'll be with me.'

Hestia doesn't meet her eyes, staring into the flames instead.

'Won't you?' asks Hera.

Her sister sighs, a long-drawn-out exhalation. 'I didn't come with you when you fled before,' she says at last. 'I didn't stand up against Zeus when you wanted to. I took my role, and made myself safe here.' She hesitates. 'And he came after you, and when you came back . . .'

Hera lets the words linger between them. She imagines her return through Hestia's eyes. Her coldness, the way she clung to her dignity and made herself regal. Untouchable. But Hestia knew what she was feeling inside. She always does.

'I'll be with you this time,' Hestia says quietly.

With an understanding between the two of them, Hera starts to allow herself to believe she really will win.

13

When he strikes, she is unprepared. He doesn't wait for her to keep her promise. He doesn't wait for Hera to bring him allies; he doesn't bring his monstrous children or Ekhidna to fight at his side. He is so sure that he can triumph alone.

Night falls over Olympus, and at once the darkness is rent in two by a rain of fire. Hera runs out to the courtyard, and he is there. Free of the pit, he seems to stand almost as tall as the mountain itself, his vast arms spread and his leathery wings unfurled between them. The flames rage in the dark pools of his eyes, and even when she screams his name, he doesn't respond. The palace shakes with each impact, each flaming rock he hurls at it crashing through marble. Smoke hangs thick and heavy, cloaking the air, and she can't see anything but flashes of heat and crimson light. She looks one way and then the other, disorientated, shouting his name over and over. The others are surging out towards her, the bellowing of the immortals creating as much of a din as the boulders hurtling through the sky.

The control she believed she had is slipping through her

fingers again. Could his impetuous assault be doomed, after all her planning? Or is he truly strong enough to win? She searches in the gloom for Hestia, but the other gods are there instead. Their panic is startling, but then, they have never expected this. They have had such faith in their mountain stronghold. She sees Aphrodite dodging a huge rock streaming with fire; it slams into Ares, who is dazed for a moment before he rallies and shoves her behind him, storming to the courtyard edge and flinging back his head. His battle-cry rings through the night and Typhon screams back, fire flickering from his mouth.

Athena slips past her, yelling instructions, but Hera can't make any sense of what she's saying. Under her direction, the others are picking up the rocks and flinging them back at Typhon. Even Hephaestus is lumbering about, the thick muscles of his back rippling.

Typhon is impervious to their blows. As the fires take hold around them, and the palace buckles and crumbles under the onslaught, masonry tumbling and blocks of marble spinning down the slopes, Athena stands tall and takes careful aim. She hits him squarely in the face, the rock smashing into his jaw, and Hera sees his black blood pouring. It doesn't slow him at all.

Where is Zeus? It's the only clear thought in Hera's mind. The line of gods is buckling against her son. He is so relentless and the rocks he pelts at them are unceasing. All around him, the winds are howling and his vast serpent-fingers hiss, and she can hear nothing else.

The mountain trembles beneath her feet, and she sees Ares hit by a boulder and then another, staggering backwards just as the wall of the palace behind him buckles. Great blocks of stone fall around him, striking the golden tiles, and Hera thinks the air itself is on fire as the dust and smoke swirl in a choking cloud. Aphrodite is clawing at the wreckage, pulling rubble away and flinging it behind her as she searches for Ares beneath it. Hera sees Demeter, her hair wild around her face, blinding her as she searches for Typhon in the gloom. He rears up again, Athena standing defiant before him, and he throws back his head and spits. Hera sees the venom searing Athena's skin where it lands. Athena's eyes flash silver and furious, and Hera knows this is her moment. The other gods are incapacitated; it is only Athena holding firm against him, and she doesn't know Hera is there. She tenses her body, poised to charge. It's right that it comes down to the two of them now, she thinks. Zeus' untouchable daughter, caught between Hera and Typhon. For all the foresight she inherited from her doomed mother, Athena has no idea of what's coming.

But neither does Hera. Just as she readies herself to strike at Athena, she hears his roar. Lightning shears the sky, and Zeus bounds towards her. He is not the sedate, regal King of Olympus now. He's not the sneering god on the beach, telling her that he will do as he pleases; there is none of the cold-eyed blankness of the stranger he was when he seized her the first time. He is a raging warrior, alive with the ferocity he once unleashed upon their father. The thunderbolt crackles in his hand as he shoves her aside, leaping up on to the ruined walls of the courtyard to face Typhon.

For a moment, the white light dancing on the prongs of the thunderbolt illuminates the two of them: Typhon's face twisted in grotesque fury, his matted hair seeming to brush the stars in the dome of the heavens, the full and dreadful extent of his monstrosity a hideous contrast to Zeus, who holds his gaze.

The hatred is palpable, raw and pulsing between them, and Hera is scrambling to her feet, but Athena's hands close on her arms and she can't free herself. Athena's fingers dig into her skin, slowing her down so that she cannot stop Zeus from raising his weapon. Typhon pulls back his arm, ready to hurl fire and rock at the god, but Zeus is faster. Lightning surges from the thunderbolt, striking Typhon in between his eyes. His scream echoes from the mountain summit. Hera wrestles herself out of Athena's grasp, and lurches forward just in time to see him topple. She clings to the jagged stone edges as he falls, a trailing plume of smoke rising from the crater in his head.

She can't make sense of what she's seeing. She can't believe that Typhon, who was so powerful, could be destroyed. Ichor slides down her arm, dripping from the wounds that Athena gouged into her flesh. The only injuries she has, from a battle that had hardly begun before it was finished.

The loss is incomprehensible. Typhon, her hope for the future, the triumphant vision she had of another life. It threatens to overwhelm her, a tide of grief swelling and rising, ready to break over her, but still some part of her keeps her from crying out. The part of her mind that is darting frantically through the fractured scenes of the fight, working out who saw her and how her actions – or lack thereof – might be construed. When she leapt at Zeus and Athena stopped her, she could have been running to his aid. When she stood and watched the rest of them pummelled by Typhon's onslaught, it could have been the shock and confusion of the moment that rooted her to the spot. Can she hope to convince them of this? Swallow down her despair and pretend that she's searching only for proof that the monster is defeated, not for a glimmer of hope that he has survived?

In the strange silence that has fallen across Olympus, she hears a soft *drip, drip, drip*. She glances up to the side, to a broken slab of marble that lies haphazardly on the pile of rocks that was once their home. A black pool has formed on top of it, and the only sound in the stillness is of the slow drops of viscous liquid spilling over the edge. She lifts her hand towards it, touches it and flinches at the burn. It reminds her of the cave, the fledgling monsters and the sting of their venom when they scraped her with their teeth in play. This is the venom from their father's blood, more potent than theirs, now splattered across the smoking ruins of the palace.

Zeus clears his throat and she spins around, her back pressed to the rough stone, her lies gathered on her lips. The words evaporate on her tongue the moment she sees his face. Above her, the black blood slides down, tracing its way across her shoulder and the torn skin of her arm. She bites back any sound of pain as it bubbles and spits, mingling with her ichor.

Behind Zeus, the other gods are gathering. Ares, freed from the rubble, with Aphrodite at his side. Demeter and Hephaestus, both looking bewildered as the falling flakes of ash swirl around them. Poseidon, grim-faced. Hestia, appalled. She arrived too late, and Hera catches her eye, giving an almost imperceptible shake of her head. Hestia cannot help, and there is no good in implicating herself in something she has had no real part in.

Athena is at her father's right hand. She casts a glance up and down Hera's body, shrewd and assessing. Hera imagines the cogs of her mind gliding into place, smooth and silver, knowing all. There is no place to hide her intentions, and so she straightens her back and tosses back her hair, looking straight past Athena to Zeus instead.

She never saw the punishment of Prometheus, only heard of it. It didn't surprise her that he could order the torment of his former friend and ally. Prometheus, who had turned his back on the other Titans to join with the Olympians, who had once made up a trio with Zeus and Metis when they planned to change the world for the better. Now Zeus is the only one of them left on Mount Olympus to enjoy what they created together. But who knows better than Hera how he can betray those who trusted him?

'You were behind this?' he says, and she can see the ripple of shock pass through the other gods. Only Athena remains smug and unruffled.

His tone is heavy with authority. Hera has seen his flaws, his greed and his carelessness, and she has thought that they have made him weak. An unfit ruler, governed by his desires and complacent in his power. Right now, though, in the flush of victory, he radiates strength. And she has no weapon remaining.

She won't let any of them think she is afraid. She won't fall to her knees and beg for any forgiveness. She takes her time, making sure her voice doesn't crack, infusing her tone with the contempt she feels. 'I was.'

The quiet takes on a dreamlike quality. The drifting flakes are like snow, settling in soft clumps on the destroyed remains of their palaces. Hera doesn't let her gaze falter, but in the corners of her vision, she can see the others looking around and taking in the full extent of the devastation. Devastation that she has wrought.

'Why?' It's Hephaestus who asks.

Hera almost wants to laugh at the question, but the burning pain in her arm intensifies, and his face is slipping in and out of focus.

'It doesn't matter why,' Zeus interjects, his words dropping like heavy stones in front of her, and she wants to protest, to take this moment to tell all of them exactly why, but the fire is spreading through her veins. Typhon's venom surges through her, tinting everything green, and her speech slides away from her.

Zeus is lying, she thinks. He knows why; he knows what he's taken from her. And now it's all in the open, she doesn't care if she joins Prometheus on his lonely crag. Send the eagle to devour her liver, she thinks, let all her pain be on display. Let it be on the outside, instead of consuming her from within.

If it weren't for the poison coursing through her body, she could have resisted Zeus' grip. Everything has been swept away from under her feet, and she is giddy with recklessness. But the venom is too powerful a force, clouding her brain and slowing her instincts. Through the veil it casts over her eyes, she can see the blisters forming on Athena's forearm where poison sprayed across her flesh. In all her rough and tumble with the infant monsters, Hera had become hardened to its sting, but the flow of it into her open wounds is too much to withstand. Neither of her surviving sons make a move to help her. Her sisters stand frozen to the spot. And the cold, bronze fetters close around her wrists and ankles – chains that might bind her to a desolate mountainside, or imprison her in the depths of Tartarus if he chooses.

She's stronger than all of them, her drowsy brain tells her. The only one brave enough to fight for what she's owed.

Whatever punishment he dreams up for her could never be enough to stop her.

* * *

She'll never know how much of it is real, and how much a fevered vision conjured by the fire raging inside: the strange, green-hued flames roaring through her golden blood. She is aware of darkness all around her. Not the close, heavy black-ness of the pit, but an endless stretch of midnight dotted by the distant stars. The chains hold her fast in the empty void. He has found a place to exile her beyond anywhere she knows, some-where beneath the solid dome of the sky where there is nothing.

Perhaps that is the horror he intends. To leave Hera, who loves solitude, in an eternity of it, with nothing but the thoughts of her failed coup to keep her company. Maybe he means to leave her here until madness threatens and she begs to return, fearing loneliness forever afterwards.

But the madness is in her already; the tide rising from her body to her brain, unstoppable and relentless. As she hangs there – wherever she is – in unbreakable chains, she sees fractured shapes and swirling movements. A chasm splits the emptiness, an abyss gapes open underneath her dangling feet, and she sees the yawning mouth of Chaos. The vast, unfath-omable confusion that Gaia once described to her. Galaxies swirl and collide, dizzying and shapeless, and Hera feels the irresistible pull of it, tugging her in every direction, tearing her apart. In her bewilderment, she thinks she can hear Gaia's voice, whispering through oblivion, and she strains to hear her words, but they're carried away in the howling winds.

She is lost in it; only the touch of icy bronze at her wrists and ankles tethers her to any semblance of reality. If she could gather herself, she could transform, become a bird and swoop away, but she can't command her sense of who she is. She's adrift, for how long she doesn't know. Her thoughts bleed into one another until they're lost in the cacophony too.

Only one breaks through, too distant and formless at first for her to catch. It's that memory of Gaia; a beam of light she tries to grasp. The epiphany, somewhere within her, that Gaia was born of Chaos – that Gaia sifted out the mass of elements and built a world from it. And as the waves of poison tainting her blood begin to slowly recede, Hera holds on to that thought. She begins to feel her own body again, bit by bit, as though she's rebuilding herself, taking shape again and knowing who and what she is. She takes a breath, and feels it in her lungs. She blinks, and sees the wheeling stars slow down and steady themselves, becoming fixed points of light once more, twinkling in place. The roaring in her ears dwindles and quiets, and she thinks she can feel the venom draining away, dissolving into the stream of golden ichor as she is restored to herself.

At her back, she can feel the stony edges of a sheer cliffside. She turns her head to the side, and sees the bronze fetters on each of her outstretched wrists. Far below her, the sea froths over rocks. Typhon was even stronger than she had realised, armed with weapons he hadn't mastered. If he had been less impetuous, less impulsive, then together they could have won. It's too late now; Typhon is gone, incinerated by Zeus' thunderbolt, and all her plans have died with him. She remembers the scent of burning: his charred flesh as he collapsed to the earth. She wonders what has become of his smoking remains.

A rustling sound startles her, and she feels a flash of apprehension when she sees it's a bird: large and grey-feathered, perched on a rocky ledge near to where her left wrist is fastened to the mountainside. For a second, she thinks it an eagle or a vulture, and she can't help but imagine Prometheus' fate, but as the lurch in her heart subsides, she realises it's a crane. He tilts his head towards her, something plaintive and beseeching in his eyes, and she recognises Hephaestus.

'Did he leave you to watch over me?' she asks. Her voice is dry and dusty, her throat crackling with the effort it takes to speak.

The bird darts his eyes one way and then another. He ducks his long neck, his shoulders hunching up: he is so very like his god-form, so unmistakeably himself. He gives a low, mournful hoot, and the discordant note makes her head ache. As a goddess, she's never known sickness. Her injuries have always healed fast, never lingered to cause her any suffering. She has no patience for it.

'Bring me nectar,' she tells him. She may be imprisoned – in chains of his making, no doubt – but the command slips out naturally. It isn't in her to ask him, certainly not to beg. She can see his discomfort, and it doesn't take much to imagine how reluctant he must have been to take on this duty.

He spreads his wings, wide and edged in black feathers, his swoop blotting out the pale moonlight as he takes flight. She leans her head back against the unforgiving rock, closing her eyes while she waits. She's sure he won't disobey her, but they are in uncharted territory now. Who knows what threats Zeus might have made to their son? Despite the dull throbbing in her temples and the weariness in her shoulders, she smiles with a bitter sort of mirth. Picturing the hapless Hephaestus torn between the conflicting demands of both his parents, unwilling to anger either one of them.

She doesn't have to wait long. She hears his heavy tread on the summit above, and the weight of his sigh as he crouches down.

'Tip your head up,' he says, and she obliges.

He's silhouetted against the dim sky. Awkwardly, he reaches down towards her, steadying himself with his other hand. It's a clumsy manoeuvre, but he manages to tilt the cup he carries close enough to her mouth that the sweet liquid pours in. Some of it splashes out, trickling down her jaw, but she can ignore the indignity because it's so delicious and rejuvenating. She cannot gulp it down quickly enough.

The anatomy of a god is a mysterious, unknowable thing. Within Hera, she can feel the entire universe – the Chaos she glimpsed in her frenzy is contained inside her, the seeds of Creation and everything that exists lives in her immortal body. But she is muscle and bone and sinew too, and they must be replenished with the nectar and ambrosia that is sacred to all gods and forbidden to any other creature. She has gone too long and sustained too much damage to be able to revive herself without this. With every drop, she is renewed. And at last, when the cup is empty, she opens her eyes and sees with clarity. The fuzzy edges have worn away; the world is sharp and clean and free of pain.

'Thank you,' she says to Hephaestus, and even though his face is shadowed, she can see the jolt of surprise spread across it.

'He only said to guard you.' His voice is low, almost sullen. He is so unhappy with this situation, and she thinks of him coming to her with his gifts of jewellery, thrilled with his own skill. He still hasn't learned what matters among the gods; he still thinks he can get by with an open heart and enthusiasm. *But he's finding out,* she thinks, *one crushing disappointment at a time.*

'He has a temper,' Hera says carefully. 'But he doesn't mean to leave me here.'

'He said—'

'Never mind what he said. He's my husband; I know him.' She tries to modulate her tone, not to speak too sharply or betray her frustration. 'He's made an example of me now, but the purpose is served.'

He stays silent, either too confused or too wary to say anything more.

'What happened was only between the Olympians and Typhon,' she goes on.

'Typhon? That was his name?'

Hera pauses. 'It doesn't matter now.' She can't speak of him, not to Hephaestus. 'It wasn't a battle like before, when we fought the Titans and all the immortals had to choose a side. No one else knows this time, except for us. And Zeus defeated him. He got to show us all how powerful he is, and that none of us can challenge him. But nothing has changed.'

'What do you mean?'

'Zeus might be angry, but he'll realise soon enough that this has given him an opportunity to show his strength to the other Olympians. It's over, and I know he'll want me back at his side before long.'

'I can go to him – plead your case,' Hephaestus begins.

'No.' Hera's voice is firm. 'I'll do it better.'

'But—'

'You can't be as persuasive as I can.' She lets him work out her meaning.

'I don't think—'

'You can't leave me here,' she says. 'Your mother. Your queen.' She can feel the agony in his hesitation. 'If I let you go . . .'

'He'll thank you.' She stops and thinks about it for a moment. 'After a while.'

He wants to release her, and she knows it. He's afraid of Zeus' wrath, but he wants the conflict to be over.

'Did you see how Ares and Aphrodite fought together?' she says.

'Did they?'

She suppresses a sigh. How like him not to notice. 'If Ares wanted to do something, he wouldn't let anyone else stop him,' she says. 'He isn't afraid of consequences.'

If she could see his face clearly, she'd know if this barb has landed. He's the humblest of the Olympians, but he's a god. She knows his ego will be his most vulnerable point.

'And Aphrodite?'

'She likes that about him.'

She gives him a moment to understand what she's saying. 'You're my son too,' she continues. 'You can be as bold as Ares, if you want to be.' *And reap the same rewards*, she doesn't say. She doesn't have to.

He takes a moment, and she doesn't know what he's going to decide. Then he reaches for the fetters at her wrists and unlocks them smoothly.

'Thank you,' she says.

'You could have transformed,' he says. 'Become a bird, and slipped out of the restraints yourself.' He hands her a tiny brass key so that she can unfasten the ankle chains too, gripping the edge of the rock with one hand while she does so. Then she hauls herself upwards, to join him at the summit.

'Then why did you unchain me?' she asks.

'So that you knew I'd do it. Isn't that why you asked me to?'

A sound escapes her throat, somewhere between laughter and tears. 'I wanted to know how far you'd go to help me. To see if I had any friends left among the gods at all, after this.' She can only imagine the anger the rest of them must feel towards her.

His face is quizzical. 'You just said it yourself. You're my mother,' he says, tilting his head to one side. 'How could I leave you?'

Is it guilt she feels? How quick she's been to dismiss her middle son as useless to her. And yet he's here, at her side when she's so alone. 'I won't forget this,' she promises him.

'Neither will Zeus,' he says.

Hephaestus can always tap into a seam of pity in her, she thinks. For a second, she wavers, uncertain. She could ask him to chain her up again, leave her for Zeus and keep himself free of his father's wrath.

It passes. She snaps on a smile, and reaches for his hand. 'Come on,' she says. 'Back to Olympus.'

14

The shriek of the eagle stops her in her tracks. Hollow and desolate, the sound of it rings across the mountaintop, echoing through the sky. Hephaestus pulls his hand from hers, and she turns to see the horror etched into his face before she feels it settle like ice in the pit of her stomach.

The eagle dives down, the tip of its wing almost brushing her face as it glides past her.

And then Zeus is there in front of them, the bird sinking its talons into his forearm and looking up at his face expectantly. He stares past it, over its white-feathered head, straight at them.

Not at them, Hera realises. His gaze, cold and assessing, is fixed on their son.

'Athena warned me you would do this,' Zeus says.

Hephaestus wrings his hands together, glancing at her, his eyes anguished.

Despite herself, Hera feels a trembling deep inside, like the shudder in the earth before an avalanche of stones tumbles down a hillside. She quells any trace of it before she speaks. 'Why did you leave him as guard, then?'

She thinks, for a second, that she sees the twitch of a smile on his lips. He beckons her forward.

She straightens her spine, tossing back her hair, and walks towards him. Her dress is dusty, the white linen stained grey from the dirt of the cliff face she has been chained against. She wears no crown, no golden adornments, no armour, but she tells herself she is no less a warrior or a queen.

He takes her wrist, his hand warm against her skin, and pulls her up the slight slope so that she can see they are at the very peak. He gestures forward.

A bay to the east sweeps around in a wide curve, the dark waters sparkling in the starlight. The tree-covered land spills out before them, and ahead, a cone-shaped mountain rises up, an ashy cloud encircling its head. She narrows her eyes, watching the tumult of glittering orange sparks, the crimson glow of heat and flame emanating from within.

'I know this island,' she says. 'Sicily.' She's been here before, many times. But this fiery mountain is new, and it gives her a creeping sense of dread to look at it.

'Your monster is buried there.' He's so close at her side, her skin stirs in little bumps at his proximity. She tenses, trying to understand what he's telling her.

'I flung his remains from Mount Olympus. He crashed through the ground, halfway to Tartarus. I heaped the earth on top of him where he fell,' he goes on. 'He was still burning, strong enough to scorch through the rocks I piled up, however high I built them.'

A wild flame surges from the peak, black smoke seething into the air as though in defiant answer to Zeus' words.

'I thought it would be a warning to you not to try again,'

he says, and he looks back towards where Hephaestus waits further down the slope.

She swallows. 'Chaining me to that rock was warning enough,' she says. She glances up at him. His expression is thoughtful, more meditative than angry now, and it makes her feel even more uneasy.

'Was it, though?' Now he meets her eyes, and she can't find any softening in the golden burn of his stare. 'Because you seem to have been freed without too much trouble.' He turns away again, and she wracks her brain for the words she'd planned to use. He's taken her by surprise, that's the problem, and before she can gather her strategy, he's calling to Hephaestus to join them.

Her son climbs the last few feet of rock. He's much broader-shouldered than his father, shorter and heavier, his bulky strength evident in the thick ropes of muscle bunched at his arms and in his back. He's built for hammering metal and hauling rock. Zeus is like his eagle; his stature is noble, his stance watchful but easy. On Mount Olympus, he assumes a patrician sort of authority, a kind of paternal dignity that can belie his ferocity. In battle, and out here, far from any other audience, there is a flicker of wildness in his eyes. A hint of something normally restrained, now loosened. Next to the coarse and trusting Hephaestus, Zeus is a gleaming predator.

'Your mother proved her disloyalty,' he says. His words are cutting but his tone stays mild, and Hephaestus nods uncertainly. 'You had a chance to show where your own loyalty lies.' He jerks his head towards Hera. 'Which of us you stand beside.'

Hephaestus starts to shake his heavy head. 'She's my mother,' he says, 'I couldn't leave her.' His eyes implore Hera to speak in his defence.

'It's clear to me now,' Zeus interrupts.

Hera looks into her son's pleading eyes, and her throat freezes up.

Zeus lifts his hand, startling the eagle, which soars away in a sudden fluster, and Hephaestus and Hera's eyes dart up, looking for the thunderbolt, anticipating the lightning strike. Instead, the wind whips around them, plastering Hera's hair across her face and blinding her. She claws it away, and sees Zeus' arm swing around, directing the gale towards Hephaestus. He's knocked off-balance, his feet scrambling as he's lifted right off the ground. And with the wind at his command, Zeus hurls his son across the valley below them, right into the fiery mouth of the volcano.

Hera sees him swallowed up by the flames and gapes at the empty space he has left behind. 'Why him?' is all she can ask. 'Why not me?'

'It still can be you.' She hears a note of real anger. There is none of the relish she could detect when he spoke to Hephaestus, no enjoyment of this moment. She stays silent, and he simmers. 'Let him find his way out,' Zeus says at last. 'Let him show himself to be a real god. Or else he can stay under there forever. I don't care.'

Her pulse is pounding. She's barely made sense of the loss of Typhon, and now Hephaestus – after the fragile moment of connection she'd felt to him – is gone as well. Two of her three sons, lost so abruptly she's still reeling from the shock. Zeus must be confident that Ares wouldn't help her in any future battle, or else he'd be under a mountain too. Under the waves of confusion and horror, she can feel her anger starting to build once more.

He grasps her shoulders, his fingers digging painfully into the bone. 'It won't happen again.'

She shakes her head. 'It won't.'

She's telling the truth. She decided it already, while she was still in chains. Overthrowing him by force isn't going to work.

She makes herself look up into his face, trying her best to convey sincerity.

He doesn't believe her. But it doesn't matter.

The other Olympians greet her with coldness, Hestia excepted. She can't blame them. They're still rebuilding the wreckage of their palaces, transforming the debris and rubble back into shining towers of marble. She notices this time that it's even grander, each god's separate halls more distinct and impressive than they were before. When Zeus sweeps her into the throne room of the new main palace, she counts twelve shining thrones and looks askance at him.

'I want to extend the council of the gods.' He sounds offhand, as though it's a casual matter, but her mind is whirring. Does he mean to invite Titans to rule alongside them? Does he want to stack Olympus with more of his own allies, to keep a closer eye on her, or to create a more forbidding opposition to any attacks she could dream up?

She doesn't ask any of these questions. She nods with as much meekness as she can muster. He must know her subservient attitude is a cloak she's wearing, one she's shrugged on and could fling aside just as easily. One that's ill-fitting, too small; one that will never keep her contained for long.

Klymene is waiting in her chamber, her smile tremulous. Hera feels a rush of affection, or maybe it's gratitude for the sight of a friendly face.

'I have a bath prepared for you,' Klymene says, forestalling anything else.

It's when Hera is reclining in warm water, and Klymene is pouring from a silver jug on to the goddess's long hair, combing it back away from Hera's face, that she alludes to what happened.

'You could have told me,' she says softly.

Hera tenses.

'I would have kept your secrets. I will always keep your secrets.'

There are nymphs nearby, folding swathes of linen, pouring perfumed oil into shallow saucers, rubbing flower petals between their fingers for a richer fragrance. But Klymene's words are lost underneath the stream of water, deliberately inaudible to anyone except Hera.

'I know,' she says at last.

But she hadn't known it, not for sure. She'd brought Klymene here as an ally, and then not dared to confide in her when it came to it. Even with everything Klymene has lost to Zeus, Hera had feared to share Typhon with her. That old distrust of the Titans, maybe. Perhaps she hadn't quite dared to believe that Klymene really would stand with an Olympian in the end – that she'd help to rebuild Olympus with Hera when she might see an opportunity for the Titans to seize power instead.

Hera breathes in sharply. Was it the same for Typhon and Ekhidna? Despite the plans they'd hatched together, was this why Typhon acted alone? Did the two of them still not trust Hera quite enough to wait for her signal?

Klymene, misinterpreting her distress, is soothing and solicitous. 'Don't worry about it now,' she urges. 'It's all over, and you're back.'

The nymphs gather, ready to help her out of the bath and dry and adorn her before she goes to her husband.

Later, in Zeus' bed, gold-framed and lined with animal furs, she tries to broach the subject of Hephaestus. Zeus is replete, lying with his hands behind his head, the sheen of sweat on his broad chest drying in the soft caress of the night air. A whole wall of his chamber is open to the skies, the vista of stars only interrupted by the marble columns that hold up the roof above their heads. If she stands between those pillars, the side of the mountain will drop away just beneath her feet. She used to enjoy that feeling, the dizzying little thrill in the pit of her stomach when she looked down through the empty space. It made her feel powerful, no doubt the reason he designed it this way. Since he chained her to a cliffside, suspending her over a terrifying nothingness, she can't feel the same way again.

Even after Typhon's assault, Zeus hasn't felt the need for a defensive wall, to put thick stone between him and any future attackers. It shows how little he worries about the prospect. How complacent he is in his invulnerability.

'I told you,' he says, his voice flat. 'It's up to him to find his way out, if he can.'

'He's your son.' She tries to make her tone coaxing, not combative. She props herself up on her elbow, the furs sliding warm and luxurious over her skin. 'Besides, all he did was bring me back to you. And hasn't that made you happy?'

A laugh escapes his throat, a little huff of mirth he can't suppress. The silver moonlight softens his face, lulling her to believe that she can persuade him now. 'You tricked him into helping you,' he remonstrates. 'This is your fault.'

She shrugs, and his eyes follow the way the furs slip further down. 'Both of us wanted to see which one of us he'd choose,' she says. 'He was caught in the middle, and now he's paying for it.' Idly, she strokes her fingers across his chest. 'But isn't it enough—'

'No.' He seizes her hand, stopping it dead. All traces of laughter are extinguished now. 'If he'd chosen me instead of you, what punishment would you think enough for him?'

Her smile dies on her lips.

'I know you,' he says, and it's the worst thing she could hear.

It's as though he can see her, into her soul, into the most vengeful and angry truth at her core, and it's so much more exposing than her nakedness. She would never have forgiven Hephaestus if he'd sided with Zeus, and he knows it. The last thing she wants in these moments with him is honesty, or understanding. She is someone else when she's with him, and the real Hera is protected. It's how she survives.

'Don't go looking for him,' he says. 'Don't defy me on this. Or you'll be sorrier than you can imagine.'

Her temper rises white-hot inside her, and she swallows it right back down again. Forces herself to smile falsely once more, her mask back in place. 'Whatever you say.'

'Good.' He's pleased.

Hephaestus will have to look after himself. Hera had known from the moment he was born that he didn't have the cunning nature required to thrive in this collection of voracious, greedy gods.

Perhaps he's learning that lesson now, wherever he is, the only way the gods seem to learn – through fire and pain and blood. Immortals so easily become fixed and stagnant. They rarely need to change and grow. When it happens, the process is a brutal one. She should know.

*   *   *

The sting of what Zeus did flares up when she hears the others talk of it. She is their queen, and she knows they're whispering between themselves of how she was fettered to a cliffside, left to hang helpless for as long as he cared to leave her there. And now he thinks he has her just as securely chained, with no one willing to come to her aid. None of them prepared to meet Hephaestus' fate.

Zeus forbids any of them from searching for the hapless blacksmith god, and Hera stands at his side while he delivers the command. She wonders what has become of her son – if he's clambered free of the volcano, if he's found somewhere else to take refuge, away from them, or if he still lies under the weight of the rock and the flames.

'What about Hera?' Poseidon demands.

'What about her?'

'Is it only Hephaestus who's to be punished? When it's Hera who set the monster on us?'

'He did chain her to a rock,' Aphrodite intervenes. Her words might sound conciliatory, but there's acid in her tones and an unusually angry set to her jaw. It sounds as though she doesn't think that was sufficient.

'Olympus is in ruins!'

'Your sea-palace is intact,' Hera snaps. 'You could go there. Besides, that's an exaggeration. Olympus is almost restored again.'

'No thanks to you.' Demeter sweeps into the throne room, a wintry chill in place of her characteristic warm glow.

Zeus turns to Hera. 'You have some amends to make.'

The long table is ranged with hostile faces. Hera smiles at them all. 'I'll do my best.'

Ares' fist slams into the oak, making the table shudder. 'That creature could have wounded one of us.'

She raises a perfect, scathing eyebrow. 'What kind of a war-god is afraid of getting hurt?'

'How can you expect us—' Poseidon growls, but Zeus holds up his hand. The sight of the thunderbolt silences them all.

'Everyone is displeased,' he says. 'But my sentence has been carried out. There will be no more discussion.' It's a highly unsatisfactory resolution to everyone but him. The merriment in his eyes suggests he's enjoying the tension.

The council meeting is shorter and more strained than usual. But none of the gods dare say anything more. Hera retires to bed early, glad to escape the stony glares of the family she betrayed.

She rises before dawn, slipping down to the courtyard where Hestia awaits. The sisters embrace.

'Zeus seems to hold no grudge,' Hestia comments.

Hera agrees. 'Not like the rest of them.' She broods for a moment. 'He could have exiled me to Tartarus, or alongside Prometheus if he'd wanted. I thought he'd be angrier.'

'Perhaps it's worked out in his favour,' Hestia muses.

'How so?'

They keep their voices low, out in the quiet courtyard. The stars are fading in the pearly dawn skies, and a soft pink warmth begins to infuse the horizon. At the edge of the world, Eos swings open the great bronze gates of her palace, and drives her chariot forward, her horses eager to ascend, the light of the morning trailing from her fingers as she sweeps through the air. Behind Hestia, through the colonnade that separates the main palace from the tiled square where they stand, Hera can see the hearth burning steadily as always.

'I think he's got everything he wanted,' Hestia says. 'And he's overcome the thing he feared.'

'Me?'

'A rebellion.' Hestia sighs, glancing over her shoulder to make sure no one is approaching. The palace slumbers on, silent and peaceful. 'He must have wondered if you would do something – in the back of his mind, he must have known you might. And a son rising up against him is the thing he's always been most afraid of, the same as Cronus was. But when it happened . . .'

'It came to nothing.' Hera finishes her sentence, her words clipped and dry.

'Now he's conquered a disobedient son—'

'And a disobedient wife.' Hera grinds her teeth for a second, then forces herself to relax her jaw.

'He's got nothing to fear.'

'And everyone knows it.' *He can carry on as he likes now,* Hera thinks. 'The others, though . . .' She sighs. 'They're not so quick to forgive.'

Hestia laughs softly. 'Are you surprised?'

'It was only Zeus and Poseidon I wanted to target,' Hera says. 'If I could explain that – but I can hardly tell them I planned to keep the rest of you as Olympians alongside me. Not without risking Zeus' wrath all over again.'

'They've probably all imagined overthrowing Zeus themselves,' Hestia acknowledges. 'At one point or another.'

'They'll get over it,' Hera says.

'Aphrodite will forget soon enough.' Hestia sits on the low wall, the sky burning behind her. 'She and Ares are angry on each other's behalf, imagining the other being hurt. But she'll move on to the next intrigue before long. Ares will storm off back to his own palace – and besides, he's always angry about something. The same for Poseidon. You've deflected their annoyance from Zeus for a while, given them something to sulk about and keep them occupied. But they won't dare defy him by coming after you. And before you know it, they'll find something else to rage about.'

'Demeter might take longer.' There is already a distance between the sisters, and no doubt Demeter is furious not only about the threat to the gods, but the damage done to the surroundings. Her precious plants and flowers, charred to ashes. Stricken crops on the ground where Typhon fought, trees split and incinerated, the soil poisoned with his blood.

'Hera?'

She shakes her head, coming back to the conversation. 'Sorry,' she says. 'I just thought of something.'

'What is it?'

The soil poisoned with his blood . . .

'Nothing,' Hera says.

She pictures those twelve golden thrones again. She has lost two of her sons; the Olympians have turned against her. She can't risk returning to her beloved monsters in Ekhidna's caverns while Zeus remains suspicious of her; she might lead him right to them.

She's defeated. Trapped in the palace, her influence diminished and her hopes buried underneath a volcano.

Unless . . . she thinks. But it's madness to entertain another plan so soon. She'll wait.

'Like Zeus said, I need to make amends,' she says out loud. 'Be a good wife. A good sister. Not cause any trouble.'

. . . his blood.

She means what she says to Hestia. She'll stay quiet and well-behaved.

But it won't last forever.

PART THREE

Now a fresh occasion has been added to her grief ... her tongue as ever ready to her rage, lets loose a torrent of abuse; "Away! Away with words! ... Am I not [Hera] the supreme of Heaven? Queen of the flashing scepter? ... Let the Gods deny that I am [Cronus'] daughter."

Ovid's Metamorphoses,
translated by Brookes More, 1922

15

Her life on Mount Olympus can't go back to the way it was before. She would never have thought she would want it to. But now she feels Zeus' eyes upon her all the time. If she leaves the mountaintop, she scans the sky for the eagle and shudders at the breath of the wind. His spies could be anywhere.

More than anything, she longs to see her brood of monsters. Her heart aches with the loss of them, and her arms feel empty. More than once, she turns her steps towards the distant plain, to the fissure in the earth that leads to their home. Every time, she turns back again.

She can't let him find them. She doesn't speak a word of their existence to anyone, and her sadness feels like a heavy stone lodged in her throat.

She sits by a riverbank, and can't conjure any tears. Every breath she draws is painful, her sorrow stuck and immovable as she lets her thoughts wander where she cannot go. The children, wondering where their father is gone, not knowing why Hera doesn't return with her gifts and her affection. Ekhidna, mourning her lover, her worst fears confirmed. Hera didn't help him. She let them down, as the viper-goddess had always known she would.

Fat drops of rain begin to fall, and she looks up, startled from her hopeless reverie. The clouds overhead are dismal and grey, and the raindrops gather pace. They splash into the river; they soak her hair, plastering it across her arms and down her back, drenching her dress. She lets it happen. Before her eyes, the river is swelling, threatening to burst its banks. As it rises higher, at last a sob breaks free in her throat. In amazement, she sees the torrential downpour slow and slacken, and the tears start to flow freely down her cheeks instead.

Zeus can stir up storms with no more than an angry wave of his thunderbolt, dark clouds gathering whenever he frowns. She never knew before that her grief could bring forth the rain.

Under the soft drizzle, she feels a loosening within. She takes a long, deep breath, dissolving the remaining tightness in her chest, and the air is cold and reviving in her lungs.

Dusk begins to fall, bleeding inky darkness through the bank of grey cloud that swallows the dwindling light of the sun. Hera stands, the shadows lengthening around her, waiting until there is nothing but starless night.

She soars, ghostlike, into the air – a nighthawk, almost invisible. Her senses tingle as she glides, every inch of her awake and alert for any sign that she's being followed.

The volcano seethes and rumbles in the distance: a gleam of fire on the island of Sicily, surrounded by night-black seas. She lands on its slopes, soundless and graceful. At the summit, fiery sparks and ash spew from the deep crater, and the flakes fall like black snow around her. Deep beneath its heavy rock and shifting molten streams, it growls and sighs like the wind or the ocean, the power thrumming wild and ferocious from its centre.

Typhon. Defeated, but not destroyed.

She stands for a while, wreathed in trailing clouds of smoke, feeling the vibrations underneath her like his heartbeat.

And then, she begins to search.

The base of the mountain, that's where she thinks she'll find it. Where his blood pooled underneath his fallen body, and flooded into the soil.

There is almost nothing that would grow here.

But she knows the legends. When the vulture flies away from Prometheus each day, the Titan's liver in his beak, blood spatters on to the mountainsides, and where each drop falls, a flower grows. Nourished with Titan blood, they bear magical properties for anyone who dares gather them. And when Cronus carved his Sky-father open, it wasn't just Aphrodite who sprung from the foam. Where Ouranos' blood rained on to the land, the Erinyes grew – goddesses of vengeance and hatred, born of his pain and suffering.

Concealed in the smoky haze, she stoops down to the ground and closes her eyes. One hand pressed to the stony earth, she lets her mind's eye roam, feeling out the shape of what she seeks.

His fury, undying and unending, pulses out, and she follows the ripples. Fire and heat, scorching through solid stone, melting it in the blaze. But underneath, a darker ooze, spreading outwards, tainting everything it touches.

She finds them growing in a clump, hidden under the shelter of a jutting overhang, beneath its mossy underside, stretching up from fibrous roots. Five thick stems give way to spiny leaves and long, drooping flowers. She lifts one with her finger, sees each creamy white petal ending in a point, the violet heart at the centre like a bloodstain. Leaning closer, she inhales the bitter fragrance and feels a shudder of memory – the nausea, the sliding vision, the odd green tinge that gave way to the collapse of her mind – and she knows she's found it.

Her fingers scrabble in the soil, digging them free, until she has every one of them. They lie limp in her palm, but she isn't deceived.

This is the last piece of Typhon: the gift he leaves her.

She flees the volcano as swiftly as she arrived, undetected in the dark, her flowers hidden in the folds of her dress. In the safety of her chamber, she hides them in a jewellery box – a fine one carved from ivory by Hephaestus.

She doesn't know yet what she'll do with them. Boil the roots, steep the petals, crush or grind them into powder? And when she has it, whatever potion or tincture she can make from the venom of Typhon, strong enough to warp a god's mind, she doesn't know how she'll use it or when.

It makes it easier, knowing it's there, that's all. That she has a weapon. That she hasn't been deserted by her monsters, not entirely.

She needs the comfort, as she's already decided the best way to convince Zeus of her obedience is to give him more children. What else would a dutiful wife do? No more squalling war-gods, diffident artists or snake-fingered demons; these next ones must be different altogether.

She tries to quell the strife and storms in her head, to think of sunshine and peace. Of the thrones Zeus has yet to fill, and the hopeful likelihood of her convincing him to give them to the children she bears him rather than those he gets elsewhere.

Hebe comes first. Cherubic, ringletted, her cheeks so rosy and her demeanour so sweet that Hera names her for eternal youth. She nurses the infant on her low couch, the sunlight streaming through her window, a far cry from the sunless cave where Typhon was born.

'How could a child of mine with Zeus be born so happy?' she says to Klymene, who can't come up with an answer, but is devoted to Hebe from the start. Klymene sings her to sleep, walks hand-in-hand around the palace with her, and plaits her hair into shining braids.

Athena brings Hebe a dress she's woven, and the little girl is overjoyed by the sweet animals she's embroidered around its hem. Poseidon wordlessly produces a little dolphin, carved from coral with pearls for eyes, and Hebe flings her arms around his neck, laughing at the tickle of his beard.

'Why would *he* give her a toy?' Hera demands, suspicious.

'Everyone loves her,' Zeus replies.

But he doesn't give her a throne. 'She can be cupbearer to the gods,' he announces carelessly when she's grown. Hebe, with her sunny disposition, never breathes a word of disappointment if she feels it. She mixes the ambrosia at the Olympian feasts and carries it around the long table, serving each of the gods, with a smile for every one of them. Aphrodite is particularly enchanted with her, and Hera often sees Hebe tripping into the goddess's quarters in the mornings to comb her hair and choose between her necklaces, selecting which shimmering strand of beads she should wear on any given day. She takes the responsibility very seriously, her studious face delighting Aphrodite as she makes her pick. Or else she's in the stables of Olympus, stroking the velvety muzzles of the divine horses that pull the chariots of the gods, and polishing the silver and gold harnesses to such a shine that they reflect her lovely face back at her.

If Hera had been surprised that Hephaestus had contrived to be so ugly, born of two handsome parents, then she truly wonders at Hebe's endless optimism.

She's doing her utmost to stay on her best behaviour. She doesn't sneak out on any more adventures. She's chopped up Typhon's flowers, drained the sap from the roots and mixed them with the dust of the petals. The resulting mixture is stoppered in a tiny jar, and it gives her comfort sometimes to take it out and hold it up to the light so she can see the green liquid trickle behind the glass. *One day*, she thinks, but she always puts it away again.

She flits sometimes between her temples. It's heartening to hear the praise and devotions that the mortals dedicate to her, to breathe in the scent of woodsmoke and flowers, and watch the quiet dedication of her priestesses as they tend the cult statues with unstinting attention. Mostly, she lets the time build up, extending the distance between her and the rebellion, suffocating in her domestic sphere until she thinks she'll go mad with boredom.

She must have Zeus convinced of her compliance by now, but she forgoes her silphium draft at the next moonrise, and before long another daughter is born. More proof of her willingness to be an obedient wife and dutiful mother. 'Eileithyia,' she tells Zeus.

'Not as pretty as Hebe,' he pronounces. 'What do you want for her?'

A throne, thinks Hera, but he won't offer it. 'The human population swells,' she says, 'and the women need assistance, more than I can offer.' She has never paid a great deal of attention to their prayers, she privately acknowledges, but as a goddess of women, she knows about them at least. And, mindful of the drawn-out pangs of birth she suffered with Typhon, she feels a shred more sympathy for the fears they have of suffering in labour for such uncertain results. 'She can be the goddess of childbirth.'

May she never resent her mantle as much as I resent mine. Let her be as simple and easily satisfied as her sister. It's the only gift Hera can give to her daughter, the last of her children. The hope that her existence will be happier than her mother's.

With her fifth child born, she thinks more often of Hephaestus. Zeus is insistent that if he's strong enough, he will rise – and if not, he doesn't deserve his godhood.

Hera remembers when he was small. The warmth of his palm when he would slip his hand into hers. The joy in his face when he discovered his talent. The catch in his voice when he said he would free her because she was his mother.

She won't do the same for him.

I can't.

She's relieved to see Zeus sprawled in the throne room most days, sipping out of a golden cup that Hebe keeps filled for him. When he's gone, soaring in eagle feathers or thundering across the earth in the guise of a bull or prowling in wolf furs under ghostly moonlight, anxiety wracks her. She never knows for certain what he's doing, though her imagination serves up plenty of lurid scenarios. When she caught him in pursuit of Asteria, she had been full of indignation that he would flout their marriage bond – the one that he had wanted so badly, not her – and now other concerns beset her. It's bad enough that he has his loyal Athena; what if he brings back another child to the heavens? She won't bear him any more children, on that she's resolute. She has had five chances now to use his offspring to bolster her power and diminish his. Each one has failed. But what if, she lets herself think, he puts the child of another goddess on one of those empty thrones, while her own daughters make do with their second-tier status, and her son endures exile? That sensation she'd had after the failure of her coup, the feeling that he had her wrapped in a too-small garment, not able to wriggle free, intensifies even more. The question begins to consume her: who will he choose, and when?

She used to feel that she could breathe freely when he was gone, but the opposite becomes true. Now she can't stop asking herself where he is.

She follows him one day, slipping out in the shape of a cuckoo, a form she hasn't taken since he tainted the creature for her forever. Now it feels inconspicuous, a small grey and blue feathered form, hopping from tree to tree as she trails him to the Boeotian mountains, to the slopes of Mount Kithairon. She hides herself in the verdant green foliage, watching as he greets the mountain-god who gives his name to the peak. The two walk together, their deep laughter rolling between the hills. Hera keeps herself back, but she's too careful, and soon she realises that she can't hear their conversation anymore. It's lost beneath the tinkling of the crystal-clear stream, its water flowing fresh and cold from the melting snows at the summit, and another sound she can hear – that of a beautiful song. The little cuckoo tilts her head, poised on a slender branch, and then she takes flight, following the melodic notes.

By a cave, its mouth framed in luxuriant ivy, a nymph sits on a rock, and here is the source of the song. The cuckoo looks around, wondering if the nymph's lovely voice has attracted the two gods but, realising she can't see them, she shakes off the guise and Hera steps forward.

The nymph gasps when she sees her, holding her hand to her throat somewhat theatrically. Hera is crowned and regal and entirely recognisable. If Zeus sees her, she won't be accused of any kind of subterfuge. She's taking a walk in the woods, she thinks, as if imagining her defence. She's not up to anything untoward.

She decides to be gracious towards the nymph. 'Your singing is quite lovely,' she says. 'I didn't mean for you to stop.'

The nymph lowers her eyes, lashes fluttering on her cheeks. 'I wouldn't dream of continuing in your presence,' she murmurs.

Hera is pleased with her deference. 'Go on,' she urges her.

'But on Mount Olympus, you must be used to far more glorious music than my humble song.'

Hera feels a flicker of impatience. It's a charming, rustic setting, but the faux modesty is setting her teeth on edge. 'Sing,' she says, and this time the nymph hears the imperious ring of command in her voice.

The forest seems to fall silent around her: a congregation of awe at the simple beauty of her voice. Birds stop mid-trill on their branches, the breeze stills, and every creeping, crawling, prowling, slithering creature appears to halt their everyday business of devouring one another or seeking their mate or scuttling away to safety, so that they can listen too. Wherever Zeus is in these woods, he's bound to hear it, and Hera hopes it has the same effect on him. But after a few notes, she stops thinking about him being drawn to the nymph's honeyed tones, and she gets lost in them herself. The song stirs something in her – a tumult of emotion that brings a sting of tears to her eyes.

As the last notes ring out, Hera draws herself together. 'What a beautiful song,' she says. 'Like one of the Muses herself.'

'I'm just an oread,' she says – a mountain-nymph, she means. A dweller in this lovely place, her duty to tend to the firs and pines, the poplars and ash trees and laurels that grow here. 'I sing to entertain myself and my sisters, that's all.'

Hera glances around. 'Where are your sisters now?' she asks.

The nymph smiles, her face honest and innocent as far as Hera can tell. 'Among the trees – we all have our own for which we're responsible, and some are further up the slopes. They'll be back soon enough.'

'Have you seen any gods? Walking past here, perhaps going deeper into the forest or up the sides of the mountain?'

She shakes her head.

Hera looks at her intently, searching for any sign of guile. 'What's your name?' she asks.

'Echo.'

'I'm looking for my husband,' Hera says.

Echo's hand flies up to her throat again. 'Zeus? Oh no, I haven't seen him – I don't think he would come to our little home.'

'He's here somewhere.'

Echo slips off her rock, her tunic falling daintily around her legs. 'I must offer you wine,' she says. 'The grapevines that grow here are quite extraordinary and—'

'Never mind.' Hera cuts her off. 'I must go.'

'Oh, please let me,' Echo implores her. 'We have no such visitors as you, and my sisters will want so much to hear about you – we've heard of your beauty, but to see it for myself. And if you wait a while, they'll be back here in no time.'

Hera weighs it up. She could carry on searching every corner of the mountain, or she could stay here, where a gathering of beautiful nymphs is shortly to converge.

She thinks she knows which option is more likely to yield sight of her husband.

'Pour me a cup,' she says, and takes the seat that Echo has just vacated.

The nymph fusses about inside the cave, mixing water and honey into the wine and pouring it into a carved goblet for Hera. It's nothing like the ornate vessels she's used to in the palace, and the wine tastes coarse and earthy, but the sunlight dapples through the swaying canopy of leaves and the stream flows picturesquely at her feet, and the nymph chatters on. Hera drains the cup and holds it out for more. 'Tell me about your sisters.'

Echo is ready, anecdotes brimming at the tip of her tongue. She weaves a tapestry of words for Hera, rich and colourful, describing their life in the mountains and the comings and goings of the minor gods who live here. Hera leans back on her elbows, and Echo keeps pouring the wine, her confidence growing as she sees how entertained the goddess is. It feels like so long since Hera has laughed like this, since she's taken such easy pleasure in conversation, with no hidden meanings to puzzle out or battle for supremacy taking place behind the words.

When she notices the shadows beginning to lengthen on the ground, she jolts upright. 'How much time has passed?' she demands, and Echo is a picture of innocent confusion. 'Your sisters,' Hera says, 'where are they? You said they would be back.'

'Perhaps they were waylaid,' Echo says. 'Distracted by

something, or maybe they stopped to rest in the heat. There's nothing to worry about, I'm sure they'll return before long.'

It's almost convincing, but Hera catches an artful glint in the nymph's eye. She draws herself to standing, and the light drains out of Echo's face as she sees the coldness in Hera's. 'You kept me here on purpose,' she says.

'Not at all – I only—'

'Did he tell you to distract me? Did he know I followed him?'

'Who?' Echo's voice, which has flowed so mellifluous and smooth all afternoon, now rises to a panicked squeak.

'You tricked me.' It's almost a relief, to let the anger well up inside her and have a target at which to aim it. She has grown so used to swallowing back bile, having it burn her from within instead of blistering her enemies with it. This frightened nymph isn't a worthy foe – hardly an equal to the queen of the heavens – but she is here, and she is helpless. 'Your endless prattling – it was all to keep me from finding him, wasn't it?'

'I don't know where he is, I swear!'

'And your sisters?'

Echo quakes. 'I don't know where they are, either.'

Hera wants to laugh. She wants to scream. When she caught Zeus in pursuit of Asteria, there were no witnesses to her humiliation. Now this silly girl with her vapid conversation – never mind that Hera had been utterly absorbed in her stories, forget that now – has seen the revelation hit her in the face. Both of them know what Echo is covering up, and Hera cannot bear that a mere oread mountain-dweller knows how Zeus regards his wife. She wants to demand that Echo tell her how often he's been here, how many times she's been left as lookout. Or if she has been one of the nymphs he's selected in the past, while another was left to watch for Hera. Certainly, her rosy cheeks and shining hair would please his eye; she's pretty enough.

In the incandescent heat of her rage, it does occur to her that at least Zeus' secrecy suggests he has learned something from her reaction to Asteria. Even if it's only that he dislikes a scene and isn't interested in an argument.

'You'll never speak a word of this to anyone,' Hera hisses, and Echo nods. Her eyes are wide and desperate; she stumbles over her promise, but Hera doesn't care what she has to say. She grabs the nymph, her hand squeezing the girl's slim throat, and she pulls her close. 'You'll never be able to.'

And she lets her go. Echo falls back, clawing at her neck. She scrabbles for air, wheezing and gasping, trying to form words to plead for mercy.

'This is a story you can't share with whoever wanders past next,' Hera tells her.

'. . . next,' Echo chokes out, and the consternation makes her look wildly around for an explanation of what's happening to her.

'You can't choose your words,' Hera says.

'. . . words.' Tears are streaming down Echo's lovely face as she begins to comprehend.

Hera smiles in satisfaction. No more quicksilver rhetoric for this sly young woman. No one will gather again to hear her sing. She can picture the nymphs returning, waiting to hear more dazzling quips and captivating stories, to find their sister only able to repeat their own words back to them.

As she stalks away, she wonders what will happen when Zeus sees what she's done to Echo. When he realises that Hera saw through his distraction, and that the nymph paid the price.

Let him see that his actions have consequences, that she is not so reined in as he believes her to be.

For the first time since he chained her to the cliffs, Hera feels a peace rolling through her. Still confined, but able to flex her muscles a little more than before. The relentless gnawing at her soul has ceased temporarily, a lull in her discontent. Her suffering is transferred to Echo, even though it will creep back in. For now, though, there is a skip in her step that could carry her all the way back to Mount Olympus.

She changes her mind on the journey home, emboldened by her little taste of victory. She won't go straight to the palace. Zeus will be distracted by the outcry when the nymphs make it back to Echo. This is her opportunity to go unseen and undetected. Taking the hawk form, she flies above the deserted plains she has shunned since her return.

She doesn't know if they'll still be there, or what reception she might find. Her elation gives way to trepidation as she makes her way down the familiar tunnels, listening out for the yaps and growls and hisses of her creatures.

'Ekhidna?' she calls out softly as she approaches. She doesn't want the viper-goddess to startle at her approach, or assume an enemy has discovered them. The walls of the cave are cold and damp, the air heavy and rotted, and Hera breathes it in with a twist in her heart. She spent some of her happiest times in here; the most joy she ever took from motherhood gleaned from beasts that would be shunned by the rest of the world. In Typhon, she had the culmination of all her dreams and all her ambitions – before Zeus snuffed him out.

She is relieved to hear the slither of snake-flesh as she

descends further down the curving passageways into the earth. They haven't all abandoned their home, then. Or been driven out by fear of discovery and retribution for Typhon's assault on the heavens.

It's quieter, though, than it was the last time she visited. She can't hear the barks and yowls she had learned to anticipate, though a deeper rumble reverberates through the rock. She reaches the final bend, calling Ekhidna's name once more as she enters the vast cavern.

The snake-goddess turns to face her. Ekhidna's eyes are fathomless pools, unreadable to Hera. She doesn't know what's in those depths: hatred, resentment, grief or indifference.

On the mountainside, in the forest, under the bright sun, Hera had felt her own power flowing through her body. Now, far beneath the surface, she has the crawling sense that this is not her world. She feels like an interloper, one who can't be sure of her welcome.

The space is vast around her. Even so, she can't make sense of her memory of Typhon here. That he was crammed in, his great shaggy head pressed to the doming roof, his neck bent and his snakes weaving their blunt heads in and out. It's the absence of their hissing that makes it so quiet.

Ekhidna's left hand rests on the mane of a creature Hera has never seen. The source of the deep rumbling she heard on her descent, she's sure. Its livid yellow eyes stare at her, its body tensed to pounce, but the touch of its mother's hand restrains it from lunging.

'The last of my children to be born,' Ekhidna rasps.

'A lion,' Hera breathes. Not one of the sleek, rangy specimens that prowl above ground. This one is bulky with strength, broader and more muscular than any of its mortal brothers.

Where their fur sparkles golden in the light, this one has a thick and matted coat, dulled by an existence buried in this living tomb. She takes in the width of its jaws, the sharp glitter of its curved incisors, and she's impressed. She holds out her hand; the lion narrows its eyes, keeping her fixed in the centre of its suspicious glare. Her voice is soft, and she keeps up a reassuring murmur as she approaches it. If any of the Olympians were here, they'd hardly recognise this eager, tentative goddess.

The lion stirs, its hackles rising. It shifts its weight from one enormous front paw to the other, and its monstrous claws scrape against the rock floor. Deep in its chest, she can hear the beginnings of its grumbling roar, but she keeps advancing, slow and steady.

Ekhidna lifts her hand from the lion's head, and watches. There's no question that she would not intervene.

The regal, vengeful queen who struck down the nymph has melted away. Hera's face is rapt as she comes closer, alight with awe as she brushes its heavy muzzle with her fingers. The lion remains cautious, hesitant for another moment, before it relaxes into her touch. Its fur is rough, scratching against her palm, but it leans its huge head towards her, seeking out more.

'Where are the others?' she asks Ekhidna, keeping her voice low and tender.

'After Typhon, they fled. It was safer for them to scatter. Besides, I couldn't keep them content catching the wriggling things we can find in these caves. They needed more.'

'Do you know where they went?'

'They'll find their own caverns underground.'

'But the lion . . .'

'He's almost ready to leave,' Ekhidna says. 'The earth won't keep him captive, though. He'll go to the surface.'

Hera thrills at the idea. He belongs in the upper world, not hidden down here. 'But will he be safe?' she wonders.

'No teeth or claws or weapon can pierce his hide,' his mother says. 'And he has no interest in the gods.'

Hera nods. 'And what will you do?'

She thinks she sees a hint of scorn in those dark eyes. Ekhidna's serpent tail flicks, black scales shifting. She doesn't answer. There is no need. She has endured for centuries. She will carry on, a monster in the darkness as she's always been.

Hera feels a fierce gratitude that even without Typhon, their brood will continue, finding the corners of the world where they can survive. She doesn't say his name down here; there is no sympathy she can offer Ekhidna. The very concept of it would be alien to the viper. Hera lets her question die away unacknowledged in the fetid air, and withdraws her hand from the lion's fur. 'I'll go,' she says.

'I knew your plan would fail,' Ekhidna says. 'From the first time you suggested it, I knew.'

'Why didn't he wait for my signal?' Hera counters.

Ekhidna says nothing.

'You told him to act alone,' Hera guesses.

Still, there is silence. Hera pivots to leave. She's glad to have seen the lion, and heard news of the others. But it's clear there is nothing more for her here.

'Cerberus went to the Underworld,' Ekhidna says, and Hera turns around, startled by what might be the first information the snake-goddess has ever volunteered.

'What for?'

Ekhidna shrugs, and the movement ripples all the way down to her coils. 'He lives with Hades, is all I know. Guarding one of the gateways to his realm.' She glides away, towards the rear of the cave, where a murky river oozes along the back wall. She dips the end of her tail into the foul water. The lion glances after her, then settles himself down on the ground, mighty head resting on his front paws. Ekhidna slides in so that the snake part of her is submerged, and she looks like a woman rising up on to a rock, long strings of black hair clinging to her body and her strange eyes staring. 'He'll survive,' Ekhidna says. 'Under the protection of the god. The rest of my children have to take their chances now.'

'If I can protect them . . .'

'You can't. If the gods don't hunt them down, men will try.'

'What mortal would dare?'

'Wait,' says Ekhidna. 'You'll see.' She pushes herself off the side, diving under the dark liquid with startling speed and sinuous grace. And she is gone, into the subterranean stream: perhaps the last time that Hera will see her.

16

Zeus says nothing to her about the nymph. Perhaps he thinks it will madden her more if he pretends he hasn't noticed. It doesn't take the shine off her victory, though. Hera rises in the sweet morning air every day on Mount Olympus, allows Klymene to tend to her hair and dress, and breakfasts on nectar and ambrosia served by her lovely daughter Hebe. She asks Iris for reports, bidding her travel to the ends of the earth to visit with the ancient Titans and bring her back any word of divine children born, rifts and arguments, or love affairs started or ended between immortals across the earth.

'Why do you take such a keen interest now?' Klymene asks her, as she fastens a jewelled comb behind Hera's ear. It gleams with pearlescent shells; a reminder of Klymene's ocean home in years gone by.

'Zeus doesn't concern himself with such matters,' Hera says. 'But I want to know what's taking place.'

'Most of the gods fear angering you now, more than ever before. Word has spread about Typhon – it's a secret, of course, but it's being talked about in every god's hall from here to

Oceanus. You can imagine how exaggerated it's become. Whispers reached the House of Pheme, and from there they multiplied across the world.'

Pheme, goddess of rumour, whose great hall is built atop a mountain not far from Olympus, can make a muttered word a mighty legend; Hera knows this. Her hall is full of windows and doorways, no barriers to entrance, and any sound you make there echoes off every bronze surface. It's always thronged with visitors, and scraps of conversation reverberate for all to hear. At first, Hera is horrified at the thought that her humiliation has reached Pheme and that all the gods know of her defeat. But Klymene tells her that it's the depiction of Typhon that fans the flames of divine imagination. Hera is the mother of a monster almost powerful enough to topple the Olympians. No one will want to incur her revenge.

Iris agrees when Hera finds her later that morning, and tells her that the legend of Typhon isn't the only rumour bolstering Hera's fearsome reputation. The story of Echo has also caused a panic, she says. Now the nymphs not only worry that Zeus might seize them, but that they might anger Hera, and she might turn her wrathful gaze upon them.

She's gratified to hear it. A whole new world is opening up in front of her: the teeming, plotting world of the immortals and all their machinations, which she can observe from above.

'Make sure the nymphs all know,' she instructs Iris. 'If they plot against me to conceal what my husband is doing, they'll suffer like she did.'

When Iris is gone in a flutter of wings, a dazzling trail of colour painted across the sky in her wake, Hera is satisfied with what she's learned. She notices Zeus striding through the courtyard towards the hall, goatskin draped across his shoulder and a wreath of olive leaves nestled in his dark hair. When he sees her, he smiles, and she can almost believe it's sincere. He looks so untroubled, no cares weighing on him. The thought bubbles up in her mind that Rhea might have watched Cronus in much the same way: the tyrant blissfully secure in his own self-belief.

He swings through the colonnaded entrance, his shoulders brushing the pillars on either side of him as he passes through. He puts his hands on her waist, shifting her aside, although the hall is wide and spacious. She bristles at the intrusion. Somehow he contrives to take up so much room, his presence so out of proportion to everything around him.

'You're here,' he says, sounding pleased.

'Where did you think I'd be?'

'I don't know,' he says. 'In your quarters, maybe. Monitoring the gods, making sure everything is running as it should.' His words call back an earlier Hera, the goddess she had been before, when she'd thought any potential opponents were outside the palace. 'Bathing in a pool somewhere, or wandering in the forests.' His tone is light, but there is a gleam in his eyes at this last part.

'Well, I'm here,' she snaps.

The door at the far end of the hall swings open, and Athena enters. She moves with the grace of liquid silver, her eyes passing over Hera with little interest and fixing on Zeus. 'Father,' she begins, and Hera pulls away from him.

'Where are you going?' he asks her.

'A new temple is being built for me,' Hera says, 'on the island of Samos. I'll go to see it, perhaps bless its construction.'

'A good idea,' he says, and turns to Athena.

Hopefully the two of them will be busy in conversation

now, for Hera has no intention of visiting Samos. What Klymene said to her earlier this morning has given her an idea.

Pheme's hilltop offers the farthest view across the earth that can be found. It's why the goddess chose it for her home – a place where she can lean out and survey the skies, the ground and the sea, ever alert to what's happening. Pheme's halls never fall quiet, are never empty. In the slow, dark hours of deepest night, her guests still huddle together in the shadows, whispering, the sound of their mingling voices like the distant waves crashing on the shore.

Hera knows, like every other god, that what you learn in the House of Rumour cannot always be trusted. You would have to be a credulous fool to believe every distorted echo, every warped reimagining of the same tale, shaped one way by the speaker and another by the one who hears it. But among the exaggerations and distortions and misunderstandings, you can grasp a shining kernel of truth – if you listen carefully enough.

She cloaks herself and veils her face before she ascends. She won't stand out like this; many visitors to Pheme arrive as anonymous strangers. Everyone holds their own secrets close in their hearts as they seek to discover everyone else's. There is a seductive quality to the sighing tides of gossip that swell and break in the interconnected halls, though; a conspiratorial air that invites confidence and urges a guest to abandon caution. It would be easy to give way, to lie back on a couch and let a tantalising fragment slip to just one enthralled listener who leans in close, holding their breath in anticipation.

Hera glides among them, shaking off the hands that reach for her elbows, that try to steer her into a corner to coax out whatever delicious rumour she might bring with her. She lets herself drift on the easy ebb and flow of the crowds, listening for any word of Cerberus or any other of Ekhidna's children. If she can find them, if she can at least hear news of where they might be, then perhaps she can keep them safe, whatever Ekhidna's doubts.

She can't pick them out of the dizzying swirl. It's been a long time since Hera last visited this place, and since then the ranks of the immortals have grown vast and staggering. Zeus' name, though, is a constant thrum in the background, soft and sibilant, relentless and insistent. *Zeus, Zeus, Zeus,* rising to the domed brass ceiling in a cloud of insinuations. But as she roams through the strange halls of hidden faces, she starts to hear an echo attached to her husband's name, a companion repeated alongside almost every mention. She turns around, looking for the source, but it's becoming a chant, surging above every other rumour that floats through the air. *Leto, Leto, Leto,* she hears, the syllables blending into Zeus' name, so often are they said together. *By the stream, in the forest, lured into a cave, a moonless night, unseen, unheard, but a nymph said . . . a goatherd saw . . . a river-god heard . . . Hera, so jealous, keep it hidden . . . don't tell . . .*

Zeus and Leto: the sound of their names drowns out every other sliver of gossip, and everywhere Hera looks, she sees lascivious smiles, hungry mouths shaping the words. She pushes her way through the gently swaying throng, searching for an exit. At last she breaks free, shoving past the figures under wide arches, into the twilit air outside where breezes wreathe around her bare arms, the breath of escaped rumours floating into the ether.

Leto, Hera thinks. She knows of Leto, of course she does,

but the Titaness is so mild and unremarkable, a quiet goddess of daylight. The feeling of unease that her name has sparked in Hera is due to her sister, Asteria.

Hera draws in a long breath. Modest and unassuming as the Titaness is, her bloodlines are rich with power. Her father was Coeus, brother of Cronus, and her mother Phoibe, both elder Titans with the gifts of intellect and prophecy. While Coeus is imprisoned in Tartarus now, Phoibe rules over the oracle of Delphi, from whom the gods themselves seek knowledge and advice. Asteria had known well enough to flee from Zeus, to transform herself into impenetrable rock to be free of his embraces. But Leto, according to the House of Rumour, has not evaded him so well. If what Hera has heard is true – even just a fraction of it – then one of the most ancient Titanesses is consorting with her husband. She can't help but think of Metis, of her prophetic gift and the bright wisdom she possessed, which made her such an asset to Zeus, and yet such a threat. And from Metis came Athena. Of all the worst-case scenarios for one of the vacant thrones, Hera can't think of much that outweighs the prospect of another god like Athena on Olympus. Another enquiring mind, another cool-headed strategist on Zeus' side. Such a child is far more likely to be born to Leto than to one of the humble nymphs with whom her husband dallies in the forests.

Hera flies back to Mount Olympus, a hawk scanning the land below. Her eyes are trained on the earth, searching for one figure alone. When she arrives, her search fruitless, she's seething. She lands on the wide sill of her bedchamber and steps into the room, hawk shape exchanged for her goddess form.

She calls for Klymene, pacing the floor until her handmaiden comes in, closing the door behind her when she sees Hera's face.

'What's happened?'

It's Hera's instinct to keep silent. But the story has already taken hold in Pheme's halls, so what point is there in trying to maintain her dignity here?

'Leto,' she says. 'The Titaness – have you heard?'

Klymene shakes her head, and Hera believes her.

'You will,' she says. Klymene's domain is reputation; she is a goddess concerned with fame and renown. If Leto becomes the mother of an Olympian child of Zeus, her name will be known across the world. 'It's Zeus.'

She watches understanding dawn across Klymene's face.

'I'm not jealous,' Hera says. 'They said I was jealous, but that isn't true.'

'Who said it?'

Hera waves her hand dismissively. 'It doesn't matter.' She's irritated by the look of sympathy in Klymene's eyes.

'He is your husband,' her handmaiden begins.

'Because he gave me no choice.' She would never have decided to be his wife if she could have been free. 'I'm not so petty as to care who he consorts with, except that it makes me look foolish.' She sits down heavily on the couch, suddenly weary. 'All wives are supposed to look to me as an example,' she says. 'He made me be the custodian of marriage, and then he behaves as though he has no wife at all.' And it's the measure of her success; that's what makes it sting. If she isn't the most perfect of all wives, then how can she be their goddess? The paradox makes her rage; it makes violence surge up in her breast, violence that can't be contained, and yet it has nowhere to go.

She can tell that Klymene is choosing her words very carefully. 'Some might see your ability to look the other way as the example.'

'But I can't.' Being the goddess of the downtrodden woman is even worse than being the goddess of marriage. They can't be the same thing; she can't bear for that to be true. 'He took everything from me except for this,' she says. 'Athena has his ear, and his respect. Poseidon has the seas, and Hades has the dead. But I'm queen.'

'No one forgets that.' Klymene hesitates for a moment. 'Even after Typhon, he took you back just the same.'

It's true, but then he makes a mockery of her when he consorts so flagrantly with Titanesses and nymphs; that's the source of the bile that burns in her throat. Their laughter, at her expense. That's what she heard in the whispering rumours: the current of delight at her powerlessness to stop him.

'It's not enough,' Hera says.

Klymene sighs. 'How can you stop him from doing what he wants? You can only find a way to live with it.'

Of course, Klymene knows the force of Zeus' will as well as Hera does, with her own husband chained in Tartarus and her son condemned to eternal torment under the weight of the sky. Hera has to wonder how Klymene lives with that, every day. It isn't for Hera, that kind of acceptance.

'Leto's sister, Asteria, ran away from him,' Hera says. 'I saw her transform, so that he couldn't overpower her.'

A wariness shadows Klymene's eyes. 'Asteria is gone now,' she says. 'She lost herself. Do you think Leto should have done the same?'

Hera sets her jaw. 'Why not?'

'After Asteria, didn't he move on to the next one?' Klymene

says. 'And now Asteria's a floating rock, the island they're calling Delos, not a goddess anymore.'

Hera narrows her eyes. 'She tried to resist – she succeeded. She saw me, and that's when she leapt into the waters. It wasn't just that she wanted to refuse Zeus, though she did. She didn't want to offend me either. There is an example there, one that perhaps her sister should have thought to follow.'

'You don't know if she tried,' Klymene says. 'You know how powerful Zeus is, how hard it is to escape.'

She does know that, from bitter experience. But it doesn't change how she feels. It does nothing to dampen her anger. Of the two sisters, only one of them is a threat to her. 'If she bears him a child,' she says quietly, 'who knows how strong they might be?'

Klymene looks grave. 'Surely there's nothing you can do about that, either.'

Hera stays silent.

Klymene knows better than to push any further. She rises to go, taking one last look at Hera before she lets the door swing closed behind her.

17

It's one thing to take the voice of a nymph no one cares much about. Quite another to contemplate any kind of attack on one of the most ancient Titanesses, and one known for her demure and gentle demeanour at that.

She'll have to watch and wait and see what happens. All she can do for now is instruct Iris to watch for Leto and report back on her condition.

It doesn't take long for the confirmation to come. 'Her body is swollen with child,' Iris tells her. 'I saw her making her way down the banks of Oceanus, too heavy now to hide from view.'

Iris perches on the low courtyard wall as she relays the information to Hera. Her wings are damp with rain, the feathers dark gold and slick, and she leans down to re-tie her sandals, her tunic clinging to her legs.

The drizzle is persistent, though the sun shines through it in weak and watery bursts. Hera looks over the wall at the world spread out below the heavens, watching where the shafts of light fall. 'How much time does she have?'

Iris shrugs, her feathers rippling. 'Not long.'

'Thank you,' Hera says.

The rainbow-goddess finishes fastening her sandal, and hops off the wall. But Hera stays where she is. She doesn't march to Zeus' quarters, doesn't make any demands or accusations. After a period of contemplation, she calls for her daughter Eileithyia and gives her an instruction.

Eileithyia listens, and frowns in confusion. 'Neither land nor sea?' she asks.

'That's right,' says Hera. 'You have the power to hold back birth, or to let it take place. It's the gift I gave you, so that you could fulfil your role.'

'To help in matters of childbirth,' Eileithyia says uncertainly. 'But this . . .'

'It's your blessing that she needs to bring forth her child,' Hera says. 'You decide when a baby is ready to be born, and in this case I'm telling you that when Leto's pangs begin, you must not allow the birth to take place. There is no island she can flee to, from Crete to Samos, Naxos or Lemnos. No mountain range that will give her refuge, no woods, no town or hamlet. Wherever she goes, even if she dives into the sea, you won't grant that blessing.'

She can read the reluctance stamped across her daughter's face.

'Swear to me, Eileithyia.' She takes her hand. 'It's my order, as your mother and your queen. No one will hold you responsible for following my command.'

Eileithyia drops her gaze to the ground. 'I swear. I won't let her give birth on land or at sea.' It goes against her instincts, but so does disobedience to her mother.

Hera is content that her daughter will do as she's told. Iris is dispatched to the House of Pheme, to whisper into the echoing bronze the edict of the queen. *Let everyone know,* she'll say, *that the Titaness Leto must be given no sanctuary. If her baby is born and you are found to have helped her, it is Hera's punishment you'll face.*

A rumour like that will take hold, she knows, and before nightfall it will have spread like wildfire raging through a forest. Every god will shun the Titaness, without Hera having to say a word.

When the moon rises, and Hera sits alone in her chamber, a goblet of wine in her hand and the gentle breeze caressing her face, she lets herself think about Leto. About the fear and panic she'll feel as her pains set in, and her baby does not come.

She ignores Klymene's knock on the door, sending her away. She doesn't go into the hall where the gods will be feasting; she doesn't visit Hestia's hearth to confide what she's done. If she does, she might waver. And if she changes her mind, Zeus' child will be born to a powerful mother and the balance on Olympus will tip even more in his favour. She can't let it happen.

Because if it isn't Leto's child, it will be another. This way, the world will see the example of the two sisters. Asteria, who fled and escaped Zeus' attentions. Leto, who didn't. If Leto is rewarded with motherhood, her son or daughter given an Olympian throne, then what will stop every nymph and minor goddess from competing to catch his eye? If Hera can't stop him from roaming in search of another conquest, then all that's left to her is to show them how much worse it will be for them if they don't do as Asteria did.

She takes a long sip of wine. In the distance, she sees a bright flash streaking through the sky. It comes closer to Olympus: the outline of Zeus' chariot taking shape and the thundering of his horses' hooves rumbling with his approach. Flames leap from the sides, a fearsome display of the returning king, and lightning sizzles as he makes his descent to the palace stables. He's back, ready to feast and drink – and avail himself of her company, most likely. She doesn't know how attuned Zeus is to the murmurings of rumour – she suspects not very – but she'll go to him tonight, make sure he is distracted from any word or memory of the Titaness.

It's likely he's forgotten Leto already, Hera thinks. It won't matter to him if Hera makes an example of her. She'll harden her heart to any sliver of pity for the Titaness. The sooner everyone understands that it's safer for them to make no threat to Hera's position, to leave the royal marriage alone, the better it will be for them all.

While Zeus sleeps at Hera's side, and she stares into the darkness, wondering how she can catch a lightning bolt, how she can pin it down and contain it, and how she'll stay one step ahead so she can prevent it from burning her whole world to ashes in one errant strike, Leto's pains take hold.

As Hera has commanded, so it unfolds. The Titaness roams, increasingly desperate and despairing, swollen beyond endurance, with no relief in sight. She seeks help and is turned away, frightened faces set against her, again and again. Her womb tightens like an iron band clamping shut around her, stealing her breath each time it squeezes.

Even if the rumour of Hera's displeasure has not yet reached every corner of the world, any goddess that Leto could turn to can see something is gravely amiss. She must have angered someone – there must be a reason why Eileithyia has turned away from this birth – and so no one will dare to intervene. Leto has heard the whisperings herself: the horrible, taunting echo as she searches for anywhere she can find respite. *Neither land nor sea*, she hears between the raindrops that hammer down from the bleak skies above. *There is nowhere for Leto's baby to be born.*

Her sister hears the words too, drifting on the black waves, insensible now to cold or pain. Deep in her rocky heart, Asteria feels the insistent rhythm of the words, and she senses her sister wandering lost across the hostile earth. With an immense effort, Asteria summons up the memory of her own escape from Zeus: the sensation of her soft flesh hardening into solid stone, the terror and the panic fading away, her thrashing limbs in the water becoming still and heavy, her pulse slowing as the ichor in her veins thickened and stopped. The faint knowledge of the girl she used to be still exists somewhere within her.

She is no island, Asteria. She isn't anchored to the seabed; she isn't held fast to the earth. And though she is no longer what she was before, her love for her sister lingers in the rock. And she calls to Leto, her cries muffled by the saltwater and buffeting winds. They don't rise to Mount Olympus, where the air in the divine halls hangs still and heavy with incense. But Leto hears. The faint words reach her and she lifts her weary head, her eyes reflecting the light of the stars as she looks out towards the sea, towards her sister's beloved voice. The rain is easing, the clouds parting so that the silvery beams of moonlight fall on the waves, tracing a broken path to the floating rock of Delos.

She plunges into the cold water without a second thought. Swimming frantically through the relentless surges of pain, she follows Selene's light towards Delos, towards Asteria or what remains of her. As the exhausted Titaness hauls herself on to Delos' shore, it seems wide and welcoming: a safe haven that invites her in, drawing her to the centre. As she stumbles forth, grasses begin to shoot from the earth beneath her feet. Trees rise up around her, sheltering her from view, concealing her from the eye of the heavens, and hills shudder forth, the ground shifting and swelling, opening caves in the new-formed slopes. Animals begin to emerge; an owl flutters to perch on a branch, and a stag lifts its head, antlers silvered by the moonlight. Flowers unfurl, spreading their petals to the night, everything cast in shades of silver and grey and black, beautiful to the amazed Titaness.

Eileithyia, who has been pacing the tiled floors of the palace, can breathe freely at last. She has felt the horrible constriction along with Leto, but now the goddess has found a place that escapes Hera's definitions. Delos is neither land nor sea. Eileithyia relaxes, and Leto feels the change as her hold loosens.

Under the cover of the trees that Asteria has summoned to protect her sister, Leto delivers her daughter. The girl is no ordinary infant, even by divine standards. Born bright, alert and preternaturally steady on her tiny feet, the child sees at once how her mother still suffers. A sheen of sweat glistens on Leto's forehead as she pants and gasps, her breath quick and shallow.

The newborn goddess lays her hand, cool and steady, on her mother's cheek, and holds her panicked gaze in her wide, dark eyes. And in the quiet circle of calm between mother and daughter, the girl guides her twin brother safely into the world.

Eileithyia sees that the babies have been born – the boy bathed in golden radiance, the girl framed perfectly in a silver ray of moonlight – and averts her gaze in gratitude. She doesn't want to bear witness to any more of it, already afraid of her own complicity against her mother's wishes.

And when Hera rises the next morning and dispatches Iris to seek out news of Leto, Eileithyia knows to make herself scarce. Hera looks around the hall, seeing only Hebe, who pours sweet nectar into a cup for her, blithe and graceful and unheeding as usual.

Zeus sweeps past, cloak flowing behind him, smiling at the sight of his pretty young daughter as he takes the golden throne beside Hera. Hestia looks up from the central hearth, leaning around one of the four pillars that slightly shield her from view, and lifts her hand to Hera. Hera is too distracted to smile in response.

Demeter comes in, taking a cup from Hebe and nodding in acknowledgement to Zeus and Hera. She leans against the wall, her elbow on the marble sill, looking out through the wide aperture at the wispy clouds wreathing past the palace. Demeter's expression is smooth and placid as she gazes out, the sunlight falling gently across her face. A sheaf of corn spills out of the basket at her elbow, bright as the sun against the sky-blue backdrop of her robes.

Athena glides through the entrance next. Hera's mood sours, but then she sees a flash of colour behind the goddess and her heart leaps.

She jumps to her feet to head Iris off, so that she can receive her news in private, but the rainbow-goddess is already here, her cheeks flushed and dewdrops sparkling on her shining sandals.

'What news, Iris?' Zeus' voice booms out before Hera can say anything. It's obvious to anyone that Iris is full of the excitement that comes with bringing a new and unexpected revelation.

It's agony to Hera to sit back down, but she can feel Zeus' gaze upon her, and she can sense his mild suspicion at her agitation. She shakes out her hair, crossing her ankles with slow deliberation as though she'd never moved at all.

'I bring a message from Leto,' Iris says. Her eyes dart to Hera, alighting briefly on the queen before she looks back to Zeus. 'She announces the birth of a son and a daughter to Zeus – the twin gods Apollo and Artemis.'

The shock is like being doused in cold water. Hera splutters, unable to comprehend it.

'Twins?' says Zeus, and she feels as though he can read every thought in her head as clearly as if they were stamped across her face. There is a dawning realisation on his own as he watches Hera's reaction. 'How interesting.'

Hera holds herself very still, trying not to betray herself any further. For all he knows, her horrified surprise is simply – and justifiably – at the news that he has fathered more children. She keeps her spine straight and her shoulders square, ignoring the flash of sympathy in Hestia's face as she looks up from the hearth, and Demeter's undisguised curiosity. Athena, meanwhile, is glowing, her radiance undimmed by any prospect of sibling rivalry.

'You can leave, if that's all,' Zeus tells Iris, and she dips her head in deference.

As she leaves, she casts her eyes back at Hera to gauge her mood. Hera shakes her head slightly, a tiny movement. She isn't angry with Iris; she knows the goddess is duty-bound to share the messages she's given with whichever god they are sent to. She can't blame her for telling Zeus.

She'll reserve the sharp edge of her anger for Eileithyia, when she finds her.

'Were you expecting Iris to bring some news for you?' Zeus asks her.

She decides that icy dignity is the best way forward. 'Anything I might have been expecting has been driven out of my mind by this revelation.' If she snaps at him, focuses the conversation on her anger at what Iris has told them, she can keep his attention on the next argument and rile him enough that he forgets to investigate any further. How angry might he be at her attempted interference? She doesn't really know. Perhaps as angry as she is right now on learning that it's failed. 'Is this what I should have expected? The announcement of your children, born to someone else, made right here in front of everyone?'

He doesn't have the decency to look even slightly shamefaced. 'I didn't know that's what she was going to say,' he says.

Up until now, Hera has been trying to understand what could have gone wrong with her plan. But the reality of the situation is setting in, and she can feel the burn creep into her cheeks. This is what she wanted to avoid: another public humiliation.

'Do you want me to send for the infants?' Athena interjects.

Zeus looks surprised. 'I don't think so,' he says, waving a hand in dismissal. 'Leave them with their mother.'

Athena rarely seems confused, but the idea that the babies might be best left with their mother makes her brows wrinkle. Hera can almost see the stream of Athena's thoughts, swift and logical, flowing to the inevitable conclusion: the children of Zeus and Leto should, of course, be brought to the palace of the gods. Exactly the reason why Hera had worked so hard to prevent them from being born.

Zeus' apparent lack of interest takes the wind from Hera's

sails. She was ready to rear up, to assert her rights and her position, but his indifference discomfits her. If he doesn't care to take them from Leto, perhaps she should hold back. As she hesitates, she sees her other daughter skulking between the far columns of the courtyard. Eileithyia, too nervous to come in, but too anxious to put it off any longer.

'Daughter!' Zeus spots her too, and calls her in. He beckons her through the columns, noticing, no doubt, how her eyes flicker uncertainly towards her mother. 'Give us your report; tell us about the birth of these new twin gods.'

Eileithyia swallows. She can't make eye contact with Hera as she speaks, staring instead with great determination at the polished tiles beneath her feet. 'The Titaness Leto suffered,' she begins, perhaps hoping this at least will appease Hera. 'She was restless, searching for a place to give birth. Until she could find a place that – that satisfied her, I couldn't help her. Not until she stopped.' Hera can see how carefully she picks her words, omitting Hera's role entirely, making it sound as though it was Leto who drove herself away. 'I didn't know what she was looking for, until she came to Delos.'

Hera narrows her eyes.

'Why Delos?' Zeus asks.

Eileithyia's cheeks flush. 'Perhaps it was because that place was once her sister, Asteria. It's untethered; it floats in the sea. It's not like anywhere else in the world.'

Hebe has drawn closer to listen. 'She wanted to be with her sister,' she says, wistful. 'Or else her sister called to her to come. I think that's beautiful.'

Hera bites back her irritation.

'I gave my blessing.' Eileithyia's voice lowers, awkward and reluctant. 'The girl was born first, Artemis. She was alert and knowing straight away. She wiped the sweat from her mother's face and calmed her, the way I've done for other goddesses before. And then the boy came. Apollo, Leto called him.'

'Well.' Zeus claps his hands together. 'In reward for the safe passage of my children, I'll fix Delos where it is,' he says. 'It won't be a floating rock any longer, it can become a flourishing island. The birthplace of Apollo, and of Artemis too.'

Eileithyia nods. 'Other goddesses have come to pay their respects,' she says. 'Dione is there, Themis too, and even Amphitrite came up from the depths of the sea. Nereids and Oceanids have gathered in the waves, and seals and dolphins have swum to the shore to see them.'

Hera nods tightly. She knows that Eileithyia is letting her know what awaits, should she think to go and punish Leto more directly, or else her twins. Powerful, ancient Titanesses, just as Leto is herself, have gathered to protect her. But it heartens her a little to hear Themis' name: Themis, who gave Zeus so many daughters once, long before Hera was his wife. Not one of them has been elevated, not one of them has made a claim to any royal status. Perhaps Leto and her children will drift on the divine periphery in the same way.

Later, Hera looks down from Olympus to see the contented joy on Delos. The boy, perched on the highest rock in a circle of seven, a shaft of sunlight falling across him as he sings a song that has just occurred to him. A snake slithers out from under one of the rocks, as though it has been lured from its hiding place by the sweet purity of his voice, and he watches it as it uncoils itself and darts past him. It's almost gone, about to be swallowed up by the trees, but the young Apollo picks up a stick that lies at his side and spears the creature before it can escape. He doesn't miss a note as the serpent writhes, dark blood trickling from the wound, and gradually succumbs to death. Among those trees, his sister eyes a boar snuffling in the rich earth, its tusks scraping the side of a tree trunk, and her hands itch for a weapon.

Zeus comes to her doorway and watches her watching Delos. She keeps her head turned away from him, though she can feel his eyes on her. She doesn't know what he is thinking. If he suspects what she did, or knows, and if he cares. If he's angry, amused or uninterested. If he has plans for the twin gods, or will discard them as easily as he has done others. The world laid out beneath her is so vast and teeming, bigger than ever before, and dense with gods and mortals, all connected in so many intricate ways that it dizzies her. Hera values nothing more than a clear head; she longs to control the sprawling mass of chaos that surely should be hers to command, but it seems intent on slipping through her fingers. Even Gaia is shifting her boundaries, extending the land that lies within the encircling ring of Oceanus, moving the plates of the earth in accordance with the endless pace of change. Whenever Hera thinks she stands on solid ground, it slides away from underneath her. She wishes that Zeus would leave her alone, but his presence fills the room, mocking and insistent. Brother, husband, king and enemy all in one, tied to her so tightly she doesn't know how she could ever be free.

18

It's Artemis who demands an audience with Zeus, in the end. She marches into the Olympian palace, the scent of leaves in her hair and dirt smeared on the hem of her short tunic. 'Give me the forests,' she demands of him. 'Let them be my domain, and all the creatures that live there will be mine to hunt as I please.'

Zeus is delighted by the intrusion. While Athena's sharp mind and composure had impressed him deeply, he finds this fearless, unruly girl quite captivating. 'You can come and go in whatever forests you like already,' he says. 'What permission do you need from me?'

Hera is there in time to hear this part of the conversation, having hastened from her quarters as soon as she heard the commotion. Aphrodite's handmaidens were all aflutter in the corridors, and when Hera gets to the throne room, Aphrodite is there, along with Demeter and Athena, and, she notices to her displeasure, Poseidon. Her brother leans back in his throne, his beard slick with saltwater and his hair rippling to his shoulders as he eyes Artemis. Hera knows that Hebe will be at the stables; she loves it when Poseidon's chariot makes the journey from his sea-palace to Olympus and she can stroke the pearl-strung manes of his bronze-hoofed horses and marvel at the gleaming shells and rosy coral that decorate the chariot sides.

'I want to be the goddess of the hunt,' Artemis says.

Zeus shrugs, exchanging a glance with Poseidon. 'The forests can belong to you,' he says. 'If that's what you want.' He sees Hera making her way forward, past Hestia at the hearth, and he clears his throat. 'I thought you'd come to demand a place here, on Olympus.'

She looks from the marble walls to the golden floors, from the gems that stud the bright thrones to the beautiful vases and delicate painted jugs of nectar, and her disdain is palpable.

Zeus doesn't look offended. In fact, he's smiling. Hera recognises the indulgence in his expression with a sinking sensation. If anything, he looks *fatherly*.

He carries on. 'What about your brother?'

'Oh yes,' Artemis says. 'He'd love it here. He could sit and play his songs and compose his poems very well in a palace, I'm sure.'

'But it's not so good for hunting,' Demeter interjects, and there is a shimmer of laughter around the hall. Hera can see Zeus' amusement is shared; the diversion Artemis is providing is clearly welcome. They're not ridiculing her – Demeter's aspect is maternal and kind, which is far worse for Hera, who makes her way to her throne at Zeus' side and sits, smoothing the long skirt of her dress around her legs.

'I'd like a bow,' Artemis says, not intimidated at all by Hera's display of queenly dignity. 'I could make my own, of course, but as goddess of hunting, I want it to be made by Hephaestus.'

At that, Zeus sits up, his hands gripping the carved arms of his throne. 'Hephaestus?'

Artemis nods. 'I spend my time on Sicily now,' she says. 'I've seen his forge, in the volcano. He makes the finest things – shields and armour – but I want a bow and arrows.'

'What's this forge like?' Zeus asks.

'I haven't gone inside,' Artemis answers. 'But the noise rings out from it at all hours – the clanging of his hammer and the anvils and the rumbling of the fires. Sparks and smoke pour from the top of the volcano; he's always working, along with his Cyclopes.' She looks surprised at the confounded reaction in the room. 'Didn't you know?'

All the gods look from one to the other.

'It seems that no one did,' says Zeus. He frowns, and then his face clears and he looks back to Artemis. 'Ask him to make you the bow and arrows; tell him I sent you if you like. Is that everything?'

She shakes her head. 'I saw what my mother endured, giving birth to Apollo. I helped her, you know.' She seems to notice Poseidon's gaze at last, and she stares back at him, her face vivid and defiant. 'I don't want that for me. I don't want to bear children, so I want you to swear that no god will ever try to take me as a wife.'

It's so like Hestia, so long ago, when she made that demand herself. Hera catches her eye, sure that Hestia is remembering the same moment. Athena too, she thinks. These goddesses are wilier than she had ever thought to be.

Poseidon snorts, but Zeus doesn't seem minded to deny his daughter anything. 'What else?' he says.

'I'll have nymphs to hunt alongside me,' she says. 'Sixty daughters of Oceanus, to be my companions. They come to the shores already, eager to train with me. Tell their father that they're to be mine, not given away to other gods.' As an afterthought, she adds, 'And I'll help Eileithyia to watch over women in childbirth. I was good at it.' Her eyes flash at Hera. 'I don't want anyone to have to suffer the way my mother did, not again.'

Hera notices the way that some of the nymphs in the halls – Aphrodite's girls, the others who flock around the gates and fill the courtyards with their gossip and chatter – look at Artemis, and she has no doubt that Oceanus' daughters will clamour to go with her. She strikes a brave and compelling figure, charming not just Zeus with her abrupt manner, but obviously casting some kind of glamour over everyone else too. The gods have probably never encountered anyone less interested in winning their favour and approval before, and the nymphs have never seen a woman who cares so little about what anyone thinks.

In Hera's opinion, the young goddess is scruffy and arrogant. Even so, she can't deny the fire that crackles from her: a wildness that whispers of freedom, the thrill of the hunt under moonlight, a spirit that won't be tamed or broken.

'I'll tell him that his daughters will serve mine,' Zeus agrees. 'Send Apollo here. I have a throne for him, and one for you whenever you care to take it.'

There is a muted gasp from the other gods, but Hera has been expecting it from the moment she saw Artemis. She takes a grim satisfaction in allowing no surprise to show on her face, nothing for Zeus to relish.

Artemis shrugs. 'The forest is my home,' she says.

'You can stay there all you like,' says Zeus. 'But you're an Olympian now, all the same.'

Hera isn't even sure it was Zeus' gift to bestow. Anyone can feel the power emanating from Artemis. But if she's not going to live on Mount Olympus, the insult of her existence will be something Hera rarely has to encounter. The brother might be more of a problem. More pressing is the news Artemis has brought of Hephaestus. Still hidden from their sight beneath the volcano, but thriving in a way she'd never imagined.

Artemis doesn't linger, now she has what she came for. 'I'll wear my tunics like this,' she calls back as her parting shot, indicating the hem that finishes above her knee. 'I can't have them flapping around my ankles while I'm running. And my nymphs will do the same.' Her eyes flicker across the drapes of Hera's finely woven skirt, falling across the arch of her golden-sandalled foot. She raises her hand in farewell, not waiting to hear Zeus' acceptance of her final demand before she's gone.

'What do you think?' Zeus murmurs in Hera's ear. His beard tickles her cheek.

'She's delightful.' Hera's tone is so dry, he can't mistake it as sincere.

A smirk plays on his lips. 'She's powerful. Did you feel it? Quite the adversary, I'm sure, if anyone wants to oppose her.'

'Why would they?' Hera asks. 'I can't imagine anyone would be interested in fighting her for the privilege of living in a forest cave and chasing down wild animals with a bow and arrow.'

'She's young,' Zeus says. 'You were once, and I remember how you used to wander in the woods.' His voice lowers even further, horribly intimate. 'Maybe you found other attractions there.' He pauses. 'But then you discovered a taste for ruling. Maybe Artemis will do the same, one day. She might be glad of the throne I've given her, and maybe I will be too. It might be time for someone … fresher. A different kind of goddess on Mount Olympus.'

The hall is still thronged with immortals, and Hera can feel curious eyes resting on her. Wondering what Zeus is whispering, trying to read her reaction on her face. She stretches her mouth into a smile, pretending she didn't hear the threat in his words. 'She's certainly interesting,' she agrees.

Zeus snorts with laughter, the contemptuous kind, and Hera keeps smiling, keeps sitting up tall. No one can see how her skin prickles at the back of her neck. No one will know how oddly stinging it was to hear him mention her youth. She's a goddess; she hasn't aged since those days. She never has to fear the creep of wrinkles; there will be no sagging of her skin, no hunching or withering, no weakening with time. But inside, she feels the ache of the centuries that have passed and the heaviness of all her extinguished hopes.

'And Apollo, he's bound to be interesting too, if he's anything like his sister,' Zeus says.

Poseidon's ears prick up at this and he leans in, the tang of salt wafting from his skin. 'It's about time we had another god on Olympus, that's for sure, among so many goddesses. Restore the balance a bit.'

Zeus inclines his head. 'Goddesses have their advantages too.' He glances at Hera. 'I am looking forward to meeting him, though.'

Poseidon grunts. 'It's about time,' he repeats.

Hera stands up, sharp and decisive. 'Send Iris for me when he arrives,' she says, before sweeping from the hall.

She stalks to the stables, her skirt billowing around her legs as she strides. It's possible that Artemis has a point about the long gowns, not that Hera will ever admit it. Hebe, as predicted, is fussing over Poseidon's horses, pure white stallions whose black eyes roll back at Hera's approach. Hebe lays a hand on the muscular flank of the one closest, and he relaxes under her touch. The other shifts uneasily, its bronze hooves clattering against the floor.

'Prepare my chariot,' Hera says, and Hebe hurries to do it.

She won't fly to Sicily cloaked in hawk feathers. She'll make her arrival as the resplendent queen of the gods. Let Artemis see her coming; she's not interested in her. Hera wants to see the workshop of Hephaestus for herself.

The noise and tumult is unmistakeable. From deep within the mountain, the echo of metal banging against metal rings out across the valleys, and the furious sparks surge and glitter from the crater at the top.

So, her son has made a home for himself here. A productive life away from Mount Olympus. Ares left, that's true, and surrounds himself with his warlike followers, brooding in his dark mansion all alone except for Aphrodite's visits, but she'd never expected it of Hephaestus. She thinks about what Poseidon said about the balance of gods and goddesses on Mount Olympus. He saw it as some kind of slight, some aberration to be corrected. But as far as Hera can see, the gods have found no barrier to freedom, to choosing the shape of their own existence. None of them seem shackled to Olympus by golden chains; they are free to wander as they please. Now Artemis has done it, she wonders if Athena or Aphrodite might follow. They roam, like she does, but they always come back, even though Zeus doesn't watch them as closely as he does Hera. Even though they don't have the same responsibilities as she does, the same invisible leash that holds her there.

She notices a flurry of movement at the base of the volcano. A boulder rolls a short distance to the side, and Artemis herself is there, pushing the boulder back into place behind her before she breaks into a steady run, her bare calves flashing in the long grasses. Hera wonders if she's already gone to Hephaestus, if that's the way to his forge, and if she's asked for her bow and arrow. What might Hephaestus make of such a request, especially with Zeus' name invoked in approval? Hera remembers how he was always so eager to make gifts for her, and all the wonderful contraptions that he would present to Athena, so proud of his own artistry and innovation. If that enthusiasm hasn't been knocked out of him by his expulsion from the heavens, she's sure he'd be happy to give the young goddess whatever she asks for.

The boulder shifts again, and Hera backs towards the sloping hills behind her. A curtain of ivy creeps over the rock to her left, and she ducks behind it, peering through the dark green leaves as another figure emerges. The broad shoulders she remembers, and the squat, stocky frame, but there is added clumsiness to his gait now. She sees, as he takes a few steps forward, that he is off-balance, his right leg dragging, and she feels her forehead wrinkle in confusion. Gods are sleek and swift, not awkward and limping. But there's no denying the evidence of her eyes. He must have been injured when Zeus hurled him. Perhaps, in the dark prison of the volcano, if he had no nectar or ambrosia to nourish him, he didn't heal like a god usually would. He keeps one hand on the boulder, steadying himself as he shades his eyes from the sun with the other and looks around, searching. She wonders if he looks for Artemis, though she's long gone now.

Anxious that he shouldn't see her, Hera takes another step back, the ivy swinging in front of her face. Her eyes take a moment to adjust to the darkness.

It's a cave, and although she's never been here before, there is something familiar about it to her all the same. Something in the air: a sourness that recalls a tender feeling in her, something comforting in the slight whiff of foulness, and as her memory catches up with her instinct, she hears the slither of scales against stone. 'Ekhidna?'

The serpent-goddess looms in the shadows: the black coil of her snake tail, the same tangled black hair falling across her woman's body, and her wide black eyes staring. 'I have waited for you here,' she says, and Hera thrills at the sound of her voice, the rasp and scratch she thought she'd never hear again.

'How did you know?'

Ekhidna nods towards the light filtering through the ivy. 'I thought you'd come to see his forge. Your blacksmith son.'

'But why?' Hera asks. She had thought Ekhidna would have disappeared back into the fetid froth and scum of the underground waters she loves.

'I found that I can't retreat from the world like before,' Ekhidna says, and Hera has the unaccountable sensation that those cold black eyes can see into her mind and read what she's thinking. 'Not with most of my children living now in the upper earth. In swamps and caves and far-flung islands where the warlike giants make their homes.' Beams of soft light fall across her tail, making some of the scales glimmer a murky, iridescent green that reminds Hera of dragonflies. 'Places where the gods never care to tread,' Ekhidna continues. 'The forgotten parts of the world, where it's still wild, where everything still belongs to Gaia.'

Hera feels her heart quicken. 'I've tried to seek out news of them, but have heard nothing. Can I see them?'

Ekhidna shakes her head, her lip curling in what Hera thinks is amusement. 'The earth keeps its monsters hidden,' she says, 'for all that Zeus thinks he has conquered them.' She nods towards the light. 'The blacksmith god has Cyclopes working in his forge, on top of Typhon's grave. I've seen the places where our children roam, and the other creatures that live there too. Zeus doesn't know half the world's secrets.' Her lips lengthen into an unmistakeable smile, eerie and strange. 'I pursued the mother of his twins, hissing through the mist and the salt spray as she ran. I chased her with the warning you whispered into the House of Pheme, so that she fled from my voice. It was only her sister that saved her.'

Hera stares at her. 'You chased Leto?'

'I know now that Typhon was wrong to attack outright.' Ekhidna's voice is hypnotic, a slow churn of black water sucking Hera into its currents. 'He is dead and you are a hostage-queen, but I am free, like all the monsters of the world. No one knows where we are, or that we are. Leto never caught a glimpse of me. But I heard your bidding, and I helped.'

Hera is astonished. 'Why did you help?'

'Don't forget there are many of us who hate Zeus as much as you do, daughter of Cronus – and have done so for longer.' And Hera remembers that the serpent-goddess has dwelt in her caves since long before the gods made their home in the clouds. There is an ancient power thrumming through Ekhidna's words, tumbling together like rocks crashing from a mountaintop. Since he hung her up against the empty sky, Hera has thought of Zeus as the strongest force the world contains. But Ekhidna isn't talking of brute force, of battles and war and weapons that can tear down mountains and boil the seas. The venom that seeps from her tongue and stains her speech, like ink billowing from a vast squid in the ocean's lightless depths, is another kind of strength. Hera feels it, as surely as if it flows through her own veins, and it makes her grateful to her terrible daughter-in-law.

She feels lighter, almost giddy as she speaks. 'I came here in my chariot, in full sight of the heavens. I won't stay any longer in this cave, in case it draws any notice to your hiding place.'

Ekhidna chuckles, the horrible gurgling of a polluted spring. 'I have so many, the Olympian Thunderer could never find me. But you need to know, before you even heard what he was doing with the Titaness, Zeus had already discarded her and turned his attentions to another – the nymph Aegina, daughter of the river Asopus. He took her from her father's home in the shape of an eagle, swooped down and caught her in his claws, carrying her off to the island that bears her name now. Her son is already born, a mortal boy, destined to be king of the island's men.'

Hera turns back, her elation ebbing away as swiftly as it had risen. 'Another?' she says. 'A mortal king?' She thinks on it for a moment.

'I've lived in the caves of the island; I've seen him walking the shore.' There's a hunger in the way Ekhidna says it, her black tongue caressing the words.

'I won't have a mortal bragging to his subjects that he's the son of Zeus,' Hera says. The imagined impudence makes her burn.

'There's a spring that flows from underground there, that gives them fresh water to drink,' Ekhidna says. 'I can corrupt it, bring a plague to silence them all. He can rule over them in the Underworld, when all of them are shades, unable to remember where they came from at all.'

'Do it,' Hera says. Mortals are so much more easily dealt with than gods. She won't have to give this one a second thought. It will be as simple as a flash of Ekhidna's tail in the spring, the ooze of her venom mingling with the crystal-clear waters. If only all her problems were solved so simply.

19

Not long after she returns, Olympus is thrown into disarray. Demeter storms into the throne room, demanding that Zeus tell her where their daughter, Kore, is.

'How would I know?'

Hera can see he's truly baffled. It's not beyond him to lie, of course. But she looks from face to face around the hall, and all the gods seem taken aback by Demeter's palpable distress. No one seems to have an answer.

'I've searched everywhere,' Demeter says. 'There's no trace of her, and none of her companions have any idea what's happened to her.'

'Has she ever vanished before?' Athena asks.

The goddess shakes her head, her hair escaping from her braids. She twists the loose curls back and forth between her fingers, tears brimming in her eyes. 'She said she felt like someone was watching her – that there was a presence. But nothing happened, and when Artemis joined her on Sicily I thought she would be safe. They're friends – and Artemis is so powerful, I thought she'd be a protector.'

'Who would be watching her?' Athena muses. There's no trace of sympathy on her face, no concern for Demeter. She looks only intrigued by the possibility of a mystery to solve, a puzzle to work out.

Poseidon snorts. 'You've kept that girl hidden since she was born, Demeter. Sicily, you say? All the times I've come ashore on that island, I never knew she was there. Perhaps someone was curious to get a glimpse.'

Demeter's face twists with disgust. Hera notices that her shoulders are shaking, her eyes wild, and she remembers making a threat to Demeter about the girl long ago, when she was newly married. She hasn't thought about her since – she hasn't needed to – but now she wonders why Demeter wanted to keep her so concealed.

'But who knew?' Demeter demands. 'You never saw her there; no one did. She lived with her nymphs, she was quiet and modest and never attracted any attention.'

'Hephaestus has his forge on Sicily now,' Aphrodite interjects. 'Maybe he saw her and decided he wanted her.'

Athena's eyes gleam with satisfaction that the problem is solved. 'That's probably it.'

'Then he needs to give her back!' The edge of panic in Demeter's voice startles them all. 'She's not his to take.'

Zeus' face relaxes. 'Go to his forge, see if she's there.'

Demeter stalks out, and Hera slips from the hall to follow her. The goddess's cloak flares out behind her, and Hera catches her by the shoulder to make her stop. 'What are you so worried about?' She recoils at the sight of the fury bubbling through Demeter; she's never seen her lose her composure like this.

'How can you ask that?'

'If Hephaestus has her, you'll get her back.'

Demeter shakes her head. 'I kept her out of the sight of the gods for a reason. You should understand that. I wanted Zeus to forget she existed, and he did. He has so many daughters, why shouldn't I keep mine out of the way?'

'You did, for a long time,' Hera says. 'But didn't you think someone would notice her eventually?'

'Zeus agreed I could be left alone after she was born,' Demeter says. 'Hestia was cleverer than me; she made sure she got that promise from him *before* he could touch her. You saw it was the first thing Artemis did, as soon as she came to Olympus. We all found a way, except for you – you didn't believe Hestia when she warned you about him the first time, and so you found out for yourself. I didn't want that to happen to Kore – not Zeus, not Poseidon, not any of them. I was waiting; I thought in time I'd choose a husband for her, but it was easy to put it off. She was happy where she was.'

'On an island that you never let her leave?'

'She didn't need anything else,' Demeter bites back. 'And now your wretched son has made his home there, and it was all for nothing.'

Hera is struggling to feel sorry for her. 'Hardly for nothing,' she says. 'You've had her to yourself for plenty of time.'

'When I think of that ugly blacksmith god putting his hands on her,' Demeter says, 'I can't bear it. Of any god I might have chosen for her, he is the very last.'

Hera's patience runs out entirely. Hephaestus is ugly, and he is exiled, but he's still a son of the two most powerful immortals on Mount Olympus. 'I should have done what I said I'd do, aeons ago,' Hera says, 'and found someone for her to marry myself. You should be grateful for how long you've had.' She thinks she might order Hephaestus to marry the girl.

She remembers how Demeter turned her away when she was fleeing Zeus, and it gives her a savage satisfaction to imagine putting Demeter's daughter in the same desperate position she was once in.

It's overdramatic, she thinks, for Demeter to cause such a fuss, and she lets her sister go without another word to try to stop her. She can't imagine Hephaestus putting up much opposition to the raging goddess, who can only cast Hera a look of thunderous fury before she storms away. If Demeter drags Hephaestus out of his volcano and up to the heavens to complain to Zeus, she doesn't know if Zeus will punish him again or welcome him back.

But as it turns out, neither happens. Demeter searches Hephaestus' forge, and can find no trace of her daughter. Despite herself, she believes him when he tells her he never noticed Kore at all.

'What was the forge like?' Hera can't help but ask, and Demeter stares at her uncomprehendingly. 'I could go to him,' she suggests, and Zeus shakes his head, implacable. His order still stands: Hera is to stay away from Hephaestus.

The council of the gods is stumped; no one has heard anything of Demeter's daughter. Iris is dispatched to every corner of the world to gather information, and she can find nothing.

Gods and Titans alike are willing to help. Demeter has favoured them all, summoning up crops and blessing the earth with her bounty indiscriminately, and so no one wants to see her despair. But she returns to Olympus each dawn, pale and weary, having searched every hillside, every clifftop, every distant cave and remote beach and verdant forest that she can find. At night, she clutches a flaming torch to see by, and the Titaness Hecate walks at her side, sympathetic to her terror. She begs for news and, disappointed again, turns back to search throughout the day.

'What's wrong with her?' Hera asks Hestia.

Hestia makes a reproving face. 'She's grieving for her child,' she says.

'But the girl must be somewhere . . . she'll find her eventually.'

'It's strange, though, that no one has seen her. It's as though she's disappeared from the face of the earth entirely,' Hestia says.

'She might find her more quickly if she would stop and rest. Take some nourishment,' Hera says.

'It's days since she took any nectar or ambrosia,' Hestia agrees. 'But she won't listen to me.'

'Then she won't listen to anyone,' Hera says. It's hard to keep the irritation from her voice. 'But she isn't the only who's suffering.'

It's only been a few days, but the pall cast over Demeter has spread to the world. Without her nurture, leaves are beginning to curl and wither and drop off branches. Flowers are dying; their heads drooping and petals fading as they shrivel away. The air tastes cold and bitter; the scent of decay carrying on the icy breath of the wind.

'She must find her soon,' Hestia says. 'I wish I could help her search, but . . .'

'You need to keep the fire burning,' Hera insists. 'She can neglect her duties, but it's no reason for you to abandon yours.'

'She can't,' Hestia says, her dark eyes serious. 'It can't go on much longer, with nothing growing, everything dying.'

'Zeus will have to command her to stop.'

'What if she refuses?'

'How can she?' The words burst from her, twisting in her throat. 'We all have to obey him, whatever we feel.' She can't hide her bitterness, the bile that poisons her voice, when she thinks about Demeter rebelling now – and maybe even winning – when she never helped Hera.

Hestia rests her hand on Hera's. She doesn't pull away, but she smoulders still with resentment.

'Demeter is determined,' Hestia says. 'The other gods underestimate her, but they're wrong.'

'Why?' Hera demands. 'She's just a goddess of gardens, of crops and flowers. Her life is simple – too simple if she makes such a fuss about this.'

'You think of her as generous and nurturing because she makes things grow,' Hestia says. 'But nature is ruthless too. It destroys as well as creates, with no mercy. I think we'll all see that side of her now.'

'She'll see sense,' Hera vows.

But Hestia is right. Demeter doesn't relent.

'Why don't you make her?' Hera asks Zeus, and he only gives her a bewildered look that angers her even more. 'Hang her up in chains,' Hera goes on. 'Don't give her the choice to carry on like this.'

'But if I do that, the earth will die even more rapidly,' he points out.

Hera flounders. How did Demeter find the courage to defy him, and how is she doing it so successfully when Hera's attempts have failed?

But Demeter doesn't seem to care. If Zeus threatened to beat her, to bind her, what difference would it make to a goddess who won't even eat? When Hera looks at the desperate

Demeter, she sees how quickly she is shrinking in upon herself, and she starts to seriously wonder if Demeter will even have the strength to bring life back to the world if her daughter isn't found soon.

At last, Helios comes to their hall: the mighty sun-god, who dwells in distant Oceanus, crowned with shining rays.

'I saw her taken,' he tells Zeus and Hera, having insisted that he speak to them alone.

'By whom?' Hera asks.

'It was Hades.' The sun-god's tones are deep and sonorous. 'I was at my zenith in the sky above Sicily when I saw him split the ground in two. His dark chariot ascended, led by the black horses of the Underworld. He took the girl – she was picking wild flowers alone in the meadow that he tore apart – and they vanished beneath the earth. It happened so quickly, no one else witnessed it.'

'Why didn't you tell us before?'

He turns his golden eyes on Hera. 'It's the dread god's business which girls he takes. I only tell you now because of her mother's behaviour.'

'What do you think he wants?' Hera asks Zeus. 'Does he seek a return from the Underworld? Is this his way of showing that he's grown tired of ruling the dead, and wants to rejoin the living?'

Zeus frowns. 'He's shown no sign of it. He's never interfered with the upper realms before.'

Helios has no interest in staying. 'Get the harvest goddess under control,' he advises Zeus as he leaves. As much as Hera also wants Demeter brought back in line, his words rankle.

'He's so arrogant,' she seethes as his chariot arcs back up into the sky, bright fire trailing in his wake. 'Perhaps he's forgotten how we, with Demeter, chained up his father in Tartarus.'

Zeus isn't listening. 'Send Iris for Demeter; we'll tell her where the girl is, and she can get back to her duties.'

'Will you tell Hades to give her up?' Hera asks.

She can tell from the surprise on his face that the thought hadn't occurred to him. 'Demeter can't find a better husband for her daughter than Hades,' he says.

'I think she'd disagree. Olympian gods can't descend to the Underworld. It belongs to Hades alone.'

Zeus waves away her objections. 'It's done now.'

Hera opens her mouth, about to protest – marriage is her realm, after all – but the vision of Demeter's closed-off face in the woods, turning her away, rises up in her mind. 'I'll find Iris,' she says.

It isn't so simple. First Kore disappeared with no trace; now it seems her desperate mother has done the same. Iris can't find her, and when Hecate draws close to the palace in the veil of evening, she has no news of Demeter either.

'Could she have learned about Hades some other way?' Hera asks. 'Has she made the journey to his realm herself, to get Kore back?'

'She would have waited for me,' Hecate says. 'I know the way.' Hera can't help but listen, spellbound, whenever the Titaness speaks. Moonlight glitters in her eyes, and her midnight cloak trails behind her as she stands, a pillar of darkness in the glorious surroundings of Olympus.

And Hera can't imagine Demeter, the usually vital and glowing goddess of plenty, attempting to navigate the shadowy tunnels, descending into the crumbling soil full of crawling, slithering things, where the nourishing sunlight can never reach.

But Demeter is not who she was. And so the merciless chill of an endless cruel winter sinks its claws into the earth. Until now, Demeter has wielded a gentle balance in the world, but without her steadying hand, a brutal famine sets in and, at length, Poseidon is moved to take action. He rises from the cold, dark waters and drives his horses through the rainy skies and squalling clouds, to the heaped snows of Mount Olympus. Soon there will be no mortals left, he complains; someone must drag Demeter out of her cave and make her halt the devastation.

'Her cave?' Zeus queries.

Poseidon's dark brows are drawn together, but his fury springs from defensiveness. 'Yes, the cave of Mount Elaios, in the Arcadian forests.'

'How did you know she was there?' Zeus is on his feet, sceptre in hand, looking for Iris. Hera, on the throne beside him, stays where she is, eyeing Poseidon with growing suspicion.

'She hasn't left since—' There is a bluster in his tone, and the air in the megaron seems to thicken as realisation dawns on the assembled gods. 'Well, come on,' Poseidon says. His thick, muscled arms are folded across his broad chest, his beard curling halfway down to meet them. 'She can't still be angry.'

'About Kore?' Zeus asks.

'She was searching the shoreline.' An angry sigh huffs from his lips, as though he can't believe he's being forced to explain this. 'She hadn't taken nectar or ambrosia, her strength was dwindling.' He casts a contemptuous glance around the room, lingering on Athena, who is staring at him with the horrified light of comprehension dawning in her eyes. 'She was always so haughty,' he snaps. 'Zeus had her once, and she thinks she's too good for anyone else.' His eyes alight briefly on Hestia, his face contorted into a sneer. 'I galloped out of the waves, a horse, and she was grateful. She climbed on my back willingly enough. She was too tired to walk further.'

Hera can't contain her revulsion any longer. 'But you didn't help her look for her daughter.' The knowledge of what he did instead hangs unspoken in the air.

He doesn't even bother to answer her. She's been hiding in that cave ever since. 'It's gone on too long,' he appeals to Zeus. 'She needs to come back. How can anyone be so stubborn?'

'You'll have to persuade her,' Hera says to Zeus. She can imagine Demeter in the cave where she's sought refuge, broken and grieving, and Hera knows that if she had had the power to bring the world to ruin on that peaceful beach after Zeus attacked her, she would have done it. 'Offer her something, to compensate for her suffering.'

Poseidon ignores the glare she directs at him.

Zeus thinks about it. 'She's made her point,' he says. 'But I can't tell Hades to give up the girl.'

'Why not?' Hera is incredulous. 'Nothing else will satisfy her, and if we don't appease her somehow, then every living thing on the earth will die.'

'Perhaps there's a compromise,' Athena suggests, and all the immortal faces turn to her. 'Demeter can't go to the Underworld to see her daughter. Hades won't relinquish his wife. We need a way to make both of them happy.'

'Only one of them can have her, though.' Zeus frowns, baffled.

Hera can see Athena working it out, strategising to find a solution that keeps the peace. 'Some kind of condition,' she muses, 'that means she can split her time between them.' Her face brightens. 'Of course!'

'What?' Hera can't disguise her impatience.

'Demeter will understand,' Athena says, as though Hera hadn't interrupted at all. 'Ultimately, she'll be glad to have her daughter honoured as Queen of the Underworld – just so long as she doesn't lose her entirely. And Hades won't mind surrendering her for a time, so long as it doesn't appear that you've forced him – or worse, that Demeter has.'

Her plan, it transpires, is to invent a requirement for Kore to stay in the Underworld only if she's consumed any food while she's been in Hades' kingdom.

'Of course she will have eaten!' Hera interjects.

'Yes,' Athena says, her eyes alight. 'So we'll make an exception. Let it be known that she's eaten, say . . . pomegranate seeds – just a handful. Zeus will be merciful: she'll stay down there for part of the year, and return to the upper world for the other part. Demeter can have her winters while her daughter is gone, provided she gives us spring when the girl comes back.'

Demeter is mollified enough to accept the proposal, perhaps because it's the only way she'll see the girl again. No longer Kore, deity of flowers; the goddess who ascends each spring has taken the name Persephone, bringer of destruction. The winters that Demeter inflicts are harsher than they ever were before, but it's a small price to pay.

That Demeter's defiance can go unpunished tastes bitter to Hera. She, queen of them all, has to cast around for subversive methods to achieve her ends, and Demeter can hold the threat of the destruction of the world over Zeus' head.

Hera smiles at Persephone's wedding to Hades, accepting the praise offered up to her and the sacrifices burned in her honour as the bride is carried by torchlight to her new husband's home underneath the earth. Hera is gracious and poised, clad in splendid robes embroidered in shining thread by Athena. A jewelled brooch glitters at her breast, a fine-tasselled belt wraps around her waist, and the soft skin of her arms gleams with perfumed oil. Earrings sparkle like stars on her delicate lobes, bracelets jangle on her wrists, and she knows that she's as beautiful and magnificent as any goddess in the heavens.

But inside, the venom churns and the black bile rises, even as she oversees the marriage rites. Her authority here feels empty; the deal was done without her assent. Hades took his bride without asking Hera, and for all the gods give thanks to her for blessing the union, she knows she had no choice.

20

In the palace, Apollo sits with Zeus – he's come at the invitation, passed along by his sister, to claim his throne – and Hera enjoys the peaceful silence down on the ground, away from Mount Olympus. She knows that he'll be singing, his haunting notes weaving through the columns, stirring the nymphs to tears, and she prefers to be here. Yesterday, over cups of wine, she listened to him brag to Zeus about Daphne, a naiad he pursued through the forests. The daughter of a river-god who had sworn, like Artemis, to eschew all men. But Apollo had burned for her, he said, his words like poetry as he described his desire, how the flames within him surged at the sight of her tumbled hair, the shape of her lips, the inviting curves of her body outlined beneath her tunic as he gave chase. She'd fled, he told Zeus, like a lamb or a deer or a dove, her fluttering panic only more charming to him. And when he finally closed his hands around her arms, she called out to her father to save her. The soft skin under his fingers hardened into bark, her arms stretched and twisted into branches, her feet were rooted to the earth by great tendrils, and her beautiful hair became a leafy crown. He could still feel the terrified racing of her heart beneath his palm as his hands roved across the trunk that was her body, and she was still warm beneath his lips as he kissed her before she stilled. It's why he wears the laurel wreath in his curls, he told Zeus, for it was a laurel tree that she became. They'll be linked forever, he said, his would-be lover now his sacred tree. The two gods laughed, regretful of the conquest that never was, but amused by the story, nonetheless.

Hera hadn't been very taken with Artemis, but she dislikes Apollo even more. She can't stay away from the palace forever, though, so it's with a certain reluctance that she makes her way back. To her surprise, as she enters through the gates, she meets a swell of immortals in the courtyard, a bustling crowd that tries her patience. On the edge of it, she spots Klymene, who is on her tiptoes, searching the faces. When she sees Hera, she raises her hand and starts to make her way across to her.

'What's going on?' asks Hera.

Klymene's hand rests on her forearm, a gentle restraint. 'Apollo has been in a furious temper – someone drove off the herd of cattle he keeps, and he couldn't find them anywhere. But he has the culprit, and he's brought him here.'

Hera makes a face. 'What does he want with a cattle thief? Couldn't he deal with him there and then?'

Klymene hesitates. 'He's the son of Maia.'

'Atlas' daughter?' Hera recalls.

Klymene nods. 'My granddaughter.'

'Well, have the cattle been restored? Does Apollo still want punishment?'

'No.' Klymene draws a breath. 'The thief's name is Hermes – and he says that Zeus is his father.'

The sinking sensation in Hera's stomach is all too familiar. 'Does Zeus recognise his claim?'

She can see the reluctance on Klymene's face, but the goddess nods.

Hera sighs. 'Maia keeps to the woods and the caves of Mount Cyllene, is that right?'

'She never ventures away from them.' Klymene's words tumble over one another in her eagerness to explain. 'Hermes says how worried she was when he disappeared – he was only born a few days before, but he was a baby like no other. Except Artemis, I suppose. He snuck out, unnoticed, and found Apollo's herd that he takes such pride in.'

Hera rolls her eyes.

'It was mischief,' Klymene says, 'that made him take them. Apollo was raging, but when he found them and was prepared to take revenge on the thief, Hermes showed him an invention – the lyre, he calls it. He cut the head and limbs from a tortoise and scooped out its innards—'

'But why?'

'To make an instrument – he stretched ox hide across it and strings of sheep gut – an ingenious device, and it makes the most beautiful music. Apollo was enchanted by it, of course. So he took it in recompense for the trick, and he brought Hermes back to Zeus.' She looks at Hera, her face open and pleading.

'So Maia has never said a word about Zeus . . . visiting her?'

Klymene shakes her head.

'She hasn't boasted?'

'She never would. We'd never have known anything about it, if it weren't for Hermes' trickery.'

'And is Zeus impressed by that?'

'He is.'

Hera nods grimly. 'Another Olympian?'

Klymene doesn't need to answer.

In the corner of the courtyard where they stand, the wind whistles over the low wall, ruffling their dresses.

'I gave him two daughters,' Hera says, 'and he denied each of them a throne. What should have been theirs was given to Apollo and Artemis. Only one throne remains, and if Hermes takes it, then there will be no other chance.'

Klymene waits. She doesn't argue her granddaughter's case, but Hera knows what the goddess has lost and how she grieves for it.

'You've been a faithful handmaiden,' Hera says. 'And friend.' She pauses. 'Maia will be left alone – I won't harm her.' She can see how relief floods Klymene's face, softening her shoulders and lifting the corners of her mouth. 'I suppose there's nothing I can do about Hermes now?'

'It's his destiny to be a great name,' Klymene says. 'Famed for his trickery and slyness. I can feel it.'

Hera's time is consumed with surveillance. Listening for the rumours carried on the wind from the House of Pheme, taking reports from Iris, pacing from end to end across the earth herself. Ekhidna is her unlikely ally, still surfacing from her caverns to help Hera where she can, her appetite for revenge on Zeus unabated. It's Ekhidna who tells her about Zeus' next victim – a nymph called Io, who he's transformed into a golden-horned heifer to keep her hidden from Hera. Ekhidna, with her knowledge of Gaia's more terrible creations, suggests that she sends Argus, a hundred-eyed giant, to kill the animal on Hera's behalf. Hera has a better idea. She steals the cow, and spirits it away under the protection of Argus so that Zeus can't find her. She'll enjoy his frustration.

How Hermes manages it, she'll never know, but somehow, he tracks down Io and her monstrous guardian, and he slays the giant.

Hera returns, gloating, to the shock of bloodstained earth and the body of Argus. She stares at the scene, not able to move until the horrified silence is broken by the scratching of a bird in the dirt nearby. He ducks his head, strutting past her, and then he stops where Argus lies and stretches his neck upwards. His deep blue feathers gleam in the sunlight, shimmering into green and back to blue again as the light catches them. As he opens his beak to give a great caw that echoes between the trees, the crest on his head quivers. Fastening his beady black eye curiously on to Hera, he fans out a huge tail behind him, extending his iridescent feathers in a great semicircle around him.

Hera presses her lips together. She won't let the giant lie here, forgotten by the world.

She kneels beside his body, and the bird comes closer, drawn by an invisible command. Hera closes her eyes, letting her mind quieten, the bird's sleek neck bowed under her fingers as she calls on Gaia, on the long-lost Rhea, on every goddess of the forests and the living world to help her.

If they hear her, she doesn't know. But a calm strength imbues her body, and one by one, she fastens each of Argus' hundred dead eyes to a feather in the bird's tail. When she's done, she loosens her hold, and the animal wakes from her spell. He folds his tail back down, and lets it spring open again, and now the giant's blue gaze is held in the magnificent display, preserved forever.

'You'll be the sacred bird of Hera now,' she tells him.

His glorious feathers sway in the breeze, his eyes uncomprehending as he struts away again.

She buries Argus on the hillside, and waits for the next time.

She hears about Semele on a crisp afternoon, with the tang of autumn fresh in the air. The advent of Persephone's descent lies ahead, and Demeter will bring about another winter, but before then, she'll oversee the bounteous harvest she granted through the warm months of spring and summer. For that glorious span, Persephone dance in the meadows and lies laughing in pools of sunlight, breathing in the fragrance of the blooms that burst in profusion beneath her feet wherever she walks. Soon, the fresh bloom of her skin will blanch again, a pallid grey leeching away the colour and draining the light from her eyes in the dreary gloom of her marital home. She will sit, cold and powerful, on her ash throne, overseeing the drifting shades, her subjects.

If Hera walks this dusty track when the seasons turn again, she'll see the offerings left at the crossroads. A flame will flicker in a small bowl, its meagre light sporadically illuminating what the mortals have left, breathless and anxious, before they flee in the encroaching twilight. A hunk of bread, glistening with honey. Chunks of blood-smeared meat. Wine. The trees will exhale a lingering breath of damp decay, and Demeter will retreat back into her sorrow. It will be Hecate who waits here for Persephone, who will reach out to take her hand, the bronze key at her belt ready to unlock the gateway between the worlds and deliver the dark king's wife to him.

But today, the low sunlight slants across the fields and

through the tall spears of the cypresses, and the scent of woodsmoke hangs delicious in the air as Hera strolls.

She comes to the banks of a wide river, fringed by plane trees, the clear waters shallow and sparkling as they lap on the stones at the edge. Further along it narrows, flowing into a dark gorge underground, but here it is broad and beautiful.

She barely notices its beauty, so preoccupied is she with the tide of melancholy that rises within her. She's heard from Iris that the plague that Ekhidna had spread across the island of Aegina, wiping out almost its entire mortal population, has been reversed by Zeus. He turned the ants of the island into humans to replace those lost, and as Aegina's son had survived, so the mortal progeny of Zeus still has a kingdom to rule over. Zeus didn't seem aware that she'd had a hand in the obliteration of the others – mortals die all the time, it's what defines them, and it didn't disturb his equanimity at all. If she harasses them again, though, he might suspect her involvement, and so another of her plans has dissolved before her eyes. At times like this, it feels that her losses stack up within her until she is nothing else. Just a yawning void, empty and desolate. It can be easier to take an animal form, to let the simplicity of animal urges soothe the turmoil in her mind. When she comes back to herself, she will remember she is a queen. A daughter of Cronus. Wife of Zeus. More powerful than anyone except for him, and feared across the world.

She chooses a low, flat rock and, shimmering from her goddess shape to that of a lioness, lies across it. She stretches luxuriously, flexing her paws, noticing the satisfying sharpness of each claw curving from the soft pads, before she folds them beneath her furred muzzle. So it is as a lioness that she hears the nymphs. They swim upriver, dallying by the rock where she is sprawled, so intent upon their gossip that they don't even notice her. The lilt of their chatter is pleasant, and she lets it wash over her as her eyelids grow heavy, until a familiar name makes her prick up her ears.

'She says it's Zeus who comes to visit her . . .'

'. . . disguised as an ordinary man . . .'

'. . . she believes him.' There's a trill of laughter.

'It could be true, though. Think of her mother.'

Hera strains forward, willing them to be more specific.

'But Semele isn't a goddess.'

She knows the name, unusually for her. There are very few mortals Hera could identify, but Semele is one of them. Her mother is Harmonia – and Harmonia is the daughter of Aphrodite and Ares. Hera has never given her eldest son's child much thought. Just as Demeter kept Kore hidden on Sicily, so Aphrodite and Ares chose to keep their daughter away from the other gods. Besides, Harmonia was wed to Cadmus, a mortal man, so surrendered any right to live on Mount Olympus with her divine family. She and her husband founded the city of Thebes, and Hera had forgotten that she even knew the names of their children until now. Semele is one of them, and a princess of Thebes – and, if the nymphs are right, the latest paramour of Zeus.

'She swears it's him, boasts about how wonderful he is . . . but . . .' The nymphs burst into laughter again, and Hera wishes she could shrug it off as blithely as they do. In this form, the urge bubbles up almost irresistibly, to run to Thebes on these fast, muscular legs and tear the girl's flesh from her bones. Her mouth waters.

She slinks down from the rock, tail swishing behind her

as she creeps into the undergrowth. There is no way she will reveal herself to gossiping nymphs, no chance she will give credence to the rumours they spread by showing her anger, although she'd love to watch them quake as they realise who has overheard their impudent musings.

She swathes her chariot in a thick cloud to hide it from view as she resumes her goddess shape and soars upwards. Not to Thebes; she won't be impulsive about this. She has to think.

Later that night, as Zeus slumbers, she rises from his bed in the pale glimmer of moonlight and sits on the low sill overlooking the world spread out beneath them. She casts a brief glance back to check that Zeus remains oblivious, and then, wrapping herself in another gauzy cloud, she slips into the dim skies. She swoops out of the misty veil as a hawk, gliding down past the slopes of the mountain, her yellow eyes fixed on the distant city of Thebes.

The palace of Cadmus and Harmonia is as somnolent as the palace of the gods, though it feels to Hera like a flimsy, insubstantial thing. She could collapse the solid stone walls with a single breath. If she strode through these dark, cramped halls as a goddess, the floors would shake beneath her feet and her voice would echo like thunder. But she wears the shape of an old, mortal woman – a detestable weakness, a body so feeble and ineffectual she can hardly stand it. She longs for the trusty strength of her lioness guise, her wide jaws and powerful legs, her speed and ferocity. Or the sleek precision of the hawk body, honed and ruthless as it dives towards its prey. Instead, she must shuffle, must peer through clouded eyes as she makes her way through this mortal home. The earthen

floor is covered with reeds woven into matting, the air thick
with an animal smell and the roof low above her head. She
imagines that this is the grandest dwelling of which mortals
can conceive, but she wonders how Harmonia can bear it.
Clumsy frescoes decorate the walls, illuminated by the leaping
flames of the torches set beside them; nothing like the grace
and elegance of Olympian artistry.

At this hour, the only people awake are slaves, their backs
bent with their relentless labour, and whenever Hera passes
one, they barely even lift their eyes to her. They have no idea
who walks the passageways of their palace, no awareness that
she has blessed them with her divine presence. They only continue with their toil.

Hera listens, filtering out the quiet noises of crackling fires
and weary footsteps, searching for a particular sound. She
moves towards the heart of the palace, beyond the paltry
throne room to the chambers of the royal family, and she hears
it. Behind a heavy wooden door, a beating pulse – young and
strong and vital – with another fluttering beat laid underneath
it. A second heart within the same body. And she reaches for
the iron handle, and swings the door open.

Semele is awake, perched on her windowsill, looking out
towards the moon. For a moment, Hera feels dizzied by the
image of herself doing the same; an unfamiliar pull towards
this young woman tugging in her chest. A moment later, the
fury explodes behind it. She imagines her bragging in these
rooms, in the courtyard outside, by the river that wound flat
beneath her as she flew here, a silver mirror in the night. This
woman, comparing herself to the goddess Hera, boasting of
her husband's attentions.

She lets the door close behind her.

Semele, startled, looks around. 'Oh, Beroe,' she says, her shoulders relaxing. 'It's you.'

It's the name of her aged nurse, the old woman Hera has disguised herself as. 'You should be sleeping, child,' she says, infusing her tone with feigned tenderness.

Semele smiles, a wistful light in her wide eyes. The falling moonbeams gleam on her loose hair, her bare arms, giving her an ethereal lustre.

'I can't,' Semele says, and her hand drops to her stomach.

The draping material across her torso has concealed its rounded shape, but as she strokes the top of the protruding bump so tenderly, Hera sees it clearly. 'Is it the baby?' she asks. Her voice cracks on the words, but maybe Semele attributes it to her age. 'Is anything wrong?'

She laughs. 'No, nothing's wrong. He's lively, that's all.'

Hera draws closer, her every step across the floor deliberate and measured. She can't betray herself, can't let her anger lend force to her movement in case she brings the palace down on all their heads. And that's not her plan. She has something else in mind. 'A son,' she croons, reaching out her wrinkled hand to stroke Semele's swollen belly. Her skin is warm through the fine wool – fine to her, at least, though it feels coarse to a goddess accustomed to Athena's weaving. Under her fingers, she feels the child move as if unsettled by her touch. Only a layer of mortal flesh shields him from her.

She withdraws her hand.

'What else would Zeus give me?' Semele says. 'A strong son, fit for the Thunderer.'

She's so smug and silly, cradling her stomach and picturing her child in the arms of a god. 'So you say,' Hera rasps. 'You say the father is Zeus. And I believe you, of course,' she hastens to add as Semele's eyes widen. 'I believe that *you* believe him, anyway. But many a young man tells stories to a girl, to get what he wants from her.'

Semele sits up straight, opening her mouth to protest, but Hera is too quick.

'If you don't think people will say you've been fooled, seduced by an ordinary man pretending to be the king of the gods, you've got no sense.'

'But my mother—'

'Your mother might be willing to believe. She knows of Zeus' . . . habits, after all. But I'm not talking about her.' Hera watches her closely, sees how she stiffens at the oblique reference to Zeus' other conquests. 'Still, what do you care for gossip when you know yourself what the truth is?'

'I do.' The dreamy cast to her expression has dissolved now, and her tone is icy. But Hera can see the hurt stamped across her face. This girl is almost too easy to read. Zeus must have found it easier than plucking an apple from its bough.

She laces her fingers through Semele's, squeezing them gently. Very gently. 'I've been your nurse all your life,' she says softly. 'I know how sweet you are. You wouldn't dream of the awful, poisonous things people talk about. It would never enter your pretty head.'

Semele frowns. 'I'm about to be a mother,' she says. 'You might still think of me as a child, but—'

'Do you think he loves you?' Hera says.

'Of course.'

'I'm old.' Hera sighs. 'And I've seen many a girl believe a man when he says he loves her.'

'He does! You don't know – you don't know what he's like when he comes to me.'

JENNIFER SAINT

'I can't imagine it,' Hera says. 'A god, in all his glory. I can't even picture what his chariot must look like. How he must blaze with divine fire and the light of the heavens!'

'Well . . . no,' says Semele. 'He doesn't come in his chariot. He comes in secrecy, of course.'

Hera pulls her hand away. 'Like a normal man?'

'In disguise! He has to be concealed.'

Hera shakes her head sorrowfully. 'So you've never seen him as he truly is? The way that he comes to the goddess Hera's bed? He's never shown himself to you like that?'

Tears are brimming in the girl's eyes and she dashes them away furiously. 'You're twisting everything!'

'I'm sorry,' Hera says, assuming a doleful expression. 'I don't mean to upset you. But listen, it's easy enough to remedy.'

'What do you mean? What do I need to remedy?'

'Just ask him to show you what he really is,' Hera suggests. 'If he loves you so dearly, tell him to swear to grant you one request – he'll agree, I'm sure.'

'He'd grant me anything,' Semele says, her voice stubborn.

'Make him swear by the river Styx. One request. When he does, tell him you want to see his true divine radiance. Why shouldn't you see him as Hera does? And then come back and tell me what a stupid old woman I am to doubt his story.'

Semele tosses back her hair. 'You *are* a stupid old woman. But I will. Just so that you can never say anything like this to me again.'

'Try to sleep now,' says Hera. 'You should rest.'

Semele lifts her face to the dome of the heavens. 'I will.' But she carries on gazing, rapt, at the star-scattered sky.

She's a simple girl, Hera thinks as she shuffles out, eager to be herself again. Maybe that's what Zeus likes – her

260

uncomplicated adoration. It unsettles her more than she'd like, that he's treated this one so differently to the others. That he's come back to her, again and again, with seductive words. She can't believe that he's developed some sort of real affection for a mortal woman.

Whatever it is, this situation is a novelty to him, and he always likes that. It's swiftly dealt with, now that Hera has satisfied her curiosity. She slips out of the palace and takes to the air, her brown feathered wings spread wide.

Zeus never knows that she was gone. When he next visits Semele, she repeats the foolish words that Hera gave her and, bound by the oath he recklessly swears to her, he has no choice. He stands before her and shrugs away the mortal skin that made him bearable to her eyes. When Semele sees the Zeus that Hera sees – his unearthly radiance, his immortal splendour – she is burned to ashes where she sits. Lightning strikes the ground, and when Semele's parents come upon the scene, they find that the fire cannot be extinguished. It burns on while they weep, and they make the patch of flaming earth a sacred shrine to their beloved daughter.

21

It plagues Hera's mind that she only discovered Semele by chance – who knows how many more there are, and where? The not knowing drives her to madness. It makes her recall the frenzy of Typhon's venom; the abyss that opened up below her to the very beginning of the world, and how she hadn't known what was real and what was not. Zeus might be pursuing a desperate nymph to the ends of the earth; he might be crooning sweet words into a mortal princess's ears and making her believe that he loves her. He might be descending with fire and fury, or he might be playing the lover, the seducer. He takes what he wants, by force or deception, by brutality or charm, and she doesn't ever know why he chooses one or the other. All she knows is that he leaves a trail of broken women in his wake, and she is the most broken of them all.

It makes her dangerous, and he knows it. It's why he toys with her then hides from her, threatens and cajoles her in an endless dance, and neither of them ever seem to gain any ground. He has his victories, but she can wound him too. She made him destroy Semele; he knows she's always there, ready to poison his pleasures.

Only sometimes she worries that she just makes it sweeter for him. That the thrill is heightened for him, if he must sneak and plot and occasionally lose. She's trapped in this unhappy game, and he keeps choosing to throw the dice.

'I should have slaughtered Io before she ever got her shape back,' Hera says to Ekhidna, in a cave behind a waterfall, a secret place where no god will see them meet. 'I let her go, to breed more mortal women like her, and Zeus won't leave them alone.'

'There's another, then?' Ekhidna's boredom is evident.

'A girl, Danae,' Hera says. 'A granddaughter, or great-granddaughter of Io ... who can keep track of mortal generations?'

The serpent-goddess remains indifferent. Hera has chosen the wrong ally to confide in. She can't tell Ekhidna that she feels a twinge of pity for this girl – pity for a mortal, she can hardly believe it.

'Semele bragged, she was impious,' Hera says. 'But Danae, she's trapped in a tower, locked up by her father. She can't escape Zeus.' She sighs. 'Besides, there are so many of them. If I punish them all, I'd do nothing else.' She categorises them now in her head. Asteria was the bravest; she managed to elude him altogether at the cost of her own life. Semele has been the worst – delighted by his attentions and eager to brag about them. Leto was a risk, her children destined to be powerful. Maia stayed silent and hidden; it isn't her fault that Hermes was born so precocious and enraging, and besides, by the time Hera knew anything of her, it was too late. Danae is only a frail mortal girl; there's no danger she'll give birth to another god. Hera could be kind, and let her live.

'Did you summon me here to talk about Zeus' women?' Ekhidna asks.

Hera shakes her head. Her mind moves on swiftly from Danae, and on to the issue that's of more concern. 'No. It's something else. There's talk of an unknown god, living on the slopes of Mount Nysa. How can that be?'

'I've heard no such rumours.'

'You have been busy,' Hera says, acid in her tone. 'The prayers have come in great multitudes recently – plagues, diseases, foul water where fresh springs have always flowed before. Mortals dying all over the place.'

'And doesn't it heap more offerings on all of your altars?' Ekhidna points out.

'It does,' says Hera. 'The more desperate they become, the greater the sacrifices. But if you kill them all, then all you do is swell the ranks of Hades, and what's left for us?'

'I dwelt for aeons in the pit of the earth,' Ekhidna says. 'Now I have my freedom. What did Gaia create me for, if not this?'

'The other gods will tire of it,' Hera warns her. 'And besides – I need you to help me keep watch.'

'Who can this new god be, then?' Ekhidna says.

'He has a great talent for making wine – the grapevines of Nysa have always been famed, and suddenly there are reports of a wine sweeter and more delicious than any that's been tasted before. The mortals are making it too; where could they learn such skill if not from a powerful god?'

Ekhidna uncoils her tail; and the scent of rotting salt and stagnant marshes breathes into the air. 'I can poison the streams on Mount Nysa so that when these wine-making mortals collect the water for mixing, they'll die. What's a god without worshippers?'

'Maybe,' says Hera. 'But maybe he'll just move on some-where else. And I want to know . . . I *have* to know . . .'

There is no pity in Ekhidna. Hera's glad of it, usually. The sympathy she gets from Hestia or Klymene irritates her some-times. She doesn't want anyone to feel sorry for her; she wants solutions. But she's starting to suspect that Ekhidna isn't so interested in providing those, either. The viper-goddess has her own agenda; she always has. Only there is a restlessness about her now, a taste for destruction.

Hera wonders if she should tell her about the flowers she gathered from Typhon's volcano. The poison she pressed from their leaves, that she keeps safe in a jar in her chamber, untouched. It would be foolish to trust her, but sometimes she yearns to say Typhon's name to the only other being who remembers him like she does.

'All you want is to outwit Zeus,' Ekhidna says flatly. 'With his nymphs, his girls, his bastard god-children.'

Hera looks at her in surprise. 'And what do you want? To pollute rivers and poison mortals? I thought you hated Zeus too.'

'Because he's a danger,' Ekhidna says. 'To me. To all my children.'

The ache she always feels when she thinks of them. She's been so careful never to ask Ekhidna anything about them. If she doesn't know where they are, she can't be responsible for leading Zeus or any other god to them. They'd slay them as ruthlessly and thoughtlessly as Hermes slew Argus, and she won't be the cause of it.

'But the more mortals there are, crowding the earth,' Ekhidna goes on, 'the fewer places there are for them to hide. The greater the chance of men taking up arms against them, trying to win the favour of the gods by murdering their enemies.' Antagonism flares in her eyes. 'There's more at stake than your marriage. Why would I care for your injured pride? Why would I carry on risking myself so you can hunt down whoever Zeus sleeps with next?'

Hera goes cold. It takes a moment for anger to seep into her bones, hardening them. 'Perhaps we can't be of help to each other anymore.'

'No,' agrees Ekhidna, the old, unmistakeable contempt infusing the word. 'Not anymore.'

And with a flip of her coiling tail, she dives into the waterfall and is gone.

For once, Hera is relieved to be back on Mount Olympus. The familiar gold and marble floors, brightly frescoed walls and soft torchlight feel comforting after that confrontation. The serpent-queen's words echo in her mind: the icy hiss, the impertinence and, worse, the truth.

Once, Hera dreamed of overthrowing her husband. Now she lurks and spies in the hopes of denying him one girl in twenty. It's petty. It's beneath her. And yet it consumes her.

In her chamber, she snatches up the little glass bottle and contemplates the livid green liquid within. What has she kept it for, all this time? If she doesn't have the courage to use it, she might as well dash it from her windowsill on to the rocky slopes below.

The door crashes open, and Hera closes her fist around the bottle, burying it in the folds of her skirt.

Zeus is buoyant, the atmosphere around him crackling with energy, a triumphant smile splitting his face.

Her stomach sinks with dread.

'Come on,' he says to her, extending his hand. 'I have something to show you.'

She tucks the bottle securely into the wide knotted belt at her waist, and follows him.

The hillside is pretty, thickly wooded with pines that give way to long grass waving in the breeze, fragrant with the honeyed scent trailing from the night-blooming flowers under the violet skies. It would be so peaceful, were it not for the raucous sounds echoing from the forest – shouts of laughter and song, the rattling of cymbals and the heavy thud of drums.

The gods, arrayed behind Zeus, look doubtful.

'What have you brought us all here for?' asks Aphrodite.

'Follow me,' he replies, and leads them between the trees.

The noise gets louder, and Hera grows more apprehensive. It's Zeus' jubilance that unnerves her. She can see that Aphrodite is enjoying it, her eyes shining in the moonlight and her lips parted in a smile, a flower she's plucked on the way tucked behind one ear. Ares walks a pace behind her, a grimly devoted shadow. Demeter is relaxed, at home in the woods and in the fresh mountain air. Poseidon, summoned from the waves, grins at his brother in anticipation of some amusing pleasure ahead. Zeus has even called Artemis to join them, and she saunters between the gnarled trunks at Apollo's side. His lyre hangs carelessly from his hand like the bow does from hers, his hair artfully rumpled while hers is tousled from running in the wind. The two of them move with a loose elegance, graceful mirrors of one another. Even Hestia has been drawn from the hearth-fire, wiping her sooty fingers on her skirt as Hermes chatters away to her.

'Behold!' Zeus declares, and he sweeps his arm through the air.

The trees give way to a clearing, splashed in silver light. There's a circle of rocks, garlanded in ivy, on which are perched nymphs and bearded goat-legged men. At the centre, rising to his feet at the entrance of the Olympians, stands a god Hera has never seen before. He's slight and pretty, with a sweetness in his face that is somehow familiar. He has an open, eager smile; his hair falls to his shoulders in wild waves and, like the others in the clearing, he holds a drinking horn, which he swings towards them in exuberance. 'Welcome,' he calls out, and wine spills from the mouth of the horn in a ruby spatter across the earth.

'My son,' Zeus says, turning to the assembled gods with a smirk. 'His mother burned to death before she could give birth to him. I snatched him up from her ashes and kept him safe within my body until he was ready to be born.' He's talking to them all, but he never looks away from Hera. 'He is twice-born: once as a feeble mortal child, and then again as the splendid god Dionysus.'

It's only because his self-satisfaction is so unbearable to Hera that she's able to hold herself in check. Above all else, she refuses to give him the reaction he craves. While her mind is whirring beneath the surface, she keeps her face calm – even slightly bored.

'Come, sit, drink with me,' urges Dionysus, and the gods need no more invitation. They're so curious, so eager for this diversion.

'Once you've tasted the wine of Dionysus, you'll never want to drink any other,' Zeus brags.

Dionysus shrugs. 'It's true,' he says.

Hera keeps a smile on her face as he talks about the grape-vines of Mount Nysa and how they ripen beneath the sun, sweet and juicy and incomparable. He inclines his head to Demeter in gratitude, thanking her for blessing them, and Hera can see that she's charmed. Zeus swells with pride in his son, though Hera doesn't know how much of it is paternal delight and how much is his enjoyment of her discomfort. His eyes keep returning to her, that infernal smirk hovering on his lips. However much she tries to hide it, he knows how she burns while he parades another son before her and the other gods – and one, she realises with a bitter dart of agony, that she has made more powerful. If she had never interfered with Semele, Dionysus would never have been reborn an immortal.

Aphrodite leans in closer, her eyes lingering on the new god. Hermes rests his chin on his hands, apparently rapt. Hestia takes a cup of wine, squeezing Hera's arm briefly as she sits beside her, a small gesture of sympathy with the anger she knows the queen is suppressing, her palm soft and warm on Hera's bare skin. But even so, she can't hide her curiosity.

Dionysus keeps the wine flowing, and the gods keep drinking. It's smooth and rich, sweetened with nectar, and the more he mixes, the funnier his stories become. Even Ares loosens his rigid posture, and his habitual belligerence seems funny too, rather than aggressive. Athena leaves before long, bidding them goodbye before she flutters off as a grey owl, bored of the growing incoherence of her fellow gods as they keep drinking. Hera finds herself draining cup after cup, hoping that the wine's sweetness will soothe the sting of Dionysus' presence.

But it maddens her more and more. Her restraint loosens, her tight grip on her emotions faltering, and the wound pulses red and raw with every sip she takes.

Dionysus, ever more energetic and joyous, gestures vigorously and his drinking horn tumbles out of his grip. Wine flows in a vivid stream, dripping on to the grass, and Hera scoops up the vessel with a smile before he can catch it.

'I'll pour you some more,' she says, reaching for the wide jug by his feet. She pours the wine, swirls in water and nectar and then, surreptitiously, she slips the tiny bottle out from where it's tucked beneath her belt. No one sees how deft she is, how quickly she moves. With Athena gone, no one else is paying attention. Handing the horn back to Dionysus, she watches him tip his head back as he drinks.

No one seems to notice the lapse in decorum, even though Hera has never poured a drink for any one of them before. They're all enjoying themselves too much.

The goat-legged satyrs are singing, one of them beating the drum again in a relentless, snaking rhythm. Their chorus is rough and raucous, nothing like Apollo's refined, melodic voice, but the god of music cheers for them anyway. A nymph drapes her arms around his neck, pulling him to his feet, and they start to dance. Hera, still seated, is suddenly aware of bare skin as the gods begin to whirl in drunken circles. Dresses slip down over shoulders, skirts are hitched up and legs flash in the half-light. Dizzy, she looks from one side of the grove to the other, and sees hair tumbling loose, Poseidon's lascivious smile, Ares and Aphrodite slipping away between two pine trees and vanishing into the shadows. Smoke streams from the fire, the flames writhing to the insistent pulse of the music, and everything happens in flashes. Artemis with her back to the gods; Apollo staggering out of the circle; Artemis pushing him aside. He crashes to the ground, rolling over on the earth, his limbs tangling together with his dancing partner's, his usual grace abandoned. Artemis dips her head to another nymph's face; they're almost touching, and the wind turns, blowing the smoke right into Hera's eyes. She waves it away. She can't see Demeter. Dionysus lifts his drinking horn into the sky, and the rich scent of wine rolls towards her, sweet and over-powering. The dancing figures, silhouetted against trees and torches, swing around and collide as the music gets faster and the chaos intensifies. Poseidon's fingers dig into female flesh, twisting and tugging, his teeth and eyes glinting in the light as the moon emerges from behind a wispy cloud, illuminating Zeus in the very centre of the clearing, surrounded by nymphs.

'Come,' says Hestia in her ear.

Hera lets her sister pull her to her feet and draw her away from the clearing, into the cool of the surrounding woods. She hears giggles, rustling leaves and snapping branches in the dark, but Hestia leads her on. She glances back once, through a gap in the trees. She can't make out the difference now between intertwining figures, melding bodies, the dance and the ecstasy.

The goddesses walk back through the forest, into the chill of the dying night. Above, the sky is fading to misty grey and the stars are disappearing. 'It's almost over,' Hera says, and Hestia nods. Hera thinks her sister is sympathetic, misunderstanding her words, thinking she refers to the frenzy they've left behind.

But Hera is thinking about Dionysus, and what she's done to him.

Hestia stumbles on a root, and Hera catches her. 'Too much wine,' she says.

'Dionysus' wine' – Hera lowers her voice in a passable imitation of Zeus – 'is not like any other.'

Hestia flings back her head and laughs, far more than the

joke deserves. Her merriment infects Hera, already a little giddy over her victory with the poison, and she laughs too, until they're clutching each other's arms, making fun of the amorous siblings they've left behind them.

Together, they make their way tipsily down the hillside, talking until the sky is ablaze with fiery pink and amber light.

Hestia, recovering herself, tries to turn the conversation back to something more serious. 'You don't seem to mind too much about Dionysus,' she says.

Hera tosses her head. 'What good would it do?' She tries to keep the glee out of her voice. She knows that Dionysus no longer presents a problem, but Hestia doesn't.

'Really?'

'What, are you so sceptical?' Hera laughs.

'You aren't worried? You don't think Zeus might make him an Olympian?'

'What throne could he have?' Hera stops dead for a moment. 'You think he'd give him Hephaestus' throne?' The effects of the wine are wearing off and, as she sobers up, a familiar doleful gloom is stealing into her happiness, casting shadows in her head again. 'He would. I know he would. Replace my son with one that another woman gave to him – a mortal woman, at that.' *It's probably what he's planning; the most grotesque insult so far. But*, she tells herself, *he won't get the chance.* 'Do you think Hephaestus will come back?' she surprises herself by asking.

Hestia thinks about it. 'I feel him sometimes, in the fire,' she says. 'Mine is a domestic flame, and his much more ferocious – but I can feel the echo of it burning. And I know how much he loves it. How happy he is in that forge, in the heat and the intensity, turning out his creations with no one to criticise or mock him.'

Hera is taken aback. 'Really?'

'We're connected,' says Hestia.

'Everyone's connected to you,' says Hera. 'You're the centre of us all.' The lingering trace of wine in her blood is making her quite sentimental. 'But you think he'll stay there, then? Never come back to Olympus?'

'I don't know,' says Hestia. 'He might fear Zeus' anger too much. Or maybe it's he who's angry. I'm not sure.'

Hera can't imagine Hephaestus angry. But then, it's been so long since she saw him. She doesn't know who he might be now; how his time in his volcanic workshop might have changed him.

'You could go to him,' suggests Hestia.

'Zeus won't allow it.'

'Is that all that's stopping you?' Hestia scoffs. 'You could steal away any time you liked. You do, at all hours.'

Hera frowns. 'He meant it, more than any other threat,' she says. 'Sneaking away, interfering with his plans – that's one thing. Open defiance is another matter.' She looks at Hestia. 'You don't believe me.'

'Should I?'

Hera doesn't answer. There is something else – a discomfort, a reluctance to face her son again. She's the reason for the exile he's suffered. And maybe before that too – it nags at her, just a little. She never loved him. Ares didn't care, but Hera fears now that she wounded Hephaestus long before Zeus did.

'Let's sit,' says Hestia, tugging at her cloak to pull her down on to the grass.

The meadow stretches around them, dewdrops twinkling like crystals on flower petals, a tiny burning centre in each reflecting the incandescent sunrise. Hera is grateful that Hestia

273

doesn't push her to talk any more about Hephaestus. The peace and stillness between them feels like something sacred; a precious calm that floods her body, a silent communion with her sister. They don't talk any more, both of them held in the moment, until gradually they relax into the welcoming cushion of the soft grass, and both of them fall asleep.

The noise blasts right by her ears; a rude intrusion into her slumber. Hera startles awake, confused by the sound that she can't immediately place. She sits up on her elbows, looking from side to side, and sees that Hestia has jumped to her feet and lifted her arms to the sky, her face alight with something Hera hasn't seen in her since the days of the Titan war.

The source of the noise is quickly apparent; a donkey lumbers past the goddesses, letting out another long, low bray. Hera squints in the bright sunlight at the distant shape fleeing in precipitate haste down the meadow: a lurching male figure in a peaked cap. A rustic god or satyr perhaps, she can't tell from the outline of his back, dark against the sunshine. She's surprised by a low ache in her skull, the lingering effect of so much wine, and she's slower to gather her wits than normal.

Hestia shouts after the figure, and Hera winces. Satisfied he's gone, Hestia flops back down on the grass beside her.

'Priapus.' It's so rare to hear Hestia snap, her usual serenity disturbed. 'Thankfully that donkey brayed just in time to wake me up before he could put his hands on me.'

Hera wrinkles her nose. 'The vegetable god?'

'He was sneaking up on me while we slept.'

Hera shades her eyes and peers in the direction of Priapus. 'He regrets it now, I'd say.'

'He'd regret it more if he'd got any closer.'

'What a fool.' Creeping up on two goddesses that are under Zeus' protection – Hestia, thanks to the oath he swore to keep her untouchable, and Hera, bound by the marriage vows he neglects. She can imagine the wildness of his fury if he found another god had tried to take what's his.

Hestia's calm is returning. 'That wine of Dionysus has a lot to answer for.'

Hera feels a little thrill rippling through her. It should have worked by now. The fresh air is clearing her mind, enlivening her again, and she's eager to get back to Mount Olympus.

'A reminder not to stray too far from the hearth,' Hera says, extending her hand to her sister and helping her up.

Hestia doesn't answer. She's preoccupied all the way back up the mountain, covering the ascent in swift strides.

Only Demeter is back from the night before.

'Where are the others?' Hera asks. 'Still on Mount Nysa?'

'Probably.' Demeter doesn't elaborate.

Hera tries to effect a casual tone. 'And do you think – when they return – that Dionysus will come with them?'

'I doubt it. Some kind of madness overtook him.' Demeter lifts her palms in apparent mystification. Hera is fairly sure it's feigned. 'He leapt up, clutching his head, screaming, and he ran before anyone could stop him.'

Hera widens her eyes. 'How strange.'

'Very,' Demeter replies drily.

Since Persephone's abduction, it's been clear that Demeter's loyalties don't lie with Mount Olympus anymore. She wouldn't care enough now to accuse Hera, or try to take her to task, or go to Zeus with any complaint. There is a hardness to her now, where once she was soft and bountiful. She shrugs and moves on, back to her fields and gardens and the nymphs that tend to them.

Hera allows herself a moment of silent exultation. Somewhere, Dionysus will be running still, trying to escape the swarming frenzy in his head. The burning red agony of madness; the torment he cannot escape, no matter where he goes. It will boil like acid inside his skull.

Hera remembers what it was like, and the visions she saw when a few drops of Typhon's blood mixed with her own. Last night, she poured his venom directly into Dionysus' wine; the poison that kills mortals and drives gods to insanity. She hopes he flees to the very ends of the earth to try to get away from the horror inside himself. She hopes he never finds his way back again.

And Zeus will understand that while he might disrespect her and humiliate her, lie and deceive and torment her, threaten her and command her obedience, she will never stop fighting back. And he will never be able to defeat her, even if he spends eternity trying.

Even if she destroys herself in the process, she will never let him win.

PART FOUR

So let that noble wife of Zeus dance, beating her foot in its shoe; for now has she worked her heart's desire . . . Who would pray to such a goddess?

Euripides, *Heracles*, translated by
E. P. Coleridge, 1938

Haste, leave the skies, fulfil thy stern desire,
Burst all her gates, and wrap her walls in fire!
Let Priam bleed! if yet you thirst for more,
Bleed all his sons, and Ilion float with gore:
To boundless vengeance the wide realm be given,
Till vast destruction glut the queen of heaven!

Homer's Iliad, translated by
Alexander Pope, 1717

22

One god can't undo what another has done.

So Zeus can't cure Dionysus' madness, any more than he can prove it was caused by Hera.

'Will you search for him?' asks Athena, when the gods gather in council.

'Any son of mine,' Zeus answers, 'can prove himself without my help.'

The glance he gives Hera across the table almost looks admiring.

'A wandering god might cause trouble, though,' Athena points out.

'Hephaestus has been in exile for a long time,' Demeter says. 'And he's caused no problems.'

'Leave them both be,' Zeus says. 'They're of no consequence here. No one should look for them. If they never return, so be it. Only the strongest gods deserve a seat here.'

Hera shifts under his gaze. It's almost as though she's impressed him with her persecution of Dionysus, although he could just as easily have been furious. He might change his mind again, at any moment. She doesn't mention the nymphs encircling him in the grove of Dionysus; he doesn't say outright that he knows what she did to his son. There is an unsteady peace between them, one that could be shattered without warning.

She won't disturb it, for the time being. She's already decided to let the mortal girl Danae alone, even when she bears Zeus a son, Perseus. She's shaken a little when the boy grows up to murder the Gorgon Medusa. Ekhidna's parting words come back to her, the warning she hissed about mortal men hunting down monsters to win the favour of the gods.

But Perseus comes back to the city of Argos, a pale and colourless king who makes offerings at the feet of the great statue of Hera, showing her proper reverence.

'Zeus has so many mortal children,' she muses to Hestia, 'and they aren't so very impressive, even if they call themselves heroes. If they honour me as Perseus has done, perhaps I can leave them alone.' *Unless he shows an inclination to seek out more monsters.*

'Demeter tells me that Dionysus has recovered,' Hestia says. 'His madness passed, eventually.'

'But he hasn't come back.'

'He travels among mortals,' Hestia says. 'Building his following, luring them with wine.'

'So long as he stays among them,' Hera says. 'He can do as he likes.'

Spurred on by her new-found tolerance, she even arranges a marriage for one of Zeus' other mortal sons, a king of Crete named Minos. She gives him the Titan Pasiphae, daughter of the sun-god Helios: another wedding attended by immortals and humans alike. If Zeus' children are to be mortal kings, they can be satisfied with their tiny realms and stay well away from her domain. She'll be strategic with her punishments. Zeus is pleased with the marriage, smiling down on the sun-splashed island where he had grown from infancy in the shadow of Mount Dicte, a boy-god learning to fight and rule.

Perhaps Zeus is lulled into complacency by her indifference towards Perseus and Minos, because as he beckons to Hebe to pour him more wine, he starts to talk with grandiosity about another son that's to be born to him. 'A son of the House of Perseus,' he brags, 'destined to be King of Mycenae.'

'He'll be born tomorrow?' Aphrodite enquires, taking a long sip of wine.

'He will.'

The mortal cities are spreading like wildfire. The gods are choosing their favoured ones, and Hera is sure that Zeus doesn't mention Mycenae by chance.

'You love the city, don't you?' Zeus says to her. 'Mycenae, Argos . . . what's the other one, Sparta?'

She's loath to admit the interest she's taken in human settlements. Mycenae and Argos lie at equal distances from her beloved sanctuary, a place so devoted to her worship that she can't resist it. But in Sparta, she loves to watch the warlike girls who train to fight each other like boys. When she sees them, glowing with victory, wielding the spears they learn to hurl in combat, sporting their bruises and scars with pride, they remind her of herself when she was a young goddess, ready to bring down the Titan rulers of the world. When she stalked the battlefield with her own spear, drenched in golden blood. It's a world away from the sedate, matronly role she plays now. She's annoyed that Zeus has noticed, and hopes he hasn't seen her silently exulting in their wrestling matches, gleeful at their snarls and the crunch of fist on bone, remembering the days that are so far behind her. It would be a violation, if he were to glimpse that side of her, the one she locked away and left behind on a lonely beach at the edge of the world. A piece of herself she never gave to him, that she wishes he would forget ever existed so it can belong to her alone.

'Hera?'

She is startled back to the conversation, forgetting the kicked-up dust in the Spartan arenas, coming back to the luxurious surroundings of the palace. 'So what you're saying is that the new King of Mycenae, part of the family of Perseus, will be born tomorrow?' she repeats.

Zeus nods.

'Are you so sure?'

'Of course.'

'Swear it, then.'

Surely he won't fall for this again, she thinks, but he's so puffed up in his own arrogance that he can't veer away from the trap she lays in front of him.

'By the waters of the Styx,' he declares, 'it will be so.'

As if he has any idea about childbirth. He's so pleased to find a way to taunt her before the other gods about his new son, that he forgets this is her domain and not his.

He pontificates more, about the hero this boy is destined to be. Hera had already decided to tell Eileithyia to hold the mother back, like she did to Leto, just to prove him wrong. She *was* intending to leave his mortal children alone. But the more Zeus talks, the more insulted she feels.

'I kept her husband at bay,' Zeus goes on. 'Delaying him on his travels and extending the night so that I could come to her in his shape. She never suspected that I wasn't him, until I lifted the cloak of darkness and allowed him to return. When he greeted her, she was confused, insisting that he'd been with her for hours already.' His smile is lascivious, lingering on the memory.

Hera glances through the columns to the courtyard, keeping an eye out for Eileithyia.

'Men all want to be heroes now,' Zeus says. 'They want to defeat the monsters that are a scourge on the earth. But none will be greater than my son.'

'What monsters?' Hera snaps back to attention.

Zeus waves a hand. 'Creatures like the Gorgon.'

Hera frowns. 'Medusa wasn't a scourge, though. She hid herself in a cave so that she wouldn't harm anyone after Athena transformed her.'

Athena looks over to them, unabashed at Hera's slightly pointed remark. 'That doesn't matter,' she interjects from the other end of the hall. 'If Perseus tells it differently – if he tells them how ferocious she was, how terrible – then that's what they will remember about her. See how he's held up now among them – all the brave, young men of the world will want to make their names in the same way.'

'The oracle foretold it,' Zeus says. 'My son will be the greatest monster-killer there has ever been. Perseus' achievements will fade to nothing in comparison.'

This elicits the reaction he was hoping for, at last. Hera can feel the colour draining from her face, and the wine goblet she holds trembles in her hand.

Zeus looks pleased at her agitation. 'What's wrong?' he asks.

'Nothing,' she says, setting down the goblet with care.

'Nothing at all. I'm simply eager for tomorrow, to see this great king born.'

Eileithyia does as she asks. Alcmene might scream and pray as much as she likes, but her baby is stuck fast. Meanwhile, Hera directs her daughter to another woman of Mycenae. Her son is still safe within the womb, only in his seventh month, but Hera is adamant.

'He's another child of the House of Perseus,' she says to Eileithyia. 'If he's born here today, he'll be the king that Zeus promised.'

And so the baby Eurystheus is delivered instead of Zeus' son. He's tiny and fragile, but he's blessed by the queen of the gods, and so he lives. Eileithyia doesn't release her hold on Alcmene until the sun rises on the next day, when it's too late.

Zeus sends his thunderbolt streaking through the skies, shaking the heavens. But his oath is binding; his son will not be king.

The first few months of the baby's life pass by, and Hera plans her next move.

'Alcmene has changed the infant's name to Heracles,' Eileithyia reports back to Hera.

Heracles. *The Glory of Hera*. 'Why?' she asks.

'She knows that it was Zeus who deceived her. She must hope to win your favour – especially after the birth took so long. She probably suspects that punishment came from you. She wants to appease you.'

Hera snorts. She's tying her golden sandals around her calves, ready to run to Mycenae. 'She should throw the baby into the sea, if she hopes to appease me.'

Eileithyia raises an eyebrow. 'I thought you only wanted him to be born late, to deprive him of the throne.'

That was to prove Zeus a fool in front of all the others for his bragging. Now, she has to deal with the problem of the child. She can't allow the prophesied monster-slayer to grow to adulthood.

She wonders if she should find Ekhidna and warn her. But the memory of their last meeting sparks her anger again. She'll stop Heracles alone.

Outside the city, she scours the ground for snakes. She doesn't have to wait long before one uncoils across the path, heavy and thick, a sinuous diamond pattern glittering on its scales in the moonlight. Its cold eyes meet hers, its black tongue flickering in and out as she reaches out with her mind, into the confines of its triangular skull. She has taken this form before; she knows what it feels like. The cold blood flowing around its body, the precision of its reptilian focus on its prey. She breathes a mist into its brain, a vision of a baby in its crib, helpless in sleep. *In the palace,* she whispers silently, and the snake moves as she directs it to move, hypnotised by her command.

She sees another, and although one serpent is enough against a human child, she decides not to take any chances.

These two will dispatch the son of Zeus. The son that, unlike Dionysus, is not protected by his father's ichor. She won't give him a chance to grow strong enough to set about hunting down monsters. The mother, Alcmene, can have more children – ones that belong to her own husband. She'd probably prefer that anyway, Hera thinks, if she really is as devoted to him as they say.

Back in her own chamber on Mount Olympus, Hera

watches and waits. Spirals of smoke drift towards her, each one carrying prayers that she lets wash over her. The teeming mass of mortals on the earth below are mostly as anonymous to her as they have ever been, but she notices now that mortal names are more readily on the gods' lips, more frequently a topic of discussion and gossip in their gold and marble palace.

Hera thinks it's undignified. Gods arguing about mortals, bestowing their affections on them, caring about their inevitable deaths. Mortals exist to worship the gods, that's how she's always regarded them. But bit by bit, some of their lives are weaving their way into her consciousness. Look at her now, sitting on the stone sill, casting her eyes down to Mycenae to see that her snakes reach the infant Heracles. She was careful to ensure that Zeus saw her in the megaron before she made her way here to watch in peace. He won't be able to prove this was her doing.

No screams shatter the air of the Mycenaean palace. *Never mind,* thinks Hera. *No one has discovered him yet.* But when Eos brings the radiant dawn and the city wakes from its slumber, still no outcry reaches the heavens. Hera expected to hear laments, howls of grief and misery, desperate entreaties to Mount Olympus to undo this tragedy. They always call for that, the grieving mothers; they always beg for the return of their little ones. As though the Olympians could pluck a soul from Hades, as though they could descend into his dark kingdom and take what belongs to him. The gods can't even call back the mortals they themselves love. The king of the dead has no mercy. But it seems there is no quashing of mortal hopes. They keep praying, even in the face of divine indifference.

There's a sound at the doorway, and Hera looks up expecting Klymene.

It's Zeus, black-browed and bearded, his shoulders filling the width of the archway into her chamber.

'What is it?' she asks, anticipating that he's heard of the baby's death, even if she hasn't.

'My son Heracles has slain his first monsters,' Zeus says.

'What?'

'Two snakes attacked him in his crib last night. When his nurse went in this morning, he was sitting upright with one strangled in each of his fists.'

Hera recalls the weight and the power of the snakes, and her mouth hangs open. 'He *strangled* them?'

'Choked the life right out of them,' Zeus confirms. 'The Mycenaeans are proclaiming it a miraculous feat – the first of many.'

She should have stayed to observe, to intervene – but how could she have foreseen this? Zeus' other mortal sons aren't so special. Kings maybe, but not inhumanly strong. No human baby is capable of strangling a snake; why this one?

Zeus saunters away, pleased to have delivered the news. She's sure he knows where the snakes came from; why else would he come and tell her personally how her strategy failed?

'I'll find another way,' she says to Klymene later, as the goddess braids her hair. She won't be beaten by a mortal; it can't be allowed. 'Though I don't understand how he survived the snakes.'

Klymene is brisk and deft, both as she shapes the braids around Hera's head, and in the advice she offers. 'You've already made him famous,' she points out. 'He bears your name, he's defeated your snakes – anything else you do will only bolster his reputation.'

'Is that what you see?' Hera asks.

'He's still a baby,' Klymene says, 'but I know he's destined for greatness.'

'I can't stop the workings of the Fates,' Hera says. 'Whatever they've determined, that's what will be. But if it's destined that everyone will know his name, it doesn't have to be for great things.'

'You've let other children of Zeus be,' Klymene says. Her voice is gentle. 'This child's parents know you are angry; let them make offerings to you to make up for the insult.'

'I'll think on it,' says Hera.

What she thinks on is how she'll take a more effective revenge next time. She bides her time, a brief interval for her that in mortal years allows Heracles to grow to manhood. He takes a wife and she bears him children. His strength is already legendary; he's admired across mortal lands for the breadth of his shoulders and the bulging muscles of his arms and chest, but he hasn't yet become the hero Zeus spoke of so confidently.

Hera has noticed the time when, still in his youth, Heracles flung a lyre at his music teacher with enough force to kill the man. A fit of pique, an accidental death – it wasn't intended, everyone knows, but it gives her an idea.

Dionysus has still not tried to return to Mount Olympus. The madness she inflicted on him has done its job; even though he shook off the frenzy after a while, the memory of it has kept him away.

A similar strategy might work with Heracles, she decides. He proved himself too strong when he killed her serpents, so it won't be his body that she attacks.

The prospect of it lifts her spirits. With Zeus so relentlessly grinding her down – alternately boasting about his victims and deceiving her, always reminding her that she cannot leave but it will be torture to stay – she needs something to occupy herself with, something that reminds her of how powerful she is. Zeus needs her too. They're both the children of Cronus. Their status together is greater than it is apart. But if she sees an opportunity to hurt him, she'll take it.

She had to poison Dionysus to bring about his frenzy, but a mortal mind is something she can twist and snap between her fingers. She can send him a vision, wrap him in a cloud and make him believe he sees whatever she guides him to see, or blind him entirely so that he lashes out in panic. What form his madness will take, she has yet to decide. Something that will ruin his reputation, bring about his downfall in the eyes of men. He may be famous, as Klymene said, but Hera will transform fame into notoriety. She'll spread his name across the world, to be hated by all who hear it.

She ponders for a while, and when she decides, it's Iris that she summons.

The rainbow-goddess listens attentively to her instructions, and nods when she understands the plan.

'Fetch Lyssa,' Hera tells her. 'My first thought was to inflict the frenzy myself, but Zeus knows I've already tried to attack his son. No god knows the workings of Lyssa's mind, nor why she chooses to send her madness to one or another mortal.'

'I'll go to the palace of Nyx,' Iris says. 'I'll find Lyssa there, and give her your decree.'

'Go with her,' Hera says. 'Make sure she does it; don't let her falter. And say nothing to anyone of this.'

Iris nods. She won't disobey a direct command from the queen of the gods. Hera trusts she'll keep her silence. With that, she is gone, in a whirl of colour, to the black halls beyond Oceanus where Nyx dwells with her ferocious daughters. She'll find Lyssa there, stalking the shadows. The great Titaness of Night has birthed sweeter children – the Hesperides of the Evening; Hypnos, who brings soothing sleep; Eros, who infused the world with passion before Aphrodite came forth from the bloody seas and took his place – but their siblings are crueller, horrors of the dark, who slip through the gloom to spread torment. Oizys, spirit of misery and suffering; Nemesis, who keeps her victims awake in the night, seething with envy and bitter hatred; Eris, who scatters strife and discord; and, of course, Lyssa, the goddess of rage and madness.

Let Lyssa be the one to bring about Heracles' ruin, Hera decides. He can't defeat a goddess by squeezing her neck like he did the snakes. This time, she won't underestimate her foe. She can sit back on Mount Olympus, her eyes round with innocence, while he is destroyed.

And when it's done, no god will be able to undo it.

23

Let him unleash the violence he already holds inside him.

It's so simple, it cannot fail.

This Heracles, even if he's named for her, is a son of Zeus. A powerful one, not some ineffectual little king beneath her notice. And so she knows that within his vicious soul, like his father, he'll contain the key to his own destruction.

He'll follow in the footsteps of Zeus and Poseidon. He's everything they are, but he's mortal. He'll kill her monsters without pity, never caring that they come from Gaia, that they have more right to live than he does. What are men, but creations of Zeus that should never have existed?

That violence, that instinct towards death and destruction, is what she'll use against him.

Lyssa knows better than to defy Hera. She follows the command conveyed to her by Iris. Hera's choice of revenge is more powerful than flinging a thunderbolt at his house, or summoning a mighty wave to crash down upon him. One touch from Lyssa has him panting like a wild bull, foam flecking his cheeks like a maddened dog, his eyes rolling in terror.

Hera doesn't see it for herself, but she hears that his rage is a thing to behold. He rampages through his house in search of his victims, swinging his club with merciless violence.

When it's over, the broken bodies of his wife and children lie in the ruins of their home. The soft light of morning clears the mist from his eyes, and he sees what he has done.

'Did you tell Lyssa exactly what I told you?' Hera asks Iris, keeping her voice low. The lamentations from Thebes, where Heracles lived with his family, have reached Olympus, and the wails ring from the marble walls.

'I did,' says Iris. 'I told her to summon the anger in his heart to the forefront of his mind; to strip away his inhibitions and give way to the darkest desires that lay within him.'

Hera nods. 'At first, I thought to send him a hallucination. I thought I could make him attack the king perhaps, imagining him an enemy or a monster of some sort that he could defeat. But it was simpler to do it this way – to let Lyssa unleash the violence he harboured within himself. I thought it would be a rival, some man who had slighted him, or that he resented for whatever reason.' She pauses. As the goddess of wives, she would prefer it if it had been that way, rather than the man slaughtering his own family.

Iris shrugs. 'They were the nearest.'

'Perhaps I should have sent her by day.' Hera sighs.

Iris looks at her, curious. She doesn't dare ask her queen if she feels regret.

If he is truly like Zeus, Hera tells herself, *they might be better off dead than belonging to him.* Her existence is bearable because she is a goddess. A mortal woman, married to a man in Zeus' image? Hera can almost tell herself it's a kindness. *He wouldn't have done it if the desire hadn't been in him already. All Lyssa did was bring it to the surface.*

And if she still suspects it might have been an injustice, she only has to think of the clutch of monsters she loved like a mother long ago. The monsters that Heracles is destined to kill, if she doesn't break him first.

Better his children than mine.

Zeus is grim-faced. 'Hermes, take my son to Apollo at Delphi,' he orders as he strides through the courtyard, and Hermes takes flight, his winged sandals fluttering as he obeys the command with haste.

'Apollo?' Hera asks, and Zeus stops, spinning around to face her, the threat of thunder in his scowl.

'I told him to take Delphi as his own,' he tells her. 'Phoibe surrendered the oracle to him – it's better that it's an Olympian delivering our prophecies through her than a Titan.'

'And will the oracle dictate how your murderous son should be punished for his crimes?' Hera asks.

'He will be cleansed!' Zeus' voice crashes across the mountain summit, loosening rocks and making them tumble down the slopes. He pauses and gathers control of himself. 'The oracle will tell him how he can purify himself from the stain of his family's blood – now that Delphi itself is cleansed of any foul presences.'

'Phoibe?' Hera is shocked.

'No, not her.' Zeus has calmed, his rage blown out as quickly as a passing storm. 'There was a snake-nymph in the caves there – an unspeakable thing, infecting the waters with slime and disease. Apollo pierced her with his arrow and left the corpse in the sun to rot under Helios' glare.'

Hera feels the blow before she comprehends his words.

It robs her of breath. She'd warned Ekhidna that the gods might tire of her killing mortals in such great swathes, and she sees with bitter clarity that of course it would be Apollo who tired of it first. He loves to bring plagues – to fire an invisible arrow into a tribe of mortals who sicken and die, begging for his mercy. Sometimes he heals them, sometimes not. Just as he's claimed the oracle as his own, so he has claimed disease.

Zeus notices her distress. 'What is it?' he asks. 'The creature – is it one of yours?'

Hera collects herself. 'Of course not,' she says. 'I have nothing to do with monsters now.' She's fiercely glad of her victory over Heracles. She's glad to have saved Ekhidna's children, hidden in the wild, lawless lands where giants live – the kind of places that brash, bold heroes might have a taste for exploring and conquering since Perseus brought back the Gorgon's head. How much can a human woman and her children matter in a world teeming with them, compared to these few solitary creatures left of their race – magnificent, unique and all that remains now of Typhon and Ekhidna? 'But what purification can redeem Heracles?' she asks. 'Who will take him back, into their towns, into their homes, knowing what he's done?'

'The oracle will guide him,' Zeus says. 'His fate can't be changed.'

Hera lets it go. Heracles will be remembered as a murderer, not a hero. Let Zeus realise that in his own time.

Hera stands on the stone path that leads to the shrine at Delphi. The low evening light slants through the mountains, and Hera can see why Apollo, who loves the sun, likes it here. The peace, the wildness, the golden light that's always so pleasing. She sees how Zeus is ousting what remains of the old order; already, the mortals praise Apollo as a sun-god alongside Helios. Artemis, so cold and elusive, is replacing Selene in some prayers as a goddess of the moon. The mightiest and most ancient of the Titans are retreating from their spheres, and here, in the very centre of the world, it could not be more evident that the Olympians reign supreme. The archer-god assuming control of the oracle, the source of knowledge and wisdom and foretelling of the future that once belonged to Phoibe, to Themis before her, and to Gaia first of all, reaffirms Zeus' desire to stamp Olympian power across the world.

She sees Heracles, stooped and shaken, making his way to the shrine, and she shimmers into a bird shape – not the ostentatious peacock she created with the eyes of Argus, nor the sleek hawk whose form she so loves, but instead the grey owl preferred by Athena. She perches on the gnarled branch of an olive tree, deliberately unremarkable. When Heracles is done here, he can walk right past her and never dream she's so close.

It's Apollo she's waiting for, and when at last he strolls by, leaving his priestess to convey his decree to Heracles, she jumps down lightly, herself again.

'What will his punishment be?' she asks, without niceties.

Apollo tosses his sleek hair out of his eyes, a smile playing at his lips. He keeps walking, and she falls into step alongside him. 'That's for Zeus to know, and to share as he deems necessary.'

He's so lofty, so impudent, so sure of himself. Hera has never loathed him more.

They make a beautiful picture, walking side by side through the fragrant air, the dark green spears of the cypress trees growing fresh and verdant along the gently rolling slopes around them. Hera's embroidered dress swishes around her ankles, her arms are smooth and bare, and her hair tumbles loose beneath her glinting crown. Apollo is louche and dazzling, his beauty feline and dangerous, sleek as a mountain lion.

'The man killed his wife,' Hera says. 'It's my business to know.'

Apollo gazes meditatively towards the horizon, and Hera bites back her impatience. 'The prophecies about him can't be defied,' he says. 'He's destined for a greatness never seen before in the mortal world.'

'Maybe the promise of that greatness is too much for a mortal to bear,' Hera suggests. 'Maybe that's what drove him to murder his own children.'

'That won't stand in his way,' Apollo says.

'He can't be forgiven for it,' Hera protests. 'Slaying his own blood, his kin – it can't be forgotten by other mortals. They'll shun him, cast him out.' *They won't worship him as a hero when he's broken their laws like this.*

'Not for his whole life,' says Apollo. 'He'll do penance for it.'

'What penance?'

'He'll be a slave to King Eurystheus,' Apollo tells her. Finally, she has it. 'He'll carry out whatever tasks the king decides to set him. When he completes the tenth, he will be cleansed. And he'll have his freedom.'

Hera considers it. She's pleased by the inclusion of Eurystheus – the boy whose birth she arranged to precede that of Heracles, so that the throne Zeus had promised to his son would go to him instead. 'That's acceptable,' she says. There's nothing so demeaning to a man who believes his destiny is to be a hero than to have to serve as a slave instead. She's denied him his birthright, orchestrated his tragedy, and now the ensuing penance is sure to break whatever spirit he has left. Not to mention humiliating him in the eyes of the world. Her pride is restored, and her monsters will be safe.

Apollo looks amused. Hera doesn't let it needle her. She's come out as the winner here, whatever he thinks he knows about the future.

Briskly, she sweeps herself back into the air, a hawk this time, and the winds bear her aloft back towards Mount Olympus. She doesn't trouble herself to say goodbye.

It never lasts for long. As soon as she finds a way to triumph, Zeus will find another way to insult her. At the palace there awaits a horrible surprise, for Zeus has been on his wanderings from Olympus as well. Soaring over the lovely city of Troy, his eagle eyes alighted on a beautiful young man out hunting with his father and his dogs. The unfortunate youth was so absorbed in the hunt, holding his javelin aloft, ready to spear the stags that fled before him in the shadow of Mount Ida, that he didn't notice when the sun was blotted out above him, when the eagle's claws reached out and fastened themselves in the tender flesh of his arms and bore him into the sky. His father cried out, his dogs barked in panic, but Ganymede was already a tiny figure in the clouds, and his beloved city shrank to nothing beneath him as he screamed for mercy.

By the time Hera returns, Ganymede is ensconced in the palace. Never, since Ixion, has Zeus brought a mortal into their home.

'He was too beautiful to leave on earth,' is all he says, as though it's explanation enough.

Hera stares at the young man, who doesn't shrivel into cinders at the sight of her. His eyes stay wide with fear as he gapes at the terrifying majesty of the palace of the gods. With a shaking hand, he pours nectar from a jug into Zeus' cup and says nothing.

'Mortal beauty doesn't last,' she says. A hideous thought seizes her; will he stop even the pretence of secrecy now, and bring all his victims here? She never thought she would be grateful for his deceptions, for his trickery, but then she'd never contemplated he would parade them right in front of her.

It seems Zeus has already thought about Ganymede ageing, of his skin drooping and wrinkling and his thick hair becoming patchy and grey. He's decided it can't be allowed, and so he has granted the boy immortality and condemned him to an eternity in the heavens. It's why he can look the gods in the face without burning to ash.

Hera can almost feel sorry for him, a trapped plaything of Zeus. She can't bear the sight of him hovering behind her husband whenever the gods gather to feast, pouring nectar or wine into his cup. Hebe still pours for the other gods, but Ganymede is there to serve Zeus alone.

Hera takes to her temples, staying away from the heavens as much as she can. She decides to observe the enslavement of Heracles, coming to the palace of Tiryns to see what labours Eurystheus will set for him. She's horrified to see him returning to the king with a lion's hide slung around his shoulders, the beast's face frozen in a snarl more ferocious than any other lion that has ever prowled across the earth before.

'The Nemean Lion!' she hears the awed onlookers gasping,

and she knows with a sickening lurch that it is the lion born to Ekhidna: the youngest son of Typhon.

Eurystheus is just as displeased as she is to see the return of the hero. 'No weapons could pierce its skin,' he complains. 'How was this done?'

And Heracles tells him how he strangled the animal, just as he had the snakes that Hera had sent him, and then used its own claws to tear the skin from its flesh. She grinds her teeth together to hear it. She'd imagined the labours that Eurystheus would devise for Heracles would be ones that disgraced him, not elevated him. This has only given him a chance to demonstrate his strength and his bravery.

And the lion is dead, nothing more than a trophy for this loathsome man. Hera had reconciled herself long ago to the knowledge that she'd never see Ekhidna's brood again. That they were safer without her, that they could thrive better if she left them alone. She had taken comfort in the knowledge they were out there, all the same.

'Don't try to intervene,' someone whispers in her ear and she jumps back, startled.

Zeus is standing beside her, wrapped in the same mist that conceals her from mortal eyes.

'What – what do you mean?' she asks.

'You've had your chance against Heracles,' Zeus says. 'Now let him succeed or fail alone.'

A host of outraged responses rise up inside her like bile, but she holds them back, settling on, 'He won't need my help to fail.'

Zeus scoffs. 'He'll prove you wrong.' The laughter dies in his throat, and his eyes darken, his mood changing like lightning again. 'But make sure you don't interfere.'

'He's had a good start,' Hera acknowledges. 'But Eurystheus won't make the mistake of giving him such a task again. He'll find something Heracles can't do.' She has faith that the mortal king won't want to be shown up – she'll wager that he will want to expose whatever weakness Heracles has, whatever will make Eurystheus shine in comparison to this hulking brute of a slave he's been given.

She overestimates him. Eurystheus sends Heracles after the Hydra, while Hera seethes at both his stupidity and the fact that he has chosen another of Typhon and Ekhidna's children as the target. But Zeus watches her so closely, she is powerless to intervene.

The Hydra hisses and spits in the warm, green waters of the volcanic lake where Heracles confronts her. Her nine heads, each grown to monstrous size, sway on their long necks, weaving back and forth, and nine sets of jaws snap and bite at him every time he comes close. He's sweating, his lion-skin cape flung on the shoreline, flattening the waving sprigs of lavender, and he narrows his eyes at the beast while he swings his sword.

Hera perches on a rock at the edge of the cave where the Hydra looms from the waters, Zeus right behind her. Her fingers dig tightly into the stone, grinding it to dust where she grips it.

Heracles lurches forwards, splashing in the shallows, and his bronze blade slices through one of the Hydra's muscular necks. But to his disbelief, and Hera's joy, the ragged wound pulses and contorts, and in the place where the severed head once was, two more sprout forth – each one more ferocious than before. The maddened Hydra swipes at Heracles, and he dodges. Again and again, he lunges, his feet slipping on the wet rock, the two of them locked in a deadly dance. He evades the curved blades of her teeth, but each time he manages to cut off one head, the same thing happens.

Hera is delighted, ready to tell Zeus she was right after all – and it only took two labours for Heracles' inadequacy to be proven. Typhon and Ekhidna's daughter now boasts multiple deadly heads and Heracles is only making things worse for himself. But before she can gloat, Heracles scrambles back towards a ledge and shouts to the friend who awaits anxiously on the shoreline.

'How can he help?' Hera says with a snort, but the man is following Heracles' instructions and lighting a fire on the bank. Heracles wades across the lake to grab a flaming branch, then, wielding it in one hand, he makes his way back to the Hydra. His sword glitters in the sunlight, and Hera sees it drop through its arc towards one of the Hydra's flailing necks with painful slowness, as though time is crawling to a halt. The head is severed; it falls into the lake. As the stump begins to throb, Heracles presses the burning torch to the wound.

The stench of burning snake-flesh fills the cave, and Hera presses her hand to her mouth. All of them – Zeus, Hera, Heracles and his friend – stare at the charred, bubbling stump of the Hydra's neck. Nothing happens.

From then, it is inevitable. One by one, Heracles cuts off her heads and burns her necks before more can grow, until none are left.

Even when Eurystheus announces that the labour cannot count as one of the ten that Heracles must complete – he had help, it was his friend Iolaus who set the fire and handed him the burning branches, and he must succeed alone – it is of scant comfort to Hera.

She remembers Ekhidna in her cave, surrounded by her infant monsters, and it grieves her deeply to think that two have now met their end through Heracles. That their lives only matter for the glory they bring a hero; their ignominious deaths collected as proof of his power.

Heracles' labours continue: a succession of beasts and monsters subdued, slain, captured, and Hera cannot intervene.

'He's making more of a name for himself every time,' Hera laments to Hestia.

'He could still fail,' Hestia says.

'But if he doesn't,' Hera says, 'I need something else. I can't have all the gods thinking this mortal has beaten me.'

'His name means "glory of Hera",' Hestia reminds her. 'Everything he does is in your honour.'

Hera makes a face. 'I don't want it.' *Not from a son of Zeus. Not from a monster-killer.*

'Then pick your own hero,' Hestia suggests. 'Find a mortal and give him your blessing; send him on quests equal to those of Heracles, and let your champion drown out his successes.'

Hera pauses for a moment. 'That isn't a bad idea.'

She starts to pay closer attention to the mortal world, looking for the kind of man she could choose as a rival to Heracles. There's no shortage of candidates eager for the kind of renown Heracles is building. Never mind the horrors of his past; never mind the tragedy he leaves in his wake. A man who slays monsters will know an echo of what it means to be a god, to be worshipped and feared in almost equal measure.

She can't bear the swaggerers, the arrogant men who drink and brawl like Heracles but with none of the fearlessness that marks him out. She finds it dispiriting, looking down from the wide windows of Mount Olympus, searching for a man who is good enough to represent her.

The clamour of grief that rises at once from Argos pulls her attention away from would-be heroes. It's the sudden, startling sound of a hundred prayers borne to the heavens, desperate and distraught. All of them imploring her by name.

She hears entreaties from women every day, but never such a collective keening of anguish, never such mass despair and sorrow.

Dionysus, the Argive women call over and over again. *He demanded our worship, he cursed us with madness, he killed our children.*

The pain. So much pain. It's almost magnificent in its scale. She could feel admiration for Dionysus in evoking a devastation so vast and wide-spreading, but . . . these are her worshippers calling out to her. They are all wives, destroyed mothers, crying out for her protection. For her vengeance.

There are some cities, she knows, that resist the worship of Dionysus, and Argos is one of them. It's amused her to see those that hold out against him, those who fear the seduction of his intoxicating cult. Those who don't want their women to run wild alongside him in the forests. Dionysus can punish them for insolence, of course, that's his right – but to attack the wives? The women that belong to Hera? These women are the virtuous ones who have held fast to their responsibilities. They're the ones who haven't shunned the sacred bond of marriage to join his maenads, the ones who pray to her and turn steadfastly away from him – just as they should.

He cursed us with madness. It makes it worse. He's used her weapon against them – he's inflicted a madness upon them, just as she did to him. It couldn't be a more pointed insult to her, and it's this that she hears as clearly and audibly as their suffering.

These are prayers she won't ignore. This torrent of outraged grief and horror is no ordinary disaster inflicted by the gods – it isn't Poseidon shaking the earth or Zeus hurling his thunderbolt, it's no famine from Demeter nor plague sent by Apollo – this attack is directed at Hera, the queen of the gods, as much as any mortal woman.

She is swift in her descent to the city walls. Dionysus is on the plain below, looking just as he did in the forest – young and beautiful – but with a cruelty in his smile that she doesn't remember.

Perhaps he's learned now what it takes to be an Olympian god.

He was an irritant to her before. Now he burns with divine rage at an entire city, demanding that they bow down to him, and Hera sees an opponent. Not just a potential threat or an annoyance, but an enemy.

For the first time, she decides, she will join a mortal war. She lifts the mist around her, looking him full in the face as she reveals herself, standing alongside the Argives. Allying herself with the city of Perseus, against Dionysus, for anyone to see.

When it's over, she stays in her great temple close to the city. It's so peaceful in the sanctuary, so calm and quiet after the skirmish. Her statue towers over the women who come to her, who come to pour libations to her and weep in the dim shadows for all they have lost. Somewhere, Dionysus is mourning too, not a victor any more than Hera is. Zeus sent Hermes to end the battle before she could rout him, but not before Dionysus' mortal bride was felled by Perseus. There is no winner, only broken women and grieving gods. Hera waits for the familiar black bitterness to poison her insides, for the frustration to gnaw at her soul, but perhaps the soothing balm of the evening air and the hushed grief of the women is keeping it at bay. Above her, the stars glimmer in the inky sky.

Her thoughts, for once, are not on revenge. The other gods have all lingered in the mortal realm far more than she ever has. To find herself on the frontline of a human war is a novelty, and somehow she can't bring herself to leave them in the aftermath. She's here in her temple, still listening to the women who whisper their thanks to her. She came to them, even if she couldn't restore what they had lost. She can't change what happened to them, and Hera has never cared about mortal tragedies enough to want to before. She would do it now, she thinks, and not just to spite Dionysus. In the gentle twilight, the shared sorrow of her worshippers moves her. She can't help them, but she is there. And she stays in the temple as night draws in, unseen but felt.

In the morning, she returns to Mount Olympus and climbs the steps to the palace, the snow-scattered slopes fading into the clouds behind her. Around her, all is quiet. The courtyards, the stables, the houses of the gods built around the central edifice – all of it shines white and gold and miraculous in the silence.

She enters through the imposing colonnade, making her way to the megaron, where she'll find the comfort of Hestia's hearth, of the living flame that will burn forever. But she catches sight of another figure, sitting in one of the twelve thrones that line the far end of the grand hall. She knows the shape of those rounded shoulders, that squat silhouette, bulging with the awkward strength that he's never known how to carry gracefully. She's surprised by the rush of gladness she feels. At last, he has found the courage to come home.

'Hephaestus,' she calls, and he looks up to meet her eye.

His face, previously so open and readable, is guarded now. There's a tightness to it, a wariness he didn't possess before. But he stands, and she notices how he leans heavily with one hand on the armrest of the throne he's just vacated.

'Does Zeus know you're here?' she asks.

'Not yet.' He sees her gaze hovering on his damaged leg. 'From the fall,' he says, gesturing to it. 'It shattered. Beyond even my ability to repair.'

There's a beautifully carved stick resting against the table. Silver-topped, the handle is engraved with animals caught in a chase – lions pursuing a herd of oxen, chased in turn by dogs and herdsmen – intricate and tiny, but so vivid with life that Hera imagines she can see them in motion.

'Have you come back to seek forgiveness? Or recompense? Or – why have you come back?'

He smiles, though it doesn't reach his eyes. 'I thought it was time.' He notices how her eyes linger on the carvings on his stick, and he speaks again. 'I brought you something.'

He gestures towards her throne, and she realises as he does so that it isn't her throne. It's been replaced, with one that's clearly his own work.

It's beautiful, polished gold like the others, but unmistakeably superior. He pulls it out from the line so that she can see the artwork on the arms and the sides, and she's wonderstruck by the detail. On each side, a peacock spreads its glorious tail:

perfectly cut pieces of blue glass inlaid on the gold, glittering in the light. The heads, carved with exquisite realism, rear up at the front, so she can rest a hand on each.

'So that everyone knows it belongs to you alone,' he says.

'It's glorious.' She means it. 'Did you make it in your forge, in the volcano?'

'And carried it here.' He gestures to it, indicating that she should sit.

'Thank you,' she says. 'Though perhaps you should have made a gift for Zeus. He's the one who was angry with you in the first place.'

'I have something for him too,' Hephaestus says, and something in his tone gives her a twinge of foreboding. It's accompanied with a little thrill of anticipation; perhaps his time in exile has toughened her son's character and made him ready to challenge his father at last.

She steps up to the throne, running her hand along the peacock's feathers. The gold is smooth and cold beneath her fingers, every join imperceptible to the touch, as though it's fused together by magic. 'You've got even better,' she says.

'I've had time to hone my skills,' he agrees. 'The things I've created – you should see them.'

'I will,' she says, suddenly eager. 'I will come to see them.' She's intrigued to discover what it's like inside a volcano, what treasures like this his workshop might hold.

'Maybe,' he says and she's not sure why he's doubtful. Perhaps he thinks she won't defy Zeus' authority, but she will. Zeus is bound to be interested himself, once he sees this creation. The gods love shiny objects, precious trinkets, anything that is the best of its kind.

Her son's eyes are intent upon her as she sits, sliding her

hands to the peacock heads and marvelling at the comfort and the grandeur. 'It's perfect,' she says.

The fetters spring from the armrests, smooth and oiled, clamping her wrists in place. At the same time, two slide out of the throne's legs and wrap themselves around her ankles. A fine mesh billows out, interlinked chains so thin they can hardly be seen, settling over her in a net so that even if she transforms to another shape, she won't be able to get out. She stares at her imprisoned limbs in disbelief, and then at Hephaestus. She thinks it's some kind of mistake, or a demonstration, until she sees the satisfaction in his smile: the first true one he's shown her since his arrival.

'What is this?' she gasps. She can't move her wrists or ankles at all. If she tries to stand, the throne will come with her, and she'll look absurd, ungainly, more ridiculous than he does. It's so stupid, and so utterly effective.

'You're the reason for this,' he tells her. He gestures at his leg, the useless one, and she's bewildered.

'Zeus did that,' she says.

'Because of you. You made me release you. You didn't care that he'd punish me. You persuaded me to do it, and you did nothing to help me.'

The words dry up in her throat. What he says is true. She did know that Zeus would be angry with Hephaestus, and she acquiesced to his demand that she stay away.

'I had no nectar, no ambrosia, nothing to heal my injuries,' he goes on. 'I lay there until I could pull myself up through the pain. When I realised no one else would come.'

She wants to point out that he's a god – not just any god, but a son of Zeus and Hera. What's wrong with being self-reliant? She always has been. She knew this about him when he was born, that he didn't have the temperament for Mount Olympus. That he didn't have it in him to scheme and fight and claw his way to power. Whatever the cost.

But now it does seem, unfortunately for her, that he might have learned at least a little. Still, she isn't afraid, not like she was when Zeus suspended her in chains. Hephaestus isn't cruel.

It's humiliating, though, to be held like this.

'I'm sorry,' she says. The apology feels strange in her mouth. It's certainly unconvincing. 'But see what you've achieved – the workshop you've built for yourself, the worship you enjoy from mortals. Even while banished from Olympus, you've become a powerful god.'

'I have.' He bridles. 'But no thanks to you.'

'You've earned your place here, without needing to do this,' Hera wheedles. She'd like to shout at him, let her voice ring from the marble pillars, order him to undo his fetters at once and not dare to lay his hands on the Queen of Olympus ever again. But she has the sense that hearing her plead is part of the motivation for him. If she gives him what he wants, it will be over more quickly. It weighs heavy in her heart to use the same strategy with her son as she has to with Zeus. But she's sure it will work.

And when it does, she can decide how she'll make him pay.

'You can impress Zeus with everything you've achieved,' she tells him. 'Rather than insulting me, his wife, like this. Surely you don't want to risk his wrath again.'

'I don't think he'll mind,' says Hephaestus. 'He might even enjoy it.'

She would fling him into a volcano herself, if only she

could get her hands free. To think she had ever pitied him. 'Why aren't you angry with *him*?' Her frustration boils over. 'I didn't help you, but he was the one to hurt you, not me.'

'Why did you attack Leto?' Hephaestus asks. 'Semele, Heracles, Dionysus and his bride? What about Io? You were angry with Zeus; why did you hurt them?'

She stares at him. 'It's not the same.'

He laughs, a harsh sound in the beautiful hall. 'You tricked me into freeing you once; you won't manage it again.' He's bent and misshapen, even more than before he was thrown from the heavens, but his hunched body looks to her now more like the curve of a flame than a broken god. Burning with the power Hestia had felt in him; a savage heat strong enough to melt iron. 'You'll have time enough to think about it,' he says. 'No one in the world can free you, except for me.'

And he walks away.

24

Hestia finds her first, coming back to the hearth. Hera calls to her, hoping that something in Hestia's affinity with fire will help. Her power is twinned with that of Hephaestus; maybe she can see some weakness in the metal restraints that will help release her sister. But the fetters are smooth and immovable, beyond Hestia's strength. Aphrodite, too, declares herself baffled – 'This mesh is so fine, even an ant couldn't crawl through!' – and although Ares yanks at the throne with all his power, trying to tear the whole thing apart, he can't even dent its shining surface. Demeter glances at it and shrugs, announcing that it looks impossible to her, and all Zeus can suggest is hurling his thunderbolt at it.

'That might destroy the chair,' Athena points out, 'but Hera with it.'

For the others, it's an amusing conundrum. None of them are trapped, so they can enjoy the absurdity of her predicament. It rouses them all to try – it appeals to every god's competitive spirit to want to prove themselves the best.

'Only Hephaestus can release me.' Hera sighs. 'Zeus, why

not send Hermes to him with an order from you that he must return and let me go at once.'

'Hermes!' Zeus cries. 'He's the god of trickery – surely he can devise a solution?'

But Hermes can't. He circles the throne, examining every inch, searching for the secret to the contraption – some hidden lever, a key, something that would release her. 'It's impossible,' he declares, and Hera rolls her eyes.

'Just summon Hephaestus,' she says.

Apollo agrees. 'I can't see any other way.'

He refuses to come. At this direct defiance of his authority, Zeus grows angry. The skies darken and thunder growls from the heavens, but Hephaestus doesn't care.

'If you bury him in Tartarus,' Hera says, 'I'll still be stuck. He knows you can't force him.'

'There are worse punishments than Tartarus,' Zeus snaps.

He might be referring to Prometheus, or perhaps the mortals that have been consigned to the pit – not just chained to the rock like the rebel Titans, but forced to endure torment for their offences to the gods. Ixion is there, still strapped to his burning wheel; Sisyphus, who cheated Hades, pushes a rock endlessly up a hill; Tantalus, who butchered his own son and tried to trick the gods into eating his flesh, is eternally dying of thirst. Does Zeus imagine something like this for his own son? Hera is truly afraid that Hephaestus would take the punishment rather than free her.

Her mind has been black with vengeful dreams, but now panic snakes in. What if he truly intends to leave her here forever?

'He's furious with me,' she tells Zeus. 'And maybe with you

too. He won't do it to please us. But the other gods – one of them might be able to convince him.'

'No one wants to risk going into his forge,' says Zeus. 'They don't want to find themselves chained up too.'

'Offer them something. A prize.' She thinks about Hephaestus, what he was like when he lived on Mount Olympus. He was always eager to please, always afraid of incurring anyone's displeasure. The opposite of his brother, Ares, who has never cared for anyone's feelings at all. Well, almost anyone. 'Tell them,' she says, 'that whoever brings Hephaestus up here and compels him to free me can marry Aphrodite.'

Zeus blinks. 'What?'

'Hephaestus was always scared of Ares. Give Ares a reason to threaten him, and really mean it.' She pauses. 'Aphrodite won't mind.' It's true that the goddess is fundamentally opposed to the whole idea of marriage, but she's never bothered to ask Zeus for protection against it like Hestia and Demeter have. She lives under Zeus and Hera's rule; she's lucky not to have been ordered to marry already. It's only because Hera has always approached her own role so half-heartedly that she hasn't been, and now it's time to remedy that. 'If she has to marry, she'll want it to be Ares, and he's the one that's going to be able to do this. She'll know he's the only one who could succeed.'

It's a rare moment of unity between the two of them. Hera supposes she should be grateful that Zeus isn't more entertained by her plight. He could have mocked her; she had expected he might. Hephaestus certainly thought he would. But perhaps Zeus is offended that another god has taken it upon himself to hurt her.

When Ares tries and fails to make Hephaestus release her,

despair begins to take hold of Hera's heart. The war-god might as well scream his threats and unleash his violence on the sheets of metal in his brother's forge. Hephaestus is as impervious to it all as his anvil would be.

Hera has brought down Titans; she has married her enemy and dedicated her life to poisoning his; she has birthed the greatest monster the world has ever seen; she has been the bane of mortals who have displeased her. A scourge of impudent gods and heroes alike, she is worshipped by scores of women who look to her to be a bastion of strength because she, too, has lived through what they have endured – she is a wife, a survivor and a queen. And this foolish trick is to be her downfall?

She wishes she had been the one to throw Hephaestus from Mount Olympus. She should have cast him out the moment he was born, mewling and weak and no use to her at all.

Alone in the hall, the skies veiled by Nyx, with only the low light of Hestia's flame flickering between the four pillars in the centre of the megaron, she thinks she might give way to tears at last.

And then Hephaestus returns, unsteadier than usual on his dragging feet.

She composes herself, sitting up tall and regal, ignoring the tired ache in her arms and feet.

As he comes nearer, she can smell the wine on his breath. Heavy and sweet, wafting out in waves towards her. His eyes are reddened, his mouth slack. She tenses.

He leans down so that his face is close to hers. She shakes back her hair and holds his gaze.

'You have to swear,' he says, and his words come out thick and slurred, 'that you won't take revenge.'

She lets the image of herself chaining him to the walls of Tartarus rise up inside her, and with a twinge of regret she lets it drift away. 'I'll swear it.'

He kneels on the marble floor and, despite his intoxication, produces a pitcher of silvery water she knows has come from the river Styx. It seems he's thought of everything.

'I swear I won't take revenge on you.' She forces out the words, and to her relief, his fingers move deftly across the fetters at her ankles, manipulating a tiny key into a lock none of the gods had even seen.

'Why did you come back?' she asks.

Someone else is at the entrance to the throne room; leaning languid and lithe against the columns of the anteroom porch. *Oh no*, she thinks.

He's smiling in just the way she remembers, but even though gods don't age, she thinks she can see the toll that grief has taken in his eyes, everything he's lost since she sent him fleeing into the wilderness. 'He was more responsive to my wine and conversation than to Ares' threats and fists,' Dionysus says.

Hera swallows. 'Why would you tell him to come back?' The thought strikes her, and she can't understand why she didn't see it before. 'You want to marry Aphrodite?'

The bindings at her ankles fly open, and Hephaestus moves to her wrists. The relief of being able to flex and move her feet again is indescribable.

'I can't take the credit for his decision,' Dionysus says smoothly. 'I gave him the wine, and let him talk. He came to this conclusion all by himself. I haven't come to claim any bride.' He glances through the fluted columns, at the crown-shaped constellation twinkling outside in the night sky.

'But have you come back to stay?' The words feel heavy in her throat.

Hephaestus pauses, his meaty hand clamped on hers. 'You won't stop him this time, will you?'

She doesn't answer.

'I think I've proven myself to Zeus,' Dionysus says softly. 'My wanderings are done.'

'Fine.' Her voice is tart. 'There's no throne for you, but lesser gods live among us too.' Hebe, Eileithyia, Ganymede, serving-nymphs and hangers-on. There's no denying that Dionysus has built a powerful cult of worship for himself, and wrought as much terror as any other Olympian, if not more. He's earned the right to be here.

Hephaestus turns the key, and the mesh slips away from her as the metal bracelets release their hold. She's free.

'I don't need you to thank me,' says Hephaestus, even in his drunkenness correctly anticipating that she wouldn't. 'Aphrodite is reward enough for me.'

Aphrodite is furious about it. She hadn't protested too much before, confident that Ares would triumph, and canny enough to see that it might be better to be his wife than to let Zeus and Hera decide later that she would be a valuable bribe for some other god.

But to marry the blacksmith god – the returned exile, the inferior brother of the magnificent Ares and laughing-stock of the immortals – it's more than she is prepared to tolerate.

Zeus gives her a choice: he can blast her from the mountain with his thunderbolt, or she can do as he has decreed.

It's the most joyless wedding that Hera has ever presided

over, swiftly followed by one that is even worse. Apollo brings news from the oracle: it's destined that the first-born son of the sea-nymph Thetis will be greater than his father. She's a glorious, silver-footed daughter of the old sea-god Nereus, desired by many immortals, and Poseidon rises up from the salty depths to fret with Zeus over such an alarming prophecy.

'Marry her to a mortal man,' Poseidon urges, 'make sure her first son isn't born to a god.'

Hera curls her lip. It's like Metis, all those centuries ago, doomed by a similar prophecy. She comments that the gods could just leave the nymph alone, if they're so afraid of the consequences, but they're baffled by such a solution.

'She's too much temptation,' Zeus explains. 'Hera, give her a human husband.'

Hera supposes the alternative is that Thetis could be swallowed alive instead, as Metis was. She does as Zeus says and finds her an unremarkable husband, a king of Phthia named Peleus, thinking he can't be too offensive.

Knowing that Thetis will never willingly agree to the match, Zeus instructs the man to attack the nymph when she surfaces with her dolphins. She loves to splash and play with them in the shallows, he says, and Peleus should wade out and seize her. He must subdue her, Zeus says, drag her on to the beach and keep hold of her however she fights, whatever creature she transforms herself into to try to be free of him.

Hera listens, wrapped in mist, as Hermes delivers this message to the stunned man on the very beach where he's to carry out his divinely ordained assault. Hermes recites it with practised fluency, the wings on his sandals fluttering in the breeze that whips the water into little frothy peaks.

'I'm the greatest wrestler of Phthia,' Peleus answers, his

head bowed to the immortal messenger. 'She won't be able to get free.'

Hera can hear Zeus' voice rumbling, can picture him sprawled on his throne as he set out the steps by which Peleus should overpower the woman.

'When it's finished,' Hermes tells him, 'she'll have to marry you. She can't refuse.'

Thetis will obey, following Hera's example, Hermes explains. This is how the queen of the gods came by her own husband, he says, and so the nymph will be no different.

Her own name, invoked as justification for rape. All this time she's spent struggling against Zeus, challenging his power, and nothing at all has changed.

The man, Peleus, stumbles over his words of gratitude. What a gift, what an honour, what a prize he's been given. He won't fail, he promises, and the hungry light in his eyes tells Hera that he won't waver for a moment.

'You won't interfere,' Zeus warns her, his thunderbolt in hand.

Perhaps the son Thetis will bear will bring his mother some honour, Hera tells herself, some kind of consolation for what the gods have decreed she'll endure.

Afterwards, the sea-nymph's outraged eyes bore into her throughout the wedding, flinty with hatred.

It was Zeus who insisted, Hera wants to say to her. *Turn your wrath upon him, not me.*

But no one ever does.

Hera hasn't forgotten Hestia's suggestion that she find her own mortal champion, a hero to bring glory to her name and dilute the supremacy of Heracles. With Dionysus installed on Mount Olympus, and Aphrodite still furious about her wedding to Hephaestus, not to mention the bitter aftertaste of the Thetis affair, Hera is glad to spend more time on earth.

It's anger that inspires her choice, in the end. A murder is committed at one of her altars – a woman clings desperately to it, howling for the goddess to protect her, and a man advances on her without mercy. Hera could strike him dead in an instant for the impiety, for the pollution of her shrine, but she holds back her revenge.

The attacker is called Pelias, and he's stolen the throne of his kingdom from his brother. Now he rules the city of Iolcus, and his brother's son has been smuggled away to grow up in safety away from his murderous uncle.

The boy, Hera decides, will be her choice. He'll go on a quest in her name, come back victorious, and enact her punishment on Pelias then. It will be a long, protracted punishment: Pelias will be shown how great a man his nephew is, left to fear what shape his revenge will take, so that he can't sleep for terror until the day he returns and delivers Hera's justice.

The nephew, she learns, is called Jason. She visits him, taking the form of an old woman, and asks for his help in crossing a river. He lifts her in his arms, wading into the stream, and even as she allows herself to become heavier and heavier, he manages to hold her aloft. At the other side, he hauls himself up the bank, setting her down as carefully as he can. She notices that one of his sandals has come loose and drifts down the river, and his breath comes in heavy gasps, but still he nods courteously to her and makes no complaint.

He'll be compliant, she thinks. He has none of Heracles'

brute charisma and outsized arrogance. He'll be so dazzled by her that he'll do anything she tells him to do.

Back on Mount Olympus, she announces the quest. Jason will gather a crew, and sail to Colchis to steal the Golden Fleece from Aeetes, the son of Helios. It's a suitably difficult task, and she doesn't care for Aeetes or any offence he might take.

The gods are more interested than she anticipated. When Jason sends out heralds to gather his crew, sons of Poseidon and Boreas answer the call; even a son of Ares joins the mission. To Hera's annoyance, Heracles makes his way to the harbour where the ship awaits – the *Argo*, a beautiful ship, the first of its kind, its construction guided by Athena – and, leaving his labours uncompleted, declares himself one of the Argonauts, as they become known. Down in the forests, Artemis hears of it and sends her own champion, a woman called Atalanta – tall and fearless, skilled with a bow and disdainful of her male companions, the very image of the haughty goddess herself.

Hera doesn't care. The greater the crew, the greater Jason becomes in commanding them. It all elevates her, in the end.

She has never been so intimately involved in mortal affairs; never cared whether a human lived or died, or for anything else that happened in between, except for when she was threatened or insulted. But this quest is invigorating. It holds most of the gods of Olympus in its grip, delighting them as their favoured heroes triumph in battle and dodge obstacles.

And even though the gods are competitive over their chosen champions, it's the most united that Mount Olympus has ever felt, all of them absorbed by this collective diversion, this amusement that Hera has conjured up for them to enjoy together.

For all the resentments, for all the wounds they have

inflicted on one another, for all the jostling for power and hatred they nurture, the gods of Olympus gather as a family over the Argonauts. It's strange to Hera that this is thanks to her. Bringing the gods together has never been her goal. But, she reflects, it's something Zeus could never do. Although he wields the ultimate authority, they obey him out of fear. She's the one who has created this unprecedented harmony, this stability they enjoy, however unintentionally it's come about.

There is a power there that Zeus doesn't even recognise, but she does.

She watches Jason retrieve the Fleece, sees Pelias suffer and die on his return, and listens as the gods cheer the completion of the mortal quest as heartily as if it's their own triumph. Hera receives their congratulations, the most triumphant of them all.

25

The attack comes in the night with no warning. A great thud that makes the palace shake, and then another and another, and Hera jumps from the bed and rushes to the wide window to see that the sky is on fire.

Zeus is right behind her, his hands closed tight around her shoulders. 'What is this?' he asks. 'Is it your doing?'

The air smells of burning; something streaks past them into the courtyard that opens up beneath Zeus' chamber and it takes Hera a moment to realise it's an oak tree – an entire oak tree, torn from the soil and set alight. 'No,' is all she can say.

The palace erupts into chaos; the immortals arm themselves and run to see where the assault is coming from.

The giants have risen from the earth. From Sicily, Thrace, Campania and Arcadia, the terrible children of Gaia have emerged from their caves to wage war on Mount Olympus. They are ranged on the plains below, far taller and broader than mortal men, if not shoulder-high to heaven like Typhon was – though in a terrible echo of him, Hera sees that serpent-scales glitter on their coiled lower limbs. One has scaled the mountain and is pulling up pines and boulders from below the palace to throw at them.

'Are they yours?' Aphrodite has to shout to be heard over the roaring flames, the crashing of trees and rocks, and the shrieking winds.

'This is nothing to do with me!' Hera turns to Zeus. 'These giants, they're creatures of Gaia – they aren't fighting for me.'

Zeus is already sprinting towards the giant on the mountain, brandishing his thunderbolt. He's swift to strike, his lightning sizzling through the giant's forehead, sending him toppling down the slopes, snapping tree trunks as though they're dry branches as he falls.

Down on the ground, the other giants roar.

'Zeus,' Athena says, 'you stay here, attack from the skies. Ares, Dionysus, Hermes, Hephaestus, Apollo – we'll charge them on the ground. The rest of you, defend the palace.'

'And me?' Hera asks.

Athena's gaze is steady. 'Whose side are you on?'

'I had no warning. They're coming for me too.'

Athena turns to Zeus. 'Do you trust her?'

'No,' he says. 'But we might need her to fight.'

'Come with me, then,' Athena tells her, and she tosses Hera a spear.

Hera has barely held a spear in her hands since the battle against the Titans, but her body remembers the sensation, Metis' long-ago training swimming up from her memory. She follows Athena down the mountain, wondering even as she runs behind her what she'll do. The gods are swift and intent, each stride they take covering vast swathes of land. The giants bellow as they charge.

Ares' bloodcurdling cry echoes from the mountains. In the

churning seas, Poseidon breaks through the waves, tearing islands apart with his fists to hurl at their attackers. Apollo is firing a volley of arrows; one pierces a giant's eye and he slumps down on to the rocky ground with a shuddering crack that reverberates across the earth. Dionysus flings his vine-wrapped spear at one opponent, bringing him down; Athena slams a vast rock into another. Hephaestus is flinging handfuls of molten metal at a giant who screams in agony, smoke rising from his charred flesh in great plumes.

It goes against Hera's instincts to battle Gaia's children, but she is in the fray. One giant takes advantage of her hesitation, grabbing hold of her waist and yanking her out of the dust and chaos. She shoves him away, but he dodges back, wrapping his arms tightly around her so she's winded, then slamming her to the ground beneath him, tearing at her dress. She hammers her fists against his chest, trying to break free of his grip, his breath foul in her face as he grasps and paws at her body.

There's a sickening crunch, and his eyes roll back in his head. His arms loosen around her, and she pushes him backwards. A bolt of lightning hits him squarely in the chest and he lies still. Behind him is a man, his club poised in his enormous fists, a familiar lion skin draped around his neck.

'Heracles?' It makes no sense. Another giant looms behind him, and she leaps to her feet, nimbly circling the hero. She stabs the point of her spear into the giant's serpent coils, pinning him. He screams in rage and pain, tumbling down in front of her. She shoves his elbow out of the way and yanks her spear from his tail, thrusting it deep into his belly. She won't give any of them the chance to touch her again.

The battle turns in favour of the gods. When the last of the giants is buried in the earth, each of their bodies smouldering from Zeus' thunderbolts and weighed down beneath a volcano, Apollo announces that he foresaw the battle would be won with the help of a mortal hero. He seized Heracles along the way, carrying him to fight alongside the gods.

Hera wipes her ash-smeared face with her forearm, her muscles aching from the effort of burying the final giant. Returning them to Gaia, is how she likes to think of it. Her torn dress flutters around her calves, stained and shredded. 'I don't think we needed him,' she says.

A shaft of early-morning sunlight pierces the white clouds above and glints off Zeus' crown as he saunters towards her through a fine drizzle of rain, one hand clasping his son's bulky shoulder. Heracles is uncharacteristically quiet, almost reverent in the presence of his divine father. Hera prefers to look at the frozen snarl of the lion cape than at his face.

'I saw my son's bravery in saving you,' Zeus says, and Hera frowns.

'I can slay giants without the help of a mortal,' she answers. Zeus is resplendent, his goatskin aegis draped across his chest. The battle has left no mark on him. Heracles, meanwhile, is damp and bruised, his lip split and the hair on his broad chest matted with blood – either his or a giant's, she isn't sure which.

'Nevertheless, he ran to your aid,' Zeus reproves her. 'And I'll reward him for his service.'

The ichor in her veins still runs warm and pulsing from the battle, the elation of the fight still lingering. 'What will you give him?'

'When he dies,' Zeus says, 'he won't go to the Underworld. I'll make him a god, like I did Ganymede. He'll marry Hebe—'

'Hebe?' Hera interjects. Her sweet, youthful daughter, married to this hulking brute?

'He will.' There is a ring of finality in Zeus' voice. Heracles turns his battered face to his father, reverent with awe and gratitude.

She could fight it. If not the promise of immortality, she could at least protest the choice of bride. She has fought Heracles at every step of his life; she could fight him to his death and beyond.

But there is such a strangeness to the morning. Opposition to Zeus, and to his troublesome offspring, usually comes as naturally to her as the ascension of dawn, trailing from the chariot of Eos. But she is fresh from a battle fighting alongside him, ranging against the snake-limbed giants that once would have been her allies. She's defended the heavens she tried to topple, and found herself on the same side as the mortal she hates more than anyone else.

Each time she has tried to bring Heracles down, she has only given him another chance to prove himself.

Finally, she looks directly at the hero. They've never come face to face before. It's only because he's a demi-god, more powerful than most of Zeus' children, that he isn't burned by her gaze. 'You've caused nothing but trouble in the mortal world,' she says. 'Holding yourself up against kings, killing and rampaging to make yourself the best among men. As a god, you will remember your place.' She lifts her arm to encompass the ravaged land around them. 'Do what you want here; I'm done with testing you. You're powerful among mortals. But remember, if Zeus keeps his promise to bring you into the heavens when you die, it will be different there. On Mount Olympus, I am queen.'

He stays silent, a little cowed by the gods around him. Athena, Apollo, Ares, Dionysus and Hephaestus have drawn closer, all of them radiant with divine power, and he looks so very ordinary in their midst.

She's had it the wrong way around, all the time. *Glory of Hera*, that's what he's supposed to stand for. By lowering herself to oppose him, she's allowed him to think of her as a rival, and every success has glorified him instead of her. She has legitimised him as a worthy son of Zeus, capable of withstanding her attacks. Better he become a minor god, serving under her rule, than remain an enemy.

A rainbow glimmers in the watery light; Iris coming with Hera's chariot to escort her back to Mount Olympus. Hera takes her place, gathering the reins in one hand, her divine peacocks harnessed and eager for the command of their mistress. She nods to the others to follow, leaving Heracles behind.

26

Mortal years pass, largely unnoticed in the heavens. Since the war of the giants, Hera has been plagued by dreams of Gaia. Robed in green, crowned with flowers, the way she had appeared to her so long ago. Hera feels the earth's reproach, her grief for the giants that Hera cut down, but the goddess won't speak to her. In her dreams, Hera tries to ask Gaia why she sent them, but she gets no answer, and she wakes frustrated and angry.

She doesn't know if Gaia still slumbers or if she sent the giants; she doesn't even know if the primal goddess cares anymore one way or another what happens among the gods, or to Hera. Somehow, without her realising it was happening, Hera's loyalties have shifted. After so long existing at the heart of the Olympians yet still feeling like an outsider, she finds that she's more like them than she ever knew.

If she's left the world of monsters behind her, if she isn't allied to the dark and fearsome creatures that Gaia nurtures, then she has to accept that the role that was forced upon her is one she's come to thrive in. The attack of the giants has reminded her that she still has a thirst for battle, but she no longer wants to spend her rage on nymphs or mortal women who've fallen prey to Zeus, or even on individual heroes who attract her ire.

Hera longs for something grander.

It comes from an unexpected quarter. Zeus makes a proposal to the council of the gods. Hera looks around the long table in the great hall, where he's summoned them all. Poseidon arrives, salt-encrusted, with his trident in hand. Ares flies from his black mansion in the shape of a vulture, which makes him all the more intimidating when he transforms back into his god-form and scowls at Hephaestus from his throne. Hephaestus has come from his forge, his hands still black with soot and ash, the scent of singed metal hanging around him. Aphrodite looks right past her husband to her lover. Athena, in her armour, waits for Zeus to speak. Demeter is there, looking almost as indifferent as Artemis, who has come on a begrudging visit to the palace and sits with one bare calf crossed in front of the other and her bow propped up beside her. Apollo and Hermes murmur quietly together at the end of the table, next to an empty throne.

'Where's Hestia?' Hera asks, perturbed.

'She asked to be excused,' Zeus says. 'This doesn't concern her, anyway.'

She hears footsteps, and thinks her sister must have changed her mind, but to her horror it's Dionysus, crowned with ivy, sliding on to the vacant throne.

'We all agree,' Zeus begins, cutting off any protest Hera could make, 'that the Argonauts' quest was a fine spectacle.'

The gods nod their heads. They all enjoyed the diversion.

'The heroes of that adventure are growing old,' he goes on.

'Mortal halls ring with songs of how they sought the Golden Fleece, and the sons of the men who did it grow restless to prove their own greatness.'

'Do you propose another quest?' Hera asks.

'Better than that,' Zeus says. 'A war.'

'There are wars all the time.'

'But this one,' Zeus says, 'will be greater. More ships than have ever sailed together, a bigger army than the world has ever seen. The annihilation of a proud city.'

The gods glance at one another, already anticipating the sacrifices and the prayers they'll receive.

'Which city?' asks Athena.

'Troy.'

'Why Troy?' Aphrodite's voice is high and urgent.

'It's impossible to take – like the Golden Fleece,' Zeus explains. 'Poseidon built the city walls himself; no mortal force can bring them down, even an assembly of all the armies across Greece.'

'The old king of Troy tried to cheat me from my payment,' Poseidon growls from his end of the table. 'I'll help the Greeks tear down the walls.' That old king is long dead, his insult to the sea-god nothing to do with the Trojans who live behind those walls now, but it doesn't matter to Poseidon.

'I have a son in Troy,' Aphrodite protests.

'I'll fight for the Greeks as well,' Hephaestus interjects. Needless to say, Aphrodite's Trojan son wasn't fathered by him.

Aphrodite casts him a disdainful glare. 'I'll defend the city,' she says, and she looks towards Ares, her meaning clear. *The god of war will fight on my side*, she's thinking, *what chance do the rest of you have against him?*

'The Greeks will have my favour,' Athena announces. 'It will take skill and foresight to bring down a city so well fortified. It's a challenge.'

'How will you start this war?' Hera asks.

'Troy is rich with treasure. Destroying it will bring the victors gold, prizes and fame that will last forever,' Zeus says. 'It won't take much provocation.'

The Greek fleet, a thousand ships strong, is magnificent to behold. Zeus was right; men have joined from dozens of separate kingdoms and cities, eager to be a part of this fight. Hera watches them, a righteous flame burning in her heart.

At first, she'd thought this would be another enjoyable diversion, like the Argonauts had been. But Zeus' choice of provocation has infuriated her. This mighty war is being fought in the name of a woman, Helen – yet another child of Zeus, born this time to a Spartan queen. Given her legendary beauty, she was already a darling of Aphrodite, who has decided to give her to a Trojan prince named Paris. The Greeks sail under the pretence of bringing her back to restore the stolen Helen to her husband, Menelaus.

What's wrong, Hera thinks, *with fighting for power and wealth? For the thrill of conquest, for the promise of glory?* She had looked forward to this battle, but for it all to centre on another one of Zeus' bastard offspring sours her pleasure in it. And if that wasn't enough, the House of Pheme spreads a rumour – that Aphrodite rewarded Paris with Helen when he chose Aphrodite as victor in a contest of the goddesses. The story whispered through the echoing bronze halls goes that Hera, Athena and Aphrodite all came to him on Mount Ida outside of the city and asked him to decide which of them was the loveliest.

'Why would I debase myself by submitting to the judgement of a man?' Hera complains to Klymene. 'It's a ridiculous fiction, to cover up for his theft of Helen. He makes it the decision of Aphrodite, instead of admitting to it himself.'

'It's absurd,' Klymene agrees – but like all rumours, it has taken root, and she hears it everywhere she goes.

'Don't destroy Paris yet,' Athena advises her. 'Lend your support to the Greeks, and let them crush him and his city in your honour.'

It's alien to her to take Athena's advice. But Athena's love of strategy and victory overcomes the distance between the two goddesses. Athena doesn't care for Hera's resentment of her; Athena only wants to win this war. Hera does too, and so she listens.

She'd like to tear the impudent mortal limb from limb and eat his flesh raw, but she agrees that Athena's strategy might yield a sweeter victory in the end.

Only Hestia seems uninterested in the unfolding of events. 'Don't you want to watch?' Hera asks her.

'War isn't my sphere,' is all she'll say.

It's irresistible to Hera. She loves to walk among the Greek camps ranged outside the walls of Troy, cloaked from mortal view, stirring up a thirst for Trojan blood in their hearts as she goes, exulting in the thanks they offer up to her. And the women they've left behind keep her altars smoking with offerings too – either to bring their husbands home safe, or to keep them away for longer. The gaze of the world – human and divine – is on those beaches, and Hera, spurred on by the offence of Paris, presides over the carnage.

*　　*　　*

Returning to the palace from the battlefield in the tenth year of the war, she sees Thetis, hurrying from the mountain. The nymph leaps into the salt sea, her body a graceful arc as she plunges. Hera narrows her eyes.

'Why was Thetis here?' she asks Zeus.

He looks guarded. 'She wasn't.'

Hera sits beside him, taking her time. She smooths out her skirt, slow and deliberate, and then she speaks. 'Her son, Achilles, sulks in his tent, refusing to fight alongside the Greeks. The Mycenean king, Agamemnon, has stolen his captive woman, Briseis, from him. His honour is insulted and he broods, determined to make them pay. I think Thetis has come here to ask you to lend your support to her son. I think she clasped your knees and begged you to back him in his refusal to fight, even though it means my Greeks will suffer. Without Achilles in the fray, the Trojans will prevail, and you know it.'

'Where did you – how did you come by such a notion?' Zeus splutters. In the face of Hera's silence, his brows draw together and his defensiveness turns to anger. 'It isn't for you to know what another god asks of me.'

'She wants her son to have the greatness he was promised,' says Hera. She widens her eyes, keeping her tone calm and betraying none of her own quiet fury. 'Of course she's asked for your help. Even though you swore the Greeks would win this war, she wants you to punish them for how they've treated her son.'

Zeus slams his fist on to the table, and across the hall Hera sees Hephaestus, who has stopped to talk to Hestia by the fire, startle at the noise. 'I'll decide what to do about this war.' Her husband's voice echoes around the room. 'You hate the Trojans more than is reasonable; you don't see anything else. If Thetis came to me, she was within her rights to do so, and I can grant her request if I see fit. I won't order Achilles to fight. I'll let the Trojans punish the Greeks on his behalf.'

'Zeus is cruel,' Athena says to Hera in private, 'to give the Trojans the advantage for the sake of Thetis. He's come to me for advice so many times, and I've always shown him the clearest path.' Her smooth brow is creased, the brightness of her eyes dimmed by her disappointment. 'For nine years, we've tussled back and forth in this war, and now the end is in sight, if not for this.' The years are nothing to the gods, but they have been so captivated by this war that they've experienced the passing of days almost as mortals do. Each one feels more precious, more urgent, as the gods pay closer attention than ever before. 'He prolongs it for her pride in her son – the greatest warrior there has ever been, who won't fight.' There is a particular bitterness in her tone at that. Athena loves a fighter, and Achilles' intransigence infuriates her. 'We should show ourselves on the plains,' she says. 'You and me. Turn the tide of the war, so that the dogs can feast on Trojan corpses tonight.'

'We'll go in my chariot,' Hera says. She hadn't realised Athena had this in her – such depth of feeling. She has always been so cool-headed and rational, so maddening to Hera. She has never envisaged riding out to battle with Athena at her side, and in defiance of Zeus' orders too.

She harnesses her sacred peacocks to the front of her golden chariot, too eager to wait for Hebe to assist her. Their bright plumage is vivid and striking, their feathers so glossy and beautiful. It's a world away from the grime and dust of the battlefields. Before they can reach Troy, Iris swoops down in front of them, and Hera's delicate birds rear up in fright, shrieking in panic as they stagger to a halt.

'He saw you leave,' Iris says. 'He sends a message.'

'What message.' Hera's voice is so weary, it isn't even a question.

'If you pass me, he'll smash your chariot with a thunderbolt, with the two of you in it.' Iris' eyes are soft with apology. 'He says that Hera knows what it is to feel his wrath, but Athena doesn't. Not yet.'

Hera feels Athena bridle next to her, and she places her hand on the goddess's wrist. 'Don't do this, not for the sake of some mortal lives.' She nods to Iris in dismissal, and the rainbow-goddess streaks away. 'Who cares which of them fall today, really? They all go to Hades in the end.'

'He's wrong,' says Athena, her eyes flashing.

'He's often wrong,' says Hera. Now Athena understands it too.

The bodies pile up across the Trojan plains; so many men, more than have ever died in one war before. Even the children of the gods themselves aren't safe. When Zeus frets about his own son, the warrior Sarpedon, Hera is scathing in her retort. All the gods care about mortals in this war, she warns him, and if all of them spirit away their favourite, then there will be no one left to fight.

'You wanted this war,' she tells him. 'Let your son prove his honour by dying in your name.'

And he does.

When the *Argo* sailed, a mortal generation ago, the gods cheered and laughed and applauded their adventures. In this war, they weep and plot and scheme and fight, swept up in a conflict Hera had never imagined they would all care about so deeply.

For gods, the world is eternal and loss is rare. The urgency of this war is compelling in a way that is new. For a time, the perfumed halls of Olympus are alive with discussions of strategy and casualties, of siege tactics and courage, of weak mortal flesh and indomitable human spirit. Achilles rejoins the fray when his beloved Patroclus dies, and his grief is transfixing. Hera has heard countless prayers born of sorrow, oceans of pain and suffering that toss her worshippers to and fro on their currents for centuries. In this war alone, the agony is constant and unceasing. But Achilles is a spectacle – his despair taking a shape so malevolent, so harrowing, that even the gods stop to marvel.

Hera felt something for the women of Argos – she was moved by their collective anguish – but she's never watched this kind of desolation up close. When Achilles chokes the river Scamander with Trojan corpses and the god of the river rises up in a fury to drown him, Hera directs Hephaestus to scorch Scamander into retreat so that the hero's life will be preserved a while longer. Saving a hero is something she never thought she'd do. Her son obeys her, as eager to serve her as he used to be, as though the gulf between them had never opened up at all. Like the softening she feels between herself and Athena, this kinship with Hephaestus is inexplicable to her. That an event in the mortal realm, even one as cataclysmic as this war, could effect a change in her – it's unprecedented.

But the war burns itself out at last. Troy falls, as is decreed by the Fates. When the celebrations on Mount Olympus die down, when the gods on the side of the Trojans are appeased and the surviving heroes scatter to their disparate homes, Hera finds the days that follow desultory. The thrill has drained away, and the gods return to their usual pastimes, their quarrels and petty rivalries over individual mortals, but Hera misses the grand scale of the war, when everything felt so heightened and so vital.

She goes to Hestia, who never cared for the war in the first place, hoping to find her sister's presence to be the same comforting anchor it's always been. 'Nothing changed for you,' she says. 'Do you think that's better, to stay out of it all from the beginning?'

Hestia's voice is distant, dreamy, when she gives her reply. 'Whatever happens, the mortals light fires. Outside their tents, in their besieged homes, wherever they stop on their journeys. They light fires and make their first dedications to me, always.'

'I know,' says Hera. 'You didn't need to get involved.' The altars of the other gods were more replete than ever during the ten years of fighting. Times of desperation are fruitful in prayer and sacrifice. But Hestia satisfies a quiet, ongoing, daily need. Warmth. Light. The safety of home, even for those who are miles away and weary, or whose homes lie in ruins. The hearth gives them an illusion of its comfort, even if it's a feeble flame kindled by an exhausted traveller on a desolate island, or a captured slave dragged to a foreign land. Hestia will be there, the promise of her twinkling hearth keeping hope alive in times of prosperity and suffering alike.

'You wouldn't have either, once,' Hestia says. 'You never involved yourself in mortal affairs. You opposed their creation to begin with. And now, you don't know what to do with yourself without a human diversion.'

'What do you mean?'

'The others are all the same.' Hestia sighs. 'Maybe Prometheus foresaw it, when he helped Zeus to create humanity. Maybe he knew that we needed them.'

Hera protests at this. 'They need us,' she corrects her sister. 'But what would we do without their worship?'

It's a baffling question.

'The strongest gods are the ones that are most revered,' Hestia says.

'Because we're the most powerful.'

'I think it's the other way around. Our strength comes from them.'

'That's ridiculous,' says Hera.

'Not to me,' says Hestia. 'I'm not interested anymore in ruling from a palace. In sitting up here on a golden throne, so high above the world that we aren't part of it.'

Hera has only ever found solace at Hestia's hearth. This change is so abrupt, and so shattering, that she can't fathom it. She has no gift of prophecy, but she finds with a sickening sense of inevitability that she knows what's coming next.

'I'm leaving my throne to Dionysus,' Hestia says. 'He has it anyway, really. He wants it, and I don't care.'

'What do you mean?'

'Artemis lives in the forests, where the hunt is,' Hestia says. 'I want to be in the cities, in the hamlets and villages – in the homes of the mortals, where my fire lives.'

'But what about the hearth here?' says Hera. 'This is your home.'

'Rhea went back to the mountains.' Hestia sounds wistful, talking about the mother they never knew. 'Gaia has returned to the earth.'

'I don't understand.'

'The world is changing,' says Hestia. 'It doesn't need us in the same way.'

'The biggest war ever fought just happened in our names,'

Hera counters. 'Designed by Zeus, dictated by the Fates. Humans died in their droves for us.'

'And now it's over, you're directionless. The other gods are searching for new adventures – Athena and Poseidon vie over Odysseus returning home, Apollo sets his sights on Mycenae, where King Agamemnon has been murdered by his wife, and you're here wondering how to fill your time.'

'There'll be other wars,' says Hera.

'But they'll happen whether you intervene or not,' Hestia says.

It doesn't make any sense to Hera. 'We rule over everything.'

'What Zeus set in motion when he created mortals,' Hestia says, 'was something no oracle foresaw. They spread in unmanageable numbers, their prayers are too numerous to hear, and when they go unanswered, the humans keep living and dying regardless. They don't learn weaving from Athena anymore; they teach it to each other. They craft their own armour, light their own fires, administer their own justice.'

'And send thanks to us when they do it.'

'But they do it all anyway, without needing us to show them how. We're the ones who need their offerings now, who thrive on what they give us. Without their worship, without their belief, we would shrivel away, become no more than spirits haunting the earth.'

'Even if that were true,' says Hera, 'there's no danger that they'll stop their worship.'

'But I'm tired of Olympus,' says Hestia. 'As long as there's fire, I'll be honoured. I've tended this hearth since we defeated the Titans. I've seen every argument among the gods, have listened to every complaint and quarrel, and watched the world transform beneath us while we struggle for power. When

Dionysus came for my throne, I realised I didn't care if he took it or not. Why should I?'

'Because it's yours. We fought for our power, and we won.'

'But my power isn't in the throne,' says Hestia. 'It never was.'

'It's madness to talk about leaving,' Hera says. 'Even if you don't want to rule.' Mount Olympus without Hestia is unimaginable. She is the centre of everything, the calm eye of the storms that shake the palace. A light that keeps burning, whatever darkness threatens to descend.

'Do you think this palace will last forever?' Hestia asks her.

She's never considered any other possibility.

'Everything has to change. Even gods.'

'Go into the cities, if you have to,' Hera says. 'All the gods have travelled. You'll see if you do that it's the other way around to what you think; you'll see how the gods are needed. And then you'll come back.' There is no alternative, she's sure of it.

'Perhaps,' says Hestia.

The conversation is more unsettling than Hera could have ever thought. But maybe it's an effect of the strange restlessness that has set in among the gods since the end of the Trojan War. Even though Hestia stayed out of it, she must have been affected by the way it seized the rest of them. It will pass, Hera decides.

She doesn't want to lend any credence to Hestia's ideas, but since her time on the plains of Troy, she finds herself drawn down to the mortals again and again. She lets Athena occupy herself with the homecoming heroes, and she drifts near the cities that she loves. Not a part of them, not in among the teeming masses of humanity, but close by, watching. On the island of Samos, she smiles upon a statue of herself – crowned and regal, the smooth stone face carved with a serene expression and round eyes. At her feet lies a lion skin, the animal's face frozen in a perpetual snarl, its hide trapped beneath the sceptre she holds. Winding around it are vine leaves, twisting and delicate. The emblems of her conquered foes, Heracles and Dionysus, only admitted to the heavens when they had endured her opposition long enough. She has made sure that Zeus couldn't fill Mount Olympus with a host of unworthy children. She's tested them, forced them to prove their mettle, and no one can deny how ferocious a gatekeeper she has been. Every challenge she's mounted against Zeus has kept him in check, reminded him of where his limits are – that they exist at all.

Olympian rule has lasted longer than any other. Maybe all the time that Hera thought she was fighting against her family, she was strengthening them without realising. And now that she's built this empire with them, the one she wanted to destroy for so long, she discovers that she is afraid of it falling apart.

The last hero of Troy reaches home. The survivors grow old and die, and their feats live on in memory, in the stories they were promised. Their ghosts will stalk the ruined city forever, made flesh each evening in song by the bards who recount their deeds and summon the clash of metal and shrieking war-cries for their eager listeners time and time again.

In the heavens, the gods reminisce too.

And Hera cannot prepare herself for the hollow desolation of the palace when Hestia finally departs, without any further warning or farewell. It had seemed inconceivable that she would really go.

The hearth that has burned since the dawn of their rule lies in cold ashes, abandoned.

And as Hera watches from above, the fires down on the earth flicker and sputter and, one by one, die down to nothing.

PART FIVE

O gods! Yet why do I call on the gods? They did
not hearken ever before to our call.

Euripides, *The Trojan Women*,
translated by E. P. Coleridge, 1891

Who says change is an impossible thing after a
certain age, when all of life is nothing but the act of
changing to grow?

Great Goddesses, Nikita Gill

27

It isn't as simple as rekindling the fire. What has vanished with Hestia is the spirit and the comfort of the hearth. The gods who would stride past her without a word, who would overlook her in their rush to jostle for authority, feel her absence more keenly than they would have dreamed. Every one of them has sought out her kindly friendship, and there is no replacement for her sacred flame. What homecoming is there for Hermes, god of travellers, if he can't sit beside his aunt and tell her of all the places he's visited that she has never seen? Why fight the wars in which Ares revels, if not for the sweetness and safety of a hearth that will always be protected? In the honest light of her fire, Aphrodite could find a moment's peace from her restless yearning; enough so that she never resented the gentle Hestia for holding herself apart from everything the goddess of desire offers. In the warm circle of Hestia's flames, even Zeus could find a welcome without struggle, a respite from the monster that surges up within him, a fire that soothes and warms rather than raging and burning and destroying.

So Hermes wanders farther, and comes back less frequently.

The tapers die out in Aphrodite's house on Mount Olympus, and she is no longer found lounging on her couches or bathing in rose petals. Hephaestus won't march on his brother's dark mansion to see if his ever-reluctant wife is there; he retreats to his workshop.

Hera goes there, at last. Zeus' edict that she never visit has long expired, but still she's never made her way beneath the fiery volcano to see where her second son has made his home.

The heat blasts across her as she enters; the heat and the noise. It takes her a moment to orientate herself. The darkness of the mountain's interior is punctuated by flashes of searing light, sparks flying as hammers beat down on anvils, furnaces roaring, bright streams of molten metal flowing. Towering figures lumber past, sweat trickling into the single eye at the centre of each one's forehead. Cyclopes.

Of course Hephaestus has made friends of the creatures despised by the gods. No surprise that they work so industriously here under his direction.

She finds her son in the centre, calling out directions, and she watches him work for a while before he notices her. Up on Mount Olympus, he stumbles and hesitates, always tripping over his words. Here, in the workshop he's built from his prison, he is a different god entirely. Not swaggering with false bravado, like the drunken god who had announced he should wed Aphrodite. But sure of himself, and at ease.

He catches sight of her and, wiping a rag across his gleaming brow, he sets down his hammer and limps over to her, clapping a passing Cyclops on the back as he goes. 'What are you doing here?' he asks, but there's no hint of displeasure in his greeting.

'It's so long since you've graced the halls of Mount Olympus,' Hera says. 'I wondered if you were ever returning.'

He beckons for her to follow him out of the busy forge, past the seething flames and hissing metal, to a quieter anteroom branching from a corridor. In here, a fire burns merrily at the hearth and a jug of wine rests on a table beside a silver chair. Hera can imagine him here, taking a moment's peace from the bustle of the workshop, sipping his wine and watching the dancing flames. Her heart catches. It's not in the nature of most gods to find such easy contentment.

'Is there something brewing?' he asks. 'A war? Another quest? Have you come to ask for armour, a shield, something else?'

'No,' she says. 'I'm here to find you, nothing else.'

His eyes are as unclouded as the summer sky. 'There's always a reason. When a god comes here, it's always to ask for something.'

'Will you come back?'

He shakes his head.

'Why not?' Hera asks. 'You won your place in the heavens again. Would you really flee because Aphrodite ran back to Ares?'

He only laughs. 'I don't belong up there.'

It's true. Like the melted bronze he pours into moulds in the forge, he has tried to take on all the shapes that make a god. He looked to his father and tried out vengeance. He followed the example of divine husbands in seizing the wife he thought he was entitled to, one who could never love him. He strategised over mortal battlefields, favouring one hero and then another, fanning the flames of carnage like the rest of them. But it's only now, when she sees him here, that he is the god he was meant to be. The son she couldn't accept, no longer apologetic or resentful.

347

'I'm needed here,' he says. 'I'm useful here. I don't care about my throne.'

She can hear Hestia's words echoing in his voice. Which other gods apart from those two have ever cared for being useful?

'You'd surrender your power, just like that?' she asks. But even as she says it, she hears the discordant note in her words. He hasn't surrendered his power at all. It breathes from him, as easily as leaves fluttering in an autumn breeze. He's found it here, and he wears it so naturally she hardly notices it.

'Without us,' Hephaestus says, 'can't you rule as you always wanted? The fewer gods on Mount Olympus, the less you have to share.' He speaks candidly, without rancour.

It should lift her spirits, not leave her with an unaccountable sensation of dread. Will they all go, until she's left alone with Zeus?

'I can see you're happy here,' she says, making her tone brisk.

'I am.'

'Then I'll leave you.'

For the first time, she feels the weight of her expectations lift away. She looks at her son without disappointment.

She doesn't say that she'll return. He doesn't say he'll come to find her again. An understanding settles between them that it would be a lie.

For all that she and Zeus have warred against each other, her children have found a peace she never could. Ares with Aphrodite, Hephaestus with his work, sweet Hebe an eternally young and beautiful bride given to Heracles when he died at last and ascended to the heavens, Eileithyia toiling ceaselessly among the women whose need for her is a never-ending well of worship and gratitude, hope and faith and love, that keeps the goddess as busy and fulfilled as her blacksmith brother.

Hera won't resent them any longer. She'll forgive them for not filling the void that aches inside her; she'll find a little comfort in their happiness. The weight of her own history drags in her wake, anchoring her where she is, the pain she's carried in her soul almost since the world began, fastening her in place so she can't follow them into their calm, contented waters. But she won't demand that they stay and scheme and fight at her side, not now. When she leaves Hephaestus' forge, she lets them all go.

Any fire the remaining Olympians light in Hestia's absence is a feeble imitation. The wave of darkness that swept across the mortal world when she left has passed, though; on earth, they have rallied and relit their own hearths. Somewhere among those glowing spots of light, Hestia moves unseen and unknown, unshackled from the heavens. Hera searches for her in every agora, in the centre of every town and village, from the tiniest hamlets to the busiest cities, where a flame to Hestia is always kept burning, no matter who the patron immortal of the settlement might be. But like their vanished mother, like the dormant Gaia, Hestia leaves no trace of herself behind.

A desultory winter passes, and when springtime rolls around again, Demeter is nowhere to be seen. Perhaps she has followed Hestia's example; perhaps her growing disenchantment with the Olympians has reached its peak. Across the world, crops fail and harvests wither.

'They'll both come back,' Zeus says, dismissive. Hungry mortals provide a boon to the discontented gods as they pray for a change in their fortunes, but when another year passes without Demeter's beneficence, hunger turns into famine, and as the populations decline, so do the offerings to the heavens.

'This isn't another endless winter, like when Persephone was taken.' Hera paces back and forth in the throne room.

Zeus rolls his sceptre between his thumb and finger, staring at the carved eagle that tops it, the little jewelled eyes staring back at him. He doesn't appear to take in a word she's saying.

'What I mean is, it's not a cataclysm,' Hera says. 'She's somewhere – not everything has stopped growing. She's still out there. You could summon her back.'

Zeus glowers.

'Why don't you?' asks Hera. 'Make them all come, a great council of the gods together. Send Iris.' She recalls the gathering at the river Styx, the division of the realms, and she pauses, looking hard at Zeus. It's hard to reconcile the god who once towered above them all, full of boundless energy, seething with raw power as he drew lots for the heavens, with the figure before her now, slumped on his cushioned throne. 'Where is everyone, anyway?' she asks, looking around at the quiet hall.

'I don't need their noise,' Zeus says. His voice doesn't crack and rumble through the marble columns. There is no shiver of thunder to his words. Only the faint edge of petulance.

Something moves in the corner, and Hera turns to see who's there. A face looks back at her, shining, gold and blank. One of Hephaestus' creations, his mechanical statues, moving figures he built to entertain the gods, to glide across their gilded floors and pour nectar from jugs, to their surprise and delight. Since Hebe and her new-god husband Heracles left Olympus for their own home, and Ganymede found a way to escape his magnificent prison in the clouds, these lifeless things have served at the gods' tables. Their inner workings – the systems of pulleys, levers and wheels designed by her son – are a mystery to Hera, but the novelty has worn away, and she's used to their silent subservience. It's only now that she finds something eerie in the vacant space where the thing's eyes should be.

It rolls towards Zeus, smooth and frictionless, a jug of wine raised in one metallic hand, ready to pour. Zeus' gaze is already clouded, and Hera doubts she'll get anywhere with this one-sided conversation.

She steps past the automaton. No nymphs fill the courtyard, no trailing perfume of roses, whispers and giggles linger in the air. They all left soon after Klymene did. Hera had granted her that request, to return to her sisters in the home of Oceanus. Klymene had served faithfully for long enough. In her wake, it seems that all the nymphs have followed down the slopes of Olympus, returning to the rivers and the forests, back to their families. It's so very quiet.

She sits on a bench, a white wisp of cloud floating past her in the otherwise empty air. No smoke drifts up towards the Olympian acropolis today. The once-cacophonous din of prayer that she could catch if so inclined has been steadily dwindling, and now when she listens, she hears only a plaintive trickle.

She should go and round up the other gods. Search the mountains and the forests and the temples to find them and call them together. She'll do it, she thinks, when she can find the energy. For now it seems easier to sit, to let her thoughts wander.

After a while, Athena comes to sit beside her.

'So you're still here,' Hera says.

'You didn't find Hestia?' Athena asks.

'No,' says Hera. 'But where are the other gods?'

'Don't you feel it too?' Athena says. 'The pull to the earth?'

'What is it?' There is something – some kind of longing, though Hera had thought it was just the nagging she's accustomed to feeling in her soul, the restless urge that keeps her moving forwards all the time.

'The mortals are cold and hungry and fewer in number,' Athena says. 'Their prayers can't reach us here anymore.'

'Why does that matter?'

'It calls us down to them,' Athena says, and Hera recognises it when she says it. The invisible draw that tugs at her from the world, the worship she craves.

'We existed before them.' Hera feels the echo of her argument with Hestia again, like she did with Hephaestus. It sounds increasingly hollow each time she repeats it. 'We came to power when there were no prayers at all, no mortals to worship us. Why would we need it so much now?' She remembers the thrill of the vitality she felt as a young goddess, how the earth spread out before her, teeming with the plants and animals and gods who lived at their command, how she would roam across it safe in the knowledge that it was hers to rule.

'Zeus swallowed my mother because he was afraid she'd bear a child that would destroy him,' Athena says. She's never spoken of Metis before. Hera has never even considered whether Athena grieves for her lost mother. To hear her allude to her now is so abrupt and unexpected that it's like the shock of jumping into a glacial pool, the waters melted from ice and snow, back in a time before any of this, when the sharp thrill of pain was a novelty, when it·felt like a game. Before she knew what it truly was to be hurt. 'He quaked at every oracle, every prophecy of powerful sons who could overthrow their fathers.'

'None was ever born to him,' says Hera. She remembers how it burned her up, that none of her children were strong enough. The old failure has lost its sting now. She's glad her children weren't like Zeus. She might even be glad they weren't like her, either.

'I've wondered if he created them instead,' Athena goes on. 'If the mortals he conjured up have grown enough to siphon his power away, without him ever realising what was happening.'

Hera stares at her.

'We all feel it,' Athena says. 'I thought it was just Hestia leaving that made it less inviting to be here.' She sounds sceptical even as she says it. Hera supposes that, of all the gods, Athena has always spent the least time at the hearth. She has been the most self-sufficient of them all. 'But I think it's the offerings, the savour and the smoke that we've learned to depend on,' she continues. 'It's not reaching us, so we have to go to it, go to where the worship is. It's only Zeus who clings on up here.'

'The gods can't leave Olympus,' Hera insists.

'Look around.' Athena lifts a graceful arm, her face as serene as always. Even when she was planning devastation on the Trojan battlefields she was above it all, abstract and calm. 'They're already gone.'

Hera is sure they'll be back. The end of a god's reign is written in fire and disaster; the sky burns and collapses, mountains tumble, and the scars are carved deep into the earth. It doesn't stutter and drift to a quiet ruin. That won't be how it ends.

Zeus still has his throne, and on the earth the mortals still huddle together and pray.

It isn't enough for Poseidon. In his deep-sunk ocean palace, he strikes the seabed with his trident in fury at the meagre offerings that come his way. He sends violent shudders through the earth, shaking the ground with his rage. Mortal palaces topple. The vast stones in their fortification walls come loose and rain down the hillsides; roofs cave in and the inhabitants either flee or die. Those who are lucky enough to escape Poseidon's indiscriminate wrath eye the destruction; they send in their bandits and plunder and steal. Cities burn, and kings fall.

Hera comes back to Zeus. 'What will you do?' she demands. 'There was already famine; now earthquakes are decimating what's left of the mortals.'

'You never cared for them anyway,' Zeus says. 'Why would you now?'

'When did you last leave Olympus?' Hera asks. 'When did you last go and see for yourself what's happening?'

His face contorts, and his fist squeezes around his thunderbolt. Hera doesn't tremble. 'I won't be told where to go,' he snarls. 'Not by you.'

'Athena was right,' she says. 'The fewer mortals there are to worship you, the less power you have.'

His grip on the thunderbolt tightens convulsively. He sits taller in his throne, his eyes dark, and he lifts his arm to hurl it at her. It streaks past her face, singeing her hair, and crashes into one of the four pillars around Hestia's abandoned hearth. The marble cracks and breaks, heavy chunks smashing into the floor, shattering tiles, each impact ringing across the polished stone and vibrating in the dusty air.

He pulls back his arm, ready to throw another, and she

dodges around the remaining pillars, to the safety of the ante-room. She knows he won't get up, that he won't chase her.

He's too afraid. He doesn't know whether he's stronger than she is anymore, not for certain. And he doesn't dare find out.

So she leaves him to his wine, and his ruined palace, and she follows the path down the slopes of Mount Olympus in the footsteps of the other gods.

It's different to the times when she's wandered before. There is a heaviness in her bones, one that seems to hold her to the ground, slowing her pace. She wonders when this switch took place. If it can somehow be that the gods became so tethered to the mortal world that it's now the source of their strength, as Athena said. Or if this is part of some kind of life cycle for immortals, as Hestia hinted when she spoke of Rhea and Gaia falling dormant and disappearing. Somehow, during Jason's voyage for the Fleece, and the long, brutal annihilation of Troy, when the ambitions of heroes intertwined with the glory of the gods who championed them, Hera forgot to look away, and now finds that she can't. And as the human world has shrunk down to this smaller scale, their land ravaged by hunger and disaster, so has her own.

Is this what happened to Gaia, when she stopped rising from the earth? Did she lose the vitality, the will to shape herself like one of the gods and intervene in their rule? Hera finds herself increasingly in a somnolent daze, a kind of waking slumber. A shadow of what she once was, in a world drained of its former dazzling hues. She lingers in her temples, where the air is dim and fragranced, where the weak sunlight slips through the columns and reminds her of Mount Olympus. The past starts to feel like one of the stories they tell, like something that might never have been at all.

The green creeps back in first, rich and verdant. Seasons that had bled drearily into one another with barely a difference in between become distinct, alive and vibrant once more. Stirring from within the statue of herself, Hera feels aware of the fresh scent of spring, of a world reawakening.

A new strength ripples in her limbs; a luxurious stretching sensation. She steps out from the oak carved into an imitation of her body, into the hawk shape she hasn't occupied for so long, and she soars through the columns, into the brightness of the day. The priestesses making their way to the temple in the vivid dawn look up, startled, as she flies over their heads.

On the summit of a neighbouring hill, she takes note of the changes. The great cities, ruled over by wealthy palaces, have shrunk away. Some have burned, some have crumbled in Poseidon's earthquakes, some have been abandoned by the once-important families that occupied them. The world has been shaken, and Hera watches for a time to see how the pieces have fallen in the centuries that she's spent half-dreaming. The villages that are left, where survivors have gathered together and formed communities, still fight for supremacy, and they still make what offerings they can to Hera for her blessing. There are still marriages; there are still women who call upon her for protection, for goodwill. The fires they burn must warm Hestia, wherever she is; what crops they can grow garner praise for Demeter. There are battles enough to please Ares, if he's watching.

On the beams of mud-built halls, Hera cocks her head and

tucks in her wings while she listens to bards singing stories of a time that seems fantastical: when the gods ruled together from Mount Olympus, when one could stride among mortals like a colossus, instead of hovering close to the altars and temples as Hera does now. When she drifts too far away, she can feel her strength sapping, and so she comes back and she listens to the songs of heroes she remembers, quests she oversaw, wars she masterminded. The faces of the listeners, rapt in firelight, send a shudder through her. These mortals dream of the kind of feats they can't imagine taking place now, of an age that has been lost.

Hera wonders, when the poets strum their lyres, if Apollo is nearby, if he's taking heart from the music flowing from their fingers. Does Dionysus draw near while the rough red wine is poured? She never sees any of them. In the night sky, lightning crackles erratically from time to time. Perhaps it's Zeus, firing his thunderbolt through the empty rooms of Mount Olympus, still believing himself in charge of this changed world that moves on without him.

No Titans challenge him. Hera listens to the recitation of their names too, as the stories unfold in the low-roofed smoky halls. She hears a poet tell of the sun-Titan Helios, jealously guarding his broad-browed cattle from the cunning mortal Odysseus, in whom Athena had taken such pride, and she sees Helios in her mind, radiant and gleaming, when he came to tell Zeus of Persephone's abduction. To picture him now, if he were to appear among these men, crammed together on their wooden benches, their own rangy animals shuffling in the sparse straw at the end of the room, feels absurd, like something she imagined rather than knew. It has been a long time since he drove his chariot through the arc of the heavens,

357

drawing the fiery sun across the sky. Apollo took the sun from him centuries ago, like he took Delphi from Phoibe, like Artemis took the moon from Selene, and Hera has given those Titans no thought since then.

She goes back to Mount Olympus to see if any other gods have returned. She asks Zeus every time, and always she receives the same sneer, the same cold stare, as he tells her no, they haven't.

'They don't dare,' he says. His voice is always thick with wine now. The huge jars lined up in the storerooms of the palace that brim with the sweetest and richest product of Dionysus' vines aren't drained yet.

'That's not why,' Hera tells him. He's been alone up here too long, with his thunderbolt and his wine and no company to distract him from his thoughts. 'Do you know how different things are now? Do you even glance down at the world to see what's going on?'

'I don't need to look down,' he says. 'The mortals look up to the skies in search of me. Needing *my* favour.'

'They do,' says Hera. 'Even now, hundreds of them are travelling to Olympia. Walking for miles, day after day, to reach your sanctuary. They're holding games in your honour, competing for victory in your name. I've seen the oxen they've penned, ready to sacrifice for you – the smoke from a hundred pyres will reach you here.'

He shifts in his throne, fractious. 'Good, good,' he mutters.

'It doesn't make you want to see for yourself?' she asks. It's an odd sense of responsibility that brings her here, that makes her deliver this news. She doesn't want to see him rove the earth again, seeking out nymphs and women, beginning all the chaos once more. By coming here, she's risking just that happening, and she wonders if it would be safer to stay away altogether. But her curiosity won't let her. She has to see for herself what his reaction will be. She came here braced for confrontation, but instead she finds herself offering the world up to him. Tempting him, if only to see if he'll take it.

He waves his hand, knocking away the sceptre that leans against the throne. 'It's insignificant,' he says. 'Remember how many oxen they used to burn for me at Troy, all the sheep, all the entreaties they sent, begging for my help? This is nothing.'

'It's not nothing,' Hera says. 'The mortal world is picking up again. It's not like it was, but there is momentum. Wherever the other gods have scattered, they must feel it too. Maybe they'll be drawn there.'

He scowls, his face darkening. 'Athena wouldn't show her face. She's wise enough to know I'd strike her down.'

'Why Athena?' Hera asks, baffled.

He takes a long draught of wine, spilling the ruby liquid carelessly over the edge of his cup, sending it in thin rivulets down his fist. 'She was born from me. It was her duty to obey me.'

Hera studies him closely. His voice rumbles with fury, but she's sure that beneath it, she can detect a seam of grief.

'Athena was wise enough to see how things were changing,' she says. 'She knew that staying on Mount Olympus was a mistake.'

He flings the cup at the wall, wine spattering across the once-bright fresco, staining the faded paint. It was unthinkable, once, that anything in their palace would lose its vivid freshness. The chill that hangs in the air, the dust that sparkles in the beams of light interspersed with shadows – it all speaks of neglect and decay, a house of immortality conquered by time.

'She wasn't going to be your loyal daughter forever,' Hera goes on.

The thunderbolt sparks in his other hand. He says nothing.

'I'm sure she hated you just as much as the rest of us, by the end.' Power thrills up inside her with every word. Not the power to tear up the world by its roots, not wild and reckless and explosive. It's something else: the anger that's choked her soul for aeons now flowing free, at last directed at the right target, at the source of all her pain. There is no one else standing in between them now.

'You were never grateful,' he snaps. 'Only jealous and vindictive, always complaining, always arguing.'

'Grateful for what? That you stole everything from me? I was a daughter of Cronus! I—' She stops abruptly. 'It doesn't matter now,' she says. 'Arguing over who had more right to rule. Your reign only lasted so long because of me.' She holds up her hand to cut him off as he starts to speak, and to her astonishment, he subsides. 'Without me to hold you back from your worst excesses, you would have brought yourself down. Without me to keep the sons you fathered under control, you would have suffered the same fate as Cronus did. But just because I was the only one who challenged you, doesn't mean you had their devotion. They all left you, the moment they realised they could.'

He slams his fists on the arms of the throne, the golden sides buckling under the impact as he moves to haul himself up, to spring at her, the thunderbolt slipping from his grasp and clattering, useless, on to the tiles. He can't free himself, and for a confused moment, Hera thinks he must be fettered as she once was, that Hephaestus has somehow snuck up here and chained his tyrannical father. But there is no fine mesh, no smoothly locking bronze. Both Zeus and Hera stare at his feet, rooted solidly to the floor, immovable.

What was divine flesh is now as hard and colourless as the marble pillars that stand around them, still holding up the sagging roof of the palace for now. Hera can see the bewilderment in his face, mirroring hers. She wishes Athena was there so that she could offer some logical explanation, tell them how a god could petrify into stone. Would she suggest that he has sat on his throne, unmoving, for long enough that he has become part of the lifeless palace around him? That his unchanging nature, his belief in his eternal power, could transform him into material that never changes, never adapts, forever stays the same?

Time freezes between them like ice sparkling in the winter sun, a thousand tiny cracks fracturing the surface as it threatens to break and let the river beneath surge free. Both of them suspended in a staggering realisation; both of them comprehending that Zeus is trapped. At the same instant, both of them see that his thunderbolt lies on the ground, just out of his reach.

Hera lets her gaze drop to the weapon, the instrument of Zeus' control, the threat he has wielded over her and all the other gods since he used it to overthrow the Titans. His sacred thunderbolt is within her grasp if she wants it, and there is nothing he can do to stop her from taking it.

She watches the thought spread across his face like the rising dawn. The horror in his eyes warms the frost in her bones, freeing her from its grip so that she can take a step and then another, only a few paces bringing her to it.

Very slowly and deliberately, she picks it up. It thrums against her palm, alive with energy. Sleek and sharp, faintly warm, fitting in her hand as though it was always meant to be there. Powerful enough that it can bring down a dynasty, shatter divine bones, hold a family of gods hostage to your every whim.

'You would deserve it,' she says. He knows what she means. That she could blast him to immortal fragments and never regret it.

'Will you?' He holds up his head, his gaze level. She doesn't know what to read in his eyes. Defiance. Loathing. Resentment. Desire. Every toxic feeling that characterises their marriage, every poisonous craving that has brought them here.

She closes her fingers around the thunderbolt, feeling it hiss at the touch of her skin. 'No,' she says. 'Not yet.'

And she walks away, leaving him behind.

28

If any other god wanted to challenge her, she has the thunderbolt. But she still sees no other gods. The sun rises every day; is it by the will of Apollo? Does Artemis coax out the moon, drawing her into her fullness each month and letting her wane back to nothing again in an endless cycle? The mortals give them dutiful praise for doing so, but Hera doesn't see them flashing through the skies in their chariots.

Until and unless any gods re-emerge, there are no immortal foes for her to quash. There are no rivals to provoke her ire, and no Zeus to rebel against. No divine family to govern.

She can't explain what's happened to the Titans, any more than she can discover the whereabouts of her fellow Olympians. She wonders if *all* the other immortals, like Zeus, are petrifying into stone somewhere. If they're slowly transforming into statues of themselves, their minds hardening with their bodies. Or if they've become one with the elements they love best, like Rhea did when she vanished into the forests, absorbed by the mountains and trees she conjured. Or if they wander, like she does, lost in the rhythms of the mortal world.

JENNIFER SAINT

She's sure that if she is to find any of them, it will be Athena. She was always the brightest, the sharpest, the most vivid of them all. Athena understood before Hera did what was happening to Olympus; wherever she is, she must know better than Hera what has become of the rest of them.

If Athena can be found anywhere, it will be in her patron city, the one she battled Poseidon to rule. This city towers above all the others, its naval fleet the fear of all of Greece and beyond. So Hera goes to Athens, in search of the goddess she once hated so fiercely. She's never cared to spend much time here before. Athena's busy, bustling city teems with men. They gather in crowds to debate the issues of the day, and cast their votes in assemblies, and Hera, cloaked from their view, studies the speakers. She remembers Athena on the rocky island of Ithaca in another age, putting on the faces of different mortals so she could guide her beloved hero Odysseus to triumph, and she looks for her now, to see if she is doing the same in her beloved city. She hears impressive speeches, but none that quite sparkle with Athena's brilliance. She doesn't feel the presence of the goddess, sleek and silver, making the air hum with her power. There are only mortals, everywhere she looks.

But perhaps she sees them differently now, because they aren't just a mass of bodies in her way. Hera notices differences: the fine purple wool of a nobleman's cloak, the dark shadows under a young man's eyes, a crooked nose that must have once been broken, a child playing with a dog. Details that she's never cared to spot before. As dusk falls, she finds a symposium, a drinking party where wealthy men of the city lie back and sip wine poured by slaves, plucking grapes from the fruit bowls on low tables beside them. When she first enters, she thinks she's sure to find the goddess here. The gilded ceiling and bronze wine cups remind her of the gatherings of the gods on Mount Olympus – a poor imitation, but the closest she can find in a mortal city where the smell of animal dung, sweat and smoke hangs heavy in the close air. It's not the polished rhetoric she listened to in the public assembly, nor the humble devotions addressed to her in her temples, nor the awestruck entreaties of the heroes to whom she gave her favour once. It's human discourse as she's never really heard it before, perhaps because she's never been interested in it. As the wine keeps flowing and the conversation slips into bawdier jokes and boasting, she's reminded a little of the Argonauts, the way they were when she'd draw close to listen every now and then, keeping an eye on their quest, and she'd find them gathered around their campfires, drinking together. The huge presence of Heracles had irritated her too much for her to linger long; he would be sprawled on his lion skin, club at his side, draining jug after jug of wine and shouting over the others. She'd always withdrawn in disdain, coming back only to ensure Jason stayed on course to bring her the glory she required of him.

A slave-boy brings out a pole topped with a small bronze disc to great cheers. Through the smoke from the tapers, she watches, intrigued, as each of the men takes it in turns to flick wine from his own cup at the disc. The crimson liquid splashes across the mosaic floor, and they cheer more loudly, flinging with greater abandon, until one of them manages to knock the disc from the pole and sends it clattering on to the ceramic tiles with a wild clang. Women file in, dresses sliding from their shoulders as they enter, and the atmosphere thickens. Athena definitely won't be here, Hera decides. It's no place for the virgin goddess; probably not for the goddess of wives, either.

Outside, the warm evening air feels cool in comparison to the heat within. The stars twinkle overhead, and Hera turns her steps towards the hill overlooking the rest of the city. At the top of its slopes, the Acropolis stands. The jewel of Athens: a great rock where the first kings of the city had once lived long ago, where Athena and Poseidon once contested each other for supremacy, where the gods have always been worshipped, and now a site for temples impressive enough to reflect the magnificence of the city.

She shrugs off the mist that hides her from view and walks through the grand entrance at the western side of the summit, flanked by tall columns. In the shadowy interior of the porch, she can make out the coffered squares on the roof above her, each one painted blue with a golden star in the centre. As she steps out the other side, on to the plateau, she sees the moonlight gleaming on the white marble pillars of the Parthenon, which stretch up towards the heavens in front of her. Everything feels fresh, new and unfinished. She remembers the construction of the Olympian palaces, the ease with which the gods rebuilt after Typhon's destruction, as she casts her eyes around the signs of human industry – piles of carved blocks of stone, partially constructed walls, evidence of the years dedicated so far, with more still to come.

A colossal bronze figure rises between Hera and the grand temple, holding a spear and shield. Hera feels her heart lift at the sight of the statue, imposing and austere, imbued with the spirit of the goddess she seeks. It has been so long that even the lifeless imitation of a familiar face feels like balm to her loneliness.

Perched on Athena's shoulder, a grey owl cocks her head and narrows her round eyes at Hera. She watches Hera walk across the earth, following her movement as she circles the Parthenon, looking up at the brightly painted sculptures on the temple pediments, her eyes running across the carved and decorated figures of the gods until she finds herself there.

The owl flutters down, shaking out her wings, and Hera recognises her just before she transforms.

'Athena.'

'Hera.'

The two goddesses stand together for the first time since the desertion of Olympus. The first immortal Hera has seen apart from Zeus. Athena, unlike her father, still stands strong and unbowed, as fierce and beautiful and glowing as she has ever been.

'I thought you must be here somewhere,' Hera says. 'I didn't think you could have disappeared altogether.'

Athena nods. 'I'm not surprised to see you,' she says.

'And the others?' Hera asks.

Athena shrugs. 'You know what's become of Zeus, I assume.'

'Have you been back?'

'I saw him,' Athena says. 'He didn't know that I was there.'

Hera wonders when it was. Athena hasn't glanced at the bag hanging from Hera's waist, but if she saw Zeus after Hera's last visit, she's too sharp not to have noticed his thunderbolt was missing. Her hand hovers close by it, just in case. They've been enemies, then allies and now strangers to one another. She doesn't know what to expect.

'Did you see anyone else?' Hera asks.

Athena still wears the same contemplative, untroubled expression that Hera used to find so maddening. 'No,' she says. 'But they're still out there, I think, in some form at least.'

'Are you sure?'

'Those of us who can adapt,' Athena says. 'Any like Zeus, still clinging on to what we lost, won't be. Those of us who came down from the heavens – we've found our own way to keep going.'

'You told me that we needed the prayers and the offerings, that we had to be closer when so many mortals died,' Hera says. 'But there are more than ever now. If we went back, wouldn't it just be the same as it used to be?'

'It hasn't worked for Zeus.' Athena's voice stays low and serious. She hasn't betrayed any particular joy at seeing Hera again. That's just the way she is, Hera supposes. Neither one of them is given to displays of affection. 'We grew dependent on worship and stronger from belief. When the human population waned, we weakened. Even with more mortals now, even with temples like this one' – she waves an arm at the Parthenon – 'I don't think we can go back. We had to change when the world did, or get left behind like him.'

'But—' Hera starts, and Athena cuts her off.

'Would you even want to?' She glances up at the painted carvings above their heads, depicting the scene of her own birth from the head of Zeus. 'To go back to the way things were?'

She wouldn't. She told Zeus as much, the last time she saw him. But then, it's all right for Athena, presiding over her glorious city. She always liked to be among mortals: teaching them, instructing them, guiding them. Hera only ever wanted to be above them. To rule as she believed she was meant to, to fulfil the destiny that Gaia laid out before her in the halls of Oceanus so many lifetimes ago. Now she finds herself wondering why.

'Stay in the city for a while,' Athena says. 'You'll find the other gods. They're everywhere – in the sculptures here, in the libraries where our names and our stories are written down on rolls of papyrus. In the theatre dedicated to Dionysus on the slope of this hill, where they perform plays not just in devotion to our names, but *about* us. In the agora, where the philosophers try to make sense of the world. You know, a man argued that the moon is only a lump of rock, devoid of any divinity at all? If she heard him, Artemis didn't care enough to strike him down. The city exiled him, but you can't banish an idea once it's been born.'

The enthusiasm in her voice makes Hera uneasy. The scene above them recalls Athena's birth; now Hera recalls that Athena is made from Metis' sacrifice. The ancient Titaness, so wise and full of foresight, let herself be consumed so that her daughter could live. The way Athena is talking, she seems to celebrate all that the mortals have learned, even if it means an unheard-of questioning of the gods, as though she'd let them consume her in pursuit of progress. 'You don't mean for them to stop worshipping us altogether?' Hera asks, exasperated.

'Just see it for yourself,' Athena says.

Hera doesn't follow Athena's advice, not straight away. Instead, when the goddesses part, Hera takes flight, sweeping long-feathered hawk wings through the skies, all the way to the banks of Oceanus.

Since she was brought here as an infant, its dark waters have churned in a vast, snaking circle around the world. Hera can't count how many times she's witnessed Eos rising from its depths in the east to cast her rosy light, before Helios would draw the fiery golden sun up above its shores and across the heavenly arch. Each evening, he used to sink back down into the western depths of the mighty river, sailing his shining boat back to the east under the dark veil of night to begin again in a harmonious cycle. The river always flowed back into itself, replenishing itself, feeding its tributaries and branches with a never-ending supply of fresh water.

She knows what she always used to see: the far bank of Oceanus shrouded in dark mist. That was the edge of the world, where the dome of the heavens would slope up towards its apex, where the walls that contained Tartarus and the Underworld would curve downwards in symmetry. This is the way it always was. Even when Apollo and Artemis took the sun and the moon for themselves, still the huge river of Oceanus remained, even after the Titans had withdrawn to their halls beneath it, not needed anymore.

Until now.

The moonlight sparkles off the broad stream, which trickles in place of the river that was. She walks, her goddess form restored, along the muddy grass at its edge, until the dark water runs underground and is lost beneath the earth. If the halls of the Titans are still under there, she can no longer see the entrance to their subterranean homes. The land on the other side rolls on as far as she can see, no longer cloaked in the black mist that once signalled the end of the world.

It has always been the case that Gaia has raised new mountains, carved out fresh rivers and opened up serpentine networks of caves and tunnels within the vastness of her body. The shape of the world that Hera ruled over changed many times during her reign. But Oceanus was as fundamental a part of it as Mount Olympus, the home of the most ancient Titans and the gateway to Tartarus and the Underworld, something she had once believed could never change.

It's gone. The liquid arms encircling the earth have loosened their hold, and Hera cannot see the solid limits that once held the world in place. She kneels on the bank, muddying her dress, one that Athena wove long ago on her loom in their palace.

It's so quiet here. The air no longer rings with echoes from the bronze halls of Pheme's House of Rumour, and only a few mortal prayers drift this far. Hera lays her hands on the damp earth, and lets her mind fall into stillness.

She can feel a low hum, deep in the soil. A slow, ponderous heartbeat, one that drives currents in the ocean and pushes continents, diverts rivers and opens up new lands. She feels the ever-present weight of the thunderbolt at her waist, Zeus' weapon with its power to destroy and enslave, and it suddenly feels insubstantial – a toy, a trick, the instrument of a king who could only break and burn what he ruled until it all ended in ruins. Somewhere, underneath Hera's fingertips, Gaia still stirs and the world moves with her breath. Gaia shaped it from nothing; she watched the Titans rise up against the sky and the Olympians bring down the Titans in turn, and now those gods have scattered and she remakes it again.

Hera unfastens the twine that holds the bag closed, and draws the slender, spiked thunderbolt from it. It only sputters now, a weak halo of feeble sparks that dissolve into nothing. She turns it over, the metal too dull to gleam in the soft light, its surface charred and blackened.

Perhaps if she tried, if she ascended into the clouds and stirred them up, she might reignite it. Maybe it's what Gaia intended, if she intends anything at all – for her to usher in the next era, a new order of the gods, expanding into the new horizons. Everything she fought and strove for under Zeus.

371

Even if Gaia did intend that, Hera makes her own choices now.

The thunderbolt shudders slightly, a feeble pulse of energy rippling through it. She lowers it into the stream and the water sizzles in shock, a brief fizz of bubbles erupting around it. She holds it under the surface until it's nothing more than cold, inert metal.

And then, she lets it go.

29

She comes to understand why Athena takes such pride and pleasure in Athens. Of all the places Hera has roamed, it feels the brightest and most dynamic, surging with curiosity and optimism, the qualities that Athena prizes most. Hera supposes that the invisibility of its women doesn't concern the goddess who has always been a friend to heroes – to restless men, driven by the thrill of discovery. The city embodies her, and Hera can see everywhere evidence that Athena has found her perfect home, the place where she belongs.

Hera, the once reluctant goddess of wives, can't find the same for herself here, but even so, she can feel its lure, enough to let herself be swept along for a time on the tides of humanity that ebb and flow in the city. This time, she doesn't float unseen in a cloud. She takes the form of a mortal man – after all, she cannot walk freely here as a woman. She's following the rules of the mortal world, without even thinking about it. She walks on streets of packed earth, avoiding the deep ruts from the carts that wheel up and down, and she feels a loosening of herself as she lets it absorb her. To her astonishment, passers-by look her directly in the face. She's so entirely absorbed into their mass that they meet the eyes of the goddess Hera and never know it. They jostle her, shoulders and elbows jabbing into her sides, and she doesn't strike them down. She almost laughs. There is a lightness in her step since she drowned Zeus' thunderbolt. It never weighed very much, but without it she is free, and she walks with the carelessness she once had when she used to roam the forests, before the golden thrones of Olympus were even created. She lets the revelation settle into her bones; she has no enemies now, no rivals by which to define herself. Zeus isn't prowling these same streets, seeking another victim to flaunt in her face. Seeing Athena again has confirmed it for her: their Olympian family is fragmented and it's left to Hera to find her own place in the world as it is.

Spring sunshine warms the air, and a procession winds its way towards the south slopes of the Acropolis. Hera falls into step with it, curious to see where it takes her.

Zeus used to like this, she recalls. He'd go with Hermes, sometimes dressed as beggars or humble men, seeking kindness and hospitality from strangers. Testing the mortals, he'd say when he laughed about it on Mount Olympus later. He'd wait for them to slip up, to violate the rules of his game without ever knowing they were players. When they offended him, he'd shed the disguise and visit ruin upon their houses.

It kept him entertained. But Hera isn't looking for that kind of diversion.

The crowds wind their way to the foot of the hill, overlooked by the Parthenon. A wide semicircle of stone benches fans out, spreading back and up the slopes. At the front, Hera is welcomed by Dionysus. Her old habits rear up; she glares at him and he stares back, impassive. It's a ridiculous statue, she decides, showing the god perched on a satyr's shoulder, holding a theatrical mask. A nod to his childhood, the one he led on Mount Nysa, hidden from Olympus, learning to mix wine and dance and sing, to lead people further into ridiculousness.

If the scale of the crowd is anything to go by, people are more than willing to be led there. They filter through, filling the stepped rows that ascend up the slope so that the audience members at the very back look down at the stage from high above.

Athena praised the plays, and here, Hera presumes, is the theatre where they take place. She halts and glances around, wondering whether she should stay. Someone barrels into her back, cursing her as they roughly make their way around her. She barely even registers the insult.

She's heard enough bards sing of the exploits of gods and heroes. This, no doubt, will be more of the same. On impulse, she makes the decision to settle herself on a stone bench, pressed in by others on all sides. The gentle breeze is welcome, freshening the air into which rises the smell of sweat and stale wine. She imagines if the other gods could see her now – if the stone Dionysus contained the god himself, looking out at her – they would find it amusing. For all her regal dignity, here is the queen of the gods wearing the form of a mortal man, squeezed between two others, watching the proceedings of humans as though it's of interest to her. The thought almost makes her rise from where she sits, either to halt it altogether or simply flee to something more worthy of her attention. She eyes the statue with suspicion. The gods are everywhere in this city, and nowhere at the same time. She should leave; Athena was wrong, there is nothing here for her.

But then the actors begin to perform, masked and

commanding, and Hera remains where she is, torn between leaving and staying. She'll just see what happens, just a few moments longer. She glances at the curved rows of benches surrounding her. Not every face is intent – some are distracted, some chatting among themselves, some shouting out at the performers – but she has the dizzying sensation of being in the centre of something they are all experiencing as one. She and thousands of mortals, watching three men on the stage swapping painted masks as they take on different characters, their voices ringing up to the farthest seats. At the front, on seats carved like thrones, sit the Athenian leaders in vivid cloaks and fine linen robes, priests of Dionysus in ivy crowns and, Hera notices, a woman draped in a finely ornamented peplos, hued in rich purple. It's almost all men, apart from her, but men of all kinds seem to be there, even some slaves in their short tunics. Eager chatter drifts across the breeze; sometimes they call out to the actors, as if to intervene. It puts Hera in mind of the gods watching mortals. The entertainment they sought on Mount Olympus when they gathered together, how deeply they yearned for pain and suffering, how they used to savour it.

In battle at Troy, she'd witnessed the collective intensity of the fighters – the heat and the determination, the rising lust for their enemy's blood that united them across both sides – but this is very different. As the play progresses, she sees shared emotions on faces across the audience – their horror as events build to a dramatic climax, their sadness as an actor takes the centre of the stage, his mask a woman's face, and delivers lines that throb with bitterness. He plays the part of Pasiphae, the Cretan queen who gave birth to the Minotaur, the victim of Poseidon's cruel trick with the bull. Hera stares in fascination as he recites the words, blaming Pasiphae's madness and suffering on both the god of the sea and her husband who provoked his wrath, and the audience recoils from the grotesque description of how she fell in love with the beast, and yet they lean closer, trying to catch every word.

Hera can remember how it happened. She remembers the tenor of Pasiphae's prayers when they reached her. She never wondered at the time how other mortals might have felt about Poseidon's justice. It was right, wasn't it, that mortals felt fear? Right that they shrank from such examples, that they made sure to honour the gods correctly. Only now she senses something different, something other than fear in the crowd, and Poseidon does not rise from the seas to sweep away this actor in a tidal wave of wrath. He carries on, unmolested, just as Athena had said the philosopher who denied the divinity of the moon never suffered the punishment of Artemis.

The tragedy comes to a close; there is death and grief, and then the spectators exhale and turn to one another in a kind of daze. The actors bring a man up to the stage, the playwright apparently, his face strained with anxiety as he scrutinises the faces of the fine-clad men in the front row for their reaction. For someone who wrote those words about Poseidon, Hera thinks he looks mild – as ordinary as anyone else she sees in the theatre, more apprehensive about the reaction of the judges than the prospect of the sea-god's anger.

She slips out of the crowd; she's seen enough. As she passes the stage, hurrying to leave, he's stepping away too, and he bumps into her elbow, catching her arm. She feels it like a brand on her skin. His eyes meet hers for a second, warm and human, and it sparks a crackle in her veins, a flash of hunger to know what's in those depths. For a dizzying moment, she can taste the sweet, clear air of the forests and hear the thundering of a waterfall, pure water tumbling into itself, when she was a goddess who was just a girl unmarked by loss and suffering.

She pulls away, startled and eager to shed the human form. As soon as she's far enough away to exchange it for that of a hawk, she flies to the top of a neighbouring hill, a flat outcrop of rock. The sense of communality in the theatre has unsettled her. All those people, all of them feeling something at the same time. And she was with them, not apart from them, not hovering above them observing, but in the thick of it.

She can leave. Athena doesn't have any wisdom to offer her now. If Hera has nothing left to be queen of, then Athena has lost her role as adviser. Why would Hera listen to her anymore? The other gods were always too captivated by this world; it's unseemly. Hera was right to keep her distance.

She convinces herself, and, as twilight descends and the mass in the theatre begins to disperse, she readies herself to fly away and leave the city behind.

Her hawk eyes catch his movement in the crowd, tiny and indiscernible if she weren't a goddess. He shouldn't stand out to her, he shouldn't be distinguishable from any of the others. But without thinking about it any longer, she swoops down from the ledge and follows him through the streets of Athens.

His house might be pleasant by the standards of the other dwellings here, but not to her. She lands gently in the tiny central courtyard around which the rest of it is constructed, and glances about. It's paved, with a small well at one end and a little altar at the other, nothing else to see. She pushes one of the doors that leads inside; it gives way easily to her hand, of course, and she steps into a corridor. Within, it feels dark and cramped; cave-like, she thinks. She runs a hand along the whitewashed plaster, listening for the household sounds. It's so quiet. Other revellers from the festival might be drinking together after the day's events, but he has come back to an empty home. A narrow staircase leads to the upper storey and she makes no sound as she climbs it. A door is ajar at the top of the stairs, a faint glow of light emanating from within. She pushes it silently, and sees him.

The room is sparsely furnished – a bed in the corner, a large wooden chest beside it, a wide table and a chair with a curved back where he sits. Papyrus rolls are heaped on the table and he clutches a sharpened reed in one hand, its nib dark with ink. His other hand is pressed to his forehead, his brows drawn together in frustration. A terracotta lamp provides the only light, a small flame flickering from the wick that floats in a gleaming pool of olive oil.

She moves deliberately, brushing against the wall so that he hears the rustle of her cloak against the plaster. He startles, turns around to face her, jumping to his feet when he sees the figure of an unknown man standing in his house.

'What do you want?' he barks.

She's used to the musical, rounded tones of the gods. The actors performing on the stage could fill the air tolerably well, but his voice sounds thin in comparison to theirs. His eyes are a richer brown than she remembers from the theatre. He isn't young, but his dark hair is still thick. It looks soft.

'How did you get in here?' He sounds both furious and panic-stricken. 'Who are you?' He looks at her more closely. 'Weren't you – did I see you at the theatre today? Did you follow me here?'

'I wanted to ask about the play,' she says.

He looks ready to explode. 'Get out,' he growls, and she can see he's sizing her up, deciding whether he can drag her from the room.

She takes another step inside, letting her cloak fall from her shoulders. As it tumbles to the reed matting spread across the floor, she lets the transformation ripple through her. Not the full radiance of her goddess form, the kind that burned Semele to ashes, but a gentler approximation of it. One that his eyes can bear.

His jaw drops, his skin turns ashen and he grips the table behind him for support.

'I want you to tell me,' she says, still advancing towards him, 'what you think about Poseidon.' Her eyes flick to the scrolls piled up on the table. 'What other plays have you written?'

He's mouthing like a fish, unable to get any words out. Eventually, he manages to stutter a response. 'My other plays? But – they never win. They're no good.'

'I liked it,' she says. 'I saw some people cry. You made them feel something. Something about the gods. About what we did.'

His eyes bulge in terror. 'I didn't mean . . .'

'It doesn't matter to me,' she says. 'I'm just interested to know.'

He's bewildered, afraid for his life, paralysed by the shock and the overwhelming dread she's caused, and she's going too quickly. She's racing ahead, a thousand questions bubbling on her tongue; suddenly, there are so many things she finds she wants to know when she never cared before. This man in front of her is only one human she's plucked out of thousands, and charged with explaining them to her.

'I'm not here to hurt you,' she says. She wonders how many times a god has said that to a mortal, and how many times they've meant it enough to make it true. 'I'm not angry.'

But she doesn't know what to be instead. And she's concerned she might have shattered his mind entirely, from the way he gapes at her still. She comes closer, and puts her hand on his shoulder, reminding herself to be gentle as she presses him to sit back in the chair. She can smell the smoke from the lamp caught in his hair, the salt and heat of his body, the woodsy scent of the papyrus. She could stand, but she looks about and sees a three-legged stool, which she draws forward and sits on, as though this is a normal conversation.

'There were so many people watching today,' she says. She's hovered in banqueting halls where poets have sung stories to fifty, perhaps a hundred listeners. But there were thousands there today, watching the same story unfold, their emotions suspended on a precipice all at the same time, sharing their grief and their horror in a single moment. And for the first time, she was among them, truly among them.

She has been alone for a very long time.

He nods. His eyes are fixed on her, still wide and anxious, but some colour is returning to his face, though he still doesn't seem able to speak.

'I want to know what it meant to them,' Hera says. 'What brought them there, why they stayed, what they wanted.' She has never asked herself this about any human, at any time in the whole history of their existence. They were there to do what the gods desired them to do; that was what mattered.

'To honour Dionysus,' he says quickly. 'The festival – that's what it's for. The plays are to please him.' And then he looks as though he wants to bite back the words he's just spoken, worried he's made a misstep, that pleasing Dionysus is the opposite of what Hera might want.

'That's not true,' she says, and he flinches. 'Tell me about the other performances. Tell me what they've come to watch before, if it's always like it was today.'

So he does, haltingly at first. He stumbles over every sentence, but while the lamp burns down, he manages to paint a picture of the annual festivals. He tells her the plays can celebrate the city's triumphs, that old stories can be brought to life to make the audience reflect on the present day, and, as he grows a little in confidence, he talks about the questions they raise, the ideas that can stir within the audience, the ways they can be inspired to think and feel. She wants to know where it all comes from; he takes her into the next room and shows her shelves stacked with papyrus rolls, a veritable library of his own, and she makes him tell her why he treasures it, what it means to him.

She leaves him when the sky turns grey and misty with morning, her mind alive with still more questions, and she's momentarily annoyed as she imagines that this is exactly what Athena wanted. It's too late, she laments; the careful distance she's always held between herself and Zeus' experiment has shrivelled away, and she's found herself behaving in a way she once would have criticised and scorned. She is immersed in the human world instead of observing from a hidden vantage point, her disdain for them melted by the insistence of her curiosity.

She didn't imagine such an inner life for models made of clay and shaped for the entertainment of the gods. She told Zeus once that mortals could never truly resemble them, not in spirit. When she'd listened to mortal stories before, she heard in them the power of the gods – that the gods strode the world, colossal and awe-inspiring, and held the lives of their human worshippers in their hands. In this thriving, restless city, she discovers they're telling stories about themselves too: passionate, angry, poignant, tragic stories about who they are. The gods created humans, but now Hera is seeing humans create gods, just as Athena told her they did: in their artworks, in their poems and plays, in their philosophising. She isn't sure now that they need the actual gods at all – only the versions of them they construct for themselves.

And the balance of power has shifted so far that it's the gods who need them.

She goes back to the playwright's meagre house, where the shadows flicker on the walls, and she can see the intensity on his face as he gains the courage to talk, reflecting the same eager yearning for answers that she feels herself. She was incredulous once when Aphrodite took Adonis as her lover, when Eos cast her gaze down on to the rosy-lit world and found a handsome mortal, but as she watches his ink-stained fingers sketch out in the air the point he's trying to make, she wants to know what his hands would feel like on her skin.

She never wanted to be a goddess of marriage, but since Zeus made it her role, she has held fast to the rules that bound her. It was enough for him to make a mockery of fidelity; she took it on as her duty, desultory as it was. It has bound her for aeons, made her body belong to a philandering god she has hated all that time.

Now she decides it's hers again, and when she touches this mortal, the world doesn't collapse. He draws back, and she laughs, asking him if he fears that Zeus will hurl his thunderbolt. Outside, the rain cascades from heavy clouds, but the skies stay quiet. *Zeus can't see us*, she says. *He'll never know*.

She's certain that nothing will happen, that she can relinquish her weary fidelity and the world will still have its goddess of wives, carved in stone and wood and ivory, set down in scrawled ink, trapped in song and verse forever.

That version of Hera still exists: a shell built around her of prayers and myth, a construction that's been made for her, made of her. But she can walk free of it now and leave it standing behind her.

She can be anyone. Vengeful Hera, wrathful Hera, the queen of the heavens, most long-suffering of wives and cruellest of punishers, will continue without her. She can slip away from the tethers of who she was, find a sweetness in love again, and, for the first time, belong to the world rather than commanding it.

In the gentle light of dawn, the world is washed clean. Hera leaves the city, leaves her mortal lover sleeping. When he wakes, maybe he'll think she was never more than a dream.

She has to make sure. One final visit to the place that was her home. One last look at her Olympian palace.

The god who ruled it is a relic now. He sits sightless, motionless, inanimate on the throne. As solid a rock as Asteria transformed into when she fled from him. As cold and hard as their marriage. All the divine vitality is long drained away, and the palace crumbles around him with no one left to sustain it. Walls have toppled, columns are broken, and the wind whips icy and harsh around the statue that used to be Zeus.

In time, there will be nothing left of him or their home. It will wear down to dust and be carried in fragments on the breeze, leaving nothing but a bare mountain summit cloaked in snow and wreathed in clouds.

Nothing lasts, that's what she knows now, even gods who think their rule will be eternal. Even Athena's beloved city won't sustain its peace and prosperity; war will come, mortals will die, but there will always be more. Everything will change, and it will always bring loss, but she moves through the world now, not above it or apart from it, and she changes along with it.

Every now and then, she's convinced she glimpses the gods who have been caught in the tide along with her. When Athens loses its hold on its empire, Hera still sees Athena: a grey-feathered owl tilting its head in the town square where men debate philosophy and rationality, striving for sense and understanding; or else a flash of silver in the eyes of someone stacking another roll of papyrus in the public library, the teacher calling his students to lessons, or the woman demonstrating how the loom works to her attentive daughter. At the lush, rolling vineyards, she sometimes thinks she spots the laughing eyes of Dionysus in a jovial winemaker selling his wares. In the forests, she's convinced she catches a flash of Artemis, running in pursuit of a stag, or else she recognises her determined jawline in a defiant girl. In smoky forges, where blacksmiths wipe the sweat from their brows, she feels the patience of Hephaestus; and she is certain that Ares still runs wild on the battlefields, filling every fighter's heart with his destructive rage. Hestia is there, of course, in every kindly friend, at every welcoming hearth.

She wonders where they see her – in rebellious wives, she hopes, in the iron souls of powerful queens, in resilient girls who find the strength to keep going.

Even when they no longer worship at her altars, she won't disappear. The mortals can determine their own lives, and she will carry on. Immortal and ageless, reinvented a thousand times, remade for a thousand narratives, throneless and wandering, but forever the ruler of her own destiny.

ACKNOWLEDGEMENTS

There were so many things I wanted this novel to be; thank you to Juliet Mushens for understanding it before I did and guiding me in the right direction from the beginning. And thank you to Rachel Neely for all the reassurance as I missed all my deadlines and descended into panic. Without both of you believing firstly that it was going to be written and secondly that it would be good, I could not have got to the end. I'm grateful to everyone at Mushens Entertainment for everything you do.

I feel very fortunate that this is my fourth novel edited by Caroline Bleeke – I now hear your voice in my head while I'm drafting, Caroline, and it makes me so much better! Working with you and with Flora Rees again was such a dream and it was so delightful to see *Hera* taking shape and becoming the book I hoped it would be when it was only the spark of an idea.

Thank you to everyone at Wildfire and at Flatiron for everything, in particular your understanding when I missed all the aforementioned deadlines – I'm sorry! Thank you, Micaela Alcaino and Joanne O'Neill, for your fourth amazing book covers, they are so beautiful.

ACKNOWLEDGEMENTS

To Elodie Harper and Susan Stokes-Chapman, for all your friendship and support, which was needed more than ever while I was writing this one! And the lovely author, blogger, classicist and bookseller community who champion my books – I hope you all know who you are because there are too many to mention by name and I feel endlessly lucky that this is the case. A particularly special mention to Nikita Gill for lending me your beautiful words for the epigraphs to Part Two and Part Five; you are so inspiring and so kind.

I am, as always, so very grateful to my friends and family for all your love and support. Thank you, Jo Murricane, for coming to Athens with me in a major heatwave for research (and drinking rosé by the lake!). Thank you, Bee and Steph, for being the best listeners and advisors.

And thank you to all my readers. I hope you love *Hera*.

ABOUT THE AUTHOR

Jennifer Saint grew up reading Greek mythology and was always drawn to the untold stories hidden within the myths. She studied classics at King's College London, where she is now a visiting research fellow in the Classics department. After thirteen years as a high school English teacher, she wrote *Ariadne*, which was shortlisted for Waterstones Book of the Year in 2021 and was a Waterstones Book of the Month, as well as being a *Sunday Times* bestseller. Her second novel, *Elektra*, and third novel, *Atalanta*, were #1 *Sunday Times* bestsellers. Her latest mesmerising mythological retelling is titled *Hera*.